Chapma
Chapman, Vannetta
A promise for Miriam /

34028080959183
BC $13.99 ocn771652947
09/04/12

3 4028 08095 9183
HARRIS COUNTY PUBLIC LIBRARY

WITHDRAWN

A Promise for
MIRIAM

Vannetta Chapman

WITHDRAWN

A Promise for
MIRIAM

Vannetta Chapman

HARVEST HOUSE PUBLISHERS
EUGENE, OREGON

Scripture quotations are taken from The Holy Bible, *New International Version*® *NIV*®. Copyright © 1973, 1978, 1984, 2011 by Biblica, Inc.™ Used by permission. All rights reserved worldwide.

Cover by Koechel Peterson & Associates, Inc., Minneapolis, Minnesota

Cover photos © Koechel Peterson & Associates, Inc. / iStockphoto / Thinkstock

This is a work of fiction. Names, characters, places, and incidents are products of the author's imagination or are used fictitiously. Any resemblance to actual persons, living or dead, or to events or locales, is entirely coincidental.

A PROMISE FOR MIRIAM
Copyright © 2012 by Vannetta Chapman
Published by Harvest House Publishers
Eugene, Oregon 97402
www.harvesthousepublishers.com

Library of Congress Cataloging-in-Publication Data
Chapman, Vannetta.
A promise for Miriam / Vannetta Chapman.
    p. cm — (The Pebble Creek Amish series ; bk. 1)
ISBN 978-0-7369-4612-4 (pbk.)
ISBN 978-0-7369-4613-1 (eBook)
1. Amish—Fiction. I. Title.
 PS3603.H3744P76 2012
 813'.6—dc23

                                                    2011050769

All rights reserved. No part of this publication may be reproduced, stored in a retrieval system, or transmitted in any form or by any means—electronic, mechanical, digital, photocopy, recording, or any other—except for brief quotations in printed reviews, without the prior permission of the publisher.

Printed in the United States of America
            12 13 14 15 16 17 18 19 20 / LB-CD / 10 9 8 7 6 5 4 3 2 1

For my sister,
Pam Lindman

Acknowledgments

When I was four years old, my sister taught me how to tie my shoes. I'm grateful she's still in my life, and she continues to have the patience to teach me things such as quilting and double crochet stitches...which are both much harder than how to knot your shoelaces. I love you, sis.

Although Pebble Creek doesn't actually exist, the village of Cashton does, and there are several folks in the Driftless region I'd like to thank, including Anita Reeck (Amil's Inn Bed and Breakfast), Kathy Kuderer (Down a Country Road), and Pete and Nora Knapik (Inn at Lonesome Hollow). Richard Lee Dawley (author of *Amish in Wisconsin*) was also kind enough to answer questions while I was conducting research.

The *Englisch* development I describe being built in the area of Nappanee, Indiana, is entirely fictional, though the Menno-Hof Museum mentioned does exist in Shipshewana, Indiana, and can be visited at www.mennohof.org.

Thanks to Suzanne Woods Fisher and the *Budget* for their endless supply of Amish proverbs. Other reference materials include *The Amish School* by Sara E. Fisher and Rachel K. Stahl, and *Herbs and Old Time Remedies* by Joseph VanSeters.

Thanks also to my editor, Kim Moore, and the excellent staff at Harvest House, as well as my agent, Mary Sue Seymour.

Mary Ellis was an encouragement to me in the writing of this book. My friends and prereaders, Donna, Kristy, and Dorsey, are a precious gift. Bobby, Mom, and kids—I adore you all.

I didn't attend a one-room schoolhouse, but I am a better person today because of the teachers in my life who cared, who were dedicated to their profession, and who encouraged a very shy little east Texas girl. I'm thankful that they did.

Prologue

Indiana
March

Gabe sat by the side of the bed, clasping Hope's hand.

The wind fought with the window panes, intent on finding its way into the small upstairs room. The rain lashed out against the night sky.

He knew when Dr. Frank left the room. He heard him in the hall murmuring to Erma and recognized the defeat in his voice as he moved down the stairs.

Gabe felt the weight of thick, heavy exhaustion pressing down on him. He couldn't have held up his head if his life had depended on it, though he would have found a way to do so if it could have saved Hope.

Saving Hope.

It had become his life mission, but that wasn't *Gotte's wille*. So the bishop had said as recently as an hour ago. So Erma was saying to the doctor as he left the house even now. Why couldn't Gabe's heart agree? Instead, he allowed his head to drop to the quilt, allowed his lips to kiss her hand—a hand that was even now growing cold, and for this moment he allowed himself to weep.

He heard Erma walk slowly up the stairs and stop outside the bedroom door, allowing him this final moment alone with his wife.

"*Mamm!*" Grace's scream tore through the house, startling in its pitch and intensity. Lunging past Hope's mother, Gabe's five-year-old daughter threw herself into the room, clawing at the bed and attempting to crawl on it, all the time sobbing and crying. "I want my *mamm*. Why won't she wake up? Make her wake up!"

He tried to pull her away, putting his arms around her small frame and murmuring in her ear, but her cries only increased.

"Silence that child!" Hope's father stood in the doorway, his face an inscrutable mask, his voice a hammer falling. Walking into the room, he jerked Grace from Gabe's arms. "Take her, Erma. Take her and silence her. I will not have such a display in my home."

Micah paused a moment, his eyes taking in Gabe's tearstained face and the lifeless form of his daughter. Briefly, Gabe thought he saw the mask of indifference slip from his features, but it was less than the span of a heartbeat, and in the dim lantern light he could have imagined it. With a scowl, the older man turned and trudged from the room, leaving Gabe alone to deal with his grief.

~ Chapter 1 ~

Pebble Creek, southwestern Wisconsin
Three years later

Miriam King glanced over the schoolroom with satisfaction.
Lessons chalked on the board.
Pencils sharpened and in the cup.
Tablets, erasers, and chalk sat on each desk.

Even the woodstove was cooperating this morning. Thank the
Lord for Efram Hochstetler, who stopped by early Mondays on his
way to work and started the fire. If not for him, the inside of the
windows would be covered with ice when she stepped in the room.

Now, where was Esther?

As if Miriam's thoughts could produce the girl, the back door to
the schoolhouse opened and Esther burst through, bringing with
her a flurry of snowflakes and a gust of the cold December wind.
Her blonde hair was tucked neatly into her *kapp*, and the winter
morning had colored her cheeks a bright red.

Esther wore a light-gray dress with a dark apron covering it. At
five and a half feet and weighing no more than a hundred and

twenty pounds, Miriam often had the unsettling feeling of looking into a mirror—a mirror into the past—when she looked at the young woman who taught with her at the one-room schoolhouse.

In truth, the teachers had often been mistaken for family. They were similar in temperament as well as appearance. Other than their hair, Esther could have been Miriam's younger sister. Esther's was the color of ripe wheat, while Miriam's was black as coal.

Why did that so often surprise both Plain people and *Englischers*? If Miriam's black hair wasn't completely covered by her *kapp*, she received the oddest stares.

"Am I late?" Esther's shoes echoed against the wooden floor as she hurried toward the front of the room. Pulling off her coat, scarf, and gloves, she dropped them on her desk.

"No, but nearly."

"I told Joseph we had no time to check on his cattle, but he insisted."

"Worried about the gate again?"

"*Ya*. I told him they wouldn't work it loose, but he said—"

"Cows are stupid." They uttered the words at the same time, both mimicking Joseph's serious voice, and then broke into laughter. The laughter eased the tension from Esther's near tardiness and set the morning back on an even keel.

"Joseph has all the makings of a fine husband and a *gut* provider," Miriam said. "Once you're married, you'll be glad he's so careful about the animals."

"*Ya*, but when we're married I won't be having to leave in time to make it to school." Esther's cheeks reddened a bit more as she seemed to realize how the words must sound.

Why did everyone think Miriam was embarrassed that she still remained unmarried? Did it never occur to them that it was her own choice to be single?

"Efram had the room nice and warm before I even arrived," she said gently. "And I put out your tablets."

"*Wunderbaar*. I'll write my lessons on the board, and we'll be ready." As Esther reached to pull chalk from her desk drawer, Miriam noticed that she froze and then stood up straighter. When she reached up and touched her *kapp* as if to make sure she was presentable, Miriam realized someone else was in the room.

She turned to see who had surprised the younger teacher. It was still a few minutes before classes were due to start, and few of their students arrived early.

Standing in the doorway to the schoolroom was an Amish man. Pebble Creek was a small community, technically a part of the village of Cashton. Old-timers and Plain folk alike still referred to the area where the creek went through by its historic name.

Miriam was quite sure she'd never seen the man standing in her classroom before. He was extremely tall, and she had the absurd notion he'd taken his hat off to fit through their entryway. Even standing beneath the door arch, waiting for them to speak, he seemed to barely fit. He was thin and sported a long beard, indicating he was married.

In addition to clutching his black hat, he wore a heavy winter coat, though not the type worn by most Wisconsin residents. The tops of his shoulders, his arms, and even parts of his beard were covered with snow. More important than how he looked standing in her classroom was the fact that he held the hand of a small girl.

"*Gudemariye,*" Miriam said, stepping forward and moving past her desk.

The man still didn't speak, but as she drew closer, he bent and said something to the girl.

When Miriam had halved the distance between them, he returned her greeting as his somber brown eyes assessed her.

The young girl next to him had dark-brown hair like her father. It had been combed neatly and pulled back into a braid, all tucked inside her *kapp*. What was striking about her wasn't her hair or her traditional Plain clothing—it was her eyes. She had the most solemn, beautiful brown eyes Miriam had ever seen on a child.

They seemed to take in everything.

Miriam noticed she clutched her father's hand tightly with one hand and held a lunch box with the other.

"I'm the teacher of the younger grades here, grades one through four. My name is Miriam King." The girl's eyes widened, and the father nodded again. "Esther Schrocks teaches grades five through eight."

He looked to the girl to see if she understood, but neither replied.

"And your daughter is—"

"Grace is eight years old, just this summer." Almost as an afterthought, he added, "I'm Gabriel Miller."

"Pleased to meet you." Miriam offered her best smile, which still did not seem to put the father at ease. She'd seen nervous parents before, and obviously this was one. "You must be new to our community."

"*Ya.* I purchased the place on Dawson Road."

"Dawson Road? Do you mean the Kline farm?"

"*Ya.*" Not quite rude, but curt and to the point.

Miriam tried to hide any concern she felt as images of Kline's dilapidated spread popped into her mind. It was no business of hers where this family chose to live. "I know exactly where you mean. My parents live a few miles past that."

"It's a fair piece from here," he noted.

"That it is. Esther and I live here at the schoolhouse during the week. The district built accommodations on the floor above, as is the custom in most of our schoolhouses here in Wisconsin. We both spend weekends at home with our families."

"I don't know I'll be able to bring Grace in every day." Gabriel Miller reached up and ran his finger under the collar of his shirt, which peeked through the gap at the top of his coat.

Miriam noticed then that it looked stiff and freshly laundered. Had he put on his Sunday best to bring his daughter to school on her first day? It said something about him if he had.

"A man has to put his farm first," he added defensively.

"Some children live close enough that their parents can bring them in the winter, and, of course, most everyone walks when the weather permits." Miriam paused to smile in greeting as a few students began arriving and walking around them. "Others ride together. Eli Stutzman lives past Dawson road, and he would be happy to give your *dochder* a ride to school."

"It would be a help." Mr. Miller still didn't move, and Miriam waited, wondering what else the man needed to say.

She looked up and saw one of the older girls, Hannah, walking in the door. "Hannah, this is Grace Miller. She's new at our school. Would you mind sitting with her and helping her this week?"

"Sure thing, Miriam." Hannah squatted down to Grace's level and said something to the girl Miriam couldn't hear.

Whatever it was, Grace released her *dat*'s hand and took Hannah's. She'd walked halfway down the aisle when she turned, rushed back to where they stood, and threw her arms around her father's legs.

One squeeze and she was gone again.

Though it was fleeting, Miriam saw a look of anguish pass over the man's face. What could be going through his mind? She'd seen many fathers leave their children for the first time over the last eight years, but something more was going on here.

"She'll be fine, Mr. Miller. We're a small school, and the children look after one another."

"It's that..." he twirled his hat in his hands once, twice, three times. "Before we moved here, Grace was...that is to say, we...well, her *grossmammi* homeschooled her."

"I understand. How about if I write a note letting you know how Grace is doing? I'll put it in her lunch box at the end of the day."

Something like relief washed over his face.

"*Danki*," he mumbled. Then he rammed his hat on his head and hurried out the door.

Esther caught her attention from the front of the room and sent a questioning look toward the man's retreating back, but Miriam shook her head. She'd explain later, at lunch perhaps. For now they had nearly forty children between them to teach. As usual, it would be a busy morning.

Gabe did stop to talk to Eli Stutzman. He wanted to make sure he trusted the man.

It helped when three girls and a boy who were the last to climb out of the long buggy stopped to wish their father a good day. The littlest girl, probably the same age as his Gracie, wrapped her arms around her daddy's neck, whispered something in his ear, and then tumbled down the steps into the chilly morning.

"That one is my youngest—Sadie. Always full of energy, but she's a worrier. This morning it's about a pup she left at home in the barn." Covering the distance between them, the older man removed his glove and offered his right hand. "Name's Eli Stutzman. I take it you're new here, which must mean you bought the Kline place."

"I am, and I did. Gabriel Miller." Gabe stood still in the cold, wishing he could be done with this and back on his farm.

"Have children in the school?"

"One, a girl—about your youngest one's age."

Eli nodded, and then he seemed to choose his words carefully. "I suspect you'll be busy putting your place in order. It will be no problem giving your *dochder* a ride back and forth each day."

"I would appreciate it."

Stutzman told him the approximate time he passed the Kline place, and Gabe promised he'd have Gracie ready at the end of the lane.

He turned to go and was headed to his own buggy when the man called out to him.

"The Kline place has been empty quite a while."

Gabe didn't answer. Instead, he glanced out at the surrounding fields, covered in snow and desolate looking on this Monday morning.

"If you need help, or find something that's worse than what you expected, you holler. We help each other in Pebble Creek."

Gabe ran his hand along the back of his neck but didn't answer. Merely nodding, he moved on to his buggy.

He was accustomed to people offering help. Actually delivering on it? That was often another story, though he wouldn't be judging the people here before he knew them.

Still, it was in his nature to do things on his own if at all possible.

Was his new home worse than he had expected?

Ya, it was much worse.

The barn was falling in on itself, and the house was not a lot better, but he knew carpentry. He could make them right. At least the woodstove worked. He'd been somewhat surprised to find no gas refrigerator, but he had found out who sold blocks of ice carved from the river. The icebox in the mudroom would do.

Gracie would be warm and fed. She'd have a safe place to sleep and to do the drawing she loved so much.

He didn't think he'd be calling on Eli for help.

He'd see that Grace Ann made it to school and church—he'd promised her *grossmammis* as much. But other than that he wasn't looking to make *freinden* in Pebble Creek. He wanted to be left alone. It was the reason he'd left their community in Indiana.

He could do without any help.

His parting words to his parents echoed back to him.

"I can do it on my own."

As he drove the buggy toward home, Gabe looked out over high ridges and low valleys. Dairy farms dotted the snowcapped view. Running through it all was Pebble Creek, no doubt a prime place for trout fishing most of the year. He'd heard the call of wild turkeys and seen deer. It was a rich, blessed area.

Pebble Creek ran through the heart of Cashton, the closest town. It also touched the border of the school grounds and meandered through his own property. It bound them together.

As he approached home, Gabe's mind was filled with thoughts

of the day's work ahead of him. He wondered where he'd find the energy to do it all, but somehow he would.

For Gracie he would.

His parents had offered to send his youngest brother along for the first year, but Andrew was needed on the family place. And, truthfully, Gabe preferred to be alone—just he and Grace.

"I can do it on my own."

"Just because you *can* doesn't mean you *should*," his mother said. She had reminded him as he was packing their things that pride was his worst shortcoming, though the Lord knew he had many to choose from when it came to faults.

Was it pride that scraped against his heart each day? He couldn't say.

He only knew he preferred solitude to company, especially since Hope died.

Hope.

That seemed ironic, even to him. She had been his hope, his life, his all, and now she was gone. Her death had happened so quickly—it reminded him of one of the *Englisch* freight trains barreling around the corner of some bend.

A big black iron thing he hadn't seen coming. A monstrosity with the power to destroy his life.

Which wasn't what the bishop had said, or his parents, or his brothers and sisters.

He slapped the reins and allowed his new horse, Chance, to move a bit faster over the snow-covered road. He'd left Indiana because he needed to be free of the looks of sympathy, the well-intentioned words, the interfering.

So he now had what he'd wished for—a new beginning with Grace.

If it meant days of backbreaking work, so much the better. Perhaps when he was exhausted, he would begin to sleep at night.

⌒ Chapter 2 ⌒

Grace came home each afternoon with a note from her teacher.

Gabe took each note from the lunch box, read it, and threw it into the garbage to be burned when he disposed of the rest of the trash.

He didn't answer them. How could he? What would he say?

By Thursday he'd quit reading them because they all said essentially the same thing. He took to removing the pieces of paper with the neat handwriting and putting them straight into the garbage can.

Grace watched with somber eyes, but she never said a word.

It was early in the evening on Friday when he heard a knock at the door. He'd just burned the bacon he was cooking for their dinner. Smoke hung in the air above the stove, and the eggs he'd attempted to fry sat in a congealed mess on the table.

Grace did not appear upset about the dinner. She was usually oblivious to such things. Curled up in the corner chair at the table, she was focused completely on the drawing on her tablet. Moments before he'd caught her staring out the window, as if something grand lay outside the dirty panes of the glass. All he could see were fields that needed work, surrounded by a fence that wouldn't hold anything, adjacent to a yard that hadn't been taken care of for years.

The drawing his daughter now sketched was something quite different. Perhaps she'd seen in those few moments before darkness fell what he'd imagined from the newspaper clipping he'd read in Indiana. "Hundred-acre farm, running creek, some woods, southwestern Wisconsin. Needs work but will produce for the right man. Small homestead on property."

What she sketched was a snow-covered field with a new fence, and, if he wasn't mistaken, a pony in the corner looking toward the woods in the distance. The building in the bottom right of the drawing could be their house, or it could be the barn. It was hard to tell because she wasn't finished, and also because their house rather resembled the barn in its current state.

When the knock sounded, she didn't look up, but a shadow passed over her face. Gabe gave her what he hoped was a reassuring smile and set the plate of burned bacon on the table next to the eggs. "Probably a neighbor about that bull. He keeps finding his way out of the field."

He didn't think to let go of the spatula or take off the apron he'd been wearing to keep the grease off his work clothes.

The knock sounded again, and he hollered, "I'm coming. You don't have to bang it down."

He opened the door with a jerk, and Miriam King practically fell into his sitting room. She'd been about to knock a third time. When her small fist found no wood to knock on, it fell forward and her arm with it, which unbalanced her. Gabe reached out to stop her fall, nearly swatting her in the face with his spatula.

"Oh!" was the word that escaped her lips as she stumbled into the room.

He held on to her arms until she steadied herself, though he didn't want to. By this point he realized what he was holding. He had absolutely no desire to be touching the soft dark-gray wool of her coat. He didn't want the smell of her soap on his hands. He didn't need to be looking down on the top of her *kapp* or see the jet black of her curls that were escaping from the bottom of her bun.

"Are you steady now?"

"Yes, of course. You startled me, was all."

"You might try standing back after you knock on a door." As he stepped away from her to wipe his hands on his pants, he found he was still wearing the apron. Realizing that embarrassed him, which served to irritate him more.

"Well, I wouldn't have had to knock so many times if you'd answered the door in the first place."

"I was cooking." Gabe held up the spatula. "Took me a bit to make it to the door."

Miriam pulled in a deep breath, stared up at the far corner of the ceiling for a moment, and then straightened her coat and pulled off her gloves. Finally she looked at him again. "I apologize. I seem to have caught you at a bad time."

"We were about to eat dinner."

"Perhaps you didn't receive my notes."

"I received them."

"Then you knew I'd be stopping by this evening on my way home from school?"

Gabe scowled as he realized what she was referring to must have been in the last two notes, the two he hadn't read. "Maybe you should come into the kitchen."

He gestured to the adjoining room, the room that still had smoke settling over it. Walking in ahead of her, he cracked the window nearest to the stove.

"Was there a fire?" Miriam asked.

"No. I had a bit of a problem with the stove." Gabe snatched the plate of burned bacon off of the table. "Could I offer you a cup of *kaffi*?"

"That would be *wunderbaar. Danki.*"

Miriam sat next to the little girl and looked at the tablet. "Were you drawing this, Grace?"

He watched the two of them out of the corner of his eye. His daughter seemed comfortable enough with the woman. Grace flipped through her tablet, showing her teacher some of her previous drawings. Miriam commented on each one, not speaking down to her as some adults did, but making specific comments about the details in her sketches.

He knew his daughter was a talented artist. He'd been told by many that she had a gift. But he understood that wasn't what Miriam King was here to talk to him about.

He poured two cups of *kaffi*, steeled his spine, and walked resolutely to the table. Gabe had known when he took Grace to the school that this day was coming. He'd known when he'd decided to move to a new community that he'd have to explain.

Best to take his medicine and be done with it.

Somehow it didn't help that he'd have to look into the unusual gray eyes of a beautiful young woman across his own kitchen table. Perhaps it would have been better to have this conversation five days ago, the first morning at the school.

But he hadn't been ready then.

And he wasn't ready now.

He brought milk, sugar, and spoons to the table and pulled out a chair, sitting across from Grace and beside Miriam. He knew that's what Grace called her, because it's what Grace wrote on her papers—Miriam or sometimes simply Teacher.

The look in the teacher's eyes right now was one he could barely tolerate. It caused the old anger to flame up, and he had to swallow the hot *kaffi* in order to tamp it down, in order to distract himself so that he wouldn't say words he might regret.

It wasn't her fault. Pity was a natural enough reaction. Still, he'd seen it too many times. Pity was the one thing he couldn't abide, and it was fairly pouring out of her.

And who was she to pity him? To pity them?

Miriam stared for a moment at the congealed eggs Gabriel Miller had left on the table. She honestly didn't know where to begin. This was not, by far, her first home visit.

But it was quickly becoming the most uncomfortable.

She tried not to notice the water-stained paint on the walls or the lack of furniture in the room. The home was clean, and she gave him points for that, though of course it wasn't her place to be handing out or deducting points at all.

Instead, she focused again on Grace, who gave her a gold star smile, and she drew courage.

"Why didn't you tell me Grace doesn't speak?"

Spinning the spoon in front of him, he finally said, "I meant to. I should have."

"But..."

"But the children started coming in. I didn't want to embarrass her."

"Surely you knew they would find out."

"*Ya.* I knew, but I thought maybe they wouldn't find out the first day."

Miriam put her hands in her lap. "And then?"

"Well, then I meant to come the second day, but...I became busy."

"And you received my notes?"

Now a look of embarrassment replaced what might have been anger earlier. He and Grace shared a look, a small secret of some sort. Gabe ran his hand over the back of his neck and then admitted, "I did receive your notes, and I should have answered them, but honestly I didn't know what to say. I still don't."

Miriam took a long drink of her *kaffi*.

Grace looked at her and shrugged, same as she always did.

Gabe looked at her and shrugged.

The father and daughter reactions were so identical that Miriam didn't know whether to laugh or scold them both. But if there was anything she'd learned in eight years, it was that scolding rarely worked.

Instead, glancing again at the congealed eggs, she had another idea.

"Would you mind terribly if I cooked dinner for you?"

"Say again?"

"I'm here and I'm hungry. I don't suppose you were planning on eating that."

"I can cook for my *dochder*." Gabe sat up straighter, a defensive expression crossing his face.

"I'm sure you can cook for Grace, but apparently you were late in the fields or the barn and had some trouble. Perhaps we could do it together this once."

Grace jumped out of her chair and ran across the kitchen to the mudroom. Miriam heard her open and close the icebox door. She came back into the room, her arms loaded with fresh bacon, eggs, and butter.

This time Miriam did laugh. "She may not speak, but she has strong opinions."

"That she does," Gabe agreed with a sigh.

An hour later they'd had a good dinner, though it wasn't what Miriam was accustomed to eating in the evening. She supposed widowers were less particular about such things. It was obvious by this time that Gabe was raising Grace alone.

So what had happened to Mrs. Miller? She would ask her *mamm* when she arrived home, though as tight-lipped as Gabe was, it could be he'd told no one as of yet.

She said her good nights to Grace, who was on the floor of the nearly empty sitting room, looking over a reader she'd taken home from the school.

Gabe held a gas lantern to light their way as he walked her to her buggy. She had to try for answers one more time before leaving.

"How long has she been this way?"

"A long time."

"Have you seen a doctor?"

"No reason. She could talk before. She's chosen to stop."

"Just like that? You just decide she's okay?"

"I've known Gracie her entire life. I appreciate your concern, but it's unfounded."

"Unfounded?" Miriam felt her temper spark brighter than the stars lighting up the winter sky. "She is one of my students, and I have every right to be concerned."

"She's my *dochder*. I'll see to her raising if you'll see to her learning."

"How am I to do that if she won't speak?"

"Gracie will speak when she's ready. Until then, teach her as best you can. Her mind works the same as before. Surely you've seen that she's a bright girl." Gabe helped her into her buggy, handed her the reins, and then took hold of the mare's harness to turn her so she was facing down the lane.

But Miriam wasn't ready to be dismissed.

She didn't drop the flap that was rolled up over the driver's side and fastened with two leather straps. As Gabe walked around to her side, she practically hung out of the buggy to continue their conversation. "Well, of course she's bright, but—"

"She can still learn math, reading, and writing."

"Yes, but—"

Gabe stuck his hands into his coat pockets. His breath came out in front of him in a frosted cloud, but his eyes—his chocolate-brown eyes—were colder than the plummeting temperatures as he challenged her. "If she were a deaf or mute child, we wouldn't be having this conversation."

"But she's not a deaf or mute child."

"I'm glad you see my point. Now you focus on your job, and I'll focus on mine. Good night, Miriam."

Reaching up, he released the fasteners that held the leather flap. It spun down, shutting out the cold and the inscrutable expression on his face. She could only see out of the front of the buggy. She could only see the lane leading away from his home.

He swatted the mare's rear, and she obediently set off at a trot down the lane.

Miriam had a good mind to pull on the reins and turn right back around.

She thought to return and explain to Mr. Gabriel Miller exactly how wrong he was. She could give him a good twenty reasons why he was wrong.

Before she'd reasoned out those twenty reasons, though, she was far down the road. In truth she had trouble coming up with so many. Each time she'd come up with one, Gracie's gentle eyes, or the way she'd hugged her father's legs that first day, or the wonderful drawings she did would pop into Miriam's mind, and then she'd discard her ironclad reason to reach for another.

By the time she'd found one good reason, she saw the gaslights in her parents' sitting room window, and her horse, Belle, had already turned into the lane.

One good reason was all she needed, though.

Grace should speak because she could.

It was their duty—Miriam's, Doc Hanson's, and, yes, Gabe's too—to help her because Grace had a voice, and Miriam believed every child's voice was a gift.

Miriam was determined that, one way or another, she would find a way to set it free.

⟨⟨ Chapter 3 ⟩⟩

When Miriam woke the next morning, her first thoughts were of Gabriel Miller—the sadness in his eyes, the way he smiled when he dealt with his daughter, and the rudeness with which he'd dismissed her the night before, in that particular order.

Her second thoughts were of Grace, the young girl who had already claimed a special place in her heart.

Those strings of thought crossed one another and became tangled as she lay in the predawn light and wavered between waking and sleeping.

Then the strings were broken, and Miriam sat straight up in bed, thinking of only one thing—her mother's cooking. Her stomach growled as the smells of frying sausage and fresh biscuits wafted up the stairs and pulled away the last remnants of sleep.

It made no difference that her meal the night before had been breakfast. This was her mother's cooking. She was home.

If she'd had any urge to roll over and bury herself in warm quilts, the image of her mother downstairs cooking the morning meal convinced her otherwise. She dressed quickly in her Saturday work dress and then hurried outside to visit the restroom. The morning was cold, fresh, and sparkling.

Miriam was aware that most Americans would probably think they were crazy for still having their toilets in a separate building from the house. Even some Amish had taken to indoor bathrooms—not in Cashton, at least not on their side of Pebble Creek, but in the more liberal districts.

She paused to gaze across the frost-covered fields. At moments like this her worries lifted and she could pull in a deep breath. She was able to thank God for all she had and for the people in her life. As she stood there, morning light tinged the eastern sky, a small flock of birds took flight, and their dog, Pepper, chased a rabbit around the corner of the barn.

All of it was God's handiwork. Closing her eyes, she whispered a short prayer for her parents, her students, and even for herself.

Miriam didn't claim to fully understand why her life was different than other women her age, but at times like this it didn't seem to matter. She could trust that God had a plan, and that He would let her in on it eventually.

A light wind pulled at her robe, and she laughed at herself, standing in the cold when a hot breakfast was on the table.

Abigail turned from the stove and tossed her daughter the same smile she'd been giving the past twenty-six years, or at least it seemed Miriam could remember it from birth. Slight like Miriam, her light-brown hair was tucked under a white prayer *kapp*, and she wore a dark-gray dress with a black apron.

Today they would cook, clean, and prepare for tomorrow's church services.

"*Gudemariye*," she said with a twinkle in her eye. "I thought you might sleep a bit later after your hard week of teaching."

"You know I can't sleep late once I smell your cooking." Miriam poured *kaffi* from the pot sitting on the stove and then kissed her mother's cheek before peeking in the oven. Biscuits golden and risen to perfection winked back at her.

"As tired as you looked when you arrived last night, perhaps I should have done my best to see that you did sleep in a bit." Abigail nudged her out of the way and retrieved the pan of biscuits. "If it's the cooking that woke you, I could have served your father porridge and cold biscuits."

"What would I have done to deserve such a thing, Abigail Ruth?" Joshua asked as he banged into the kitchen. He barely managed to hang his hat on its peg before Miriam engulfed him in a hug.

She paused at the back door only long enough to glance out and see that Pepper had followed her father to the house and remained at the back step, ever vigilant and faithful to her family. The German shorthaired pointer had been the smallest of a litter born one spring when Miriam was sixteen. The dog had grown into a beauty and won the entire family's heart.

"You deserve sausage, biscuits, and more," Miriam said to her father, walking him to the table and pouring him a hot mug of *kaffi*. "I was complaining to Mother that the smells from the kitchen woke me."

"Doesn't sound like my girl to be grumbling about anything, much less a hot meal," Joshua said, smiling. He ran his fingers through his coal-black beard, which had begun to show streaks of gray the last few years.

Miriam received her size and skill with knitting needles from her mother. From her father she'd inherited her black hair and a rarely seen but volatile temper.

Joshua reached for the sugar bowl and added a single, level teaspoon to his mug. She'd never thought of her father as old, but a recent visit to the *Englisch* doctor had revealed he suffered from borderline diabetes. He'd taken the doctor's advice seriously and cut back on all of his refined sugars, though apparently he was still eating everything else he was used to.

"Your *bruders* will be here in another hour," Abigail said to Miriam as she placed platters of sausage, scrambled eggs, and the hot biscuits on the table. "They're going to help prepare the house for the church service tomorrow. Your *dat* especially needs extra hands clearing out the barn for the luncheon."

"Simon's coming later today?" Miriam asked, trying to stuff a biscuit into her mouth, take a swallow of *kaffi*, and reach for her napkin at the same time.

"*Ya*." Abigail pulled the syrup across the table to add a dab on the corner of her plate before passing it on to Miriam. "He asked for time off at the store and worked extra all week so the owner wouldn't mind him being gone today."

"It's hard to believe he'll be married in the spring." Miriam scooped eggs on her plate and added a single piece of sausage. Sinking back in her chair and pulling her mug of *kaffi* toward her, she thought of Simon marrying and having children. For reasons she couldn't explain, the idea brought to mind Gabriel Miller.

"Your brother has turned twenty-two. He's plenty old enough to marry." Joshua's gaze traveled from her to the plate of biscuits and then back to her again. "You tumbled into bed as soon as you arrived last night. Was school more difficult than usual last week?"

Miriam stared down into her *kaffi*. She had wanted to talk to her parents about Gabe, but now that she had the perfect opportunity, she wasn't sure exactly what to say.

His parting words to "focus on her job" rang in her ears, and she once again felt the anger she'd struggled with as she'd driven to her parents' home.

"Do you know Gabriel Miller? The man who bought Mr. Kline's farm?"

Joshua studied her, and then he returned to eating his meal in silence. Miriam decided that perhaps he wasn't going to answer her question. With her father, it was often that way. Sometimes he merely moved on to another subject.

This morning, though, after he had finished his breakfast, he looked out the window, out over the fields covered with snow, and said, "I went by and met the man. He didn't have much to say."

"That farm is a near total loss," Abigail added. "Everyone around these parts knows that—Amish or *Englisch*. Your father offered to help him, but apparently he wasn't interested."

Joshua shrugged, stood, and set his dishes in the sink. "The man has a right to do things his own way."

He paused long enough to kiss his wife on the cheek. "I wasn't aware Miller had a child in the school. Is that what this is about?"

"Yes. He has a girl, eight years old. Her name is Grace." Miriam thought of adding that there had been no sign of a Mrs. Miller. She considered telling her parents that Grace didn't speak. And she wanted to admit she wasn't sure how to handle the situation, especially after last night's visit at the Miller home.

As the morning light bathed the kitchen, her father said, "We'll be the best neighbors we can be to them." Then he turned, retrieved his hat, and walked back out into the cold morning.

Her mother began clearing the dishes, humming to herself as she worked.

That was the way things were with her parents. They had the ability to accept things as they were—something Miriam hadn't quite mastered yet.

But her father's words echoed in her mind as she cleaned the floors, scrubbed the counters, and then helped prepare lunch for her three brothers. Later that afternoon she went out to the barn and spent twenty minutes with Pepper—brushing him, playing fetch, and enjoying the feel of him flopped across her feet. Even while she was resting, her mind went back and dwelled on what her father had said. Being good neighbors was the most they could do at this point—and being a good teacher should be her main goal at work.

At least until Gabe was willing to let them do more.

Perhaps tomorrow's service would reveal additional information about the mystery of Grace and Gabe and the missing Mrs. Miller. Would it be useful in helping Grace?

That was something she'd have to wait to find out, and Miriam was learning a truth about herself—besides not wanting to accept things as they were, she was also not good at waiting.

Gabe would have preferred to stay home on Sunday morning.

Saturday he had worked from before sunrise until late into the evening, as he did every day, pausing long enough to feed Gracie, compliment her drawings, and peer into the small wooden box she was hovering over. It held a mouse. He'd suggested she add some straw and a bit of cheese and water if she was sure she wanted to keep the tiny gray thing.

Her smile was all the answer he needed.

He knew there was no avoiding church Sunday morning. The bishop had been by earlier in the week and all but exacted a promise from him.

The promise he'd given to Bishop Zeke back in Indiana was something he considered a serious matter. More important even than that, though, was the vow he'd given to both his mother and Hope's mother. That memory weighed on him heavier than the work that waited to be done. He'd given his word that Grace would be brought up properly and raised correctly in the faith, and he'd see to it that she was. The fact that he'd have to endure the looks of strangers and the sympathy of yet another community was a small thing.

He'd endured worse.

Running his finger under the collar of his best shirt, the same shirt he'd worn to take Gracie to school the first day, he went through a mental checklist before they left the house.

The fire was banked in the stove.

He'd taken care of the animals for the day.

Gracie wore her best clothes and waited patiently by the front door, studying him curiously.

Gracie.

He'd meant to talk to her before they set off for the service. Walking across the sitting room, he stopped in front of her and crouched down so that they were eye to eye. As usual, when he looked at her like this, when he stopped to slow down and consider how quickly she was growing before his very eyes, she reminded him of her mother. Gracie had Hope's warm brown eyes and beautiful features—a petite nose, small chin, and even the same smattering of freckles across her cheeks.

The single difference was the color of her hair. Hope's brown hair had been quite light, almost blonde, where Gracie's was dark-brown like his. The morning she was born, when the midwife had placed their new infant in Hope's arms, his wife had gazed up at him and whispered, "Isn't she a little angel, Gabe? Her hair is like the chestnut pony's, and like yours."

Looking into his daughter's expectant eyes now, it seemed as though Gabe could feel his wife's hand on his arm and hear her voice in his ear.

He drew in a deep breath and focused on what needed to be said.

"You know we're going to church this morning?"

Gracie nodded.

"And you remember the way church services are done from our time in Indiana?"

This time Gracie smiled and held up the Bible she carried. It had been a parting gift from his mother.

"*Ya*, that's *gut*, but what I mean to say is that you'll be sitting with the women and children, and I'll be sitting with the men." When concern wiped the smile off her face, he hurried on. "Today's service is at Mr. King's place. He is your teacher's *dat*, so maybe you'll be able to sit with her or with some of her family."

Gracie stood completely still now, almost as if she were playing frozen angels out in the snow, except Gabe couldn't remember a time he'd actually seen her playing outdoors with other *kinner*. He pushed the thought aside and concentrated on preparing her for the morning.

"The bishop will introduce us. When he does, I want you to come down and stand with me. I've asked him..." Gabe stared out the window, out at the farm that was to hold such promise. "I've asked him to tell no more than he feels he has to about...about your *mamm*, but I didn't want you to be surprised when you heard him speak her name. I know it's not something we mention often." This last part he added in almost a whisper.

Quiet enveloped them.

He thought for a moment Gracie might speak—a hope that was always in his heart—but she didn't. They stood there, watching each other, mirroring each other's loss. Gabe slowly became aware of the soft crackling of the fire he'd banked inside the iron stove, a light breeze stirring a branch against the roof of the house, one of the horses neighing in the barn.

Gracie surprised him when she set her Bible on the floor, placed both of her hands against his cheeks and pressed her forehead against his. They remained that way for another moment, until they both seemed to sense that it was time to go.

She combed her fingers through his beard once, the way she often had as a small child, and then she retrieved her Bible and walked ahead of him out into the bright winter morning.

Gabe wished with all that was within him that he knew what was going on within the child's mind.

As he drove the buggy toward the Kings' home, his mind went back over his conversation with Miriam on Friday evening. Was he wrong? Would it be better to take the child to an *Englisch* doctor? But his heart told him there was nothing physically wrong with Gracie. And as for the emotional things—well, they were both wounded, and wounds took time to heal.

Pulling into the lane that led up to the Kings' house, he resolved to hold his stance against the schoolteacher. No doubt she meant well, but he'd spent the last three years suffering through the attentions of people who meant well, both Amish and *Englisch*. He and Grace had come to Wisconsin to escape that, and he wasn't going to let one snippet of a girl, even if she was a teacher, stir up that particular nightmare all over again.

≈ Chapter 4 ≈

Grace listened to the words of the *Loblied*, the second hymn of praise sung in every church service she'd ever attended. Though the service was conducted entirely in German, she had no trouble following along. Her *grossmammis* had taught her well in the old language.

All of that had been before she'd attended her old school.

Before she'd learned to stand against the looks of other children—the looks and harsh words.

Before her family had decided to teach her at home. Years before they had moved to this new place, with its colder winter and different ways. Here in Wisconsin, even the sounds were different in her ears.

But the words to the hymn—the old language—she recognized and knew.

Hearing them was like being wrapped in one of her *grossmammi's* familiar worn quilts. Not the new ones packed and waiting in a chest for the next wedding. No, Grace preferred the old ones, with the occasional stain or worn spot. When she was covered with them, she was surrounded by the smells of people she loved—people who loved her.

That's what the words of the *Loblied* meant to her, and though she knew her dad would rather have stayed home and worked in the sad old barn, she preferred being here.

The voices around her rose in a chorus of sound, and it seemed to Grace as if she were singing with them.

She didn't.

At moments like this, she had to make sure she pushed her teeth together, lest some noise escape that would embarrass her father. The last thing she wanted to do on this day was cause him more hurt. She'd seen by the way he spoke to her that the morning would be difficult enough.

For her part, Grace liked new things and new people. She even liked the sad barn and the droopy house.

She had looked forward to church since they had arrived in Pebble Creek eleven days ago.

But this morning there had been no time to draw a picture and tell him that, so she'd done the next best thing—she'd put her hands on his face and tried to tell him with her eyes.

He'd seemed to understand, for he'd smiled at her and his eyes had grown crinkly the way they did when the crops grew tall or the rain came down in proper amounts.

As the song ended and they sat on the long wooden benches brought into the house for the service, Miriam's mother smiled at her. Grace liked sitting near Abigail. That was the name she was supposed to say—though of course there was no way for her to say it. Abigail smelled nice, like pies and soap and quilts all at the same time. Grace wondered what it would be like to crawl onto her lap, but she didn't wonder about it for long. Best to push such thoughts away or they would come back to keep her awake late at night.

Instead, she stared at the tops of her black shoes and thought of her mouse, whom she'd named Stanley. Miriam was reading them a story at school, and it had a boy named Stanley in it. That Stanley was always getting into trouble, but Grace's mouse seemed to behave well, other than the time he escaped from his box and ran into the kitchen. Her dad had nearly stepped on Stanley then.

He'd hopped and hollered and Stanley had run for his life.

Grace smiled at the memory.

Stanley wasn't quite as nice as Pepper. Grace had spent a few moments with the dog when she'd first arrived. Her father had looked at her and shook his head no. She didn't need a voice to tell him what was in her heart—he'd known! A dog would be an amazing thing to own, even if you had to go to the barn to see it. For now, though, she would be happy with Stanley in his box.

At that very moment Abigail looked down at her. She patted Grace on the knee and smiled.

Grace could tell that her teacher hadn't told Abigail about how her voice had gone missing. That's the way she always thought of it—as if it had disappeared like the tabby cat they had in Indiana. Muffin just walked out into the fields one evening. He didn't even say goodbye. Grace would sit out on the stoop and watch for him until dark, but her dad said that old cat wasn't coming back until he was ready—that it might be days or years.

She figured her voice was the same way. It wasn't coming back until it was ready.

One time she had tried to force it back, to make a sound come out. She had been frustrated with her dad that day because he didn't understand what she was trying to tell him. She'd become cross and tried to make him see. What they'd argued about wasn't even important.

It was just about clothes she didn't want to wear because they didn't fit anymore. He had wanted her to hurry and dress, but when she'd tried to find something to write on and tell him why she couldn't, he'd only hollered—and he never hollered. So she'd tried to holler back. What came out sounded like the old squeaky hinge on the barn, only worse and louder.

She still remembered the look on his face. He'd seemed more afraid at that moment than he had when her mother had died.

Grace could remember that day too. The day the angels took her *mamm* with them.

It was the same day her voice walked away.

Abigail reached over and squeezed her hand. "Bishop Beiler wants you to join your *dat*," she whispered. "Do you want me to walk with you?"

Grace shook her head, hopped off her bench, and started toward the front of the room. Then she remembered her Bible. Turning around, she hurried back for it. The Bible was the last thing her *grossmammi* Sarah had given her. She'd told her to take good care of it.

She retrieved it from her seat and then rushed to the front of the room.

The Kings' home had looked far less crowded from her bench. Once she stood beside her father with her hand in his, it seemed as if there were a thousand people staring at them. Grace was good at math, and she knew there weren't actually a thousand people, but there were maybe a hundred.

Her heart started to hammer in her chest like the wings of a baby bird. She looked up at her dad and the bishop, who both seemed unusually tall all of a sudden.

"I beseech you to pray for both Gabriel and Grace as they find their place within our community," Bishop Beiler said. His voice was very serious, and when she glanced at him he didn't smile the way their old bishop did. His words were nice, though, and she could tell he meant them. You could tell when people meant what they said and when they didn't if you listened close enough.

"It's difficult to experience loss in this life, but God doesn't leave us alone. He brought the Millers to us for a reason. I know you all will be family to Grace and Gabe—a mother to Grace and friends to them both. For we are one community and one family, *bruders* and *schweschders* in the faith."

Grace couldn't see Bishop Beiler's face well. She could see he had a gray beard. She thought the words he said were just right. When she closed her eyes, they washed over her like starlight.

Since her voice had gone, she'd learned to tell a lot from people's voices. Bishop Beiler's voice was very serious. Some kids thought that was bad, but it wasn't always. Bad was someone whose voice said one thing when their face said another. Bishop Beiler's voice was solemn—that was a word they had learned in school, but it matched his face. She could see his face now that he'd moved over a few feet. His face and voice matched up, so he was all right with her.

Now everyone was singing again.

Grace stood there, wondering what it would be like to sing with them. She sang in her head, but it wasn't the same.

Then the service ended and people were coming forward, shaking hands with her father. Some patted her on the head and others shook her hand as if she were an adult. She could always tell if someone knew about her voice or not by the way they looked at her.

A few people spoke to her and waited for a response, but generally adults preferred quiet children.

Some kids made fun of her when adults weren't near, but if she ignored them they went away.

Soon she was being hugged by Miriam's mother, who pulled her away from the front of the room and toward the tables where the food was being served.

As she stood in line for lunch, two boys began to rib each other and giggle, pointing at her and speaking behind their hands.

"She's mute," the taller boy said.

"No, she's not. She's stupid."

"Bet she's not either. Bet she'll squeal if we poke her with a fork."

She pretended not to notice and moved forward in the line. She hoped the boys wouldn't poke her. She was fairly sure she wouldn't squeal. She'd cut her hand once on a rusty nail when she was playing in the barn back in Indiana. The *Englisch* doctor had been surprised and said, "Not even one peep. You definitely deserve a sticker or a lollipop."

She ignored the boys and tried to think about Stanley.

As she reached the table with the plates, Hannah stepped in between her and the boys. "Hello, Grace. I was hoping you'd sit with me today."

Grace smiled up at her new friend and the boys settled down.

Maybe the bishop was right. Maybe it would all work out, the way things did in a family.

≈ Chapter 5 ≈

Sensing that he might try to cut out early, Miriam kept her eye on Gabe Miller. Which wasn't easy to do because she was refilling dishes in the food line—as the plate of sliced ham emptied, she'd whisk it off and replace it with another. When the basket of fresh bread was down to the last slice, she put another in its place at the same moment Eli Stutzman put his hand forward for a piece.

"Nice timing, Miriam."

"*Danki*, Eli."

"How are the *kinner* doing? I never have much time to speak with you when we're at school."

"They're doing well." Miriam followed him down the table, pushing forward the asparagus casserole that wasn't being emptied out quickly enough. Almost against her will, she glanced up and scanned the room again looking for Gabe and Grace.

"I believe Miller went to the barn, if that's who you're looking for." Eli had lowered his voice, but Miriam could still detect a note of teasing.

"Did he take Gracie with him?" Miriam asked.

"Actually, I think Gracie went first." Eli dumped cranberry dressing on the side of his plate.

Miriam absently straightened a dish.

"She left with Hannah," he added. "Are you worried about the girl?"

"*Ya*. The children are teasing her a bit," Miriam admitted. "It happens sometimes when a student is new. Grace is so young, and..." she fumbled and stopped, trying to think of how to explain about Grace or even *if* she should explain about Grace.

"Sadie told me about the girl's silence," Eli said. "Is there anything I can do?"

Miriam shook her head, unsure if she should add anything else, and continued to scan the room as if Gabe and Grace might reappear next to the pot of *kaffi*.

"I believe she went looking for Pepper." Eli popped a piece of a roll into his mouth and chewed it thoughtfully as two women stepped around him. When they'd passed, he held up a finger, as if he remembered another important piece of information. "She seems quite taken with the dog."

"You're probably right. Still, I'd like to check on her." Miriam surveyed the tables of food and the ten or so people left in line. Her mother and aunt were still working in the kitchen, but it looked as if they had the first round of helpings under control.

"I'll explain to your *mamm*, and if they need any other help I'll stay—or call my Mary over to lend a hand." Eli stepped back as she wriggled out from behind the tables.

"*Danki*. I'm sure Grace is fine, but I'd feel better if I could see that for myself."

"Some women are born worriers," he mumbled as he reached for a piece of fresh pumpkin bread.

Miriam heard him, but she didn't slow down.

She grabbed her coat off the hook by the back door and hurried outside and across the yard to the barn. She didn't know why concern bubbled up her spine like water surging out of a teakettle. There was no need to worry about Grace if she was with Hannah, and Gabe Miller could take care of himself.

Something seemed to be wrong, though. Perhaps it was that she had caught the look Hannah had given the Lapp boys. No doubt they had been teasing Grace as they had on Friday.

Miriam pushed open the door of the barn and instantly relaxed. She couldn't help it. The odors of hay and animals and leather had that effect on her. Closing her eyes for a moment, she pulled in a deep breath. When she did, the sounds of the young people gathered there calmed her nerves.

She opened her eyes and blinked twice, adjusting to the dim light that shone in rays down from the high windows. Wood smoke filled the air, but she knew the stove in her dad's office would do little more than heat the corner area.

Not that the December cold seemed to be bothering anyone.

At least a dozen of her students had abandoned their food and were playing volleyball. Several of the younger children were sitting in a circle being coaxed by older siblings to finish their meals before they ran to play. And, of course, a group of older boys sat off to one side, on wooden crates, talking among themselves and throwing glances at the girls.

Miriam scanned the room twice, but she saw no evidence of Grace or Gabe or Pepper. She spotted Hannah helping with the younger children.

Checking the room one last time, she walked over to Hannah and crouched down beside her.

"How's the food?"

"*Gut*. Have you eaten already?" Hannah grabbed a cup of milk a second before the youngest girl, Lily, knocked it over.

"Not yet. I'm looking for Grace and her *dat*. Have you seen them?"

"They came in with us. Grace was walking with me, but she seemed to want her father to come along. Then Sadie Stutzman joined us."

"Sadie's playing volleyball." Lily looked up at Hannah and turned on her brightest smile. "I wanna play too."

"Of course you can, but your *mamm* said she wanted you to eat first. Sadie ate already. Can you finish what's on your plate?"

"Okay, Hannah." Lily's smile vanished, but she picked up her fork and went to work on the food.

"They were here a minute ago," Hannah said.

"Kittens!" Lily exclaimed around a mouthful of ham.

"Swallow before talking, please." Hannah handed her a cloth napkin to wipe her mouth with.

Miriam had an urge to tell the girl it was fine to talk with her mouth full. A manners lesson could wait. Instead, she waited for her to chew the giant piece of ham she'd managed to stuff into her mouth.

Kittens? Did they have kittens? She didn't remember.

"New kittens are in the back," Lily finally explained. "Sadie told Grace about them, and Grace took her *dat* back there."

Lily pointed toward the back of the barn, where Miriam's father used to keep a Shetland pony she'd had when she drove a small buggy as a *kind*.

Lily pushed a spoonful of casserole into her mouth. Rather than wait on another round of chewing so that she could explain more, Miriam stood, brushed off her dress, and muttered her thanks.

Kittens? No one had mentioned kittens to her.

She made her way around the volleyball game and walked toward the back stall.

They always had barn cats. Maybe her dad hadn't seen these yet. A moment later she noticed Pepper curled up in front of the last stall door. She knelt and rubbed him between the ears once, whispered "*Gut* boy," and then stood to survey the scene inside the stall. Someone had known the mama cat had birthed her litter there.

Grace sat cross-legged near a crate that had been turned on its side and stuffed with an old blanket.

Gabe stood against the wall, his legs crossed at the ankle, still eating from his dinner plate. His attention was split between the food and his daughter, which probably explained why he didn't notice Miriam watching them.

"I didn't take you two for the back-of-the-barn type," Miriam said, resting her arms against the open half door of the stall.

Gabe stiffened immediately, but then Grace glanced up, a look of wonder covering her face, and he instantly softened. "I hope it isn't a problem," he said. "Another little girl told her about the kittens, and then—"

Grace hopped up, ran to the door, and reached for Miriam's hand.

"How many kittens are there?" Miriam asked.

All five fingers of Grace's right hand flashed out.

"I didn't even know they were here." Miriam entered the stall and knelt down in the straw in front of the crate. Grace settled beside her. For some reason she was keenly aware that Gabe was still watching them both.

"They're tiny, Grace." Miriam touched the mama cat gently. "I'd say they're not more than a week or so old."

Grace reached forward and her hand hovered over a gray-and-black kitten.

Settling back, Miriam waited.

When she didn't speak, Grace looked anxiously from the kitten and then back to her several times. Miriam wondered if she was beginning to feel dizzy.

"I believe she wants to ask you something," Gabe said somewhat sarcastically.

"Hmm." Miriam understood Grace wanted one of the kittens, but suddenly the teacher in her sprang forward. She knew at times it was best not to jump in, but rather to wait.

Grace scrambled up on her knees and wiggled closer to the kittens, which were sleeping against the mama cat.

"I think she wants to—"

"Perhaps we should let Grace speak for herself, Gabe." Miriam heard the sharp intake of his breath and sensed his shift in position, but she was too intent on watching his daughter to pay close attention to him.

Grace's eyes had widened, and her fidgeting had stopped as if she'd frozen to the spot. Then she turned to look Miriam full in the face.

Miriam smiled at this child she was already learning to love. Stubbornness was something she admired in a pupil. It had helped more than one student overcome a handicap or difficulty, but she instinctively knew she was going to have to prove herself as willful as Grace or they would make no progress this year.

"Do you have a question for me, Grace?"

Now the girl peered around, as if she might find her drawing tablet, but she hadn't brought it with her this morning.

Miriam didn't realize Gabe was standing directly behind her until he leaned down and spoke quietly into her ear. She nearly jumped out of her apron and squealed. Grace clapped her hand over her mouth to stifle a giggle.

Did she giggle? Did she make sounds when she cried or laughed?

"I'd like to speak to you, Miriam. Alone."

Miriam rolled her eyes. She realized Grace saw that too when the girl glanced away and at the kittens, a smile now spreading completely across her face.

Standing as gracefully as she could while covered with straw, Miriam followed him out of the stall. They walked away a few feet before he let loose the anger that had been building probably since she'd stopped by his house on Friday evening.

"What are you doing?"

"I'm speaking to your *dochder*."

"That's not what I mean. We discussed this. You're trying to trick her into talking. That's despicable. She'll talk when she's ready."

"Why should she—"

"What?" He had been pacing between the two rows of stalls, but now he turned on her, exasperation consuming his expression and raising his voice.

Pepper uttered a low growl from his place in front of the kitten's stall.

"It's all right, boy." Miriam turned back to Gabe. "I was saying, why should she speak if she has you to interpret her every wish?"

"That's the stupidest thing I've ever heard."

"Is it? Why? It's the very thing you were about to do."

"I was helping my *dochder*."

"You think that's helping?"

"More than what you were doing."

"I disagree." Miriam tried to ignore the intensity of his gaze, as well as the fact that mere inches now separated them. But she refused to back down. Someone needed to be objective here. Someone needed to stand up for Grace.

Gabe clenched his hands at his side, took one step closer, and fought to lower his voice. "Do you think today was easy for her?"

"I don't—"

"Do you have any idea what it's like to be among strangers?"

"Well, no."

"To be without someone you love?"

"No, but—"

"And to have no chance of getting them back?"

Miriam pulled up short, his words hitting her with the force of a bitter winter wind, stopping any argument she might have offered.

He was right.

She had no idea what he and Grace were enduring. She'd never been among strangers, and she had never lost someone she loved.

He walked to the neighboring stall, put his hands against the door, and pulled in two deep breaths. When he seemed to have calmed himself, he walked back to her, his voice icier than the pond behind their home.

"I'll thank you to not experiment with my *dochder*, Miriam. I know what's best for her. You don't. You are a girl who has no idea what life or love or loss is about. You know books and nothing else."

He turned and stormed back into the stall where Grace waited.

By the time Miriam caught up with him, he stood in front of his daughter and the crate of kittens, looking down at the message she'd written in the dirt floor of the stall.

She'd found an old stick and scribbled it into the ground. "May I keep Stormy?" Beside that she'd added the word "Please."

Grace seemed immensely pleased with herself. She'd found a way to make herself heard.

Gabe looked miserable.

Miriam pulled in a deep breath, stuffed her wounded feelings deep inside, and walked over to the little girl. Kneeling down in front of her, she reached for the strings of her small prayer *kapp*, straightened them, and then finally looked into her brown eyes.

"I suppose Stormy is the dark-gray kitten."

Grace smiled and nodded.

"He'll be ready to go to your house by the end of the month if your *dat* says it's okay."

She didn't turn to look at Gabe Miller. She couldn't have borne to see the pain in those eyes one more time. He must have said yes, though, for Grace smiled once again, threw her arms around Miriam's neck, and hugged her tightly.

Then she ran to her father.

Miriam heard them leave the stall and walk down the length of the barn. She remained there a few more minutes, watching the kittens, Pepper now at her side, and wondered how much damage she had managed to do with her well-intentioned ideas.

⬿ Chapter 6 ⬿

G abe told himself there was no reason to feel guilty regarding the scene in the barn. He told himself that while he herded the bull back into the pasture and mended the fence yet again. He repeated it to himself while he worked on the leaking roof of his barn in the biting wind. And he tried muttering it yet again each time he opened Grace's lunch box and found it empty of any notes.

He could justify his actions to himself as much as he'd like. The guilt still had a way of worming its way into his mind. His words had been harsh, and he had not been raised to speak in such a way. Moreover, as Gracie's drawing tablet was filled each night less and less with the scene outside their kitchen window, and more and more with kittens, school, and her new favorite person, Miriam, he realized if there was a bright spot in his daughter's life he should be grateful for it.

All of which explained why he had trouble remaining angry on Wednesday.

Grace struggled out of Eli's buggy, her arms loaded down and barely able to see over the top of what she was carrying.

"Miriam sent the basket," Eli explained. "I offered to help Grace with it, but she assured me she could handle it."

Gabe had noticed that Eli referred to Grace as if she spoke, and indeed it was as if Grace had her own language. Problem was, most people were too busy to catch on to it. The fact that the older gentleman took the time and had the patience to "hear" her softened Gabe's attitude quite a bit. He'd refused the man's offer for help twice already—once on the fences and another time on the barn.

He refused partly because he was determined he could do it on his own, and partly because he didn't want to be indebted to anyone.

"Grace has a stubborn streak," Gabe admitted, leaning against the door of the buggy. "She'd nearer fall over than ask for help carrying something."

He reached down and took the basket from her, wondering what in the world the schoolteacher could have possibly sent home. Given the way they had parted on Sunday, he wouldn't be surprised if it was a basket of rocks with a note telling him she'd been for an evening walk, spotted the pile, and thought of his brain. He smiled at the thought. It would serve him right.

"Guess today's work went better, given that grin on your face." Eli adjusted his coat—a not too subtle hint at how cold it was with the door open.

"Absolutely," Gabe said. "I only had to chase the bull half the morning, and I didn't fall off the barn's roof once."

Eli laughed. "If you change your mind about wanting some help, say the word."

"Sure will." Gabe was surprised to find he meant it. Not that he expected to ask for help, but if he ever did, Eli would be the man he'd want beside him. If he could trust Eli with his daughter, he could certainly trust him with a fence or a roof.

Waving as they walked away, he glanced down at Grace and wiggled his right eyebrow. "Basket, huh? Doesn't feel like there's a kitten in here. Don't think anything's squirming."

She shook her head so hard her *kapp* strings circled back and forth.

"Not sure what it could be if it's not a kitten. Maybe we should throw it over the fence to Snickers. She'd like a surprise."

Grace nearly dropped her lunch box, and then she ran in front of him so she could turn and walk backward.

"What, you don't want me to give our horse what's in this basket? So it must be...food?"

The smile that spread across his daughter's face told him he'd guessed right, though he couldn't imagine what type of food Miriam might have sent. Poison popped into his mind, but he didn't think he'd angered her that much.

Then again, the woman did seem to have a temper.

No, if he was honest with himself, it wasn't anger he'd stirred in her. It was hurt. He'd set out to wound her, to convince her to back away from him and Grace, and he'd succeeded—at least for a few days.

Apparently, based on the size of the basket, she was back.

Miriam set aside the stack of English papers she was grading. They were interesting enough. She'd asked each student to write about their fondest Christmas memory. Even the youngest of her students had amusing stories, but when she reached Grace's, her worries had consumed her once more.

> My bestest Memory is being with my mamm and
> my dat before The verY Bad night.

The words "very bad night" were written in tiny letters.

> Mamm had sewed me a very pretty green dress.
> I sat on the couch between them in my dress, and
> knew I was the Luckiest girl in the world. Then
> dat Pretended he heard a Knock at the dooR. When

he opened it, a small box Was there and it had my
name on it. I opened the box and found a doll with
a dress exactly like mine—same coloR, same style,
even same kapP. I knew my mamm made it. I could
tell the way her Eyes got all crinkly when I hugged
her. That's my Bestest memory.

P.S. I still Have that doll.

Miriam wandered over to the window. Darkness had fallen more
than an hour ago, so there was little that she could see other than
the quarter moon and a hint of her reflection in the pane of glass.
She certainly couldn't see any answers to the questions troubling
her heart.

"It's not as if he's going to return the casserole dish and dump it
on our doorstep tonight." Esther glanced up from the quilt top she
was nearly finished with. Somehow she'd managed to complete all
her grading while Miriam had been worrying over Grace—over Gabe,
if she were honest with herself.

"Of course he won't. He'll wait until morning when all the children can see him reject my cooking—"

"Our cooking."

"*Our* cooking. What difference does it make?" Miriam flopped
onto the couch, which separated their sitting area from the bedroom
they shared. "It doesn't matter who cooked it. The man is stubborn
and determined not to accept help."

"Remind me again why *we* cooked a delicious chicken casserole
and sent it with Grace?"

Miriam didn't answer at first, mesmerized as Esther's needle
quilted perfect stitches across the fabric. She had always been a good
quilter, but her impending wedding added an urgency to her sewing. At least if the teachers were ever trapped in with a winter storm,
they wouldn't want for covers.

"Miriam? Hello?"

"*Ya*. I'm still here. Just unfocused a bit."

"I'll say. I'm usually the one losing the thread of the conversation." Glancing up, Esther gave her a teasing smile. "I'm not letting you off the hook so easily. Explain to me why we sent food you think Gabe Miller won't eat."

Miriam waved Esther's skepticism away with her hand even as she slipped off her shoes and pulled her feet up beside her on the couch. "You would have sent food too if you had seen how the man cooks. I actually thought there was a fire when I first walked into his house."

"That bad, huh?"

"Yes. I guess his *mamm* never taught him how to cook."

"He probably didn't need to learn. His *fraa* cooked for them before..." Esther's hands paused and she looked up, concern coloring her young features. "Do you know how long it's been since Grace's *mamm* passed?"

"No. I don't believe he's told anyone."

"Do you think it has anything to do with Grace's not talking?"

"I've no reason to believe it does. Certainly it is traumatic to lose a parent, but children do. I've never known it to steal one's speech."

"We had that boy last year who reverted to thumb-sucking." Esther stared across the room. "It was always worse after lunch. As soon as one of us would start reading, he'd pop his thumb right into his mouth."

"Isaiah. I remember him very well. I wonder how they like their new district."

Esther resumed her quilting. "I'm sure they like it fine. I've heard the northern districts have good farmland and lots of it. Your giving him paper to draw while we read—that was a smart idea."

"It's hard to suck your thumb while you're busy."

"And where did you find the book about thumb-sucking? What was the name of it?"

"*The Berenstain Bears and the Bad Habit*, which was actually about nail-biting."

"But he understood."

"Yes, and I think it helped him to laugh about it."

"Where did you find that book?" Esther glanced up at her.

"The librarian in Cashton recommended it. I was out of ideas, so I went and asked her." Miriam ran her fingers through her hair, combing out the braid that had held it all day. "Books can sometimes help us find our way out of a corner we've walked into."

"Maybe you could send a cookbook home with Grace. Then her father wouldn't need our cooking." Esther looked pleased she had thought of the idea, but something told Miriam that Gabe Miller would not take the time to read a book she sent with Grace.

Same as he hadn't read the notes she'd sent the first week Grace had been in school, and that was before she'd made him angry.

"I shouldn't have pushed so hard and so early. He probably does know what is best for his *dochder*. They needed time to adjust. How long have they been in our community? Less than a month? But I expected him to trust me with my new ideas."

Esther didn't say anything. Instead, she set aside her quilting, walked into the kitchen, and returned a few minutes later with two cups of hot herbal tea. Sitting next to Miriam on the couch, she handed her one.

After Miriam had taken a sip, which made her feel better, she said, "That's it? That's all you have for me? Hot tea?"

"No. But I thought I'd let you stew a little longer before I straightened you out."

Miriam laughed for the first time all night.

"You're a *gut* teacher, Miriam. You know that and I know that."

"You are too—"

"Listen. Don't talk." Esther's eyes danced in amusement over her cup as she took another sip of the fragrant brew. "I'm a fair teacher, and I know it. I enjoy working with the older *kinner*, and it's been a *wunderbaar* thing for me until my time to marry. But it's different with you."

Esther tucked her feet underneath her. "You love your students as if they were your own. That's why you pushed Grace and why you pushed her *dat*. He pushed back. So what? Let him lick his wounds. He's a big man. He'll be all right."

Miriam studied her friend for a moment and realized again how much she would miss her next year. "You're sure?"

"About which part?"

"All of it."

"Oh, yes. I'm sure." She set her empty cup of tea on the end table and then moved back to the rocker to resume quilting.

The night settled around them. Miriam picked up a book and began reading it. She'd almost put Gabe Miller from her mind when Esther started giggling.

"Something funny about that quilt?"

"I was trying to imagine how mad he was on Sunday."

"Pretty mad. Face scrunched up, creases between the eyes, jaw clenched...you know the look."

Esther quilted a few more stitches. "Any idea if he's keeping pigs?"

"Pigs?"

"*Ya*. I was thinking if he's still as angry as he was, he might be feeding our casserole to his pigs. Wouldn't that be a sad use of our cooking? We try to do a good deed by sharing our dinner—using up the extra we were going to cook next week—and Gabe Miller feeds it to the pigs."

"I don't see why that's so funny."

"Maybe you could write a story about it." Esther kept sewing and rocking. "Submit it to the *Budget*. And you could give it to Grace to illustrate. Who knows? It might be the thing to get her talking again."

"I don't believe they print fiction."

"Your story could be the first, and it wouldn't exactly be fiction."

Miriam might be a good teacher, but she recognized a terrible idea when she heard one. Putting her and Gabe Miller's fight into the *Budget* was not something she would be doing—even in fictional form. But Esther's idea did start her thinking about Grace and ways she might coax the girl into talking.

Nothing that would anger Gabe of course. She wouldn't want to repeat that encounter. Perhaps she could think of a way to motivate the little girl. She'd learned from experience that every child was inspired by something different. She'd already figured out that Grace was a teacher-pleaser. All she had to do now was come up with a way to combine her teacher-pleasing urge with what Miriam wanted—what deep down inside Gabe wanted.

Put those two things together, and the result might be a little girl's beautiful voice.

❧ Chapter 7 ❧

Three hours after she'd gone to bed, Miriam continued to toss and turn beneath the covers. She'd flopped back and forth so often she was sure she had the quilt wrapped completely around her like one of the ancient Egyptian mummies the older Stutzman boy had given a report on last week.

Her younger students enjoyed listening to the reports from Esther's older students. Miriam knew it was partly a bit of hero worship—the younger boys looked up to the older boys, even though they were shy about admitting it. And the younger girls trusted the older children completely—both boys and girls. They made a nice, extended family in their little schoolhouse.

And like every family, they had their share of problems.

Staring up at the ceiling in the darkness, she forced herself to remain still and focus on a solution.

What was the problem, though?

Gabe Miller? Or Grace Miller?

An image of the young girl popped into her mind, and Miriam relaxed. Grace was a good student. She completed her assignments eagerly. She played well with other students.

Miriam tossed onto her right side.

Grace played well with other students, but not all students played well with Grace. There had been several times in the last two weeks that she had heard other children teasing her—heard and corrected them. The trouble was that she couldn't always be present to defend Grace, and neither could Gabe.

Problem number one—Grace needed her voice so she could defend herself.

Miriam knew her students very well. The students who teased Grace weren't bad children. Misguided perhaps, but not bad. They did what the young do in every species—Miriam had watched young bucks at play—they picked on the weak. She'd thought it was terrible when she'd watched a wounded yearling being harassed by other young bucks. She was fifteen years old at the time, and her father had asked her to keep him company as he studied the deer grazing in his oat patch a week before the start of hunting season.

"Why must they treat the hurt one that way? Nature's so cruel."

"Maybe," her dat replied. "Or maybe by pushing him away, by nudging him constantly, even by running at him with their antlers, it causes him to grow stronger."

When she only looked at him skeptically, he'd shrugged and then continued. "His defenses grow stronger. His hurt leg heals faster because it must or he won't eat."

"But it's wrong, dat."

"Deer don't know right or wrong. They only know survival and instinct."

At the time, the thought had depressed her for some reason, but as she'd grown older she'd replayed that scene in her mind many times. Sometimes driving home from school she'd come across coyotes feasting on a deer carcass, usually one that had been hit by an automobile. Occasionally as she watched the boys play in the fields after church, she'd notice one of the smaller ones being left out. Even on the school grounds children were teased.

She always stepped in and defended the child, but in her mind she heard her father. Did such behavior make the child stronger?

She couldn't say. She only knew teasing was wrong and she wouldn't abide it.

Over the years the ones teased had grown strong—and she thanked God for that. They found their place within the community and childish differences were put away.

For Grace that path seemed blocked because she wasn't able to speak for herself.

Tossing over onto her back, Miriam tried again to see the ceiling of the room. The answers weren't there, but they were somewhere. There was a side of this problem she was missing, just out of her vision.

She had prayed each night and each morning that God would help her attend to Grace's needs. Since she had started teaching, she always prayed before beginning her school day. She'd heard about the *Englisch* schools where spoken prayer was no longer allowed, but she imagined most of those teachers prayed silently before approaching the front of their classroom as well.

Esther had once said that a room full of students had a way of bringing out the believer in you, either that or it would convince any woman to take up baking bread, knitting scarves, or even making cabinets. Without faith their job would be impossible.

So what was she missing?

Helping Grace find her voice would allow her to defend herself, but there was something more. Miriam's mind flashed back to the three times she'd caught students teasing the young girl. Each time it had only been little singsong names, and twice other children had rushed to Grace's defense before Miriam had managed to intervene. What else had she seen?

A turtle! That was it.

She sat up in bed in the pitch-dark room, the connection so perfect that she wanted to clap her hands and wake Esther. She wanted to share it with someone.

Grace's attitude each time had been that of a box turtle. Shoulders slumped, head down, body turned slightly—it was as if she'd thought she might be able to disappear, and then the others would leave her alone.

Yes, Miriam wanted to help Grace find her voice.

But in order to do that, she first needed to help Grace find her confidence.

Lying back down and turning over to her right side, she suddenly had two good ideas for how to accomplish both things. The question was whether Gabe would allow it.

Gabe rose well before daylight, which had been his custom in Indiana. The only thing that had changed since their move to Wisconsin was he had twice the work to accomplish each day.

Pulling his suspenders over his shoulders and then reaching for his coat, he trudged through the kitchen. He paused long enough to look longingly at the *kaffi* pot on the stove, but decided he didn't have the time.

The forecast called for snow, possibly record amounts. He was hoping the repairs he'd done to the roof of the barn would hold, but it would depend on how much snow fell and how heavy it was.

Glowering at the dilapidated structure as he tramped toward it, he decided he'd like to meet the man who built it. He'd happily give him a free lesson in construction, especially construction for northern climates.

First off, the pitch was wrong. It was much too flat and couldn't possibly stand the weight of a heavy snowfall. Apparently it hadn't stood the weight in the past, which would account for the portion of the roof that had fallen in. Why it had never been repaired was another question.

The house had stood empty for nearly a year, according to the Realtor who sold it to him. Though it was dirty from misuse, it was fundamentally sound. The amount of damage in the barn could not have occurred in twelve months. Had the previous owner stopped farming before he'd moved? How long had the structure been abandoned? And why?

Gabe was late returning from the barn, which justified burning breakfast—again. At least it did in his mind, and Grace didn't complain. She didn't complain verbally. She did squirrel up her nose and leave half of the oatmeal in her bowl, but then again, maybe she wasn't hungry.

Sometimes he interpreted her silence in his favor.

Today he'd give himself a break because the snow was still falling and the roof on his barn hadn't fixed itself.

"Ready for school?"

Grace nodded and ran for her coat, pausing at the back door long enough to retrieve Miriam's basket, which had held last night's dinner.

It wasn't until they were halfway down the lane that he noticed she'd put on a few pounds since breakfast—quite a few.

"What's under the coat?"

She gave him her most innocent, wide-eyed look.

"That might work with someone who hasn't known you all your life, Grace Ann, but it won't work with your *dat*. What's under the coat?"

As her luck would have it, Eli's buggy pulled up at the end of the lane, and Grace tugged on his hand.

"I don't want you to be late either," Gabe agreed, "but that doesn't mean you're going to get away with what you're doing."

He allowed her to pull him toward the horses and buggy. Because they were the farthest farm from the school, Grace was the first student picked up and the last one dropped off, other than Eli's own kids. They sat at the windows, waving at his daughter as she hurried up the steps.

"Hold it," Gabe said, when she would have taken her seat without finishing their conversation.

Rather than share her secret with the others, Grace stepped

closer to him, close enough that he could smell the children's shampoo he'd bought for her at the general store.

"Show me," he said.

With a pronounced frown, she unbuttoned the top of her coat, revealing Stanley's box.

"Why—"

She stopped him with a finger to his lips and then quickly rebuttoned her coat and ran to her seat.

"Heavy snow coming," Eli noted.

"Heard it could be up to twelve inches."

"*Ya*, I heard the same. That would be a lot for us, especially if it fell all at once and so early in the winter."

Gabe nodded and stepped away from the buggy's door, but Eli didn't shut it. Instead, he looked toward him, and then he leaned forward and glanced past him to where the roof of his barn was just barely visible. "If you need help bedding your animals down until you have time to repair the barn, I could come back after I drop the *kinner* off."

Gabe stared out at the snow piling up on the ground. It was a beautiful sight now, at less than an inch. If it continued to fall all day and into the night, he wouldn't be thinking it looked so nice.

"I appreciate the offer, but I'm sure you have your own place to tend to."

"I do, but I wouldn't volunteer the time if I couldn't afford to give it."

Gabe knew he should accept the man's help. Maybe it was pride, stubbornness, or the fact that he didn't yet know how to judge when he was in over his head, but he raised his hand and waved goodbye to Grace. "We'll be all right, but *danki*."

Something passed between the two men then.

Gabe wasn't sure what it was. Perhaps a moment of raw honesty. All he knew was that he had to turn away from the look in Eli's eyes and turn back toward his barn, which was even now falling in on his animals. Back toward his day of work and the cold, burnt oatmeal on his stove.

He hadn't come here to make friends, and he was determined he didn't need them.

He'd find a way to do this on his own.

Somehow he'd become convinced it was better for Grace and better for him this way—alone and independent.

At this point, he doubted he'd ever feel different.

⌒ Chapter 8 ⌒

Miriam and Esther allowed the children to play outside for twenty minutes after they had eaten their lunch.

"Do you remember the time your *bruder* Noah ambushed the Stutzman twins on the way home?"

"Remember?" Miriam gazed outside at the snow, the children, and the fun they were having, and suddenly it seemed she was seven years old again. Seven years old and riding home in the buggy with her brother. "Noah made us all help with his snowball stockpile. It took us three afternoons because we had to do it on the way home and still get there in time to do our chores. We thought he was *narrisch* when he'd piled up more than two hundred and fifty snowballs."

"That many?" Esther laughed so hard some of the younger children who had chosen to stay inside and play checkers turned to look at her in surprise. "Did you actually count them?"

"He made me. He said he wouldn't build a new pen for my puppies unless I helped him. My job was to count while the others made snowballs. We were like the furniture factory over on the interstate, only we specialized in snow!"

"Why was he after the twins?"

"I didn't find that out for years. They had bested him the summer before...that time it was buckets of water, set up for when he walked out of the barn. He'd, um, been spending some time in there with a certain young lady."

"Oh, my. So it was revenge?"

"Of a sort," Miriam said, not adding that the young lady was now her brother's wife. "When the twins came walking around the corner, they didn't stand a chance. Back then their parents owned a farm that was less than a mile from here, so they often walked. He had my other brothers lined up where the road narrows, and they each had a huge pile of snowballs."

"Your brother became the king of snow fights." Esther sighed as she looked out at the white flakes still coming down.

"Don't worry about the storm," Miriam said, patting her on the arm. "Even if it is as bad as they say, at least it will make for a good three-day weekend."

"So no school tomorrow?"

"Probably not. We'll have the children write notes this afternoon saying school is closed on Friday, and whether we open Monday will depend on the weather. Someone from the school board will be by later this afternoon to give us a final decision, and then we'll be ready to sign them. I'm sure our students will be terribly disappointed."

Esther smiled. "Oh, *ya*. I always hated snow days."

"No doubt you still do. Think of it this way—it'll give you an extra day to sew."

"And it'll give you an extra day to decide what to do with Stanley."

Miriam shook her head, the strings of her prayer *kapp* falling forward as she did. "I've received a lot of gifts since I began teaching, but never a mouse."

"The note was very sweet."

They both stared at the sheet of paper Miriam had pinned to the board near her desk. Written in Grace's young penmanship, which was improving by the day, it read,

Miriam,

I'd like to give you Stanley. He is the Bestest thing I own.

GRACE

"I'll think of something," Miriam murmured. "I don't think my *mamm* or my dog would appreciate a mouse in the house."

As she rang the bell to call the children inside, she realized what she needed to do. It was a bit manipulative, but because she had decided it was in Grace's best interest, she didn't feel too badly. So much of teaching was directing students' behavior. You did it for their own good, and because they didn't always want to do what was best for themselves.

Not all students wanted to study arithmetic, memorize multiplication tables, learn to spell correctly, or commit to memory the states and their capitals. So teachers gave grades and came up with rewards, which worked much better than punishments.

She'd make a deal with Grace, one that she hoped would return Stanley to Gabe Miller's home and, in the process, move Grace one step further along the path she'd planned out for her.

Grace scribbled a question on her tablet. "You don't want Stanley?"

"I do want him. I like him very much." Miriam ran one finger down the back of the little gray mouse as the children put away their school books and prepared the building for the long weekend—what would be at least a three-day break because the snowfall had increased throughout the afternoon. "But I'm afraid my dog wouldn't like him very much. He would smell him. You know dogs have a keen sense of smell, right?"

Grace had been scuffing her toe against the floor, but when she heard this, she looked up in interest.

"Pepper doesn't just smell well, he's actually a hunting dog, which means he smells *very* well—almost as well as you draw."

Grace smiled broadly now.

"Pepper isn't allowed in the house, of course, but he'd smell Stanley, and he'd probably sit outside the door and howl so loud and so long that he would keep the entire family awake."

Grace began to giggle, though she didn't make any sound. She covered her mouth with her hand and her eyes almost squinted shut.

"I thought I might ask you to take care of Stanley for me, as a favor. Because you gave him to me, and he is my mouse now. I would appreciate it an awful lot."

Grace's eyes widened at the request, and Miriam pushed on.

"I have one more favor too. You know we've been practicing our Christmas music. I thought I might send home the words to these songs, and you could look at them and think of a way you could help us."

Now the little girl's expression turned to one of panic.

"I'm not asking you to sing, Grace. I'm only asking you to think of a way to help the other kids. They like you, and it would mean a lot to me if you would stand with them when they perform. I'm sure you can think of a way to participate."

Miriam waited a few seconds, giving her a chance to say no. When she didn't, Miriam added, "Okay? To both requests?"

Grace threw her arms around her teacher's neck and then planted a kiss on her cheek. For a fleeting second, Miriam thought she heard an "umm-umm"—like the sound you make when you hug someone tight. Then the young girl was running to put on her coat, snuggling Stanley, in his box, safely inside.

Miriam and Esther were only a few minutes behind Eli's buggy. They closed the school up tight before making their way through the rising snowdrifts—Miriam to her buggy, which the boys had hitched to her mare, and Esther to Joseph's buggy, which was waiting.

He raised a hand to wave to Miriam, and then he leaned out the front of the open buggy. "Need me to follow you home?"

"No, thank you, Joseph. I'll be fine."

Nodding once, he turned to Esther, made sure the blanket was wrapped snuggly around her lap, and then giddy-upped to his gelding. The horse trotted off through the falling snow.

The scene was picture-perfect, but Miriam wasn't fooled. The temperature was cold, and the snow was falling fast.

She would have liked to drop off another dinner at the Millers', but at the rate the drifts were accumulating, Miriam knew she needed to drive straight to her parents'.

Something told her this storm was going to be worse than anything they had experienced in recent years. She climbed into her buggy and made sure the leather flap was closed beside her. It didn't provide complete protection against the cold, but it helped. Wrapping her own blanket across her legs, she picked up the reins, murmured to Belle, and hurried toward home.

Gabe Miller would have to feed his own family.

No doubt he'd managed for the last several years, or however long it had been since Mrs. Miller had passed. For some reason that image bothered her more than the storm outside her buggy. She focused on pushing it away. The last thing she needed to do was involve herself personally in Gabe's problems. Of course, she would fulfill her Christian duty—that was the right thing to do.

And her professional duty as Grace's teacher. It was natural to care for her students.

Strictly Christian and professional. Not personal.

Maybe she could talk her dad into driving her over in the morning if the snow had stopped. Her mother always overcooked when there was a snowstorm. It would be neighborly to share some of the extra food with her newest pupil.

When Miriam woke Friday morning, the first thing she noticed was how quiet everything was. True, it was early. Try as she might on weekends, she couldn't seem to sleep past her normal six a.m. Though the sun wouldn't rise for another hour, when she went to her window to look out over the farm, there was enough light to see the miracle awaiting outside.

Enough for her to draw in a sharp breath and understand why she'd woken to that muted quiet.

An unmarred blanket of white stretched as far as the horizon and beyond—covering fields, trees, barns, and even Pebble Creek in the distance. It muffled the normal winter sounds of birds in the trees.

The morning wasn't completely quiet, of course. Now that she stood with her nose pressed to the window, peering out at the story-book scene, she could see the redbirds hopping on the branches of the sugar maple tree outside her window. When they hopped, the snow would tumble from the branch, making a slight *swish* sound.

And then she heard something else. Something that had her grabbing her robe and making her way downstairs and outside to take care of her morning bathroom needs. It was the sound of the oven door closing, bringing with it the aroma of fresh cinnamon rolls.

⪥ Chapter 9 ⪤

Miriam was sidetracked.

She'd headed to the outhouse, as planned. On the way there, she'd had to stop to put on her boots, coat, scarf, and hat with earmuffs.

The outhouse itself wasn't as cold as she'd feared. Her dad had built it with consideration for the Wisconsin winters—so he'd sheltered it from the north wind by building it on the south side of the house, behind the woodshed. In addition, he'd built an awning over the building which kept the majority of the snow off the structure. Lastly, he'd rigged it to receive some of the heat which vented from the big stove in the kitchen.

It was almost comfortable.

No, the main problem wasn't walking to the outhouse or even around the mounds of pristine snow accumulating at an alarming rate. Though the snowfall had stopped momentarily, Miriam could tell by the lowness of the clouds and the weight with which they seemed to press down that more would be falling soon.

She had hurried into the outhouse and was on her way back to the kitchen, back to hot *kaffi* and her *mamm*'s warm cinnamon rolls when she was sidetracked.

Pepper's bark pealed across the morning, bright and clear, like the sound of the *Englischer*'s church bell. Glancing toward the barn, she saw the dog jumping up and down as if he had treed a prize animal after a long hunt.

What in the world?

His yapping grew more urgent with each leap.

Miriam gazed longingly toward the house as she turned and trudged along the path to the barn her dad and brother had already made in the snow. Simon lived with their older brother, David, because his place was closer to town and Simon's job. He tried to come home most weekends to help their parents. She was relieved he'd made it before the storm closed in on them.

Now what was wrong with her dog?

Pepper didn't usually tree an animal unless he was set on its smell. At the moment his silky brown ears were bouncing with each jump, his bark pronounced as he went up into the air. Each time he popped up, he gained a good height of two to three feet.

When he saw that he'd earned Miriam's attention, he ran toward her and then shot back toward the tree near the barn. He continued sprinting back and forth—tree, Miriam, tree, Miriam, tree, Miriam.

My, but he was excited.

If he had treed a squirrel or a coon, it would faint from fear before she could pull him away.

"What is it, Pepper? What have you found, boy?"

Once Miriam was standing under the tree, Pepper flopped at her feet, a whine escaping from his throat as he waited for her to set things right.

She stared up and into the branches, looking for eyes or ears, but she saw only snow.

Then she couldn't see snow because it was in her eyes.

Pepper barked once as she wiped it away, and that was when she heard a tiny *meow*.

Stormy, Grace's kitten, had somehow escaped the barn and scampered up the tree.

"How did you get up there?"

Pulling her coat more tightly around her, Miriam began to carefully climb the tree. Even in her boots it wasn't that hard. She'd climbed it a hundred times as a child.

She had made it to the middle limb and grabbed Stormy, earning herself a nice scratch across the back of the hand in the process, when her dad walked out of the barn.

"Aren't you a bit old to be playing in trees?" He stood beside Pepper, a smile plastered across his face. Both of them looked up at her as if they were expecting an answer.

"It's the kitten's fault."

"*Ya?*"

"I couldn't leave her up here."

"Why's that?"

"She would freeze."

"She found her way up there. Chances are she would find her way down."

"Oh, *dat*. It's not so simple."

"Why not?"

Miriam clutched Stormy inside her robe. She could feel the kitten shaking as she made her way back down and out of the tree. She reached for her dad's hand as she jumped from the final limb, landing in the soft snow.

Suddenly, she didn't feel so cold as she stood there, holding her father's hand with the cat purring against her and Pepper pressed against her legs. As she surveyed their home, it occurred to her that it looked like an illustration out of one of the children's storybooks—wrapped in snow and only two weeks before Christmas. It almost seemed as if it were a picture-perfect morning—except for the scratch bleeding on her hand, which was a small price to pay for Stormy's safety.

Hot *kaffi* and a warm breakfast, and she'd forget the scratch.

The scratch and her rumbling stomach.

Her dad must have been thinking the same thing.

"How 'bout we put that little guy back in his stall and head inside?"

"Do you think Pepper chased him out?"

"I doubt it." They walked together to the back stall of the barn. When Miriam placed the kitten down beside the mother cat, she began licking him immediately. "I suspect the stall door didn't latch tight when your *bruder* brought in that pan of milk."

"Pan of milk?" Miriam peered over at the foil pan as Joshua nudged her out and toward the house. Pepper curled up in front of the stall door like some sort of sentry. "I've never known Simon to care whether a barn cat had milk or not."

"Could be I sent him in with it," her dad admitted.

"You?" she linked her arm through his.

"*Ya*, well. It being cold and all. Say, tell me about your week at school."

"Now you're changing the subject."

When her father grunted, she let it slide.

"The children were good, except for the middle-grade boys who thought it would be fun to put snowballs in the girls' mittens at the end of lunch. Within an hour the snow melted and water was everywhere."

"Did you make them clean it up?"

"Yes, I did, and they had to write apology letters."

"*Gut* girl."

"The three days off will do everyone good."

"Storm could be bad." Joshua reached for the back door to the kitchen, pulled it open, and let her enter first.

"How bad?" Miriam stopped in the mudroom. Her stomach was telling her to move on, but suddenly her mind was filled with images of Gabe Miller and his dilapidated barn.

"Worst we've had in ten, maybe twelve years."

Miriam slowly unwound the scarf around her neck and placed it on her hook under the window.

"Worried about someone in particular?"

"Gabe—I mean, Grace."

"He knows how to contact us if he needs anything." Joshua

smiled at her, the expression wrinkling the skin around his eyes. "And if I'm not mistaken, that's your *mamm's* cinnamon rolls I smell. They weren't ready when I went out an hour ago, but I'll bet they're toasty brown and piping hot now."

"Do not put that in your mouth."

Miriam heard the teacher's tone in her voice, but she couldn't have stopped herself if she wanted to.

At the moment she didn't want to.

Fortunately, Simon heard the tone as well, and though it had been years since he'd been in a schoolroom, he stopped, the cinnamon roll inches from his mouth.

"Why?" His smile widened as he prepared to take a bite of the thick gooey roll.

"You know why. It's the last center roll. I like the middle ones too." Miriam fought to keep her voice low, but with little success.

"Now, Miriam, there are plenty of others. And oatmeal as well." Her *mamm* set raisins and brown sugar on the table and then pushed an empty bowl toward her.

"Edge rolls." Miriam picked up her *kaffi* cup instead. "Don't you take a single bite until I get back."

"But—"

"Not one!"

When Simon reluctantly set the roll back on the plate, she turned away from the table, walked over to the stove, and filled her cup.

"You're being a bit hard on him," her mother whispered.

The only answer Miriam gave was *the look* she had perfected.

"I'm just saying..." Abigail raised her hands in mock surrender. "I'll let you two work this out. You are both adults."

"*Ya*. Only *kinner* would fight over a sweet roll." Her *dat* sprinkled a small teaspoonful of brown sugar on his oatmeal and reached for the smallest edge roll—one with hardly any frosting on it that Abigail had made especially for him

"How could he eat both middles and..." Miriam paused to count. "Two edge rolls? That's what I don't understand—"

"I was hungry," Simon explained.

"And to be fair, I didn't bake as much as I used to. I'm trying to help your *dat* watch his sugar intake." Abigail moved the sugar bowl to the other end of the table, out of temptation's reach.

Simon eyed the roll Miriam wanted, which now rested on the plate between them. His fingers drummed a beat on the table.

"We could split it," he offered.

"Split it?" Miriam shook her head. "Terrible idea."

"But I'm still hungry, and that one was mine. I had it nearly in my mouth when you walked in the door."

Miriam could sense him caving. In truth, all of the sugar he'd already had was no doubt hitting his bloodstream about now, and the large amount of bread and yeast was settling in his stomach. He probably wasn't even hungry anymore.

It was only a matter of saving his pride.

Then again, she'd watched him put away more than his fair share at Sunday gatherings.

She needed to play this just right, or she would be eating an edge roll. Since she was a child, she had always loved the middle of anything baked—soft and moist and sweet.

"I'll make you a deal." She turned her *kaffi* cup in her hands, staring down into the black liquid as if what she was about to offer were difficult for her. "I'll brush your gelding this morning if you'll give me that roll."

Simon sat back in his chair and ran his hand up and down the length of his suspenders. "Why would you do that? It'll take at least an hour to care for Rocky. All for one roll?"

Miriam shrugged. "I suppose I have a sweet tooth."

"Done! But no changing your mind." He slid the plate across the table and stood. "I guess being a teacher doesn't make you the smartest one in the room after all. One roll for an hour's work." He rubbed his stomach as he walked out of the room. They could hear him in the mudroom, putting on his outside gear and whistling.

Miriam ate slowly, savoring every bite, aware that her parents were watching her.

"Worth it?" Abigail asked.

"Oh, yes." She stood and carried her plate to the sink.

"Are you going to tell Simon I'd already asked you last night if you'd care for his horse today?" Joshua asked.

"Why would I tell him that? He's happy. I'm full. Everyone got what they wanted."

"Indeed," Joshua said, following his son back out into the cold.

But as Miriam and Abigail began cleaning the kitchen and set to work preparing the stew they would have for dinner, she couldn't help thinking again of Gabe and Grace and wondering if they were ready for the approaching storm.

Chapter 10

By the time daylight had completely pushed back the darkness Friday morning, Gabe had managed to move his horses, bull, and the few dairy cattle he owned to the side of the barn where the roof hadn't caved in from the night's snowfall.

Things were crowded, and his arms ached from the work. He was certain the coming day only promised more of the same.

If he could read a Wisconsin sky the same way he would have read one back in Indiana, more snow would begin to fall soon.

The question was, what time would Grace be up today? She usually slept at least an hour later on Saturdays. He studied the sky standing on the side of the barn he'd moved all the animals away from, gazing up through the gaping hole where the barn's roof had been.

Why had he come here? Did he really think running away from prying eyes would make his life easier? Did he really think hard work would ease his pain?

He'd heard about the Cashton Amish district. Some people had warned him folks here clung to old ways, and many families chose to leave rather than abide by the rules. Others claimed he would like it, that fewer choices made life simpler. The folks in this group tended to reminisce about the era their parents had lived in, a time they thought was truer to what the founders of their church had envisioned Amish life should be. They reminisced while using their gas stoves and gas refrigerators. Their opinion might change if they had to chop a block of ice out of the river.

All Gabe knew was that the distance from Indiana to Pebble Creek had seemed right and the price of the farm had been something he could afford. Staring at the structure that was literally collapsing around him, he now understood why the price had been so low.

Beyond that, though, past the roof that had fallen and the walls in need of repair, were fields more fertile than any he had worked in Indiana. He could tell this even in the midst of winter.

He'd pored over brochures before they had moved. He knew the *Englischers* called Cashton and most of southwestern Wisconsin the Driftless region. They claimed the terrain had been bypassed by the last continental glacier. Instead, the area contained the largest concentration of cold water streams in the world.

Gabe couldn't testify to glaciers that might or might not have been. Perhaps he'd ask God about that when his day came to depart this world, or maybe they would be busy discussing other things. What he did know was that the rivers and streams—like Pebble Creek—meandered through a rich soil that could and would grow good crops.

If he could survive the winter. If he could protect his animals until spring. If he could be both father and mother to Grace and still tend to all that needed to be done.

The bull let out a long, low call as he knocked up against the pen Gabe had fastened together. It wouldn't hold unless the beast settled down. Striding toward it, Gabe dumped more feed into the trough and then moved on to tend to the other animals. By the time he'd finished more than an hour had passed, and he glanced up to see Grace trudging through the snow, making her way outside to the outhouse.

Outhouse!

His grandparents had an old outhouse at their place, but both his parents' home and the home he'd shared with Hope had indoor bathrooms. That his daughter had to go outside, in this weather, tore at his heart.

Had moving here been the right thing to do?

The bishop's rules were harsh. Gabe didn't understand why the buggies were open, why the bathrooms were outside, or why the ornament on the roof of his barn had to be changed within a year of his buying it. He liked the bishop well enough as a man, and he would follow the *Ordnung*. He understood this was more than the will of Jacob Beiler. The bishop seemed like a fair man, though stern and hard to read.

Fine with him. He wasn't one for talk himself.

The *Ordnung*, and even the bishop himself, voiced the will of the church. Both represented the district, the community Gabe had chosen to live in and to raise Grace in until she was old enough to marry and choose her own path.

Grace began the walk back to the house, and as Gabe made his way toward his daughter to scoop her up and carry her high on his shoulder, he vowed to himself that he would find a way to make their new home work.

Everything appeared harder in the winter. He knew this from experience.

Hadn't it been winter when illness had forced Hope to bed?

He pushed the memory away in the same way he locked the hurt out of his heart each night. As he walked through the mudroom, Grace scrambled out of his arms and knelt down beside the box she'd made for Stanley. He'd finally drawn the line on the rodent and told her firmly that he couldn't sleep in her bedroom any longer. The mudroom had been a compromise.

"Breakfast in ten minutes," he said as he pushed past her into the kitchen, trailing snow and some dirt and hay as well across the floor.

With no woman around to fuss, he'd become lax about cleaning his boots before entering the house.

"One of the only advantages of living without a woman," he muttered, as he picked up the *kaffi* pot and stared at yesterday's sludge.

The fire he'd banked earlier was still warm, so he added wood to it and moved the pot to the back. Wouldn't hurt to heat it up. It had tasted bad yesterday. It couldn't taste much worse today.

But what to fix Grace? His oatmeal skills weren't improving, and he needed to hurry back to the barn before the snow started falling again.

She solved the problem by appearing at his side with milk and cheese from the icebox.

"If you're thinking grilled cheese for breakfast, we don't have any bread."

Shrugging, she walked to the bread basket and uncovered two of the biscuits left over from Miriam's dinner. Then she pulled open a drawer and found a knife and cutting board.

"I get the idea. Run and get dressed while I warm the biscuits."

She started out of the room but then came back to hug his legs. Her arms around him sent a surge of warmth straight to his heart, as they always did.

Kissing the top of her head, he muttered, "I suppose that means you want a sliver of cheese for Stanley."

Instead of answering, she skipped out of the room and down the hall.

Of course she didn't answer. He'd stopped expecting her to.

Had he been wrong about that? He had never questioned himself until the scene in the barn with her teacher.

As he heated up a little bacon grease and split the biscuits, he ran a hand over his jaw. Perhaps Miriam was right. Certainly, she dealt with more children than he did. Unfortunately, his daughter hadn't come with an operating manual like the gasoline engine on the windmill pump. It was one of the few modern conveniences the bishop allowed them.

As Grace settled back at the table, Gabe realized he'd given up long ago trying to figure out what was wrong with her speech. He'd learned to accept her as she was.

Wasn't that what God wanted him to do?

And why couldn't the teacher do the same?

His temper threatened to spark like the grease in the pan heating the biscuits. Getting angry wouldn't do a bit of good, though, so he pushed his anger down and ignored it the way he ignored so many of his feelings. Hope had always laughed at him in the evenings as she ran her hands through his beard and coaxed him into talking. She said feelings were like rocks in the field—if you didn't clear them out, they would break something.

He smiled at the memory as he slipped the hot biscuits onto a plate and topped them with cheese.

Grace looked up at him in surprise.

"What? Can't I give you a breakfast that isn't burnt without earning a surprised look?"

She shook her head, *kapp* strings flying, and bit into the biscuit. She didn't say *danki*, but the contented look on her face was all the thanks he needed.

He checked the stove, made sure everything was away from the fire, and then wrapped his own biscuits in a cloth napkin and took a gulp of the *kaffi* he'd poured. Grimacing, he realized he should have taken the time to make some new—it actually did grow worse each day. Interesting.

Glancing outside, he saw that his fears were confirmed. Snow was falling once again, already covering their tracks.

"Grace, I have to go back to the barn and try to settle the animals. If you have to use the outhouse, you hold on to the rope to get there. Understand?"

She nodded but remained focused on her drawing. That was another habit he needed to break—drawing while she was eating. One thing at a time, though, and today the animals needed to come first.

"I'll be back by lunch. You'll be okay?"

She still didn't look up, so he squatted beside her chair, placed his hand under her chin, and forced her to look at him. When she did he was reminded once more of his wife, but this time he realized—maybe for the first time—that Grace was no longer the baby he had held in his arms. She was growing up with a look and a personality uniquely her own.

Now she cocked her head and waited patiently.

"The storm is quite bad," he explained. "The fire will keep this room warm, and I'll be back as soon as I can."

Grace reached up, patted his cheek, and smiled. Then she turned back to her cheese biscuit and her paper.

That was what he'd remember later—the feel of her hand on his cheek and the smile in her beautiful brown eyes.

∼ Chapter 11 ∼

G race had every intention of minding her dad.

She did well for the first hour or so, but there was only so much drawing even she could do.

The snow continued to pile up outside until she had trouble even seeing the broken fence that bordered the pasture where the grumpy old bull was supposed to stay.

In some ways she understood how he must feel. She could sympathize, another new word they had learned in school. He was so big and had so much energy. It must be hard to be told to stay in one place. She wasn't big, but her feet were restless. They tapped a rhythm on the wooden floor as she drew the final details onto her drawing of the picture outside the window.

Turning the page, she considered starting another picture, but her hand was a bit sore from clutching the pencil. She thought she should take a break. Looking around the kitchen, she wondered what she would do if her mom were here. Probably they would be baking cookies or making bread. She needed to learn to do such things, but her dad was too busy to teach her. And besides, his cooking experiments didn't turn out so well.

She walked over to the stove and picked up the pan he'd set on the back corner of the stove, away from the warmth of the fire. The grease had chilled and hardened.

It looked icky.

She stuck a finger in it and stirred. It didn't look like something you would want to eat. She knew when you put it into some foods it added flavor. Grace had watched her *mammi* Sarah do that when she cooked back at their old house.

But she didn't know if she could figure out how to do such things. She had helped to separate beans before, looking for the occasional bad one and scooping the rest into the pan. The kitchen had been full of people and the oven full of good things to eat. *Mammi* Sarah had set her in front of the beans and shown her what to do. When she'd finished, the beans had gone on the back of the stove in a pot filled with water.

Grace didn't know how to soak beans. How long did you keep them in the water? Did you put some of the grease in while they were soaking? Did you add salt or pepper to the water before they started to cook? Maybe she could ask Miriam for a book that would explain such things. Her reading was much better now than when she'd left Indiana.

Maybe Miriam's mother, Abigail, would have time to show her a few simple dishes.

Taking her breakfast plate to the sink, she washed it clean and placed it on the drain board. She had to stand on the stool her dad had made to help her reach the faucet handle, and the water that came out was ice-cold. She knew it was better to use hot water, but she didn't know about boiling water on the stove and then carrying it to the sink. Instead, she had scrubbed the plate extra hard.

Even so, when she was done it hadn't taken much time. She walked back to the window and peered outside. Nothing had changed, except maybe there was more snow. She wasn't sure.

Snow or more snow. It all looked the same.

She pressed her face to the window and noticed how her breath fogged the glass.

Last year she'd gone outside in the snow and made angels with her cousins. They'd even had a sled that they'd ridden down the hill over and over again.

With her finger, she drew a hill on the frosty window and set a sled halfway down it.

What had her dad told her?

To stay in the kitchen where it was warm and to follow the rope if she needed to go to the outhouse.

She didn't need to use the outhouse again. It was a funny place, not at all like their bathroom at their old house.

But if she did have to go, she could walk in the snow, and maybe play in it just a little.

The idea made her feel less sad. Which was a good thing, because sometimes the sadness felt very, very big.

Grace knew when it felt like that she needed to do something or pretty soon she'd be in her bed crying like a baby, and she was *not* a baby.

So she went into the mudroom, which was little more than a back porch, but she liked the word "mudroom" better. After glancing around, she pulled on her boots and coat and scarf and mittens.

And that was when she saw Stanley's box.

She opened the top and inspected Stanley's world. The mouse squinted back at her, his little nose twitching. He ran down one side of the box and then turned and ran up the other.

Grace began to laugh, and her sad feelings slid away like snow melting on a sunny morning.

Tugging off one of her mittens, she ran her finger down Stanley's back. He wasn't as soft as Miriam's kitten, but he was very funny. His whiskers tickled her skin, and then he was off again, burrowing under the pile of hay she'd placed in the corner.

As she started to close the lid, Stanley poked his nose out, his tiny dark eyes staring up at her, and it seemed as though he was pleading with her.

She could almost hear him.

What if he wants to talk but can't? What if he wants to go with me?

"You can come." Grace's voice was a croak. It was scratchy and tickled a little.

Stanley didn't look scared like her *dat* did that last time she had made a sound—the time they'd had an argument and she tried to speak. Stanley didn't even seem surprised at the sound of her voice. He only twitched his nose and waited.

So she reached into the box. Her mouse hopped onto her outstretched hand and let her put him in her pocket. Grace forgot about how her voice sounded. She forgot about the fact that she'd even talked. All she could think about was the snow outside and playing and Stanley.

She even forgot about how she was supposed to stay inside the house.

⌖ Chapter 12 ⌖

B y the time Gabe stopped for lunch, large drifts of snow completely covered his path back to the house. Visibility was worse, and there was no sign the storm was lessening. But all wasn't lost. The barn was in slightly better condition. At least he thought the animals would survive the night. God willing and if the snow would let up.

If the rest of the roof would hold.

Too many ifs.

Now it was well past lunchtime. He knew that and felt bad about it. Breakfast hadn't been nearly enough, though Grace had eaten it like the tough little gal she was. Not one to complain, his Grace.

Once again, he reminded himself she hadn't complained because she couldn't—correction, *didn't*—talk. His irritation with Miriam King flared again like a fire that had received a burst of wind. He'd not questioned the way he was raising his daughter until the teacher had made her opinions known.

Knocking the snow off his boots, he opened the back door and trudged into the mudroom.

His hand froze on the door, still holding it open.

Something looked wrong. What was it?

Then he spotted it.

One of Grace's mittens was lying on the floor. He picked it up and stuffed it into his coat pocket.

Okay. She usually put her things in her cubby. Actually, she was very careful about it, but maybe she'd gone to the outhouse. Maybe she hadn't noticed she'd dropped one. He scanned the room and then noted that her coat, scarf, boots, and other mitten were gone.

Inside or out?

He hadn't seen any tracks in the snow, so she must be inside.

"Grace? Are you in here? I found your—" The word "mitten" died on his lips. The kitchen was empty. Had been empty for some time by the looks of things. He turned around and retraced his steps through the mudroom to the back door.

Only one set of prints were in the snow, and those were his.

Hurrying back through the house, he called her name again, checking each room quickly, but those rooms were dark and cold. The only light was the one he had left burning in the kitchen, and she wasn't there. Her drawing tablet and pencils were on the table.

So where was she?

He forced down the panic, though it wanted to claw up and out of his throat. His heart was beating faster than if he'd run from the pasture. Looking out the kitchen window, he tried to see what she would have seen, but the snow was falling so hard he couldn't even make out the fence.

He closed his eyes and prayed for guidance, for God to protect his child, for forgiveness. This was his fault.

When he opened his eyes, he looked out the window once more and saw what she had smudged there with her fingers.

What was it?

A hill? And a sled? Had she been remembering the area behind his parents' house? There was a small hill there where the children used to play.

Had she gone out to play?

Anger sprouted like corn in the summer fields and fought with his panic, but he tamped them both down.

She wouldn't disobey him that way.

Grace was a good girl. He'd told her to only go to the outhouse. Could she be out there? Could she be stuck in the small building? Stuck in the snow?

This time he didn't pause as he rushed back through the mudroom and out into the storm. The guide rope he'd fastened was still in place and still led to the outhouse. He could barely see the outline of the structure through the snow that was now falling even harder than it had been ten minutes earlier. He called her name as he went, the wind whipping the words away as soon as he spoke them. Stealing the words as each second that passed stole the hope from his heart.

He yanked open the door to the outhouse, but he knew before he did that she wasn't there. In fact, he had trouble opening it, the drifts were so high. He had to dig the snow away with his hands, calling out to her the entire time.

There was no answer. But how would she answer him?

The question was agony in his heart, sending pain so deep that he had to stop and rub at his chest. Was this what it felt like to have a heart attack? But he was too young, and God wasn't through punishing him yet. First his wife. Then this travesty of a farm. Now his daughter. What had he ever done to God to deserve this?

He stood in the doorway of the outhouse as the wind bit at his cheeks and the snow continued to fall.

Why had he left her alone?

Hadn't he realized the danger to her, how badly the snow had piled up between the house and the privy?

Had she come looking for him?

He walked back outside the outhouse, not thinking to shut the door behind him. It knocked against the doorjamb.

Bending into the wind, he made his way through the blizzard, and it was a blizzard now, he admitted to himself. Probably had become a blizzard hours ago when he was tucked inside the barn.

Gabe stood on the back steps and studied his farm. How late

was it? Two o'clock? Three? Realizing that each second he hesitated meant one more second Grace spent in the freezing weather, he walked inside and stared at the clock. Three twenty in the afternoon. It seemed impossible. But the old clock over the sink, the clock his dad had made, didn't lie.

How many hours had she been out there? Two? Three? More?

He was wasting time.

Walking back outside, he scanned from right to left. He would search each building. He would find her.

Half an hour later Gabe had been through every building, and most of the day's meager light was gone. Panic consumed him, sending sweat down his back and causing his heart to hammer in his chest.

Should he keep looking? Should he go for help? Was he too late?

Hurrying to the barn, he pulled Chance from his stall. The gelding was the best thing he'd bought since coming to Wisconsin. At fifteen and a half hands high, the dark bay with white tips was a beauty. Gabe didn't take the time to harness him to a buggy. Instead, he threw on the Western saddle which had been part of the purchase, led him out of the barn, and carefully fastened the door.

Though it pained him to do so, he galloped to the house, secured the horse to the porch rail, and ran inside long enough to leave Grace a note.

He also pumped up the lantern so that it would shine brightly. He set it on the hook over the kitchen table, near the window she looked out of most often.

Maybe she would see the light. Maybe she would find her way home.

And maybe she wouldn't.

Outside, he murmured once to Chance and swung up in the saddle. The horse seemed eager to run and he was grateful for that. He didn't know his neighbors well. He hadn't wanted to know them well. Certainly he had no idea what to say when he showed up on their front step.

What he did know, what he was now convinced of, was that he couldn't find Grace alone.

⌒ Chapter 13 ⌒

Miriam stirred the stew. It smelled heavenly—a rich dark broth, seasoned with herbs they had dried just a few months ago and flavored with vegetables she'd helped to can.

"Should we put the cornbread in now?"

"*Ya.* I think your *bruder* and *dat* will be ready for it. They'll be mighty cold when they come in." Abigail whacked her piecrust with the rolling pin and reached for the jar of apple preserves at the same time.

When Miriam first heard the banging outside, she thought it was her mother thumping the dough into submission. Then she realized, at the same moment Abigail did, that the sound was coming from the front door.

"What in the world—"

"That couldn't be *dat* or Simon," Miriam said, following her mother through the sitting room to the front door. Even before they had answered his knock, she saw Gabe pacing back and forth in front of the window and his horse winded and tied to their front rail.

Her heart beat faster because she realized two things in the second before her mother opened the door—Grace wasn't with him and something was terribly wrong.

"Gabe, come inside," Abigail said as she reached for his arm and pulled him through the open door. "Tell us what it is. Where's Grace?"

"That's why I'm here. I tried to find her. I can't. I looked everywhere. I just—it's growing darker and colder, and I don't know where else to look." Icicles had formed in his beard, and his eyes darted back and forth between them and then around the room, settling on nothing. He reached for the doorknob. "I have to go back. I can't stay. I only came to ask—"

His hand began to shake on the door. The tremor traveled up his arm to his shoulders until the sob overtook him.

"I'll run for *dat*," Miriam whispered. She didn't wait for an answer but turned and fled across the room and out the door toward the barn.

The last thing she saw was Gabe, a man she had come to think of as distant, big, and strong—but now he was broken.

A short time later they were all in the kitchen. Abigail had managed to press a hot cup of *kaffi* into Gabe's hands.

"We have to go." Gabe's voiced teetered on the brink of panic. "She's out there freezing. She's eight years old and out there freezing, and I'm here drinking *kaffi*!"

He pushed the cup away.

"We've rung the bell," Joshua reminded him. "Wait ten more minutes. Then this room will be full of help, and together we'll accomplish more than you can alone."

Gabe nodded once and raised his eyes to Miriam's, but he didn't say anything else. He didn't have to. The storm outside said it all. Her heart ached to witness the agony written all over his face. She might not agree with his ways, but there was no doubt his daughter meant everything to him.

And to think of Grace—scared, cold, and alone.

She closed her eyes and prayed as they waited.

The murmured conversations were interrupted by the arrival of not one but many buggies. Abigail stood and began pouring hot *kaffi* into Thermoses. Within five minutes the kitchen was crowded with men from their district. Miriam didn't know how they had managed to arrive so quickly through the storm.

But she understood how their system worked.

When her brother Simon had rung the bell outside their barn, its call had carried to at least four other farms. They in turn had sent out a similar cry for help, which had reached still more farms. No one stopped to ask questions. The call was enough.

One call sent out a ripple through their people.

One call and all would come.

Folks parted as Bishop Beiler made his way to the center of the room and placed his hand on Gabe's shoulder. Miriam's mind flashed back to six days before when Gabe and Jacob had stood at the front of their Sunday meeting, when Gabe had joined the church and Grace had stood beside her father to be prayed over. It had been here, in their home, but no one could have known then that the girl's life would be at stake a few days later.

"I didn't know it was Grace, but I knew someone must be missing for the call to have gone out. I spoke with the *Englisch*," Jacob said. "They are sending people out to help, but because of the storm the roads are impassable. The road crews have been sent to clear a path, but it will be a few hours before the *Englisch* officers arrive at your farm."

"In the meantime we go to your place to start searching on our own." Joshua stepped forward and set his *kaffi* cup on the table. "It's not hopeless, son. Every man here knows these winters, has experienced these storms, and has a *dochder* or *schweschder* at home. We'll find your Grace."

Gabe nodded and Miriam thought he wouldn't speak, but then he stood and cleared his throat. "*Danki.* I appreciate what you're doing. I...I need to remind you that my Grace...she can't...that is... she won't talk."

He looked from man to man and then continued. "She's not slow minded. She's lost. If she sees you, she'll make a signal so you can see her, but I don't think she would cry out. I don't think she would speak. I thought I should let you know."

Each man confirmed their understanding with a gesture, nod, or word of encouragement as they filed out into the gathering darkness and into the snow, which hadn't slowed in its assault.

Gabe was walking out with Miriam's oldest brother, Noah, when she thought of Pepper. She hurried to catch up with them before they were out the door and reached forward to snag Gabe's sleeve.

He glanced back at her in surprise.

A few other women had come with the men. They were moving supplies into boxes, and boxes into buggies.

"Simon is coordinating supplies," Noah said, pushing out through the front door, but Miriam pulled him back.

"It's not that. It's Pepper. I think he can help."

Gabe shifted from foot to foot, his eyes on his horse. Someone had given the gelding a few oats in the barn and then brought him back around. Miriam knew she would need to explain quickly if she had any hope of Gabe and Noah hearing her out.

"He's a good hunting dog. He's familiar with Grace. At least give him a chance. What can it hurt?"

"We're not hunting, Miriam." Gabe's voice was more tired than angry.

"He's a German shorthair, he operates off scent, and he's spent time with your daughter. What harm is there in allowing him to help?"

"You may have a point, but we can't wait for you to get him ready. Bring him with Simon and the supplies." Noah pulled on his gloves and walked out of the house.

As Miriam was about to turn away, Gabe stopped her. "Here. Take this." Cupping her hand in his, he reached into the pocket of his coat, and pulled out something small, knitted, and blue. Slipping Grace's mitten into her hand, he closed her fingers around it.

He paused long enough to look deeply into her eyes, to share with her what he'd been careful to keep hidden since she'd known him—the pain, the loss, and the loneliness.

Then he disappeared into the storm.

≈ Chapter 14 ≈

Grace kicked the snow out from under the branches of the tree. She needed to go to the bathroom, but it was almost completely dark. She kept her hand on her pocket, on top of the buttoned flap, on top of the place where Stanley was safely sleeping. At first she had been a little angry at him. It was his fault they were here to begin with. At least that's what she told herself, but she knew it wasn't true.

She should have left him in the box. She should never have taken him outside. And once outside, she should have zipped up her pocket.

It was a miracle she'd even caught him.

But now what? Once she'd chased him through the snow, past the buildings and into the woods, once she'd caught him and realized she was lost, she had found shelter under the circle of trees. Her grandpa had taught her to do that. "If you're ever lost, don't keep running around in circles. Sit still and wait for us to come find you."

She'd been younger then, really only a baby—barely six. But she remembered *pappi* Mose making her promise. What she didn't remember was ever being this cold, and she'd never been lost before. She peeked out from under the tree branches again.

How would her dad see her scarf wrapped around the tree's

branch? She could barely see it. And the snow was piling up higher and higher. When she became thirsty, she tried putting some of the snow in her mouth. It worked a little at first, but now she needed to use the bathroom awfully bad and she was hungry as well as cold.

All of those things kept her from thinking about how scared she was. She'd never been afraid of the dark before, but then she'd never been outside alone in the middle of a blizzard. Crawling back under the tree branches, she sat down with her legs crossed. Unbuttoning her coat pocket enough to slip her hand in, she ran her fingers over Stanley.

She needed to be brave—for Stanley.

And for her father.

The last thing she wanted was to be crying when he found her.

So instead, she lay down, and pulled her knees up to her chin. Maybe if she went to sleep for a few minutes, when she woke up she'd be warmer.

≈ Chapter 15 ≈

Gabe couldn't believe the amount of buggies lined around his barn and pasture fence. He might not be able to see the fence through the blizzard, but there was no mistaking the buggies. As each man arrived, Miriam's youngest brother, Simon, took charge of stabling the horse after directing the man to Gabe.

He didn't want to think about where Simon was putting the horses, because the barn certainly wouldn't hold them all.

Joshua had insisted that Gabe stay at the house and coordinate the efforts. Gabe had argued with Miriam's father about that, and it wasn't in his nature to contradict his elders. It went against his nature to sit still. He wanted to be out walking the fields, looking for his daughter.

"I understand, Gabe. I do, but that's the reason you need to be here. No one knows this spread like you do. If there are any questions, you're the one who can answer them. And when we find Grace, you need to be here to greet her." That last reason had stolen any other argument he might have offered.

So he'd taken Grace's drawing pad, made a rough sketch of the place, and begun marking off sections as teams went out into the storm.

His kitchen hardly resembled anything he recognized, there were so many women about. Actually, it was only Miriam and two others, but with all the activity the place seemed as busy as a hive.

When he was sure there couldn't be anyone else coming, another buggy would arrive outside the window. A man would hop out and hand the reins to Simon, who would be standing there almost before the horse had stopped. Miriam or one of her friends would be at the back door as the man knocked the snow off his shoes, and then someone Gabe didn't know, someone he couldn't even remember from Sunday, would be assuring him that everything would be all right, that they would find his Grace, and that he was ready to go search.

Gabe would consult his sketch and assign an area of the farm, and before he could thank the stranger—no, before he could thank the neighbor—Miriam would have filled his Thermos with hot kaffi and sent him on his way.

And though he couldn't abide the thought of eating, though he'd had nothing since the cheese biscuit nearly twelve hours before, he was grateful something delicious was baking in his oven. The men working deserved to be fed.

Noah appeared in the doorway between the mudroom and the kitchen, but he didn't walk into the room. Beside him was Pepper, who barked once, and another man whom Gabe couldn't place. In fact, he was sure he'd never seen him before.

In his twenties, clean shaven, and with a pleasant smile, Gabe noticed that he made eye contact with Miriam before reaching down and settling the dog with a single hand gesture.

"We're ready to go out with him," Noah said. "Gabe, this is Aden Schmucker. He lives a couple of districts over. His parents own the farm next to mine, and he happened to be there visiting this weekend."

"Thank you for coming."

"Ya. Of course."

Miriam stepped forward. If he wasn't mistaken, there was a slight blush to her cheeks, but it could have been the heat from working in the kitchen. "Aden's one of the best hunters in these parts. He helped to train Pepper when we first bought him."

"He's a *gut* dog," Aden said. "It was a *gut* idea to use him to look for your little girl."

Gabe nodded but didn't add anything. There were dynamics at work here he didn't understand, and truthfully he didn't care. All he cared about was finding Grace.

"Do you have something he can get her scent off of?" Aden asked.

Gabe glanced toward Miriam. She pulled Grace's mitten out of the pocket of her apron.

"Has your daughter worn this recently?" Aden asked.

"*Ya,*" Gabe said. "She has. I found it on the floor in the mudroom. I think she dropped it as she went out."

Aden squatted down beside the dog and spoke to him softly. Gabe couldn't make out exactly what he said, but after a moment Aden placed the mitten in front of Pepper and spoke two short commands.

Pepper began to walk around the mudroom, his nose to the ground. When he reached the back door, he barked once.

"All right. Let's go." Aden pulled on his gloves and Noah wrapped his scarf more tightly around his neck.

Opening the door, they both stepped out into the night, the wind pulling away any words they might have shared.

Gabe stood there watching them go, feeling helpless and hopeless. Wanting to believe and afraid to believe.

"It's going to be all right, Gabe. They'll bring Grace back to you." Miriam placed her hand softly on his back. He remembered when he had opened his front door and she had fallen through it.

He remembered the feel of her in his arms.

All he wanted right now was Grace back in his house, but it helped to know that the woman standing beside him also cared about his daughter. She understood what it was to watch Grace struggle each day in her unique way, struggle and overcome. Maybe those daily battles would give her the strength to survive until someone found her.

He stood there longer than he should have, connected to her by their feelings for Grace. The others were helping because it was the right thing to do, but he and Miriam were the two who knew Grace, who understood her even if they had come to different conclusions about what was best for her future.

He thought of apologizing, but he knew that it wasn't the right time.

So instead he pulled in a deep breath and asked for more *kaffi*.

Miriam didn't think her feelings could become any more jumbled. She was so worried about Grace that one more drop of *kaffi* would send her stomach into somersaults. Every time she looked at Gabe, it was as if she experienced his sorrows with him. Plainly his heart was breaking with each moment that passed. The man had been through so much and now this. Physically he was big and strong, but it was obvious that emotionally he was near a cracking point.

She had heard Aden Schmucker was in town for the weekend, but when he'd appeared in the doorway, her emotions had nearly bubbled over. Her relationship with Aden was complicated, and she'd made no attempt to clarify things. In fact, she'd been ignoring the situation for more than two months, ever since the fall festival.

Ignoring had seemed simplest.

She handed Gabe his *kaffi* and then moved back to the other side of the kitchen to stir up another batch of biscuits.

"It's a real blessing Aden is here this weekend," Ida murmured. Her sister-in-law had arrived with Noah, explaining that the children would be fine with her parents. They had built a *grossdawdi* house next to theirs, and Ida's mother and father often came over to lend a hand with their seven children.

"He's *gut* with Pepper," Miriam agreed as she measured the ingredients for the biscuits.

"He seemed happy to see you as well." Eva Stutzman, Eli's sister, peered over her glasses as she pulled a pan of bread out of the oven. In her fifties, she was the midwife for their families and often worked in conjunction with the *Englisch* doctors. Miriam never quite understood why Eva hadn't married. Though she had a pronounced limp, that certainly wouldn't have stopped her from having a husband and a family.

"*Ya*. I'm sure I saw him smile at you, Miriam. Didn't you go out with him several times during the fall festival?" Ida and Eva kept their voices low as they moved efficiently about the kitchen.

Miriam didn't think tonight, while Gabe was worried about whether his daughter was alive or not, was the right time to be talking about her dating prospects—or her lack of them.

She glanced over at him to make her point and then shrugged her shoulders as she finished mixing the biscuits. She was surprised Ida and Eva had thought to bring the ingredients for making biscuits and bread. How had they known that Gabe wouldn't have all that was needed? Perhaps they had guessed because he was a widower. Or perhaps they'd heard talk?

"Don't worry about him," Eva said in a low voice. "I doubt if he'd hear a workhorse clomping through the sitting room. We're background to his agony, is all. If anything, the normal sounds of women's work is a balm to his spirit."

She pulled another fresh loaf of bread out of the oven and placed it on a cooling rack, covered it with a cloth, and put more dough in the pan. When she had it in the oven, she perched back on the chair she'd pulled over from the table and resumed knitting. "So tell us about Aden."

"There's nothing much to tell," Miriam admitted, but she couldn't stop the heat rising in her cheeks.

Ida smiled at Eva, which only made it worse. Older women. It seemed to Miriam they were always imagining romance where there was none.

"Think I'll see if Gabe wants any of this bread." Miriam swept the loaf off the cooling rack onto a plate and then swiped a knife from the counter where Ida had been chopping walnuts to put into a walnut-banana bread batter. She turned and walked toward the table near the window, aware as she did that both women were murmuring in an amused way.

Let them murmur, as long as they kept baking.

When the men arrived back with Grace, everyone would be mighty hungry.

≈ Chapter 16 ≈

When Grace woke up, she couldn't see anything.

At first she thought she couldn't see across her room, but then she remembered she wasn't in her room. She couldn't see the trees she knew were standing tall all around her. She couldn't even see her fingers when she wiggled them in front of her face.

She slipped her hand into her pocket to check on Stanley. Her body must have been keeping him warm. The little mouse nudged her fingers and then scampered to the other side of her pocket.

Grace buttoned the pocket closed, sat up, and rubbed her eyes.

How long had she been sleeping? And why hadn't her dad found her yet?

She pulled her wool cap down tighter around her ears, over her prayer *kapp*, and then she tried to crawl out of the shelter on her hands and knees, but all she did was bump into a wall of snow. Falling back onto her bottom, she rubbed the top of her head.

Something was wrong. Why couldn't she get out the same way she had before?

Her heart started thumping faster, like when she played "statue" with her cousins back home in Indiana. This wasn't Indiana, though, and she should be able to crawl out from under the trees.

Reaching forward with her hand in the darkness, she tried to push out from under the trees. This time her hand hit the wall of snow.

It was as though she'd been buried alive. How was she able to breathe?

She reached up over her head and felt tree branches. So the trees had protected her?

Maybe she could crawl up and out. Or maybe she should stay put.

Grace sat back down where she thought she'd been sleeping before, and she started to cry.

She didn't want to cry, because it made her feel like a baby, but she was really afraid. Maybe more afraid than she'd ever been. *Even more afraid than when* mamm *died*—the thought whispered in her head, a terrible thing she didn't want to be there.

Once she realized how afraid she was, it was an idea that grew and grew. It was scarier than anything else. Scarier than all the tree limbs around her or the darkness or the cold.

What if her scarf was under the snow? What if her dad didn't find her? How long could she live in a snow cave?

The tears sliding down her face made her cheeks burn, so she scrubbed them with her hand, the hand without a mitten. She'd been keeping it in her pocket—the pocket Stanley wasn't in. But rubbing her cheeks made them hurt, and that made her cry harder.

Now she didn't only feel like a baby, but she was being a baby.

She'd done a lot of stupid things before—drank sour milk once by accident, ate a worm on a dare, and even touched the stove when it was hot and burned her finger.

She knew it was stupid not to talk. She heard kids call her stupid, and mostly she didn't blame them. It was just that once she stopped, she didn't know how to start again.

But this? This was beyond stupid.

Why had she gone outside? Why had she taken Stanley out of his box? Why had she managed to get lost in a blizzard?

Her throat was dry and scratchy and she wanted something to

drink—anything to drink, but she didn't want to put any more snow in her mouth. She was crying so hard she could feel Stanley running back and forth in her pocket. Her cheeks stung like the time she had sunburned them, and that didn't make any sense to her.

She must be going crazy.

Maybe that's what happened right before you froze to death. First you imagined you were hot, and then you heard voices.

What a horrible way to die, especially if you were only eight. She wished she could write a story about it and warn the other students in her class. She would title it "Freezing: The Worst Way to Go."

First your cheeks sunburn. Then you hear voices. And last you dream up a dog.

This dog sounded awfully close. Why would she be hearing a dog?

Grace tried to stand up, but she couldn't do that under the tree limbs. When she did, clumps of wet snow fell down on her. Then she had an idea. Maybe she wasn't dreaming. Maybe she actually was hearing voices. Scrubbing the tears off her cheeks, she crawled forward until she bumped into the tree trunk.

She couldn't stand up, but she could reach up and shake the branches. If snow fell down in here, maybe some snow would fall down on the outside too. Maybe someone was on the outside—and maybe they would see the branches moving and the snow falling.

Shaking the branches made her arms ache, and it made the snow fall on to her head and shoulders.

But it didn't bother her because suddenly she was filled with hope.

She was sure she heard voices now and the sound of a dog. She'd only met one dog since they moved here to Wisconsin. That dog was Miriam's dog, Pepper, and he liked to find things.

It seemed to take forever, but soon she could hear two people calling her name. They were saying things like, "Don't worry, Grace," and "We're almost through."

And best of all, she heard one man say, "Praise *Gotte*. What a smart girl to hang her scarf on the limb."

That made her feel warm all over when the man called her smart. She knew pride was a sin—she'd heard her bishop in Indiana preach on it before. She could pray for forgiveness later. Right now it was good to know she'd done one thing right on this terrible night.

Finally there was a tunnel through the snow, and the first thing she saw was Pepper's nose poking through.

Someone pulled the dog back and made the hole bigger. Pepper barked once very loudly, and then he did it again. This time when Pepper came through, no one stopped him.

He licked Grace on the face, and Grace threw her arms around him and buried her fingers deep into his silky fur. She'd never felt anything so warm before, anything so happy. She put her cheek against Pepper's neck, and then she started crying again, but this time it was different. It wasn't a sad crying.

When they pulled her out from under the trees, no one seemed to mind about the tears. In fact, she noticed that the older man wiped at his eyes, but it could have been because of the wind. No one was angry with her, and no one pulled her away from Pepper.

They bundled her in a warm blanket and offered her something warm to drink. She'd been thirsty for so long. When they handed her the warm Thermos she almost jumped for joy. Then she took a sip. It tasted like the *kaffi* her dad liked. She swallowed it even though she wanted to spit it out. Then she handed the Thermos back.

Turned out she wasn't as thirsty as she thought.

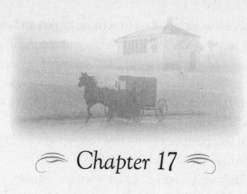

⧉ Chapter 17 ⧉

Every time a team of two men trudged back through his mud-room, hope surged through Gabe's heart, but it only took one look at their expressions to know they had no good news for him. They had found no sign of Grace.

It was as if she had simply vanished.

Bishop Beiler walked in with an *Englischer*, an officer named Jack Tate. In his mid-forties, he seemed efficient enough, though he admitted there wouldn't be much they could do until morning. He'd had a difficult time making it out with the roads closed, driving his car as far as he could and then finally riding with the bishop in his buggy. He explained to Gabe that it would be impossible to assemble a search crew before sunrise.

He seemed to understand their ways. He didn't ask for a photo-graph of Grace, which meant he knew the Amish didn't take pic-tures, and he never questioned why Gabe would have allowed Grace to go to the outhouse by herself.

After he'd taken Gabe's statement, he accepted a Thermos of *kaffi* from Miriam and prepared to go out to cover the last area of acreage Gabe had to assign, accompanied by Simon. Miriam's brother had been working all night settling horses and caring for the buggies, and he was eager to be actively participating in the search.

"You've done everything I would do," Jack said as he zipped up his coat. "At first light we'll put a helicopter in the air and more crews on the ground. For now, I might as well be out there with a team. Ready to go, Simon?"

"Sure. Are you positive I don't need to go back and find that *Englisch* car of yours?"

"Nope. Can't feed it oats or cover it with a blanket. I suspect it'll be fine where I left it." As each team came in, the plan had been for Gabe to send them back out again, but so many men had shown up that it was no longer necessary. They had covered every route on his map—covered some twice.

The men's faces were somber.

The baking Miriam, Ida, and Eva had done smelled *wunderbaar*. Yes, Gabe had learned their names. He'd even heard some of their conversation, though the words had only flowed over him, making no impression—just background noise to his nightmare. Now he noticed that the conversations around him had dropped to low murmurs and no one was eating.

There seemed to be nothing to say. And certainly no one had an appetite.

Glancing at the clock, he saw the time was pushing on toward three in the morning.

Officer Tate hadn't said it, didn't need to, but they both knew the truth. With each hour that passed the odds of Grace's surviving were less.

Then three things happened nearly simultaneously.

A dog barked. Miriam's eyes met his. And he heard someone say Grace's name.

Standing so quickly he knocked his chair over, Gabe rushed through the crowd of men gathered in his kitchen, who parted for him like wheat parted for driving rain.

He was at the back door the same moment that Noah and Aden

appeared out of the darkness. Pepper pushed his way between them, and Noah carried Grace, bundled in a blanket, her arms around his neck.

Gabe had never seen anything more beautiful in all of his life than his daughter's face. Her nose and forehead were reddened from the cold, and he thought her cheeks might be frostbitten. Brown hair, matted and somewhat wet, tumbled out of her *kapp*. Tired eyes blinked once and then again.

Gabe had to reach for the wall when his knees threatened to buckle out from underneath him.

Grace had looked sleepy as Noah had approached the door, but when she saw her father's face, her head snapped up. Her mouth formed a small O, and her arms came out.

He bridged the distance between them in a second, in less time than it took all of the fear in his heart to flee, and he caught her up in his arms. The room around him went silent. The moment froze as though every person was caught up in that heartbeat of grace.

Then they were all talking at once. He heard men slapping one another on the back. The women put food on the table, and this time there were plenty of takers.

"Bring her closer to the fire, Gabe." Miriam worked another blanket around Grace's shoulders. "Let Eva have a look at her."

Pepper barked again as Gabe moved with his daughter out of the mudroom.

"Can the dog come in?" Aden asked.

Grace's arms tightened around Gabe's neck, so he nodded yes. He'd never abided animals in the house, but he knew this time was different. He knew, without hearing the story, that somehow Pepper had brought Grace home.

Miriam suddenly wanted to walk away from the kitchen, crawl into her buggy, and go home. She did not want to see the naked look of joy and gratitude on Gabe Miller's face. It was more than she could bear.

Maybe it was fatigue.

Maybe it was her worry over the girl. Had she honestly begun to doubt that God would protect her?

Maybe it was the women's teasing over Aden, and the knowledge in her heart that he was a good man. Maybe it was the confusion that came with that knowledge.

Whatever it was, she didn't know what to do when Gabe stared at her with such thankfulness. She certainly didn't know how to react to such adoration as she saw when he looked at Grace. She was accustomed to seeing parents who were proud of their children, even parents who were sometimes disappointed or angry with their children. And she'd been to the funerals of parents who had lost their children.

Somehow, Grace Miller had wound her way into Miriam's heart. Perhaps because she presented such a unique challenge. Or because of her dark eyes, winning smile, and talent with a drawing pencil. Or because she was motherless. What woman's heart didn't open up for a motherless child?

She knew, though, as Eva checked Grace, applied salve to her frostbite, and pronounced her in "remarkably *gut* shape," that she needed to keep her distance. She needed to be objective and treat all students the same. And she did not need to respond to the looks she was receiving from Grace's father.

Things were safer when he treated her as though she had a contagious disease.

The glances he was sending her way now—well, they made no sense. It wasn't as though she'd been out in the snow looking for the girl.

"Eva, do you need me to go after the doc?" Officer Tate held his open Thermos in one hand and a hot biscuit in the other.

"No. She has good circulation in her fingers and toes, and surprisingly there are no blisters on her cheeks. The snow cave they found her in must have protected her from the worst of the cold." Eva glanced up at the men. "*Gotte* was watching over this one. I think she's all right. I'll write out some instructions."

Miriam closed her eyes and began giving her thanks to God even as Eva continued speaking.

"I've already written out directions to Doc Hanson and the closest medical center if her pain worsens. And I brought aloe vera cream and ibuprofen with me, which I'll leave. Gabe, if you see any signs of infection, you take her straight into town."

"*Ya*, of course I will."

"But I think she's going to be fine."

"Good to hear." Tate squatted down in front of Grace. "You're one lucky little girl. I suppose you had angels watching out over you."

Grace nodded and then reached for Pepper, who was resting under her chair. She had already made sure Stanley was safe and secure back in his box.

"Angels and one very smart hunting dog. You be careful and get lots of rest. Okay?"

Grace nodded, her eyes round and blanket pulled tight.

"*Danki*, Officer." Gabe reached out and shook hands with Tate.

"You're very welcome. I'll be seeing you at the school Christmas special. Miriam always invites me."

Miriam finished wiping clean the last dish and handed the officer a half loaf of bread wrapped up to go.

"You didn't have to do that," Jack said, grinning. "But I'm not going to be rude and turn it down."

"We were worried. We bake too much when we're worried."

"I'm happy to take it off your hands."

She again met Gabe's eyes as the officer turned and walked out of the house. The rest of the men were gathering their supplies and heading home, each stopping to say a word to Gabe and Grace.

She checked the kitchen once more to be sure everything was in place, and then she put her own supplies into her bag. She'd ride home with Simon, and suddenly she was bone tired. The thought of her bed and snuggling beneath her quilts was enough to propel her outside into the snow to brave the cold trip through the dark night.

"I'd like to talk to you before you go." Gabe's voice in her ear nearly caused her to drop her bag of supplies. "I didn't mean to startle you."

"No. You didn't," she hedged, pulling on her gloves. "It's only that I'm tired and didn't hear you come up. I thought you were with Grace."

"She's in her bed. Eva is checking on her one last time."

"That's *gut*. Eva, she's *wunderbaar* with the young ones. She'll be able to tell you exactly what to do."

"I wanted to talk to you about that." Gabe ran a hand around the back of his neck, and Miriam was struck again by how much of a toll the evening had taken on him. "First I need to apologize."

"Of course you don't—"

"I do, and I need to do it now while the sting of my arrogance is fresh."

"What do you mean—"

"If I had listened to you earlier, maybe this wouldn't have happened. If I had been working with Grace and insisting she learn to speak again, then she might have been able to call out for help." Gabe walked over to the counter and picked up a plate of biscuits wrapped in a dish towel. He held it in one hand, as if he were weighing it.

He held it, as if he were waiting for her to speak.

"You can't possibly blame yourself for what happened tonight," Miriam said, but she could tell he wasn't listening.

He set the plate on the counter, carefully, as if it might shatter.

She kept talking, faster now, reaching for words that might break through his thick skull. "Listen to me, Gabe. I know I'm young. I know I don't know what you know about children."

"I shouldn't have said that."

"You were right, but I do understand that you can't keep an eye on them all the time. It's impossible. Even a well-behaved child like

Grace will have mishaps. Everyone saw the guide rope you had from the house to the outhouse. You did all you could."

"But if she could talk. If she'd been able to call out for help—" he stopped abruptly, and then he turned his piercing brown eyes on her. "You do still believe she can speak?"

Miriam hesitated, not wanting to add to his burden, but she was unable to lie. "Yes."

"It's settled, then."

"What's settled?"

"You figure out what we need to do and let me know."

"How am I supposed to do that?"

"I don't know." Again the fatigue, the hand across the back of his neck.

Simon stuck his head into the kitchen, nodded at Gabe, and offered to help Miriam with her bag.

"No, I've got it."

"All right. I'm ready to leave when you are."

Eva came through then, holding up a sheet of handwritten instructions she wanted to go over with Gabe one more time.

When they were alone again, he stepped closer to Miriam and lowered his voice. "How about you send a note home in her lunch box next week? When you figure out what we should do next."

"And you'll read the note this time?" Miriam regretted the words as soon as they were out of her mouth.

To her surprise, Gabe smiled, touched her elbow, and turned her toward the mudroom. "*Ya.* I'll read the notes this time. I'll even send one back. Together, maybe we can find a way to help my *dochder* speak."

⌁ Chapter 18 ⌁

Miriam wasn't sure what she expected Monday morning. She knew she was glad to be back at school. Three-day weekends were nice, but the last three days had not been normal by any means. After the long night spent searching for Grace, she'd slept a few hours late Saturday.

But in all honesty, she'd kept herself busy most of the day and weekend, trying to make some sense of her conflicting emotions. The conversation with her mother, though, kept playing through her mind even as she prepared for classes early Monday morning.

"Shouldn't you be happy he's willing to help the child?" her mother had asked as they'd changed sheets on beds and given the house a good cleaning. Laundry would take all day Monday, so they did everything else they could on Saturday.

"I am happy. Of course."

"Except..."

"Except when I first made the suggestion, I didn't have a particular plan of action in mind."

"So..." her mother snapped a clean sheet across the large bed she and her father shared.

Miriam caught the end and tucked it neatly into her side. "So now I don't want to let him down." She paused and corrected herself.

"I don't want to let Grace down. She's been through a lot, and this will no doubt be hard for her."

"She's a beautiful child," Abigail said as she slid fresh cases over the pillows on her side.

"Yes, but I've never dealt with this sort of situation before, *mamm.*" Miriam pulled the blankets and quilt up—a double Light in the Valley pattern her mother had sewn when she was younger than Miriam was now. It had stood the test of time. The stitches were sturdy, like the marriage Abigail had envisioned as a girl. Both the quilt and the love she shared with Joshua had nurtured a family of four children and twelve grandchildren.

Miriam plopped down on the bed and tried to wrap her mind around that idea. Would she ever know that kind of love?

Abigail walked around the bed, sat beside her, and placed her hand on her back. Together they looked out the window and over the tremendous amounts of snow that had threatened Grace only a few hours before. In the day's sunlight, the snowdrifts held no danger. The path from any building back to the house was clear. But in the darkness, the cold and the snow could pose many problems, especially for a small child.

"Is that what's bothering you? Your inexperience?" Abigail reached out and took Miriam's hand in hers.

"Yes. No. I'm not sure."

"You realize God has put you in Grace's life for a reason."

Miriam felt heat rush to her cheeks. She was surprised to see a look of amusement on her mother's face.

"But—"

"But what? God uses each of us in different ways. He uses you with the younger children as He uses Esther with the older ones."

"Teaching is one thing. This is another. I don't know what she went through with her mother's passing. I don't know why she stopped talking or even when, exactly. I don't know how—"

"Miriam, stop focusing on what you don't know." Abigail stood to finish covering the pillows with fresh cases. "Grace is a lovely child."

"You said that already, *mamm*." Miriam gave her mother a baffled look.

"Did I? She has the most expressive eyes. During church last week, it almost seemed as if she was trying to tell me something simply with the way she looked at me." Gathering the dirty linen in her arms, she turned and walked out of the room.

As Miriam wrote the children's lessons on the board Monday morning, she smiled, recalling her mother's gentle powers of persuasion. She wasn't one to actually make suggestions. No. She guided your thoughts in a more roundabout way. Miriam had spent the rest of the weekend focusing on what she did know about children and what she'd learned about Grace.

By the time she'd arrived at the schoolhouse on Monday, she had an idea. Before she could write Gabe about it, though, she'd need to contact Doc Hanson. Glancing at the clock, she saw she had fifteen minutes until classes were scheduled to begin. Hurrying to her desk, she sat and wrote the note she'd penned several times in her mind.

Eli would deliver it for her.

With any luck, she'd have an answer by midweek. In the meantime, she'd begin working with Grace for ten minutes each lunch break. As Esther bustled in with a "Good morning" and students began to file into their seats, Miriam said a silent prayer that Gabe hadn't experienced a change of heart. They would need everyone's full participation in order for her plan to work—Grace's most of all.

Throwing on her coat, she whispered to Esther that she would be back quick as a stitch. As she hurried out the school's front door, Eli was just pulling up. Children tumbled out, reminding Miriam of different leaves falling from the maple tree. She'd heard *Englischers* comment on how Amish children all looked alike, but personally she didn't see it. Yes, the dresses which reached past knees were similar in style, but they varied in color—though all were dark according to the standards of their community. The youngest girls wore black *kapps* while the older ones wore white, all covered by a dark outer bonnet. Some wore black overcoats and some wore dark gray.

As for the boys, they varied so in height, build, and facial characteristics she had no trouble telling them apart. Different color shirts—brown, blue, and green—peeked out from the tops of their black coats as they shuffled past her murmuring "*gudemariye.*"

They were good children, good students, and she enjoyed her job very much, which was part of the reason she didn't regret not marrying. Part of the reason she kept putting off Aden Schmucker. How could she ever leave all these children? Gabe Miller's face popped into her mind, probably because she held a note about him in her hand, but she shook her head, cleared her thoughts, and hurried toward Eli's buggy.

She ignored two of the older boys, who happened to be putting snow down one another's backs. They would be squirming from their wet shirts for the next hour. That should be punishment enough. No need for her to get involved.

Two minutes later she was back inside, ringing the school bell and watching the children sit up and come to attention.

Esther read the morning devotional—a short verse from the Psalms. "As the mountains surround Jerusalem, so the LORD surrounds his people both now and forevermore." It was one of Miriam's favorite verses. A nice positive focus for their week. Simple enough for the younger ones to understand, and yet with enough wisdom for the older students.

After she'd waited an appropriate amount of time, Esther nodded to her students, who filed to the front of the room for the singing.

Miriam kept a close eye on the younger ones, who followed along but didn't know enough *Englisch* yet to sing the more difficult hymns. After the older children had sung the two songs they had picked out last Thursday, Miriam clapped her hands and the younger classes scrambled forward.

Once in place, she guided them through "Christmas Hymn," which they had been practicing for the last week, and then they all sang "*Stille Nacht*" in German—which everyone was quite good at because they had sung it in church. It sounded particularly good with only children's voices proclaiming "*Stille Nacht! Heilige Nacht!*" Good practice for the Christmas program to come.

Satisfied that everyone was awake and focused for their day, Miriam signaled they could sit down. That was when she noticed that little Sadie Stutzman was holding Grace's hand. That wasn't unusual among the younger girls, but she hadn't realized they had become such fast friends. She smiled at them as they took their seats.

Because it was Monday, she directed the younger children to complete their arithmetic lesson as Esther worked with the older children on grading their math homework. One of the things Miriam enjoyed about teaching was how well their classroom worked *together*—her children often pausing in their lessons to listen while one of Esther's students stopped to ask questions regarding a more difficult problem or to help another student who didn't understand one of the assignments. She thought it was part of the learning process and helped to teach them every bit as much as she did.

The morning flew by, and at lunch they allowed the children to go outside in spite of the snow that still remained on the ground.

"Remember to bundle up," Esther cautioned them. She pulled out her sandwich and sat down beside Miriam. "It's amazing to me that they want to be out in the cold. I'm happy right here beside the stove."

"*Ya.* I feel the same. Though I understand the need to go outside and make some snow angels."

The young girls sitting around them glanced up from the game of Uno they were playing.

Sadie stared at her cards another minute, and then she set them down and grabbed Grace's hand. "Let's do it. Let's go make snow angels."

Grace's eyes widened, but she didn't answer yes or no.

"Sadie's right, Grace." Lily also put down her cards. "Making snow angels is fun."

Both girls stood now, pulling on Grace's hands. Grace allowed herself to be coaxed over to where their coats hung. As Lily and Sadie giggled, they all managed to put on their outer gear and then escaped into the sunshine.

"She seems to be doing well," Esther said.

"So you heard?"

"*Ya*. Joseph was one of the ones who helped to look for her."

"That's right. I'd forgotten."

"What a miracle she was found. Joseph said Pepper is the one who found her in a snow cave."

Miriam nodded, pushing away the fears that still crowded into her dreams at night. "The best part is that Gabe wants to try therapy for her speech problem now. I believe it frightened him that she couldn't call out for help."

"How terrifying."

Esther and Miriam ate in silence.

"But how—"

"I'm not sure."

Outside, Sadie tapped on the window and then ran forward a few yards. Holding Lily's hand on one side, and Grace's on the other, all three girls fell backward. They reminded Miriam of a string of paper dolls she'd had as a child. When they began scissoring their arms up and down, Esther started to giggle.

"They're making their snow angels a bit deep. I'm not sure they will be able to stand up now." But just then Hannah happened along, and she helped each little girl to her feet.

"You know, maybe there isn't a solution to Grace's problem."

"Huh?" Esther frowned as she unwrapped two oatmeal cookies and offered Miriam one.

"Maybe there isn't *one* solution. Maybe there are several."

Taking the cookie to her desk, Miriam sat down, pulled out a sheet of paper, and began writing out Grace's new lesson plan.

∼ Chapter 19 ∼

Gabe checked Grace's lunch box after school on Monday, but there was no note.

He would check it again as soon as she arrived home on Tuesday, but he was worried that Miriam had given up on the both of them. She'd seemed confused by his request.

Maybe she didn't know what to do with Grace.

Maybe he'd been so rude when he'd confronted her that day in her father's barn that she didn't want to help them.

Maybe she was busy, being a teacher to all those children he'd seen in the schoolhouse.

He scolded himself for thinking she could drop everything and put his needs—Grace's needs—first. He drove the nail into a two by four with one slam of the hammer.

"Did that board personally offend you, or are you just feeling particularly energetic this morning?" Eli Stutzman passed another two by four his way.

Four of the men from their church district had shown up Monday morning to help reframe the barn. Gabe had been stunned—because of the weather, because surely they had their own work to do, and because this wasn't exactly the season for a barn raising.

"Not raising it," Efram had noted, pulling away a rotted board.

"Patching it." Joseph had climbed up on the roof as if the weather weren't biting cold and the barn wasn't covered in snow. Sometimes younger men had an energy that irritated Gabe, but he wasn't going to point it out right then.

They had finished the patch on the roof to the barn this morning with the help of Miriam's father, Joshua. This afternoon Joshua was attending to things on his own farm, and Joseph and Efram had errands in town, but Eli had returned to help with the side wall that was caving in.

"Maybe being around those younger guys had a positive effect on you—or maybe you like swinging that hammer as if it's a wrecking ball." Eli grinned as he spoke. Gabe was learning that the man didn't own a bad mood, which was probably a good thing since he drove a buggy full of kids and needed more than a bushel of patience.

"Guess I was worrying, is all." Gabe continued to hammer in the nails that would hold the board into place. He'd been amazed at how much faster the work went when he wasn't doing it alone. Of course, he should have known that, but somehow his pride had helped him forget.

"Anything you want to talk about?"

"Don't know that it would help."

"Will it hurt?"

Gabe thought about it for a few moments, and then he reached down and took a long drink from the jug of water at his feet. "I asked Miriam to help me with Grace. Help find a way to..." He stumbled over the history and the hurt. "Help her find her voice again. I thought I would have heard from her by now."

Eli nodded, not answering immediately.

They added two more boards to the wall before he enlightened Gabe with what he knew. "Maybe that's why she had me go over to Doc Hanson's yesterday."

"Doc Hanson?"

"Ya. It was about something very important. She came running out of the schoolhouse like it was on fire with a note she needed him to have that morning, so I said I'd take it. But Doc isn't in his office on Mondays—only the nurse is. I guess Miriam forgot that."

"He wasn't in?"

"That's what I said."

"But you still took the note?"

Eli removed his hat and then repositioned it on his head. "Maybe you need to take a break, son."

"What happened then?"

"When?"

Gabe set his hammer down on a sawhorse and took a step back from the wall. "After you took the note in."

"Nothing happened. He wasn't there."

"Did you read it?"

"'Course not. It wasn't to me."

"Right. Okay. So you took it in, but he wasn't there."

"*Ya.*"

Gabe waited, but Eli had already picked up another board and seemed to be done with the conversation.

"So I guess he'd be in today."

"Doc?"

"Who else?" Now Gabe suspected the man was messing with him, especially when he started grinning so that his beard took an upturn.

"Why, sure." Eli scratched at his beard. "Doc's always in the office during the week."

"Except Mondays."

"*Ya.* Except Mondays."

They moved down the wall, replacing boards, with the December sunshine stealing the chill from the afternoon.

"Good man?" Gabe asked. Now the boards seemed lighter, and he wasn't worried anymore. At least he knew Miriam's silence wasn't because she was angry at him.

"Doc Hanson? Oh, yes. A very good man. Seen him a few times myself."

The rest of the day went quickly. By the time Eli left, the barn was starting to actually resemble something that might withstand a winter's storm, or even a spring one for that matter.

When Grace hopped out of Eli's buggy an hour later, she waved her lunch box.

"Something in there you want me to see?"

Grace was walking backward, staying a few steps in front of him as they headed toward the house. Her cheeks were beginning to peel from the slight frostbite she'd suffered, but he still thought she was the most beautiful thing he'd ever seen.

When they reached the house, she thrust the lunch box in his hands and then dashed ahead. He resisted the urge to open it and read the note while he stood there in the cold.

Best to go on inside first and see that she had an afternoon snack to eat. Food had been popping up in his house the last few days as well. Every time one of the men showed up to help with the barn, it seemed they brought a basketful of something baked. He might have argued with accepting the gifts except for the delight on his daughter's face every afternoon when she came home and checked the cupboard.

His thoughts returned to the unread note, Miriam, and Doc Hanson. What would their plan be? What would it mean for Grace?

Whatever it was, they would confront it together.

Miriam wanted to speak quietly with Grace before their afternoon meeting. Unfortunately, her students had other ideas. Most days, teaching in a one-room schoolhouse was calm and things went according to plan.

And then there were days like Wednesday.

The rain had started falling steadily before she rang the eight thirty bell, which meant that everyone tracked in mud along with the last of the remaining snow. She didn't understand how it could be raining when they had just had a blizzard, but somehow the temperatures had continued to warm through the day yesterday and even throughout the night. Esther had told her as they readied for class that the rest of the week would be in the low forties, which meant drizzly rain and thirty-eight students who could not go outside.

Once the children had come inside and spent fifteen minutes cleaning up the mess they had tracked with them, Esther had led them through their Scripture and the Lord's Prayer. Miriam had started to harbor hope that the day would find its natural rhythm. Then they had progressed through the singing, and the Lapp boys had begun to squirm.

They hadn't made it through the second song when something popped out of the younger boy's pocket and Miriam's girls fell out of line with a squeal—all except for Grace, who wanted to get closer to see better. That should have been her first clue that the boys had brought mice into the classroom. The older children had helped to catch them and deposit them out the front door—she'd thought Grace would actually speak at that point, but the young girl had written notes madly on the side. Hannah explained to her that these mice weren't like Stanley—they were plain field mice the boys had caught in their dad's barn.

While Esther moved the Lapp boys to the back for a private conversation and an extra writing assignment on schoolroom behavior, Miriam had started the arithmetic assignment. Younger students handed their papers to older students for grading. Older students exchanged with one another. Grade 2 students started their next reading lesson, while grade 1 students filed back to the front of the room for their oral reading lesson—though they kept glancing around as if a mouse might pop out from behind Miriam's desk.

Things finally settled down, and she even forgot about the patter of rain against the window, but then it was time for recess and bathroom breaks. She kept a close eye on the Lapp boys as they tramped outside, but they had been sufficiently chastised. Their father gave them plenty of chores at home, and they would have enough trouble completing one extra assignment. A second dose wouldn't be something they would want to carry home. No doubt the mice had been meant for the restroom break and had escaped early.

So she relaxed slightly, and that's probably why she wasn't quick enough when one of the older Stutzman girls turned too quickly on the boardwalk they set over the bigger mud puddle outside. The rain was still coming down steadily. They had two lines going out of the schoolhouse—girls out the front and boys out the back.

Later she heard the real reason Katie Stutzman slipped off the board and fell, bottom first, into the large puddle of water. Apparently she'd been trying to get a better look at Amos Hershberger. It was December—only December! Too early for spring fever and the dance between boys and girls and long looks. Besides, Katie was only twelve years old. She was much too young to have boys on her mind.

Miriam hurried outside, helped a crying Katie out of the puddle, and guided her upstairs. Though Esther's clothes were several sizes too large, they would work for the rest of the afternoon.

Katie missed recess, and Miriam missed her chance to speak with Grace. They did make it downstairs in time for another hour of lessons—this time Esther's older classes worked on reading and comprehension while Miriam's students tackled new problems from their math workbooks. Perhaps it was the rain, or the morning they had experienced, or the text Esther's classes had read. Whatever the reason, Miriam's little ones repeatedly looked up from their numbers, pencils paused and eyes staring at their older brothers and sisters.

She finally motioned for them to close their books and listen in as Esther and her students focused on the final chapters of *Little Women*.

"Now that you've answered questions about the facts of the novel, I want you to interpret the meaning of the story and think about what the author had in mind when she wrote it." The older children began to squirm as they stood in line, waiting for their question.

"Hannah, this book was written more than one hundred and forty years ago. How can students today relate to it?"

Pulling on the strings of her *kapp*, Hannah stared at the board for a moment, and then she began to speak—softly at first, but more confidently as she grew sure of her answer. "It is an old book, but some things don't change. Jo's family had four girls, and most of us have at least that many." There was a bit of laughter among the students. "What I liked was how each character was different. Some people think when you grow up in a large family that everyone is the same, but you're not. Jo, Meg, Beth, and Amy all had very different personalities. The author was able to show that through their mishaps, and I think any reader can relate to the characters, even if the book was written a long time ago."

"Good," Esther said. "Amos."

The boy stepped forward—tall and gangly. Miriam knew him to be a good reader.

"What is in this book for a boy?"

"Not much."

Everyone laughed out loud now.

Amos ran his hands under his suspenders. "But when you're reading about Jo, it's almost as if you're reading about a boy."

"How so?"

"She likes to do things boys like to do rather than things she's supposed to like to do. She wants to fight in the Civil War with her father, when actually he's gone to be a chaplain. That shows how little she understands." Esther nodded her agreement, so Amos continued. "Even her name—Jo instead of Josephine—shows she has trouble accepting her place in their family."

"Know anyone like that, Amos?"

"If I did I wouldn't say. She'd box my ears."

Again laughter filled the room as Esther nodded for him to step back and the next student stepped forward.

The discussion continued until Esther glanced at Miriam, and Miriam stood and rang the bell for lunch. Everyone returned to their desks, and Esther dismissed the room by rows while Miriam oversaw hand-washing at the sink at the back of the room. Some students then picked up their lunch boxes, which they had stored near their coats, while others made their way to the stove where they had placed potatoes to cook.

Within fifteen minutes everyone had eaten and games of checkers and cards were set up.

"This rain *cannot* last all week," Esther said, as she snapped her fingers at two of the boys who were chasing two of the girls in a game of Bear. Boys were the bear. Girls were lunch for the bear.

"*Ya.* Not everyone is happy playing cards, but they have to use up their energy somehow."

"Maybe they could play Duck and go float around the school building."

The teachers savored their sandwiches and hot tea as the rain continued to drum a pattern against the window.

"It's so odd for the weather to be warmer this week."

"Joseph heard in town that it's a warm front being pushed by a much colder front that will hit again this weekend."

"*Wunderbaar.* Just in time to keep us inside on Saturday and Sunday."

"Did you know our record high in December was sixty-two?"

"I did not." Miriam studied her. "Let me guess. Joseph told you that."

Esther smiled. "He enjoys studying such things for the animals."

"You two seem as if you are going to be very happy together."

"*Ya.* I believe we are."

Esther studied the rain for a moment, and then she turned to Miriam with a mischievous smile. "There's supposed to be a singing after church. You should come. That is, if it isn't canceled because of too much rain or too much cold."

"I'll think about it," Miriam said. She would, to be kind to Esther, but she didn't think her mind would change about attending the after-church singing for single folk. She was watching out the window at the steady flow of rain, wondering if Doc Hanson would make it. Somehow, she managed to lose track of time, and she completely forgot about the need to speak with Grace about the doctor's appointment later that day.

Chapter 20

Grace stared from her dad to her teacher to the *Englisch* man who looked like pictures of a big bear she'd seen in a book.

The *Englischer* had no beard. That surprised her more than his size. She'd seen plenty of men without beards—all the younger men at church didn't have them. But she'd never seen an older man without a beard.

His skin was all wrinkly, like *mammi* Sarah's, and he had white eyebrows.

She'd been so surprised when Miriam told her to stay and not to leave in Eli's buggy. Then she'd peeked outside and seen her dad walking toward the school door.

Was this a good thing or a bad thing?

She knew the *Englisch* man was a doctor because he had a black bag like the doctor in Indiana. Only this man's bag had funny stickers all over it. That was a little odd. Some of the stickers were animals, and she would rather like to have a better look at those, but she wasn't about to move closer to him in order to do so.

What was he doing here? Was he here to see her?

The thought made her squirm in her seat.

Maybe it was about her frostbite. Her cheeks still itched a little, but not so much as to make her uncomfortable. The cream Eva had given her helped a bunch, and she'd been surprised when the other kids didn't make fun of her. Actually, they had been nicer this week.

Grace rubbed the end of her nose. Why had they been nicer this week? She suddenly wished she had Stanley in her pocket.

Instead, she sat at her desk and stared at the spot where Sadie had drawn a flower on her desktop. They had erased it right away, but she could still see the outline. It looked like a friendship flower, and it reminded her of spring.

Hard as she focused on the drawing, though, she could still hear her teacher talking to her dad.

"What do you mean you didn't tell her?"

"I meant to, but then I got busy."

"Busy?"

Dad shuffled his feet the way he did when he wished he could be done talking about a thing. "I could see that the rain was about to start, and the barn was nearly done, but not quite."

When Miriam only stared at him, he added, "I read your note, like I said I would."

"You didn't just take it out of her box? You read it?"

"'Course I did. I told you I would."

"You didn't throw it away this time?"

Grace had to cover her mouth so she wouldn't giggle. The doctor looked at her when she did that, so she tucked her hand back into her lap. Maybe giggling wasn't allowed at this meeting. It sure was funny, though, how her teacher talked to her dad as though he were a student.

"I thought you would talk to her," he said.

Miriam straightened a few things on her desk. Only thing was— everything on her desk was already in order.

The *Englischer* had walked over to the door and was speaking into his small telephone.

"I meant to, yes." Now Miriam was fussing with her *kapp*. "However, the day was very busy. All of the children were stuck inside because of the weather, and then there was an episode with some mice, and Katie fell into the mud...but those are only excuses. I should have found the time to speak with her."

Miriam glanced up, caught Grace staring at her, and smiled.

Something was not right. Not good at all.

Grace tried to think back over the last few days to see if she might have done something wrong, but nothing came to mind.

The doctor pushed a button on his phone and put it in his pocket. "Okay. I apologize. My nurse had a question, but it's all tended to now." He walked forward and offered his hand to her dad. "My name is Doc Hanson. Thank you for taking time out of your day to stop by. I realize how much work there is on a farm and that it's difficult to leave it."

Dad shook his hand. "Thank you for traveling out to see Grace."

Grace nearly popped out of her seat at the mention of her name. Why? She'd already figured out that the doctor was here to see her. He wasn't here to see her dad or Miriam.

Everyone turned to stare at her.

And everyone smiled.

Uh-oh.

Grace stood, walked over to her dad, and slipped her hand into his. The fast thump-thump-thump of her heart slowed down a little.

"Hi, Grace. I'm Doc Hanson." The *Englischer* paused a moment, but he didn't look surprised when she didn't speak. He motioned to the front of the room, where Miriam had placed four chairs next to her desk. Three chairs were grouped together, and one chair faced the other three.

"Shall we have a seat?" Doc Hanson chose the chair next to Miriam's desk, where he'd placed his black bag and some papers.

Grace chose the chair between her dad and her teacher. That seemed like the safest place to be sitting if she couldn't be in the buggy behind Chance. She told herself that soon she would be home, sitting at the table and drawing. Whatever this was about, it couldn't last long.

Whatever this was about, it wouldn't be worse than the snow cave.

"Grace, if it's okay, I'd like to ask you a few questions. Now, Miss Miriam has told me that you don't speak, so you answer as best you can—nod your head or such, and we'll see if we can write up a kind of medical history. Sound okay to you?"

Grace nodded her head slowly.

She wanted to reach over and hold her dad's hand again, but she didn't want to look like a baby, so instead she sat in her chair and held on to the sides of the seat.

"Does your throat feel sore?"

Grace shook her head no.

"Scratchy or tickly ever?"

She hesitated, looked sideways at her dad, who was watching her curiously. Slowly she nodded her head.

"All right. Now, I know you're young." He looked at another sheet of paper in his folder. "Eight years old, right?"

Yes.

"Can you remember the last time you spoke?"

Yes.

"You were able to say exactly what you meant without any stuttering or problems?"

The color rising in her cheeks, Grace nodded. *Yes.*

"How long ago was that, Grace?"

She wished she had some paper and a pencil, but she didn't, so she held up three fingers.

"Months?" Doc Hanson asked, but something in his eyes, which were blue and nice even if he was an *Englischer*, told her he knew it wasn't months.

She shook her head.

He set down his pen. "Years then?"

Yes.

Doc looked to her dad for confirmation.

"That would be about right. It happened when her *mamm* died."

Doc nodded as if that made sense. "Was there an accident of some sort?"

Grace knew he was asking her, but she didn't know how to answer. The thing he was asking about was a memory she didn't allow herself to look back on. It was one place she never went. The door was closed. That was how she thought of it.

"No accident, no. Not like you mean." Her dad's voice was very sad. She reached over and put her hand in his. That didn't make her feel like a baby at all. It made her feel that they would be okay. She always knew the two of them together would be okay. He was the one thing in her life she was sure of—her dad, and now maybe Miriam.

"And she spoke normally before?"

"Ya."

"Cough a lot?"

Grace shook her head at the same time her dad did.

"Trouble swallowing?"

Grace shook her head so hard her black *kapp* strings twirled.

"She eats her meals fine," Gabe offered.

Doc Hanson opened his black bag which was sitting on Miriam's desk and pulled out a black instrument. He held it up and showed it to her. "See this? It has a magnifying glass on one end and a light on the other. Come over here and you can look through it."

Grace glanced at her dad and then at Miriam before sliding out of her seat and walking over to stand in front of Doc. That's how she was starting to think of him—just Doc. He held the black thing up in front of her eyes.

"When I push the button, the light will come on. You should be able to see my wrinkles really well."

He was right! His wrinkles looked like the crinkles in her blankets when she woke up in the morning.

She smiled at him.

"Sometimes when a person has trouble speaking, it's because their throat is hurt. If you open your mouth and let me shine this light inside, I'll be able to see pretty far down and check it out. Would that be okay with you?"

Grace's heart started thump-thump-thumping again. She'd always wondered if maybe she'd broken her voice. Could that light-thing tell Doc?

"Good girl. Now stick out your tongue like you were mad at one of the boys. Uh-huh. One more second. Perfect. Do you mind if I peek in your ears?"

Grace grinned. What did her ears have to do with her throat? She shrugged and turned sideways. It tickled a little when Doc placed the instrument in her left ear and then her right. He made funny, "Uh-huh. I see," sounds, but nothing too alarming. She forgot all about being afraid.

He dropped the light-thing into his bag.

Wriggling his bushy white eyebrows, he confessed, "I didn't see anything in there I've never seen before, Grace. Mind if I touch your throat? Sometimes my eyes can't tell me everything. Sometimes I have to trust these old hands."

She thought of how she'd crawled around in the snow cave, feeling her way with her hands. She'd had to depend on her sense of touch then. She'd love to tell Doc that story.

Turning toward him she raised her chin high, making her neck as long as possible, as long as a giraffe's neck.

His fingers were soft and reminded her of the old sheets on *mammi* Sarah's beds. He gazed off across the room as he squeezed gently, up and down her throat. When he was finished, he leaned back in his chair. "You can sit down now, child."

He fastened the black bag and closed the folder he'd been writing notes in. His attention moved from her dad to Miriam and then finally settled on her. "I'm going to be honest. I don't know why your voice stopped working. I could send you to a specialist over in the city, and they could run more tests. Maybe they could tell you."

Her dad fidgeted in his seat.

"Sometimes a thing has to work itself out. Other times we have to help it a bit. Your voice hasn't been used in so long that I believe it's going to need help from you, Grace. It's going to need exercises like my legs would need exercises if I hadn't walked on them in three years. At first they would be very weak, and they wouldn't want to carry my weight."

Grace reached down for the hem of her apron and ran her fingers along the seam.

"Your teacher is good at working with students who need extra help. Some students need help because their mind can't catch up. You need help because your voice can't catch up." He paused and glanced at Miriam.

"I'll be happy to work with Grace," she said.

"I brought along three sheets of voice exercises. They are what we might use with someone who has experienced physical trauma, say, surgery or a prolonged throat illness."

"But Grace hasn't been sick." It was the first time her dad had spoken since Doc had begun examining her.

"You know that and I know that, but Grace's voice doesn't know that. We're going to have to coax it back into shape." He handed one copy of the sheets to Miriam and another to Gabe. "Now, your teacher and your dad will help you, Grace, but the real work will be up to you."

He stood and picked up his black bag, the one with the funny stickers. She could see now they were actually patches with pictures of different animals—dogs, cats, and even horses. "It might feel funny at first. It might even embarrass you some."

Her eyes found his when he said the word "embarrass." How did he know?

"Sometimes, when I haven't worked on something around my house, it'll squeak. Say, maybe the gate on the fence. It gets rusty because I don't go out the back way often. My wife reminds me that I need to go out there and take care of it, so I take my tools and go pay attention to it. Isn't the gate's fault, but I'm a little embarrassed at first that I've let things go and all."

He reached down and put his hand on top of her head. She was reminded of Bishop Beiler and standing at the front of the church. Doc smiled more than the bishop did.

"After I work with it a while, the gate comes around. I suspect your voice will too."

He walked to the door with her dad, and Miriam showed her the sheets he'd given her. Grace didn't pay much attention to the words and pictures on the sheets. She was listening to what her dad and Doc were saying.

"How long do you think this will take?"

"It's hard to say. Adopt the pace of nature. Her secret is patience."

"*Ya*. I know the old proverbs, but this is my *dochder* we're talking about."

"I realize that, Mr. Miller. I do. I wish I had a better answer for you." Doc ran his hand over the top of his head. "If you decide you want to do those tests, give me a call and I'll arrange them. My number is on the bottom of those sheets. You have any questions at all about the exercises, feel free to call me."

He walked out the door and into the rain.

Grace didn't know what to think, but there was one thing she was sure of. Things were about to change.

~ Chapter 21 ~

M iriam exchanged a knowing look with Esther when Grace closed her lunch box and stored it in her cubby.

"Do you think she'll speak today?" Esther asked.

"I can't be sure, but she's not going out to play with Sadie and Lily." Miriam cleaned off the corner of her desk and pulled out Grace's folder with the exercises Doc Hanson had left.

"I'll go outside with the students." Esther stood and reached for her coat.

"You don't have—"

"I want to give you two privacy. And I really could use a walk around the school yard. All the quilting I've been doing has cut down on the amount of exercise I get."

"The amount of baking the parents are sending doesn't help." Miriam frowned at the stack of baked goods accumulating on the table near the stove. It seemed every student wanted to bring them something sweet this time of year. If they weren't careful, both of them would be bigger than her father's largest heifer.

Grace moved to the front of the room as Esther slipped out the back door.

"Are you ready for our exercises?"

Grace nodded her head up and down, her chin nearly touching

her chest in her enthusiasm. They weren't supposed to work until Friday after school, but it seemed Grace had her own schedule, and it included ten minutes at lunchtime. Not that yesterday had produced any sounds. Grace had opened her mouth, but she simply shrugged when Miriam was the only person making the sounds on the sheet.

"All right. Let's do this."

They stretched their necks, flapped their arms, and worked their way through page one of doc's sheets. Soon they were halfway down page two, and Miriam was sure it was going to be another day of her pushing out vowel sounds solo fashion.

Grace participated. She had her arms stretched wide and her mouth open, but so far not a peep had escaped.

Miriam was giving it all she had, hoping her enthusiasm would be contagious.

She had practically sung her way through "ma," "me," and "mo."

Wait...had Grace spoken? She looked up from the sheet. Grace's brown eyes were staring back at her.

"Let's try that from the beginning. I believe we might have rattled something loose. Together, or do you want to repeat after me?"

Grace held both of her hands together.

"All right. Ma, me, mo..." Miriam held the note and listened, but there was only her voice in the room, so she moved on. "Mu."

And then she was sure and so was Grace.

The young girl's eyes had been closed as she focused, but they popped open, as round as her mouth, making a perfect O.

They both held the "mu" sound for three...four...five more seconds.

When they ended the syllable, silence filled the room, and then Miriam couldn't have stopped herself. She opened her arms and Grace practically jumped into her embrace. She held the young girl tight.

"You did very well, Grace! I'm so proud of you. That's the best 'mu' I ever heard."

She thought Grace might be embarrassed, might pop back into her turtle shell, but instead the little girl hugged her teacher one more time, and then she turned and skipped back to where the coats were kept.

Apparently their lesson for the day was over.

As she watched Grace run out to the playground, Miriam marveled that one sound, a single syllable, could make such a difference in both of their lives, but it had. It had opened a gate that for Grace might lead to an entirely different life.

She closed the folder and slid her hand across the front of it, and then she bowed her head and thanked the Lord for today's victory with this very special child.

The plan had been for Gabe to work with Grace each morning as they readied for school and each evening before bed. Miriam would work with her Tuesdays after school was out, which meant Gabe would have to drive in to pick Grace up. This wasn't so bad, as he probably needed to drive into town once a week anyway, and the school was on the way in.

If he was honest with himself, he'd been avoiding town and the possibility of running into people. But now that he knew so many members of the district, and so many good-hearted men had been working on his barn, he found himself actually looking forward to stopping in at the general store for a little conversation.

Miriam would also work with Grace while she closed up the school on Fridays, and then she would drive her home.

Two afternoons a week working with Miriam.

Every morning and evening working with Gabe.

That sounded like a good plan. Only Gabe wasn't holding up his end of the bargain.

On Friday morning, he called to Grace one more time. The cinnamon rolls Miriam's mother had sent over the day before were piping hot, and he'd poured fresh milk into her cup, but still no Grace. Where was she?

"Grace Ann, get in here or you'll be late for school."

He ate a roll while he waited, standing up, his work boot tapping out an impatient rhythm. When he finally heard her dragging her small book bag across the sitting room floor, he looked at the clock and saw it was time to leave. Wrapping her breakfast in a dish towel, he thrust the cup into her hands.

"Drink this. Quick."

She did as she was told, her big brown eyes staring into his. She did not offer any explanation for her tardiness.

"Why are you so slow this week?" He grabbed her coat from the mudroom and helped her into it. "The rain's stopped at least."

Bright sunshine filtered through the cold morning air as they walked down the muddy lane.

"We're supposed to be doing these exercises. Last night you fell asleep practically facedown in your soup. Yesterday you slept in same as today. Do you feel like you're coming down with a cold?" He reached out to feel her forehead, but she ducked away and shook her head no.

"Listen to me, Grace. That doc—he knew what he was talking about, but we have to do our share. Now let's practice..." He fumbled in his coat for the sheet of paper and had barely unfolded it when Grace tugged on his arm and pointed toward the end of the lane.

Eli was bringing his buggy to a stop.

Hugging her dad briefly, she took off running toward the buggy, where Eli's children were waving.

Gabe was left standing in the middle of the lane holding the sheet of paper.

As the buggy pulled away, he waved at Eli and hoped that when Miriam showed up this afternoon she wouldn't quiz them on how much progress they'd made.

He'd yet to hear Grace utter a single sound, much less a word. It had been more than thirty-six hours since they met with Doc Hanson. The man's cautionary advice to be patient echoed in his mind as he walked toward the endless work that needed to be done in the fields and the barn.

He supposed it was possible that Grace had been unusually tired this week. There was also the possibility she was avoiding him. Tonight he would speak with Miriam and compare notes. One thing he was sure of—his daughter wouldn't be able to avoid the teacher's attempts at the exercises on the ride home this afternoon.

That thought cheered him up, and he found himself whistling as he began mucking out the stalls in the barn.

Gabe didn't exactly clean up for the teacher's arrival later that afternoon. A man had to wash up and change into fresh clothes some time, and he just so happened to finish working a few minutes earlier than normal. As he sat on the front porch steps and watched Miriam guide her buggy toward his house, it occurred to him that she would make someone a fine wife.

Why had she never married? Why was she still teaching? Why was he thinking about these things? They were none of his concern, though he did appreciate the extra time she was taking with Grace. No doubt she was as tired from her workweek as he was from his.

She didn't look tired as she waved at him from the buggy.

In fact, she looked rather fresh and perky.

Grace on the other hand, looked done in. Her cheeks were red, and she seemed somewhat exhausted.

Gabe walked forward and reached for the harness of the mare. "Whoa, Belle."

"Gabe." Miriam smiled and handed him a plate of cookies. The women in this district were going to cause him to gain ten pounds before spring.

Grace hopped out of the buggy and ran inside the house, not even throwing a glance his way.

"What's with her?"

"I believe she's tired and maybe a little embarrassed. We worked fairly hard on the way home from school." She smiled and added, "I may have driven slowly to give us more time."

"Huh. I haven't managed to coax a single sound out of her."

"You don't say." Miriam cocked her head, much like that hunting dog she set so much store in—the dog that had saved Grace's life. He wouldn't be forgetting that. He needed to save the mutt a meat bone next time he cooked up something decent.

"I put some hot water on to boil. Would you have time to come in for a few minutes? I know it'll be dark soon, but I'd like to talk to you...about Grace, if you have time."

"Certainly I do."

She set aside the blanket that had been across her lap, accepted his help out of the buggy, and walked beside him up the steps. He offered to shelter her mare, but she shook her head. "I can't stay as long as that. My parents will be expecting me for dinner."

Disappointment surged up inside of him, but he tamped it down. What had he thought she would do? Stay and prepare a meal for them as she had that first evening?

"Surely one cookie won't ruin your appetite."

"One cookie and some *kaffi* I can handle."

Gabe expected to see Grace in the kitchen, but it was empty. Her coat wasn't on the hook in the mudroom, but her lunch box was on the counter. His daughter, however, was nowhere to be seen.

"I wonder where she got off to," he mumbled as he added *kaffi* to the water and set it toward the hot part of the stove.

He turned back toward Miriam as she removed her coat and outer bonnet. Perhaps that was the first time he saw her as a woman, the first time he didn't see her as only the teacher or, more pointedly, as a possible threat. Now it was difficult to remember why he'd ever felt that way.

The last of the day's light was coming through his kitchen window—a window he'd scrubbed clean when he'd first moved into the farmhouse. The week's rain had splattered it again with mud and dirt, but not enough to block the light. Not enough to detract from what he was staring at.

Some of her black hair had escaped from her white *kapp*, curling and dancing down the side of her face. Her cheeks were flushed from the cold and her eyes—soft, kind, gray eyes—were framed by dark brows. A nose with a bit of an upturn and somewhat high cheekbones rounded out the picture.

Miriam King was truly a beautiful woman. He found himself wondering again why she'd never married.

Did she not realize what a relationship between a man and a woman could offer? And he didn't mean just the wedding bed. He meant the companionship, the laughter, the sharing of burdens, the quiet togetherness that one looked forward to at the beginning and end of each day. Marriage was a gift from *Gotte*, a blessing to both man and woman.

She looked up at him suddenly and the idea crossed his mind that perhaps she could read his thoughts, but that was silly—a child's worry.

He turned, pulled two mugs from the cabinet, and carried them to the table along with the plate of cookies, which he could tell now were ginger—one of his favorites.

Walking out into the mudroom, where they kept the smaller icebox with the cold items they used daily, he pulled out a little pitcher of cream. "I believe this is still good. Do you need sugar?"

"No. Cream only is fine. *Danki*."

Gabe couldn't think of anything else that needed doing, so he drew in a deep breath and forced himself to sit beside her. They hadn't been alone before, except the time he'd confronted her about the kitten. Actually, his words had been about her ideas regarding Grace, but it had begun with the kitten Grace wanted.

He felt awkward now, even though Grace was in the house. He didn't know what to do with his hands, so he picked up the empty mug and turned it round and round, staring down into it as if he might find answers there or at least a way to begin the conversation.

"Tell me how she's been since seeing Doc." Miriam's voice was quiet, without any judgment, and perhaps that's why he was able to spill his worries.

"I thought she was fine. She seemed all right while he was examining her. Didn't you think?"

"Yes."

"I was relieved when he didn't find anything wrong." Gabe looked up when there was a light tap on the window. Grace waved and then dashed off across the yard. She must have dropped off her lunch box and then run outside again through the back door. "The little imp. I can call her in—"

"Or you could let her play. She's been inside most of the day."

Gabe nodded, stood, and fetched their *kaffi*. "So I thought everything was fine when we left the school Wednesday afternoon. Except that we haven't done the exercises a single time. She either falls asleep at dinner or is late in the morning, which is not like her at all. Usually she's waiting on me."

"Could be she's avoiding you." Miriam reached for a cookie, broke off a corner, and popped it into her mouth.

"Why would she do that?"

"I don't know, so I won't guess. We can ask her later."

"Ask her? Has she spoken to you?" Gabe had raised his mug to drink from it, but he nearly dropped it at the idea that Grace had talked to her teacher.

Miriam reached out to pat his hand resting on the table.

"Patience. Remember?"

"She hasn't spoken?"

"We've done the exercises three times—"

"But I thought—"

"Yes, I know. That wasn't the schedule, but it seems Grace has her own ideas about when and where she wants to do things. The first night I was here I believe you implied she's a bit stubborn."

"*Ya*, that she is."

Miriam pushed the plate of cookies toward him. "My cooking is *gut*, Gabe. You should try one."

"Oh. Right." He ate one of the cookies in a single bite, the taste of molasses and ginger and cinnamon filling his mouth. Suddenly he was overcome with memories of home, fall, and his mother's cooking.

"Is something wrong with the cookies?"

"Hmm?"

"I was wondering if something was wrong with the cookies. You seemed to disappear on me for a minute."

"No. They're *gut*. You were right about your cooking." Gabe ate another, and tried to move the conversation back on track. "I can't figure why Grace would work on the exercises with you and not with me."

Miriam took another sip of her *kaffi* and broke off another corner of the cookie. Why did women eat cookies that way? They weren't that big. Gabe stuck another whole one into his mouth and stared out the window.

"I think I have an idea." Miriam stood and walked through the mudroom as Grace climbed on the fence across from them. Sticking her head outside the door she called out, "Grace, could you come inside for a minute?"

When she walked back in the kitchen, her cheeks were rosy from the cold. "Let's see if we can show her we're working together on this."

She sat back down, and though her eyes were twinkling, Gabe knew in that moment that Grace didn't stand a chance. He might be busy and distracted and tired trying to pull together a run-down farm and raise a child alone, but Miriam King?

Miriam King had her mind set on teaching Grace to speak.

⇜ Chapter 22 ⇝

Miriam had worked with a lot of parents the last ten years, ever since her first year as a teaching assistant. She'd even worked with a few widowers. She had never had any difficulty maintaining a professional distance, keeping her emotions out of the equation, and remembering she was the teacher in the room.

Watching Gabe Miller practically swallow her cookies whole and seeing his tension melt away as he relaxed and forgot to worry about Grace for a moment, she'd felt her professional lines blur. Who could sit in this kitchen and remain distant? Especially after the last two times she'd been here—first cooking dinner for them and then the horrible night they had all worried Grace might be lost for good.

She shook the memory away as the little girl stomped the mud off of her shoes and walked hesitantly into the kitchen.

"Cookie?" Miriam asked.

Grace glanced warily from her father to her teacher and back again. In the end the cookie won. She pulled out a chair across from her dad, accepted the cookie, and took a tentative bite.

"Have some apple cider with it," Gabe said, pouring her a glass. "It'll help clear your throat."

Grace's eyes widened, but she continued nibbling around the

edges of the cookie, reminding Miriam of the little mouse she'd brought to school.

"Grace, I need to get home to Pepper before it grows too dark outside. You remember Pepper, don't you?"

Grace nodded, and a smile erased the worry from her face.

"I imagine Pepper remembers you as well. You two are *freinden* for life after last weekend." Miriam sipped her lukewarm *kaffi*. "Before I go, I thought we should run through the exercises. Your *dat* told me you haven't had a chance to work at home, but I told him you've done well at school and you would want to work extra hard this weekend. After all, the Christmas presentation is next week, and we had talked about your participating."

Grace began to crumble her cookie onto her plate rather than eat it.

"So let's run through what we did in the buggy on the way here. You don't need to do as many repetitions, but let's do each exercise once so your *dat* can see how it's done."

Grace nodded ever so slightly, though it was hard to read her expression because her face was now almost parallel with the table. They were actually staring at the top of her *kapp*, which had come unpinned while she was running around outside. It had slipped halfway back on her head and brown hair, no doubt carefully braided this morning, tumbled down, obscuring her face.

Miriam could sense fear coming off the child in waves, and she longed to know what that was all about. What had caused Grace to stop speaking three years ago? What had kept her from speaking in the time between? And what was she so afraid of now?

The one thing she was certain of was that the girl could not be afraid of the man sitting across from her. Miriam had encountered a few abusive parents. *Englischers* liked to portray the Amish culture as perfect, but it wasn't. Amish adults experienced anger and depression the same as adults did in any other community. Occasionally they had poor parents who were neglectful, and once in a while they had a father or mother who seemed to Miriam like bad people—but she'd always left those problems to the school board, the bishop, and the deacons.

She had learned to recognize the signs of abuse and neglect. It was an unpleasant part of her job—the misplaced bruise, the flinching when she placed a hand on a child's shoulder, the inability of a student to make eye contact. She saw none of this with Grace. Moreover, Grace was happy and relaxed in her home environment.

Normally.

At the moment, she seemed to be trying to disappear into her chair.

"Let's start with the hum. Repeat after me. Hummmm."

Grace's voice was quieter than a hummingbird hovering above a spring flower. "Hummm."

"A little louder, dear."

She didn't glance up, didn't stir at all, but she did crank up the volume. "Hummmmmmmm."

Miriam felt more than saw Gabe's excitement. She held up a hand to hold him off—she so wanted him to see all Grace was capable of this afternoon.

"Excellent. Now head up! Let's do some exercises. We'll do them with you. Shoulder rolls first."

Grace rolled her eyes, but she complied.

Miriam rolled her shoulders forward several times and then back. When she noticed Gabe was only watching, his eyes widened in amazement, she said, "It helps if *everyone* participates."

"Huh? Oh. I thought we were supposed to be *talking*."

"That comes in a minute. Did you even read the sheets?"

"Yes. Well, some of them. That is, I looked at the list of words."

"That was sheet three." Miriam turned back to Grace. "*Wunderbaar*. Neck back and open your mouth."

They all stared up at the ceiling. Miriam noticed it needed painting, but of course she didn't mention it.

"Now side to side." She thought Grace might be giggling, but who could tell? The only sound so far had been the light hum.

"Yawn." She'd found when they had done the exercises earlier that it was incredibly hard to yawn on command. They all stared at each other. Gabe started laughing first.

It was a sound of joy, and Miriam knew in her heart it came from hearing that earlier hum from Grace. She knew and rejoiced with him, but she scolded him nevertheless.

"Not helpful."

"You both look like fish with your mouths wide open, waiting for a big fat worm."

"*We* look like fish? Well, you happen to resemble a baby bird I once saw."

Grace tapped on her arm, mid-yawn.

"Oh *gut*. Let's see, deep breathing is next."

"Is this all necessary?" Gabe asked as Grace popped out of her chair and began taking giant gulps of air, her hand pressed on her tummy.

"Is it necessary? If your horse were injured, would you take it out and run it full trot or would you carefully exercise it first?"

"If my horse were injured, I'd probably shoot it."

Grace stopped mid-breath and stared at her dad as if he'd taken the rifle out of the gun cabinet and fired it in the kitchen.

"What did I say?"

"Never mind." Miriam realized it was too late in the day for analogies. "Promise me you'll do the exercises with her."

"I promise." Gabe popped another cookie in his mouth. "You're doing such a great job. Sure you can't come over tomorrow? You could bring more cookies."

"I have papers to grade tomorrow."

"Oh."

Miriam turned her full attention to Grace after straightening the three papers, which she had set on the table in front of her. "Hands on cheeks. Let's make the brrr sound just like Belle."

"Brrrrr..." Grace's voice joined hers, a bit stronger than the earlier hummmm.

Gabe forgot about the cookies and leaned forward, eyes glued on his daughter.

"And the letter M followed by all the vowel sounds. Ready?"

"Ma, me, mo, mu, may..." Each one they managed to drag out a bit longer than the last, until "may" lasted a full five seconds, like the ending note of a song.

And indeed it did sound like a song to Miriam. She had dropped out with *mu*, so Grace's voice rang through the kitchen—solitary and beautiful.

Beautiful. Suddenly Miriam remembered her mother's words. *"She is a beautiful child."*

Had she and Gabe been so focused on what was wrong with Grace that they had failed to appreciate her for what she was? Another of *Gotte's* miracles.

The little girl stood there, in her kitchen, arms spread wide, eyes closed, and *may* falling from her lips.

Miriam glanced at Gabe, and then she had to look away at the tears in his eyes and the mix of raw emotions on his face—pain, confusion, and pride.

Pride won.

He hopped out of his chair and scooped up Grace in his arms. "You did it! You spoke!"

Grace's eyes had popped open. She peeked over her dad's shoulder at Miriam, surprise and embarrassment reddening her cheeks.

When Gave set her down the pushed the cookies toward her, they were all giggling.

"Perhaps he thinks you worked up an appetite, Grace."

"Those exercises would work up an appetite in a grown man." Gabe sat back in his chair, fingering his *kaffi* mug and thumping the table with his big hand.

"She did it. Did you hear her? She was singing like a little bird."

"I heard."

They sat at the table, grinning at one another.

Finally Miriam asked, "So you'll do the exercises?"

"*Ya*, of course we will. Won't we, Grace?"

She nodded as she chewed a mouthful of ginger cookie, no longer nibbling around the edge. Was it relief Miriam saw in her eyes? Hard to tell. There were so many emotions, so many different dynamics at play, and it wasn't her place to know the hidden stories between the lines. It was only her place to help where she could.

"I should go. It'll be deep dark soon."

"Let me help you with your coat."

"I'll see you at church, Grace. Remember, try and describe your pictures while you're drawing."

Grace nodded, but it wasn't until Miriam and Gabe were nearly at the front door that she jumped up, ran to where they stood, and threw her arms around Miriam's waist. One tight hug, sending a river of warmth rushing over her, and then the child was gone, back to the kitchen, back to cookies and drawing, and—if she wasn't mistaken—a bit of humming.

They stepped out on to the porch.

Gabe stood with his hand on the railing.

"Is it that simple? Would it have been that easy all along? A few exercises and she would have been talking?"

"It's *gut* that she's making progress, but I suspect it's a combination of factors. No doubt last Friday's incident affected Grace as much as it did you."

"Also, she wants to please her teacher. That's a strong incentive."

Miriam smiled but didn't respond. The hug had unnerved her. The entire visit had. She was becoming much too close to the Miller family.

"I don't say that lightly, Miriam. *Danki*, for everything."

"*Gem gschehne*." The words were a whisper, but she knew from the intensity of Gabe's look that he heard her.

Accepting his help, she climbed into her buggy and turned Belle toward home. This evening was so different from that night two weeks ago, but her emotions were no more settled.

Why did Gabe Miller have such a strong effect on her? Why did he cause her to question so many decisions in her life? Why couldn't she be satisfied with what she had?

As Belle trotted into the evening toward her nice warm stall, Miriam tried to focus on the good things in her life, on the breakthrough they had just experienced with Grace, and on all the blessings she'd received from God.

She tried to ignore the aching place in her heart.

Chapter 23

Miriam trudged into the barn wearing her brother's mud boots, the oldest work dress she could find, and her father's discarded winter coat. It had been placed in the charity box, but she'd pulled it out, dusted it off, and rolled up the sleeves.

So what if she looked ridiculous? It wasn't as if anyone would see her.

And one more minute in the house cleaning floors would drive her completely *narrisch*. She needed time in the barn.

She'd barely begun mucking out Belle's stall when her dad leaned against the half-opened door. "What are you doing out here, Miriam girl?"

"If you can't tell, I must not be doing it very well." She plunged the apple picker into the soiled wood shavings.

Joshua wasn't put off by her foul mood. "I suppose you're doing a fair enough job. I'm just wondering why you're even bothering, is all. Your *bruder* is home this weekend, and he will take care of the stalls."

"One less for him to do." Miriam picked up another pile of shavings, shook it so the clean pieces fell to the floor, and dumped what was soiled into the wheelbarrow. Something about the burn in her muscles and the pungent smell eased the restlessness she'd been suffering from all day.

"There are three more when you're done with that one, if you're so inclined."

Miriam paused and gave her dad her teacher's look. Unfortunately, he didn't even blink. "You're teasing me, but maybe I will clean the other stalls. I can do men's work. Doesn't take a Y chromosome to shovel horse manure."

Joshua reached up and ran his fingers through his beard, slowly and deliberately. Finally, he walked into the stall, turned over a crate, and sat on it. "I wouldn't know about chromosomes, but I do know that when someone mucks out a stall by choice, probably something is bothering that person. Care to talk about it?"

"Nothing to talk about."

She stopped and wiped away the sweat that was pooling on her forehead, and then she unbuttoned the oversized coat and laid it across the door.

"Usually you would be inside grading papers on a Saturday afternoon."

"Done."

"Or helping your *mamm*."

"She shooed me out."

"Huh. I thought I was the only one she sent to the barn."

Miriam dropped more manure into the barrel and then stopped and leaned against the stall wall. "I've never heard her send you to the barn."

"She can do it with a look."

Staring down at her brother's boots, Miriam thought about all the things knotted up inside her. She didn't know how to begin to explain them to anyone, let alone her father.

"I think you're happy about the progress with the Miller girl."

"*Ya.*"

"Christmas is next week."

Miriam glanced up at him and tried to smile. "Now you're just poking around, trying to hit on what's bothering me."

Joshua didn't deny it. "Ever have a sore place along your jaw but can't quite figure out which tooth it is? Your tongue insists on darting around, testing every one, probing and checking, trying to figure it out. It isn't as though your tongue can fix it or set it right, but it is as if you have a need to know."

"Parents are like tongues?"

"In some ways. We're always wagging about one thing or another."

Miriam rolled her eyes and returned her attentions to cleaning the stall. Then her dad began to speak again, slowly, and quietly as if he were talking to himself. His next words surprised her more than if she'd stepped outside and found a field of spring flowers instead of the light dusting of snow she'd tramped through on her way into the barn.

"There was a time when I wasn't sure what to do with my life. We weren't living in this area then. When your *grossdaddi* first moved to Wisconsin, he settled in the Medford area. There weren't many Amish in Wisconsin in the nineteen twenties. Your *grossdaddi*, he married your *grossmammi* in Pennsylvania, heard the land was cheap here, and that it was *gut*. Within a year they had packed up and moved."

Miriam stopped shoveling and sat down on top of the pile of clean wood shavings. She'd heard this story many times before, but she never tired of it. She'd read much about the Great Depression, and Esther taught the historical period to the students at school. It was hard to imagine her grandparents making a move during that time.

"Your *pappi* Abel started with a small place, worked hard, and added on as *Gotte* provided. Because I was the oldest, I knew it would come to me. Maybe that was why I wasn't sure I wanted it."

Miriam looked at him in surprise.

"One indecision led to another." Joshua removed his hat and dusted some dirt from the top. "I couldn't decide if I wanted the

farm, so when I met your *mamm*, even when I knew I had feelings
for her, I couldn't decide if I wanted her and the responsibilities of
kinner. I didn't know what to do about any of it."

"You had doubts about *mamm?*"

"Not so much. Not about her. My doubts were more about myself."

"I've never heard any of this before."

Joshua's look was tender. It reminded her of the way she knew
she looked at a student who still had much to learn. "Maybe you
never needed to."

Miriam sank her hand deep into the clean shavings. "What
changed?"

"Nothing, right away. One of the ministers in our district was
putting a group together to move to Cashton, and suddenly I had
a way out."

"Not exactly a *rumspringa*."

"No. I wouldn't say I was rebelling as much as I was looking for
something I couldn't put my finger on, something I wouldn't have
recognized if I'd bumped into it. I fell in love with the land here as
soon as I saw it. Work was hard, winters hard, a smaller community...
we struggled at first." Joshua stared down at his hat. As he turned the
brim round and round in his fingers, Miriam noticed the wrinkles
and sun spots on his skin. It seemed to her he was aging before her
eyes, but only last year he'd been such a young man. Why couldn't
everything stay the same? She wasn't ready for what came next.

"Everything here was as I could have hoped for, and more. Still,
the restlessness hadn't gone away. I don't suppose it ever would have.
I heard another group was forming, ready to push on north and west.
I considered joining them and selling this place."

"Selling it?"

"*Ya*. Then your *grossdaddi* died and I was called home for the
funeral."

"That must have been a shock."

"It was. He wasn't an old man, and I'd always pictured him living
well into his nineties. He'd been bringing in the crops and had an

accident in the silo. I'd always looked at my parents as parents, never as a man and a woman. That week I was back, I saw my *mamm* as a woman who had lost her other half. I knew she would be fine. *Gotte* would provide, and I had nine *bruders* and *schweschders* still there to care for her." He replaced the hat on his head. "I guess having been away, I saw what I'd always taken for granted—their love for one another, the tenderness with which she touched his clothes as she folded them for giving away, the love in her voice as she explained to the *grandkinner*, the way she held me when I first walked into the house."

Miriam didn't speak. She didn't dare break the spell of his memories.

"When I saw your *mamm* at the funeral, I knew."

His grin brought her back to Saturday in the barn, to the smell of wood shavings and manure. "I knew what I'd been running from was being *in lieb* and commitment and maybe one day knowing heartache such as my *mamm* was experiencing when my *dat* passed— all the things *Gotte* gives us to make life wondrous. I was running, but *Gotte* didn't allow me to run far."

He stood and returned the crate to its upright position.

Miriam refocused on her work. Joshua was nearly out of the stall when she voiced one of the questions that had been plaguing her all morning. "If I ask you something, do you promise to be honest with me?"

Nodding, her father met her gaze directly.

Tears stung Miriam's eyes, but she blinked them away. "Are you ever disappointed...in the choices I've made?"

"Not even a little."

She knew it was the truth, that he wouldn't lie, and though it didn't answer the other questions, it provided a measure of comfort in the same way that working in the barn used up some of the energy she needed to be rid of.

Now, if she could figure out who or what she was running from.

She walked out into the sunshine, fetched Belle from the pasture, and led the mare back into the stall. Running her hand down the length of her mane, Miriam felt a portion of her own tension fade away. Belle nudged her pocket, looking for a treat, and Miriam pulled out some dried apple slices that the mare greedily devoured.

A clean stall and a little bit of fruit. Horses were easy to please. Hearts not so much.

⌒

"Owww."

"I'm sorry, honey. I don't know how your hair becomes so tangled. It's as if knots grow in there while you're sleeping."

Grace began to giggle, which was at least better than the near tears of five seconds ago. Girls' emotions changed so quickly, and often Gabe had no idea what caused the change for better or worse. He thought he'd be used to it by now, but he wasn't.

"Owww!"

Grace's speech was like a stream uncovered in the desert. She'd only been speaking for three days, and her responses were short and gravelly, but there was no stopping the flow of words.

"Maybe we should cut your hair off." Grace stopped wiggling, suddenly as still as a fawn caught in an *Englischer*'s headlights.

"Uh-uh."

"*Ya.* Your *mammi* Sarah used to say short hair is quickly brushed."

Grace's hand reached back behind her waist until her fingers located and touched her long brown hair. Gabe continued to comb through the tangles, which was easier to do now that she was holding still. "All done. Time to braid you up."

When they had lived in Indiana, Hope's mother had done the braiding. As soon as he'd begun to look in the *Budget* at the land deals in Wisconsin, she'd made him take over the chore. "My *gross dochdern* all go out of their homes in a presentable manner. You won't be sending Grace to school or church with anything less than perfectly braided hair and a well-kept *kapp*."

He'd learned quickly. Braiding Grace's hair was no different than braiding a rope for the pony—other than the rope held still and didn't whine.

Surveying his work, he realized Hope would be proud of him.

The thought pierced him as acutely as if a knife had been thrust into his side.

It was the way of things, since he'd lost her.

He could go hours, sometimes days, without feeling the burn of the loss. Then something as simple as preparing Grace for church would drive his loneliness abruptly home.

"You're ready to go. Want to check how I've done in the mirror?"

"*Ya.*" She hurried off to her room—half skipping, half walking.

Like the rest of the house, her room was simply furnished, but he had placed a small mirror on the wall near the door so she could be sure she'd dressed properly. Humility was important, but so was correct attire. There were many things a small girl couldn't check for herself, and though he didn't want her to grow up and be preoccupied with her reflection, neither did he want her unaware if she was walking around with shoofly pie on her face.

She walked back into the room, a smile on her lovely face and her Bible tucked under her arm.

"Ready?" he asked, grabbing his black Sunday hat off the peg by the door.

"*Ya.*" Her answers were brief, but each one brought true delight to his heart, mixed though it was with the bitterness of missing his wife. He recognized that this was a day he had much to thank the Lord for. Grace had made great strides since seeing the doctor. Though her throat was still hoarse from lack of use, and though she still tended to choose silence over words, the exercises were going well.

He could hardly wait to talk to Miriam about it.

Chapter 24

C hurch was held at the Schmuckers' farm, the elder Schmuckers'—Aden's parents. Gabe had wanted to ask Eli if something romantic was going on between Miriam and Aden, but he didn't think it was his place to pry. He had only noticed that one glance between them the night everyone was searching for Grace. He could have imagined the look and unspoken words.

Gabe hadn't been to the Schmuckers' farm before, but he knew where it was. Eli had described the place to him, and he'd driven by their lane several times.

Pulling up to the barn, he tamped down the feelings of envy that naturally rose. Aden's parents had a large spread, and it looked as if every acre of it was in tip-top shape.

Joseph Bontreger, another young fellow who had shown up to help look for Grace, was on hand to take Chance and lead him into the barn.

"Large place," Gabe said as he helped Grace out of the buggy.

"*Ya*. You've not been here before?"

"No. This is our first time."

"But you have met Clemens Schmucker." Joseph patted Chance as he nodded toward a group of older men standing outside the main house.

"I suppose I have. Is that him? Standing with the bishop?"

"Ya. He would never miss a church meeting, so I'm sure you have met him. Probably you just haven't put all the names to faces yet."

"I expect it will take me a while." Gabe had started toward the house with Grace when Joseph called him back.

He was a pleasant enough kid. Gabe suddenly recalled that Miriam had mentioned he was to be married to the other teacher, the younger one, in the spring, though they hadn't published their intentions yet.

Probably his youth was why he said what he said next. Young ones, they didn't always buy into the Amish ways of silence. Or maybe there was more to it. Maybe he was trying to warn Gabe. Later, riding home, Gabe would remember the conversation and wonder.

"Clemens can be a bit overbearing at times. Don't set too much store by anything he says. I don't believe he means any harm, but sometimes...well, sometimes he doesn't understand words can be as blunt as a tool."

"Humph." Gabe glanced over toward the front of the house and then back at Joseph. "See you inside then."

"Sure. See you inside."

As he walked toward the front steps, Grace tucked her hand in his. He noticed she did that whenever they were in a new place or if a situation unsettled her—like with the doctor. It didn't bother him. She was growing up quickly, and he might not ever have another *boppli*.

Both men were shorter than Gabe. The bishop was on the thin side, whereas Clemens had a few extra pounds on him. Not soft exactly, but not lean. Both men were graying in their beards and possibly old enough to be Gabe's father. It was hard to tell, and he wasn't going to ask.

"Morning, Gabe." The bishop offered him a handshake, which Gabe returned.

"Morning."

The bishop didn't smile, but then Gabe was learning he rarely did. He didn't set any store by it. Jacob was a somber man, was all. He'd treated him fairly since he had arrived in Pebble Creek. The world would look strange if everyone went around grinning like a fool.

"You remember Clemens."

"Yes, of course." They shook hands as well.

"I need to go and speak with the deacons. I'll see you both inside."

"Beautiful place you have." It was proper for Gabe to compliment Clemens' spread, though in their focus on humility it would have been awkward for them to dwell on it. It would have been hard not to mention it, standing at the steps of his rather large house and looking over the perfectly tended buildings. Gabe counted eight of them from where he stood. There were two barns—the larger one would have easily housed three of his.

And the double silos looked to be in excellent condition.

Clemens stared at him a moment and then said, "Didn't you purchase Kline's homestead?"

"I did. Yes."

"Falling to pieces, isn't it?"

Gabe looked Clemens directly in the eye. He didn't detect any malice in the man's words—merely a statement of fact, which it was.

"The place needs work," he admitted.

"Be better off to level it and start over, though I doubt you can afford to do so or you wouldn't have purchased it in the first place."

Without waiting for a response, Clemens turned and studied Miriam, who had walked onto the porch to say something to her father. "I never have understood why that woman hasn't married. Must be hard to find someone now, because for years she has refused to consider any man related to *kinner* in her classroom. I believe the board should consider hiring another teacher. Then perhaps she can find her proper place in the home."

Despite Joseph's warning, Gabe's mind was reeling from Clemens' manner and his words. The man's criticism of his place was spot-on but harsh. Had he actually suggested leveling the entire thing? Gabe shook his head, trying to clear the confusion away. And what about Miriam? She wouldn't consider courting anyone whose children or relations she taught. Was that true? Then like a third wave, Clemens' last statement washed over him.

"But she's a *wunderbaar* teacher," Gabe protested. "You can't just up and fire her."

Clemens shrugged. "Teachers are easily replaced. A woman's place is in the home. Scripture says as much. Generally we hire an older girl for a year or two until she weds. Miriam King should be married and raising *bopplin* like the rest of the women in our community."

Putting his hands into his pockets and gazing out over his acreage, Clemens continued. "I'll be frank. I've seen the glances you send her way."

"I don't know what you're—"

"It's best to put such thoughts behind you. My own son moved to a different district, hoping he might have a chance with her if he did. Aden thought she might consider him in another light when he came back."

Gabe was dumbstruck. He could not believe that this man he barely knew would be having this conversation with him, and he was stupefied at the things he was saying.

Clemens shook his head. "Makes no difference to me who Aden marries, only that he does and soon. But if he can't win her, with all this—" The man's hand came out to encompass his fields, barns, and house. "Then I would think you'd be wasting your time as you try to resurrect Kline's place."

Scowling, he turned and walked across the front of the house, stopping to greet another family who had driven up.

Grace tugged on his arm. He'd forgotten about her as he watched Clemens strut away. Strut was the only word for it, rather like a peacock. He'd seen some of the birds once, and the man acted in exactly the same way—feathers plumed out and hoping all would see. There was an *Englischer* back in Indiana who kept several of the birds on his farm. He was a city guy, and his wife insisted on purchasing them because they ate snakes. Gabe had told the couple that snakes weren't a big problem in their area, but the wife had wanted them anyway. She said she felt better tending her garden when she looked up and saw those peacocks strutting around.

The memory made him smile and eased the tension and anger that had begun building since Clemens first started talking.

When Gabe leaned down to see what Grace wanted, she whispered, "He's grumpy."

"Think so?"

Grace nodded, her *kapp* strings bouncing.

"Then let's head inside and find some happy people. I know a certain schoolteacher who is going to want to see you." When they walked through the door, though, it was Hannah who snagged Grace away and led her to the women's and children's chairs.

Gabe walked to the men's side, making small talk about the weather and the projected cost of seed on his way. But he had trouble focusing on the conversations swirling around him, and twice he had to ask people to repeat what they had just said. He kept glancing over to the other side of the room, trying to catch a glimpse of Miriam. When he finally did, she was standing beside Aden and laughing.

Aden Schmucker, whose father owned this prosperous spread—yet Aden had moved to a different district, a more liberal district from what Gabe had heard.

She was smiling and talking with Aden, whose father had correctly pointed out that Gabe's own place was tumbling down around his ears. Who had told him Miriam would never consider a relative of a student. Who had said they should find another teacher because she belonged in the home.

Those thoughts collided in his mind and bumped against the feelings that had been growing in his heart. It would crush Miriam to lose her job. It wasn't fair for Clemens to decide such a thing. She should be able to teach as long as she felt called to do so.

He focused again on Aden.

A young man, he was pleasant and kind. He'd shown up to help look for Grace when he didn't even know Gabe or his daughter. And now he was home for the holidays. If Gabe wasn't mistaken, it seemed he was home with a specific purpose in mind, an agenda, almost—a very pretty agenda who was wearing a forest green dress, a white apron, and a white *kapp* that covered beautiful hair the color of a moonless sky.

Miriam excused herself from Aden just before the service was about to begin. She hadn't wanted to be rude, but she wished to sit next to her family. She had hoped to be able to speak with Gabe and Grace. She smiled at the little girl, who she saw was tucked in under her *mamm*'s wing.

No time for talking, though, as everyone stood and began singing from the *Ausbund*. They had sung through the first hymn and were well into the *Loblied*, the German words rising around her and erasing the aggravation she'd felt at not being able to speak with Gabe, at not knowing how to answer Aden, at so many questions. The voices rising in unison had a calming effect on her. They always had, and she supposed they always would.

Such simple beauty.

Their voices joined together until she couldn't distinguish any single one, only the blended sound, reminding her of something natural, like the wind in the trees. The second hymn ended, and Grace held the final note a second longer than everyone else. Though she was only humming, and surely Miriam was the only one who heard it, the sound was charming and added an extra measure of peace to her heart.

She reached down and ran a hand over the back of the young girl's *kapp*, momentarily forgetting her promise to keep a professional distance. Detachment was difficult in this setting. Though the Schmuckers' house was quite large compared to her parents', it was still Plain and known to her in the way that stepping into any Amish house was familiar.

The custom of their community was to rotate the location of the church meeting place. It fell to each family to host church approximately once a year. It mattered not if your home was small or large, if you were poor or if *Gotte* had provided abundantly. Miriam had never given such matters much thought. Amish life strove to emphasize humility. Her students dressed the same. Each walked to school or came in a buggy of the same style or rode in Eli's buggy because their parents lived at the furthermost edge of the school's reach.

As the first sermon began, Miriam found her mind wandering. Generally their houses and farms were similar. Some spreads were smaller and some acreage had a harder time producing good crops, but if anyone fell on difficult times, others pitched in to help. In the last few years the majority of families supplemented their farming income with cottage industries—things such as carpentry, crafts, and services.

It was rare for a family to be in serious want. She'd had occasion to deal with only a few. Times of sickness or injury, in which case the deacons held auctions to help. There had been a case of need involving a moral issue with the father of the family. She'd never learned the exact details in that situation—and she didn't want to know.

The husband had eventually left the church and filed for divorce. Under their rules, the woman was unable to remarry, but they had all provided for her. Eventually she had sold their farm and moved back to Ohio with her parents.

Miriam glanced up when the first sermon ended. Had thirty minutes already passed since the singing? Scriptures were read and they knelt for silent prayer before the main sermon. Miriam knew she needed to pray for guidance. The realization that she had heard none of the previous sermon was proof that her heart was troubled.

Why did Aden's *dat* have so much? And why did Gabe have to struggle so? Was this the way of things everywhere? Was this *Gotte's wille*?

Questions whirled in her mind as she considered her place in the group of people assembled in the room, her place in the community.

Was she running, as her *dat* had suggested? And if she was, running from what? Tears pricked her eyes as confusion clouded her thoughts. Each time she prayed, she only had more questions.

As the pastor stepped forward and began to preach on the birth of the Christ Child, her heart began to settle. Grace scooted closer to her on the bench. Her *mamm* looked over the top of the girl's head and smiled.

"You will conceive and give birth to a son, and you are to call him Jesus. He will be great and will be called the Son of the Most High." The pastor continued to talk about the Scripture and how Mary was the perfect example of *gelassenheit*.

Miriam didn't think calmness and composure came easily to Jesus' mother. She supposed Mary was as confused as she would have been on hearing those words. Some things didn't change with the times.

Grace began to fidget, and Abigail pulled a small picture book from her bag and handed it to her. It was amazing to Miriam the things her mother thought to bring to church, but then, with her number of grandchildren, no doubt the years had taught her to come to the service prepared.

Glancing up, she caught Gabe watching them. Then she saw him nod his thanks. How hard it must be for him to sit across the room with his daughter among strangers. Only they weren't strangers—not anymore. She smiled in return, pleased they could ease his worries. Tuning in again to the sermon, she managed to focus easily on Christmas and Mary, the Christ Child and *gelassenheit*.

She was surprised, a short time later, to find that the service had ended, her *mamm* was waking Grace, and it was time to help with the lunch preparations.

Chapter 25

G race decided there were some things about talking she liked, and there were some things she didn't.

Going through the food line, it was easy enough to shake her head at the dishes offered that were terrible—and several were. Broccoli casserole? Uh-uh. Turnip greens? No way. But sweet potatoes weren't so bad, and she knew her dad was keeping an eye on her plate, so she had to add some things he would be happy about.

Talking came in handy when she hit the dessert table.

"Shoofly pie?" Esther asked.

"Yes, please."

Esther smiled, but she didn't say a word to show she was surprised. Grace wanted to run around the table and hug her for that, but she didn't.

"There you go. Come back if you're still hungry."

Her voice was soft, soft, soft—like Stormy, the kitten she hoped was waiting for her at Miriam's.

She hoped she hadn't forgotten. She hoped her dad would still allow it. She hoped maybe Stormy could be her Christmas present.

"Will you be okay by yourself?" Her dad stood there with a big plate of food heaped high. How could he eat so much? It would take her a week or more to fit all of that inside, and then her stomach would burst open like a water balloon the boys sometimes played with in the summer.

"*Ya.*"

"We're going to the barn, Grace. Want to go?" Sadie shifted from foot to foot. "The Schmuckers have a special barn with baby animals you can pet, and we can go there after we eat. Aden said we could."

Something crossed over her dad's face, like when he was mad at the bull, but it disappeared quick as lightning across the sky.

"If you want to, you can go with Sadie. I'll come find you later."

Grace did want to see baby animals. Why would they even have babies in the winter? She thought that only happened in the spring. Maybe she could ask Miriam or Esther about it. And she could ask now instead of having to write it.

That was another good thing about talking. You didn't have to search around for a piece of paper and a pencil every time you had a question or wanted to say something.

She walked down the front porch steps with Sadie, careful not to spill her plate or her drink. The girls crossed over to the barn and picked out a quiet place in the corner. They were just sitting down on one of the overturned crates when the Lapp boys came up.

"Uh-oh," Sadie said. She stuffed a piece of baked turkey in her mouth as she poked Grace in the ribs with her elbow. "Look. Here they come."

The boys had left their plates on the other side of the open room. This was the biggest barn Grace had ever been in. She looked up and saw skylights in the roof at the top. They were way up there.

"Look at Grace and Sadie. Always sitting together."

"Someone *has* to sit with Grace since she won't talk!"

Both boys started giggling.

Sadie and Grace glanced at each other, rolled their eyes at the same exact moment, and then scooted closer together. Maybe they could form a barrier that would keep the boys out.

"One's tiny," Adam said, poking a finger at Sadie. He was the taller one and a year older than Grace. She sure didn't think he was any smarter.

"Yeah, and one's stupid." Luke was shorter, probably Grace's height, and he was very skinny. She was thinking she could push him over without too much trouble.

"Hey, Sadie. I kind of wanted some of that pie, but I forgot to get any." Adam reached for Sadie's plate, but she held it out of his reach.

"Yeah. Apple's his favorite." Luke walked around to the other side, intent on helping his brother grab it.

Why had they decided to sit off all alone? Anyone watching might think they were playing, but they weren't. These boys were big bullies, and someone needed to teach them a lesson.

"Stop!" Grace shouted. She stood up and pushed Luke at the exact moment he grabbed Sadie's plate out of her hand.

He went tumbling into a pile of hay, scattering food all over his clothes.

Grace's shout had attracted everyone's attention.

Luke jumped up and began brushing the hay and apple pie off his Sunday clothes.

Adam pointed his finger at Grace and said, "Look what you did! You knocked my *bruder* over. Pushing is wrong. It's a sin. He was only trying to say hi to Sadie and you pushed him over into the hay."

Grace's throat started to close up. She knew, just knew, that she wasn't going to be able to say a word to defend herself. Sadie was crying. Grace didn't know what to do. She glanced up and saw Lily making her way around the edge of the crowd along with Sadie's older sisters and her brother.

"That's not how it happened, Adam Lapp." Lily put her arm around Grace. "I heard you and Luke teasing them. You're always teasing and you should be ashamed."

"Was not."

"Were to."

"Was not—"

"Stop it. Both of you." Sadie's brother John stepped into the middle. "We're not even an hour out of the service and look how you're acting. Did you not hear a word that was said?"

Both boys stared at the ground. Luke even kicked at the hay, which Grace thought was stupid, but she didn't say anything.

"Adam Lapp, tell me the truth or we'll take you over to your *dat*. Before you speak, remember lying is a sin too. Did Grace Miller push you over for no reason at all?"

"No." Adam's voice was small, as small as Grace's voice.

"What happened?"

"She was trying to save Sadie's pie."

"We were only teasing," Luke explained. "Only having a little fun. Girls cry about everything."

"We do not!" Sadie scrunched her face up and looked madder than Grace had ever seen her, madder even than the week before when she'd lost her paper with a gold star on it.

"The way I see it, we can handle this ourselves or we can take it to our parents." John waited for the boys to choose.

"Ourselves," they mumbled.

"Luke, because you're covered in hay and pie, you need to go and get cleaned up. That means instead of eating or playing, you'll have to go around to where the water trough is and let one of the older girls try to get those stains out of your clothes. And while they're drying, you'll have to sit there and wait."

"But, John—"

"You agreed."

"I'll take him," Sadie's older sister Katie said. "And I'll be reminding him of his manners while I'm seeing to his clothes."

Luke looked miserable as she led him off, and Grace almost felt sorry for him, but then she remembered how many times he'd teased her and Sadie. Why were boys like that? And when did they change and become nice like Sadie's brother John?

"Adam, it seems to me you were as guilty as Luke. You just didn't get caught in the way of the pie."

Adam stared at his shoes. He was all bluster around girls, but most of it went out of him when he was around the older boys. Grace had noticed that before.

"Agreed?"

"I suppose you're right."

"I want you to walk back into the house and get another plate of food for Sadie."

"Her food is fine. We only messed with her pie."

"Because you started this mess, her food is now cold. You're lucky I'm not having you bring all of us new lunches." A murmur went through the group at that idea, and Adam stopped mumbling.

"All right. I'll do it."

"You be sure and get everything she needs, and be polite about it. If Grace needs anything, you fetch that as well."

"All right, John."

"Both of you boys will bring the girls written apologies on Monday, and there'll be no more of this meanness. We don't have that kind of school at Pebble Creek."

"All right." Adam's misery deepened with each *all right* he murmured. He turned and started out of the barn.

"One more thing, Adam."

The boy turned back, maybe hoping there was something good in store, but John wasn't finished. After all, he would graduate in the spring. He was nearly a man, and he had learned, it seemed to Grace, how to scold and punish exactly like an adult. "No joining the afternoon games until your *bruder* is able to join. That's only fair."

Adam didn't even protest. He pushed down his black hat more firmly on his head and walked out the barn door.

"Come sit by us, Grace," Lily said.

"Before you go, I'd like to talk to the both of you." John stepped forward and sat down across from the girls.

Grace and Sadie moved closer together.

"You're not in trouble, so don't act as if you need to protect one another, but I want to talk to you about pushing."

Grace reached out and clasped Sadie's hand.

"You've heard the pastor speak on our lifestyle of peace, *ya?*"

Both girls nodded their heads.

"What the boys did was wrong, but, Grace, you shouldn't have pushed Luke. The Bible tells us to live at peace with everyone and to not take revenge. Are you old enough to know what that means?"

Grace shook her head no. She didn't look at Sadie, but she thought Sadie was shaking her head no too.

"It means that we don't strike back if someone hits us, and if someone tries to take your pie, Sadie, you let them."

"But, John, it was my pie—"

"I know it was, and it was wrong of him." John sighed. "I'm not saying that I have it all figured out either, and you'll want to talk about this to *mamm* and *dat,* Sadie, and your *dat,* Grace. They can explain it better. And, Grace, I'm glad you called out so we could come help, but it isn't our way to push. Our way is peace—always peace."

Grace nodded. Some little part of her had known it was wrong to push Luke, even though it had felt good. It was only that he made her so mad, and pushing him had made him stop. But what if John hadn't stepped in when he did? Her pushing Luke might have made him even angrier.

The entire thing confused her.

She probably should talk to her dad about it.

"It's *gut* the boys are sorry for what they did. When Adam brings your food over, you might want to tell him you're sorry too."

"Sure, John. We can do that." Sadie let go of Grace's hand and slipped her arm around her waist. "We'll tell both boys together."

"Great idea," John said. "Until then, you and Grace come sit with us. We didn't see you walk in, but we sure heard Grace shout." John smiled at them both as he began moving the group back to the middle of the room.

It was at that moment that Hannah came in—Hannah, who had always looked out for Grace, who had been something of a big sister to her since the first day when Miriam had asked the older girl to sit with her and help her. Grace could barely see her now, surrounded as she was by all the other schoolchildren, but she could hear her, and there was no mistaking the note of worry in her voice when she said, "Is everything okay in here? I just passed Adam, and he looked as though he had a stomachache."

"No stomachache," John said. "But you missed the excitement."

"I was stuck at the vegetable table. It's the slowest because some of those casseroles people do not want to eat."

Grace started giggling, and then Sadie started giggling, though she couldn't have known what was so funny. She couldn't have been picturing the broccoli casserole and turnip greens, and Hannah pushing them forward to each person who passed by.

It felt good to laugh.

Even after the tussle, and even though Luke was sitting behind the partition without his clothes on, probably shivering like crazy. She was old enough to know that boys did stupid things and then regretted them later. Maybe she even regretted pushing him. She knew she regretted getting lost in the storm last week.

Another thing that felt good was being part of the group.

And if it took being bullied and then pushing down Luke Lapp and then being corrected by John for that to happen, maybe she was glad all of it had happened.

～ Chapter 26 ～

M iriam hurried to catch up with Gabe as he made his way across to the barn. She'd been trying to have a word with him all day. If she didn't know better, she'd suspect he was avoiding her.

"Beautiful afternoon," she called out to him.

He turned and studied her for a moment—as if he was deciding whether he should wait or push on. Waiting won, and she arrived at his side a little out of breath.

"It is," he agreed. "Hard to believe the blizzard was just last weekend."

"And Christmas in one week."

They looked out at the bright sunshine melting the snow on Clemens Schmucker's pastures, fences, and barns. As it did, it revealed a splendid scene. It had always been that way here at Clemens' place—everything in pristine condition for as long as Miriam could remember. He had enough sons and hired help, and plenty of money to keep it that way.

"Yes, Christmas in one week." Gabe continued on toward the barn.

"I suppose you'll be missing your family."

"Both my *mamm* and Hope's *mamm* sent a care package that

arrived last week." His eyes twinkled as he held open the barn door for her. It might have been the first time he'd mentioned Grace's mother. She couldn't remember. "They're both excellent cooks, so it was nice to receive the goodies, but it won't be the same."

"Spend Christmas with us." The words were out of Miriam's mouth before she could think to ask her parents. "It's always a big, noisy affair with all my nieces and nephews."

Gabe pretended to consider the matter carefully, and then he laughed. "Your *dat* already asked, and I said I would—*danki*. Only the afternoon though. We'll spend the morning time at home."

Miriam nodded as if she understood, but she couldn't help picturing that as a lonely affair. Would it be? Or did they have their own private traditions that they kept?

"Huh. I thought they were in here eating." Gabe stood in the middle of the large room, turning in a circle as if that would help him find the children.

"They went to the other barn to see the newborn animals."

"I heard someone mention that Clemens artificially inseminated some of his stock in order to have young goats and sheep to market all year. As conservative as your—" he stopped and corrected himself. "As conservative as *our* district is, I'm surprised the bishop allows him to do so."

"I don't know all the details, but I've heard it's only allowed on a selective basis."

"Ah."

Miriam wondered what was included in Gabe's *ah*.

"We can walk through this barn and out the back door."

"Oh. How do you always seem to know where the children are?"

"I suppose I have a sense for it, just as you have a sense for planting. For instance, I heard that earlier Grace got herself into a little skirmish."

Gabe turned suddenly. "What? And you didn't come find me?"

She immediately wished she'd phrased the news differently. "No. It wasn't like that. What I mean to say is, Hannah came and told me afterward that Grace stood up for herself. By the time she walked in on the situation, everything was resolved, and it seemed Grace had made even more new *freinden*."

Gabe stopped for a moment and turned away from her to face a stall. When he turned back, he had a rueful grin on his face. "I'm sorry. I seem to always be jumping down your throat, and always outside of horse stalls."

"It's no problem."

"It is. You've done nothing but help Grace, and I should know better than to doubt your judgment."

Miriam's cheeks warmed. Why did his praise mean so much to her? It did, though, and she was pleased that his opinion of her had changed greatly since their last encounter outside a horse stall. The thought nearly made her laugh.

"I take that smile to mean you accept my apology."

"Of course."

They continued walking. Miriam had forgotten exactly how big Schmucker's barn was. The length seemed to extend a good quarter mile.

"What's it like?" she asked.

He raised an eyebrow.

"Having someone you care about as much as you care for Grace. I know that must sound *narrisch*—"

"You care about people, Miriam."

"Yes, but it's not the same."

"Why do you say that?"

Now she stopped. When she did, a silver-dapple gelding came forward and stuck his head out of his stall, beckoning her. She walked over to him and began stroking him down his long, silky neck. He leaned forward more, as if he had an itch she couldn't quite reach, and they both laughed.

"He likes that," Gabe said.

"Indeed."

"Explain to me what you want to know."

Miriam took her time answering, searching for a way to put her recent aches, her recent restlessness and questions into words. "I've worked with many children, parents, and families. Maybe it's that I have kept myself distant, or maybe I didn't pay attention when I thought I did."

Gabe leaned against the stall and studied her, but he didn't interrupt, so she pushed on.

"I've had...single parents before." She patted the gelding and glanced at Gabe uncertainly. "It's only that I don't understand what it's like..."

Gabe's grin was slow and grew until his eyes nearly shut. "How could you?"

"But—"

"How could you know until you've experienced it?"

"I understand plowing, and I haven't plowed. I understand history, and I haven't lived during those times. I understand—"

Gabe raised his hand to stop the list she was determined to share. "Raising and loving a child—one who is your flesh and blood, or even one who isn't but you've taken under your care nonetheless—isn't something you can understand by reading about or even by watching."

Miriam fiddled with her prayer *kapp*, turned from the horse, and resumed walking.

"Don't be embarrassed," Gabe said. "It's a natural enough thing to ask."

"It's only that...when you're with Grace, or even when you talk of Grace, there's an intensity about you. It's as if you have this special *thing* you need to protect."

"I do."

They pushed out the back door of the barn into the fading December sunlight.

Now they were standing directly across from the nursery barn. Instead of continuing to it, Gabe walked to the fence and studied Schmucker's pastures.

He understood what Miriam wanted to know. Not what she was asking, but what she truly wanted, and it tore at his heart. He'd come to care for her in the last three weeks more than he had realized. As he'd watched Aden stare at her during lunch, he'd become even more convinced of the reason for the young man's trip home.

It synced up with what Clemens had told him in his rough way. There was no doubt that Aden wanted to court Miriam King.

Looking out at the pastures, barns, and buildings of Aden's father, he knew he would be a fool to stand in the way.

What did he have to offer her? A broken-down farm, an orphaned daughter, and a heart that hadn't yet healed.

Moreover, he honestly wasn't sure a whole home was God's plan for him. Perhaps he was to learn to be satisfied with the piece of happiness he had—with his daughter, a roof over his head, and good health. Reaching for more seemed selfish. He'd had more once, and he'd lost it. Did he even want to risk that happening again?

He wasn't sure, and he wouldn't be bringing any of that up in their conversation.

Instead, he turned to her and tried to answer the other part of her question, the surface part, the part that spoke to her desire to have a *boppli* of her own. Maybe a desire she didn't even recognize yet, but he saw it in her face every time she paused to help Grace.

"It seems to me there are many things you can earn...a *gut* farm, respect of people you work with, even the love of a man or woman." She gazed at him as if she were hanging on his every word, and that bothered him. He didn't need anyone looking at him with such adoration. He knew too well how certain it was that he would mess up— not once but many times.

Looking out over the pasture again, he prayed for the words, the right words that would help Miriam see what God wanted her to see. When he turned back, he held his hands together, as if he were cupping water from a stream. "The love of a child, your own child, comes to you all at once—like a package on Christmas afternoon. You want to hold it to you, to treasure it and protect it, but that child is much like water."

He spread his hands apart slightly.

"You can't hold it," she whispered.

"No. Much as you try, you can't. The child grows, faster than you would believe possible—as quickly as water slips through your fingers."

She moved next to him. They both stood there, looking out toward the western fields.

"Perhaps that's what you notice when you see me looking at Grace. You see me trying to pour my love over her as she slips through my fingers."

His eyes met hers for the briefest of moments, and he had a nearly overwhelming desire to reach out and touch her, to soothe the worried look on her face.

But he didn't.

They walked toward the nursery barn then, and when Gabe opened the door, the sounds of laughing children stole away the somberness of the moment.

"*Mamm* never explained it that way," Miriam admitted. "She only said having a *boppli* was a terrible pain for a few hours but worth it in the end."

Gabe grunted. "Your mother is a practical woman."

"Maybe that's whom I take after."

"And your *dat?*"

Miriam smiled as Grace ran up to them, grabbed both of their hands, and whispered, "Come see."

"*Dat* pretends to be practical, but deep inside I believe he's a dreamer."

"Perhaps you are a combination of both." Gabe fought to keep the lightness in his voice, but if the first barn and the grounds hadn't convinced him of what he should and shouldn't do, the nursery barn certainly did.

He saw pens, stalls, feeding and watering troughs, and good ventilation. And, of course, everything was solidly constructed.

Miriam King deserved the best, and there was no doubt in his mind—from all he was seeing and everything he had heard—that Aden Schmucker was the man who could give it to her.

≈ Chapter 27 ≈

I t feels like he's avoiding me." Miriam held up the shawl she was knitting for her mother and studied it in the lamplight. She had chosen to use a triangle pattern that measured fifty-six inches across. A fast knitter, Miriam knew she could finish it before Christmas.

Her mother wouldn't have needed a new shawl, but Pepper had destroyed her favorite one a month ago.

Miriam had slipped out the back door to use the outhouse and neglected to shut the door tightly. Pepper had snuck inside and proceeded to climb into the rocker and make a nest on top of the shawl. If that wasn't bad enough, he'd pawed a big hole into the middle of it. Her mother hadn't made a fuss, but Miriam had seen the fire in her eyes when she'd ordered the dog *out*!

A new shawl for Christmas was the least she could do, and the blue and brown yarns were beautiful.

The trouble wasn't with the pattern or the yarn. The trouble was with her knitting.

"Problem with that shawl?" Esther asked.

"*Ya*. I dropped another stitch. In fact, I dropped several." Miriam sighed and began unraveling the last row.

"Maybe you're distracted."

"I am distracted. I'm telling you, Esther. Gabe Miller is avoiding me."

"Did he pick up Grace after her speech lesson?" Esther moved the light so she could better see her embroidery. With Christmas only six days away, they both had several projects to finish. Needless to say, neither was assigning homework that would require grading.

"He did, but he didn't even get out of the buggy. He waited outside."

"Maybe he was in a hurry."

"That was the first time he waited outside, though. He always comes in to talk about how she's doing."

"How is she doing?"

"Terrific." Miriam dropped the knitting needles in her lap. "It's remarkable how much she's improved in such a short time."

"*Gotte* is *gut*," Esther murmured.

They continued working in silence a few moments before Miriam brought up the subject again. "I think it's because of the conversation we had on Sunday."

"The one about babies?"

"What other conversation would I be talking about?" Miriam threw her friend an exasperated look.

"Oh, I don't know. I thought maybe you talked about crops or weather, or maybe even who the new minister might be since the Kiems family is moving in the spring."

"Esther Schrocks, if I didn't know better I'd think you were teasing me."

"And what's to tease?" Esther pulled the black thread from her needle and changed it for a pretty yellow-gold. "It would be normal for you to take a liking to Gabe Miller. He's a *gut*-looking man and he has a fine *dochder*."

"Is that what you think this is about?" Miriam gave up any pretense of knitting. She dropped the balls of yarn and the needles into her basket and stood. She suddenly needed to move, even if it only meant walking around their small upstairs apartment.

"What do you think it's about? Worry over missing a parent meeting you never even scheduled?"

Miriam stopped in her pacing, walked back to her chair, and perched on the edge of it. "I'm worried he thought I was baiting him, as I've sometimes seen girls do, with my questions about *bopplin* and families and all. I don't even know what came over me. Why would I ask him such a thing? There are plenty of women in my family I could have asked."

"But you didn't want their perspective. You wanted his." Esther glanced up from her needlework and smiled. Miriam found herself envying the young woman—there was such simple contentment in her expression.

"When did you become the wise one?" she asked softly.

"I'd hardly call me wise, but when you're first *in lieb*, it's like walking across the fields on a foggy day."

"I would not say I'm *in lieb*—"

"And when there are two men involved, things are doubly complicated."

"Now you sound *narrisch*." Miriam picked up her knitting and resumed with the speed of the freight trucks that sped down the Cashton highways.

"I do?"

"You do."

"Yet there are two men troubling your heart, and it's best to admit it." Miriam waved her words away, but Esther continued. "You blush when I mention Gabe, yet you rode home from the singing with Aden."

"You know very well I accepted a ride with Aden because my *bruder* abandoned me."

"Mm-hmm."

"Abandoned might be a strong word, but Simon wished to be alone with Emma, and I hated to deny them a private buggy ride."

"Kind of you."

"I didn't even intend to stay for the singing. It seems I was tricked into that. I helped with the dinner cleanup, turned around, and my parents were gone. Gabe and Grace were also gone."

"Would you have ridden with them?"

Miriam ignored the last question. "David and Noah were gone with their families as well, so then I had to stay."

"I'll bet you were heartbroken."

"I wasn't looking forward to it, though in the end it wasn't as bad as I expected."

Esther stood and stretched. "I can't remember the last time you stayed for singing. It was good to have you there. I know for a fact that several men were watching you. Would you care to know who?"

"I would not."

"Oh, Miriam. Are you not the least bit interested?"

"They are boys, Esther. You're forgetting my age."

"Except for Aden."

Miriam slowed in her knitting, tugged fiercely on the ball of blue yarn, and then increased her speed to make up for her slack. "Except for Aden. I hope I didn't lead him on by staying and by accepting the buggy ride."

"A buggy ride isn't a promise." Esther walked to their kitchen and set the kettle on the back of the stove.

The night grew quiet around them. When Esther returned with two mugs of hot tea, she asked softly, "They're both nice men, ya?"

Miriam didn't answer her. She only sipped her tea and then returned to her knitting with a vengeance.

Little learning took place at school the rest of the week. By Thursday preparations for the Christmas program seemed to be consuming their every minute. Miriam was grateful Esther had taken over the planning of this year's program. After eight years of teaching, she needed some fresh ideas, and Esther had plenty.

She handed the younger teacher her collected materials from

previous years and told her to shout if she needed help. This was their third year to teach together. As Miriam watched her direct the students in decorating the schoolroom, she realized anew how much she would miss her the next school year. She was happy for her and excited about her upcoming marriage, and she trusted that God would provide another assistant teacher.

But change was always difficult.

Well...maybe not always.

Change in the Christmas presentation was a good thing. Esther's ideas were fresh and fun but still in line with their commitment to simplicity and maintaining the correct focus on the proper meaning of the holiday.

"Do you like our snowflakes?" Lily held up a light blue sheet of paper. Grace and Sadie popped up next to her, each holding several blue snowflakes. The younger children had been cutting decorations for the last hour. Last year Miriam had them cut snowflakes from white paper and all one size, but Esther had thought to vary the sizes, from small enough to fit in the palm of your hand to a full sheet of paper.

The effect was dazzling.

"It's *wunderbaar*."

"Mine too?" Grace asked, her voice a bit stronger than the day before.

"Yours too. Do you need help putting them in the windows?"

"I'll help them." Adam Lapp stepped up with a roll of tape and a stepstool. When they both turned to look at him in surprise, he added, "It's my assigned task. Plus I wasn't very *gut* at cutting."

"*Danki*, Adam."

The boy had certainly settled down in the last week. Miriam had an idea it had something to do with whatever happened in the barn at the Schmuckers', but she wasn't sure she wanted to know the details. As the three moved off toward the nearest window, Miriam remembered that she needed to speak with Grace.

"Grace, can you come back over here for a moment?"

Handing her snowflakes to Sadie, Grace hurried to Miriam's side.

"Do you remember when I asked you to think of ways you could help with the program?"

"*Ya*." The girl's *kapp* strings bounced as she nodded her head.

"You did a fine job on your drawings."

"*Danki*."

"And I'm very pleased you've decided to sing with the students in your grade."

Grace's smile was all the answer Miriam needed.

"I was wondering, however, if there was one more thing I could ask of you. One of the girls still hasn't regained her voice from being sick on Monday, and I was thinking—"

As she whispered her request, Grace's eyes grew wider and her cheeks pinked, but she didn't even hesitate. She accepted the slip of paper from Miriam's hand, nodded again, and hurried away to Sadie's side. Heads together, she shared with her friend her newest assignment.

Was she pushing her? Perhaps, but Miriam's instincts told her it would be for the best.

Things were coming together as they should. A few of the middle-grade students stood at the front, practicing the lines for a skit.

Esther was helping Hannah draw a welcome greeting on the blackboard.

Four of the older boys trooped in through the front door, and Miriam turned to see Efram Hochstetler standing there, waiting for her.

"I have your extra benches. Set them up in the usual place?"

"Yes, that will be fine. *Danki*."

"It's no problem. The children look as if they are ready for the program. Maybe you can give them tomorrow off," he teased.

"Oh, we're not ready yet," Esther said, passing by holding a beard in one hand and a tail in the other.

"Need help?" Miriam asked.

"No, I think we have this."

"She wants to do it on her own," Hannah explained as two of the students crowded after her. "But Luke's beard won't stay put, and he's supposed to be an old man in the skit."

"What's with the tail?" Efram asked.

"Donkey. Someone stepped on it, and it came off. I should go help."

Miriam turned to find that the boys had already placed the extra benches against the side walls and along the back.

At least there would be a place for everyone to sit, and she knew from past years they would need it. The room would be packed with parents, family, students, and teachers from neighboring schools.

She would see Gabe then. At least she didn't think he'd try to sneak away. She had begun to question if he would still show up at her parents' for the afternoon meal on Christmas Day.

It could be she was overanalyzing what had happened on Tuesday. Grace had climbed into the buggy, and he'd set the horse off at a trot before she'd managed to walk out of the schoolhouse door.

It could be he had work that needed tending back at his farm. Images of his farm brought a smile to her face. Yes, there were plenty of things that needed his attention there, though hurrying wouldn't take care of them all. That would take many months and careful planning.

It could be she'd imagined his brusqueness and the way he'd looked at her before glancing away.

But she didn't think so, and if there was one thing she'd learned over the years, it was to trust her intuition.

The other thing she'd learned was that time would tell.

What she still hadn't learned was to be patient.

∽ Chapter 28 ∽

Gabe put on his Sunday clothes, though it felt odd to do so on a Friday evening. He checked his reflection in the mirror, making sure he'd shaved correctly. He was thirty-two years old, and he'd been shaving since he was seventeen, though he could have easily waited a year or two past that.

He still remembered his father teaching him how to do so properly and explaining to him their traditions. Why he needed to be clean shaven until he married, and why, once he was married, he would no longer shave—except for the mustache area. No Amish man would have a mustache because that facial feature had a long history of being associated with the military. Being Plain meant standing for peace in every way.

Peace was one of the cornerstones of their life, and yet so often it seemed elusive in his heart.

Gabe ran his hand along his jaw, combing down his beard with his fingers and then checking the area over his lip. There was one place he tended to miss, on the left side. He ran his finger lightly over the spot, felt the stubble, and smiled. Hope had always teased him about that spot.

Hope.

Always Hope at every corner.

He shaved the stubble, tossed the towel over the basin, and went in search of Grace.

She was downstairs, tapping her shoe against the hardwood floor, her coat already on and her present for Miriam beneath her arm.

"Ready?"

"*Ya.*"

"Excited about the program?"

"*Ya.*"

"Guess it's turned out to be a pretty *gut* school year."

"Uh-huh." She skipped through the late afternoon as they made their way to the buggy.

"Glad we moved here?" he asked.

She shrugged. "I miss *mammi* Sarah."

"I do too. Up you go." He helped her into the buggy and then climbed in after her.

"I like school." Her voice was still gravelly, still soft, but at least she was sharing her thoughts, and for that he was grateful. That was a huge improvement over their situation back home in Indiana.

Would she have talked again if they were still there? Maybe.

Or maybe it had been Miriam's doing, which wouldn't have happened unless he'd moved here to Pebble Creek.

The last possibility was that it was God's doing, *Gotte's wille*, that he and Grace be here at Pebble Creek, that they be in this community, and that Miriam be a part of their lives.

Guilt gnawed at his stomach.

He'd been wrong to treat her rudely three days before, but she couldn't have known how beautiful she looked standing in the doorway of the little schoolhouse. And Sunday outside Schmucker's barn had nearly been his undoing. Gabe had been surprised when she'd brought up the subject of babies, but once he'd gone home, once he'd lain in the dark and replayed the conversation, it all made sense to him.

Miriam had too much to offer someone not to marry, and he

wasn't talking only about her outer beauty. He was referring to her heart, her way with children, and her attitude toward life. Perhaps she'd been hiding away in the schoolhouse up until now. But something had awakened her.

Maybe Grace had awakened her.

Whatever it was, it had brought a blush to her cheek and questions to her heart.

Questions that he had tried to answer on Sunday, but he dared not answer any more. It created a false intimacy between them that wasn't proper. Best that he keep his distance. Best that he let her find her answers with Aden Schmucker.

He'd attend the Christmas program because it meant so much to his daughter.

And he'd go to Christmas dinner at her parents' house because he'd already told Joshua and Abigail that he would. It would not be neighborly to back out now. And there was the matter of picking up Grace's gift. After the holidays, though, he would distance himself from Miriam King.

It wasn't until his daughter tugged on his coat sleeve that he realized he was driving past the little schoolhouse full of buggies. There were even three *Englisch* cars parked out front. He'd expected a big crowd to be there for the children's presentation, and he was right. Looking at Grace's face, he didn't have to guess how excited she was.

As he called out to Chance and turned the buggy around, worries about Miriam fell away. He resolved to enjoy the evening. Time was fleeting. He knew that all too soon that Grace would be out of school, off courting, and then one day having children of her own.

It was important that he remembered to slow down and enjoy the moment.

Tomorrow would provide enough time to deal with its own trouble.

Ninety minutes later he found himself standing and joining in a Christmas hymn. It had been the best school presentation he'd ever seen, and he'd seen a few. He'd attended the programs that his nieces and nephews participated in every year. He remembered his own as well. Tonight the children had done an excellent job.

He was sure Miriam and Esther had done quite a bit of directing, though they were not part of the actual program. He thought perhaps Esther was behind the curtain hung at the front of the room to separate the children who were preparing to perform next from those who were reciting. One of the smaller children—one younger than Grace—had called out to her at the beginning, ducking her head under the curtain. An older student had pulled her back into line and helped her with her part in the skit.

After that, things had gone smoothly, other than the scene with the donkey. First the donkey's tail fell off. Not to be deterred, the lad playing Joseph had picked it up and thrown it over his shoulder as if it belonged there. The Christmas story continued along its correct path until the girl who was Mary tried to slide off the donkey and tripped, causing both parts of the donkey to fall over and Mary to take a tumble, nearly wiping out Joseph.

The audience took it all in stride, perhaps seeing it as one of Christ's first trials, and the students went right on with their lines, which was the only part of the program recited in High German— the passage coming straight from the Gospel of Luke.

He couldn't help being especially proud of Grace. Not only were her drawings a special part of the props for several scenes, but she also sang in one number and recited a line in another. True, her voice was soft and he had to strain to hear her, but she stood there proudly and spoke as if she wasn't nervous at all. He'd be writing home about the entire program in his weekly letter.

Gabe was also impressed with how clean and festive the schoolroom looked—blue snowflakes taped in the windows, winter drawings posted around the room, and a detailed welcome scene chalked on the front board. It seemed they had used everything at their disposal to make the crowd feel welcome, and there was quite a crowd. He was lucky to snag a corner of a bench next to Eli and his family.

Once the final note of singing faded away, the members of the school board stepped forward and thanked the students, teachers, and audience for coming. They wished the group a blessed Christmas and then invited everyone to enjoy the refreshments set up in the coatroom.

"One last thing," Samuel Gingerich said, stepping forward. Gabe remembered him as the father of Lily, one of the little girls who played with Grace on Sundays after church. He realized now that he must be on the school board. Bishop Beiler stood next to him, as did Clemens Schmucker. Beiler moved to the center of the room to explain.

"The parents wanted to present both teachers with a Christmas gift. Would both of you ladies come forward, please?"

Esther came out from behind the curtain, and Miriam stood up from her place in the third row. They met together at the side of the podium. Gabe couldn't help smiling. They looked so uncomfortable, and yet they stood at the front of the room every day.

"Esther, I believe the younger children are bringing in your gift now." Coming up the left aisle, four of the students carried a quilt. "The ladies have explained to me that the quilt contains a patch done by each family represented at the school, and across the top is a picture of Pebble Creek school done in appliqué."

There was a round of applause as Esther accepted the quilt and hugged it to her chest.

"We needed some of the older boys to bring in your gift, Miriam. The school board and the parents appreciate another fine term of service from you, and we wanted to express that gratitude with something special, so we had—"

Gabe was watching Miriam. He saw her hand go to her throat, heard her "Oh, my," and was aware that Beiler had stopped speaking.

Everyone in the room turned to the right aisle, where two of the older boys were carrying in a blanket chest.

"We had Daniel Lapp make it, and the families contributed to pay for materials and Daniel's time. Because Daniel was a previous student of yours—"

"Now I have a *boppli* of my own," a young man shouted from the back of the room, followed by a smattering of laughter.

"No doubt it will have sentimental value." Beiler directed the boys to leave the four-foot chest next to Miriam.

"*Danki*," she said softly, a blush creeping up her neck and coloring her cheeks.

Gabe could see from where he sat that the chest was made of oak and was good craftsmanship. The young man would do fine in his woodworking business.

"The children asked that we leave it open so that they could place their handmade gifts inside." The boys opened the top of the chest and then stepped back to their places at the side of the room. "Now, if you'll join me in our closing hymn, we'll finish with refreshments."

There were many things different about the Cashton community, many things he hadn't considered when moving Grace. Standing there beside Eli and singing the old familiar carol he'd grown up hearing, singing in the way that was distinctively Amish—with no instruments but with the traditional sliding musical way they had—he felt at peace. He finally understood that their two communities still remained more alike than they were different.

As he spied Grace standing with her classmates, he felt good about moving here for the first time since he'd ridden into town with her on the *Englisch* bus.

Unfortunately his feeling of contentment wouldn't last through the night.

~ Chapter 29 ~

Miriam was proud of her students.

They had done an excellent job performing their songs, skits, and poems. More importantly, they had proven they could work together as a group. The teasing and bumps of the winter months had given way to the Christmas story once again. It left her pleased and prepared to enjoy their holiday weekend.

As each student came by and placed his or her homemade gift into her new blanket chest, she thanked them and wished them a good Christmas. The younger ones hugged her. The older ones nodded or shook her hand. All seemed pleased with the evening.

Grace dropped in a rolled-up scroll, secured with a satin ribbon.

"May I look at that now?" Miriam asked.

"Nope." Grace enfolded her in a tight hug. "Wait, please."

"All right. I'll wait until Christmas Day. In fact, I believe I'll see you in the afternoon. Right, Gabe?"

"Right, Miriam."

Gabe smiled and directed Grace toward the refreshment tables so the gift line would keep moving. At least he was speaking to her tonight, and if she wasn't wrong, there was real amusement in his eyes.

It could be she'd mistaken his distance on Tuesday afternoon.

It was something she'd have to think about.

More students filed through the line, and she lost track of the Millers until she made it to the back of the room, reached for some punch, and found a cup in her hand.

"We saved you some." Gabe nodded toward the bowl, which was nearly empty. "Grace was afraid you wouldn't get any."

"I'm sure they'll make more."

"*Ya.* I told her that, but she insisted that we put back a cup for you."

"Then I owe her. My throat is quite dry from thanking all the students for their lovely gifts."

Gabe didn't laugh outright, but he looked as if he didn't believe her.

"What?"

"Nothing."

"Yes, it's something." The Lapp boys were using their cups to throw a wad of paper at each other and catch it. "Outside, boys."

"It's dark," Adam said.

"There's a lantern by the front door. We can call it shadow ball!" Luke was out the door before his brother had decided whether to follow him.

Gabe shook his head.

"You're doing it again," Miriam said.

"I am?"

"Yes. It's that look of disbelief, the same one you had when I mentioned the students' gifts."

He moved closer toward her to allow one of the families to scoot by him and out the door. "I was thinking of how many gifts you must have received if you've taught for..."

"Eight years." Miriam saved him from doing the math. "For two years I was a mother's helper, trying to decide what I wanted to do. When I turned sixteen, I became a teacher's helper, like Esther is, and I did that for two years before I became a teacher...for the last eight."

"So you're twenty-six." Gabe wiggled his eyebrows.

"And you're excellent with numbers." Miriam couldn't help laughing.

"So eight years of teaching, and each year at Christmas you could fill up a chest with their gifts? Plus maybe they bring some at the end of the year, ya?"

"I see your point."

"So what do you do with it all?" he asked, leaning in closer so he could lower his voice.

"I treasure each gift, of course."

He again raised an eyebrow but didn't say a word to contradict her.

"Space can become a problem at times," she admitted. "It might be that I have to share with others once in a while if I receive too many macramé items or pot holders."

Gabe began nodding his head, as if she had confirmed exactly what he thought.

"But I treasure each gift before I give it away."

"Your secret is safe with me, Miriam."

"Secret? You two are sharing secrets?" Simon, Miriam's brother, walked up, with Emma close at his side.

"Eavesdropping, bruder?" Miriam offered him a cookie, which he swallowed in one bite.

"Not exactly, but say...I did hear something odd when I was standing near the Englisch fellow."

"Doc Hanson?"

"No." Simon shook his head and reached for another cookie. "I know Doc Hanson. This fellow wasn't quite as old as Doc."

"The only other Englischer we invited was Officer Tate."

"Ya. I saw him as well." Emma wound her finger around the string of her kapp. "Remember, Simon? They were standing together, talking."

"Arguing's more like it."

Miriam set her empty cup of punch down on the table. "I should go see if there's a problem."

"I'll go with you," Gabe said.

"We can all go." Simon fell in line behind them.

So many people were moving in and out of the schoolhouse that Miriam wasn't sure how they would find anyone, except Officer Tate tended to wear a ball cap when he wasn't in uniform. Perhaps she could find him if she could see over everyone's head, which she couldn't.

She tugged on Gabe's arm. "Look for a dark-green ball cap. It's what he wears..."

"Got him." Gabe went across the middle of the room, which was when Miriam finally saw Officer Tate, standing near Bishop Beiler. Both were frowning and looking out a window of the school, where the curtain had been pulled to the side to allow parents to admire the children's decorations.

Tate stopped midsentence when their group walked up.

"Officer Tate. Bishop." Miriam greeted the men and then waited a moment while everyone nodded and murmured hello. "I'd heard there might have been a problem with one of the *Englischers* visiting tonight, but I didn't realize there was another *Englischer* here. Is there something I should know about?"

Tate turned to Beiler, who nodded as if giving him permission to share what he knew. Miriam didn't have a lot of experience with the man, but she could tell from the frown lines around his eyes that something had upset him, and she understood from the first words out of his mouth why he'd gone to the bishop with his concerns.

Gabe stood near the edge of the group, watching and listening. He'd only meant to give Miriam her cup of punch, as Grace had made him promise, say his good-nights, collect his daughter, and head home. The temptation to tease her had been too great, or possibly it was that she was so easy to tease. Either way, it had landed him here, in the middle of what?

"The person you're referring to is Byron Drake," Tate explained. "He happened upon the school program and walked in just before it began."

"Oh. Well, we are not rude to outsiders. I'm sure he meant us no harm." Miriam scanned the room, which now held half the people it had during the program. "Is he still here? I don't see anyone I don't recognize."

"No, he left, but he remarked on some ideas after the program that I didn't think your community would like, so I shared his comments with Bishop Beiler."

"And I thank you for doing so, but what the *Englisch* man does is his business and none of ours." Beiler's expression remained neutral. Gabe was learning it rarely changed. Perhaps that was simply his way, though there had been that frown when they had first approached them.

Tate took his ball cap off his head, rubbed his hand over hair that was quite short, and then replaced it. Now that Gabe thought about it, he remembered that the officer had removed it during the program, and he was dressed properly enough. Tate had been sitting a few seats down from where he and Eli had sat. Apparently, as soon as refreshment time had started, the cap had come out of his back pocket.

"The man sounded pretty determined," Tate said.

"Determined about what?" Gabe asked.

"Starting a tourist attraction here in Cashton."

"Perhaps the bishop is right. Why should we care about what happens in Cashton?" Miriam glanced back at Simon and Emma, who shrugged. "We don't often go into the town proper."

"I would agree with you. In general more tourism is a good thing for everyone, but the reason he stopped was because he saw all of the buggies." Tate stuck his hands into the pockets of his trousers and jingled the change there. "The plans he was so excited about had an Amish theme."

"Amish?" Miriam sat down at the desk next to her.

"What is an Amish theme?" Emma asked.

Gabe pinched the bridge of his nose, memories of trouble in Indiana washing over him like a wave.

"There was a lot of mumbling," Tate admitted. "I didn't catch everything he said, and then he was gone."

"Exactly what did he say?" Gabe glanced from Beiler to Tate. He was new here and had no influence, but he did have a stake in the community where he would raise Grace, and he needed to know.

"He kept saying—'*Perfect, this is just perfect. A schoolhouse, children. Tourists love children.*'"

Miriam bounced out of her seat. "We can't have tourists in to interrupt the children every day."

"Then he mentioned the old hotel in downtown Cashton and he left."

"That place has been closed for years," Bishop Beiler pointed out.

"True, but I had heard at the council meeting last week that they have a possible buyer." When no one spoke, Tate added, "I believe I just met him."

Gabe stayed a few minutes longer, but Tate didn't know anything else, and Beiler was set against becoming involved. Miriam's attention soon turned to thanking the remaining parents and students. It wasn't hard for Gabe to find Grace and slip away.

He drove through the country roads, lightly dusted with snow, with Grace curled up on the seat beside him. While she hummed and played with the popcorn ball the teachers had handed out, he couldn't stop his mind from sliding back to Indiana. They had experienced conflict, disruption, even families torn apart, all because of an *Englischer*'s business plans. Or maybe it had been their fault. If they had acted sooner and stepped up and involved themselves, much of what happened could have been averted.

But it wasn't their way to participate in the town's affairs, or so the older members had argued.

Perhaps he should talk to Joshua and Abigail about what had happened there. He didn't want to taint their Christmas celebration with needless worries, but he also didn't want to let matters spiral out of control.

He'd learned that lesson before, and though he didn't consider himself the sharpest tool in the wood-carver's box, he wasn't the dullest either. Perhaps it would be wisest to tell what he knew and let the community decide.

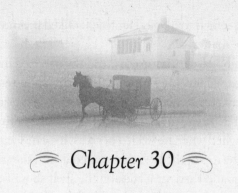

⤳ Chapter 30 ⤳

Grace didn't think anything could be better than the school presentation, but Christmas was.

When she was younger—only five or six—she would lie awake nights thinking of Christmas afternoon when they exchanged presents. This year she was still excited about that. She went to sleep at night dreaming of Stormy. She also snuck moments at the table while her dad was outside in the barn to work on her father's present. She didn't want him to see his gift before it was complete.

But Christmas morning was better every year. Her dad was out doing only what work had to be done in the barn. He had explained to her the afternoon before that things were different here than at their old home in Indiana. As if she hadn't already figured that out.

No nativity scene at the church. No candles in the windows. But the school presentation had been a huge success.

Grace skipped into the mudroom, sat on the floor, and pulled Stanley's box down into her lap. "I'll still love you," she whispered. "Even if Stormy comes here this afternoon."

She liked the sound of her voice now. Maybe that was her best Christmas present—it sounded like a soft breeze. Some people's voices were big like a strong wind. Some were screechy like a bird's cry. Hers was soft and that was okay.

Her dad seemed to like it. Her teacher liked it. And she liked it. What else mattered?

Stanley nibbled at the crust of bread she dropped in his box and then ran to the other side where the cheese from yesterday still sat.

"This afternoon is our big day. Our feast day. I'll bring you something special from the meal. I promise." Brushing a finger over his back, she laughed when he tickled her with his whiskers. Placing the lid back on the top of the box, she secured it with the string her dad had given her and then set it back on the shelf above her coat peg.

Stanley had plenty of air holes, windows she'd carved and covered with wax paper, even tiny trees she'd created for him from limbs and leaves. He had a nice place to live on his shelf. Sometimes she wondered if maybe he needed another mouse to play with and keep him company. She'd have to keep her eyes open in the barn.

Walking back into the kitchen, she made sure her dad's *kaffi* was on the hot part of the stove. This morning their meal would be small because it was Christmas. Miriam's mom, Abigail, had sent Noah over with fresh bread. Grace had taken some cheese out of the icebox and placed it on a platter with a knife, though she wasn't allowed to cut things when she was alone.

Maybe next year. Some things had to wait.

She'd also brought in the milk for herself. It would be their only meal until later this afternoon.

You'd think that would be a sad thing, but in a way it was fun. It made the Christmas celebration all the more exciting. She glanced across the counter, where she'd placed the food she'd chosen from their pantry to take to Miss Miriam's. She'd picked out her favorite vegetables, canned by her *mammi* Sarah and *mammi* Erma at their old home—golden butternut squash, bright-red stewed tomatoes, and green beans seasoned her favorite way.

The back door slammed and she spun around.

"*Gudemariye*, Grace Ann."

"*Gudemariye*." She'd wondered if her dad might be sad this morning. Sometimes holidays made him miss her mother worse. She missed her mom too, but the hurt was less every day—like her frost-bite. She wondered if that made her a bad person. Before she could think about it too long, he'd scooped her up into a hug.

"It seems there's something I'm supposed to remember about this day, but I can't quite recall what it is." He spun right and then left, with Grace hanging over his shoulder like one of the sacks of feed he carried into the barn. "I thought I might remember while I was in the barn, but nope—"

"It's Christmas!"

"What's that you say?"

He dropped her onto the floor and placed his hands on his hips.

"Christmas." Her giggling bubbled up and out.

"Huh. Are you sure?" Rubbing his beard, he clomped over to the calendar on the wall and stared at it a moment in disbelief. "Seems that just yesterday was the school presentation."

"That was Friday. You worked in the barn yesterday!"

"*Ya.* Now I'm remembering. Must be old age stealing my memory." Gabe patted his stomach and glanced over at the counter. "And I see you have a special Christmas breakfast ready for us. What a good *dochder* you are."

Pride swelled in Grace's chest. She'd known he was kidding about forgetting it was Christmas morning. No one forgot that. But he wasn't kidding about the breakfast. She could always tell when he was serious because he pulled down on his beard and his face went all soft.

Skipping across the room, she hugged him tight.

No doubt about it, she had the best dad in the world.

They ate their breakfast slowly because they didn't have to hurry anywhere. Her dad wouldn't be working anymore until it was time to feed the few animals they had in the evening. It wasn't a church Sunday, and because it was Christmas everyone was staying home with their own families.

So they enjoyed their bread and cheese. Gabe sipped his *kaffi* and then had a second cup, which he hardly ever did. They were usually hurrying to meet Eli's buggy for school. Today he refilled the mug and sat back down beside her. Snow was falling outside, but it was a light snow and he said it would probably stop by afternoon.

"Can I sled later?"

"I bet you can. Should be lots of kids at Abigail and Joshua's."

Grace thought she would know some of them from school, but there might be a few from other schools. She wasn't as worried about meeting new people now that she could talk. It didn't seem that kids teased her as much as before.

She took another bite of her bread and cheese. It was odd eating it for breakfast, but that was what he'd told her to lay out when they'd talked about their Christmas meal the day before.

"Do you know why we eat simply on Christmas morning, Grace?" She shook her head.

"I suppose it's to remind us that Mary and Joseph didn't have much in that stable when Mary was giving birth to the baby Jesus."

Grace took another bite of the bread. This time it tasted differently to her.

"Probably Mary carried some supplies with her, or they could have bought some things along the way, but it's doubtful they could have stopped and cooked something in a barn, especially with her giving birth." He turned the mug of *kaffi* in his hands. "I probably shouldn't be drinking this. I don't know if Joseph was in the habit of drinking *kaffi* or not. He probably drank hot tea. Either way, I imagine he could have used a good strong cup that morning."

They talked another few minutes while she finished her food. Things started making more sense to her, especially as she remembered the skits and poems on Friday night. It had been funny when the donkey had fallen over, but she'd ridden a real donkey before and it wasn't all that comfortable. Wasn't nearly as comfortable as riding in their buggy behind Chance.

"How about I clean up these dishes and then we'll read the Christmas story from Luke? You want to get your *mammi* Sarah's Bible?"

Grace thought that would make the morning perfect. She helped him carry the dishes to the sink and then went to retrieve her Bible from its special place on her dresser.

The morning went like that, not in a speedy blur, but flowing slowly. She almost didn't want it to end.

When it was time for them to leave for Miriam's, she stopped him at the door, reached up, combed her fingers through his beard, and whispered, "*Danki*."

"For what, my Grace?"

"For a *wunderbaar* Christmas morning."

They both knew it wasn't perfect, but it was their best one yet since they'd been alone. She walked out into the afternoon sunshine with high hopes that things could only get better.

⤳ Chapter 31 ⤳

When Gabe pulled up to Abigail and Joshua's house, he thought perhaps he had his afternoons mixed up. Maybe there was a Sunday church meeting going on. Buggies were lined up along the fence bordering the pasture, though all the horses had been taken into the barn. He counted more than a dozen.

How many children did Joshua and Abigail have?

Of course, a few friends would be invited as well, like himself. He glanced over at Grace to see if she was intimidated by the size of the crowd. A grin was splayed across her face. She tugged on his coat and pointed toward the small hill situated beside the barn. A large group of children were lined up with their sleds and saucers. A few off to the side were engaged in a snowball fight while they waited their turn.

"Want to come inside first?"

"Uh-uh."

"Okay. Do you need me to help you with your sled?"

"Yes, please."

He was unloading her sled from the back of the buggy, which was one they had bought for her when she was smaller and probably wouldn't last another year, when Hannah appeared.

"Hey, Grace. Merry Christmas."

"Merry Christmas, Hannah!"

"Headed to the hill?"

"Uh-huh."

"So am I. Want to walk with me?"

"Can I, *dat?*"

"Sure. Think you girls can drag this sled over there?"

"No problem," Hannah said. "I have six *bruders* and *schweschders.*"

"Pulled a lot of sleds have you?"

"*Ya.* My fair share."

He watched as they shuffled off through the snow. It wasn't very thick, not more than a foot. They'd had only a few light snowfalls over the last few days, but the children would make the best of it.

Squeals and laughter followed him as he carried the box of vegetables and the gift he had for Abigail and Joshua inside. He stopped and checked his pocket to make sure he had the ribbon, and then he nearly bobbled it and dropped it in the snow.

"Is that red ribbon for someone special?" Noah asked, slapping him on the back.

He thought of Miriam but bit back the words. "*Ya.* It is." He stuffed it into his pants pocket. "Merry Christmas, Noah."

"Merry Christmas to you. Glad you could make it."

Gabe glanced back at the row of buggies. "Are you sure there's room for two more?"

"There's always room for two more. Come on inside. I'll have one of the boys see to your gelding. It helps that the weather is good enough to let the older children play on the hill. Otherwise we would have to shoo them into the barn."

As they walked into the main room, Gabe understood what he meant. Every chair and couch was occupied by women, men, grandmothers, grandfathers, aunts, and uncles—and many of them were holding babies. Miriam was rocking one of them. She glanced up, her eyes locked with his a moment, and then she looked away.

"Welcome to the family," Noah laughed.

"I didn't realize there were so many Kings," Gabe joked.

"Half of us go to our church district," Abigail explained as she accepted the box of goodies. "And the other half belongs to the district on the other side of Cashton."

"A divided family," Joshua muttered as he swiped a cookie off the counter.

"Now, Pop, you're not going to start that again, are you? We're a mere buggy ride away—and Pebble Creek runs through both districts, keeping us united." Extending his hand to Gabe, the larger version of Joshua added, "David King. Middle son."

"Nice to meet you, middle son."

"You must be the brave man who bought the Kline place."

"I am."

"I want to hear how that's going. Kline's land was good, but he never took proper care of it." Unlike his conversation with Clemens Schmucker the week before, Gabe could tell there was no animosity in David's comment.

"You're right about that. Maybe you could give me some ideas on what to do with the south pasture."

"That I could."

The hour passed quickly until the food was served, and it wasn't as much a meal as it was a feast. Gabe would have been embarrassed about the vegetables he brought, but Miriam complimented him on them and Abigail asked, "Did your *mamm* put these up, Gabe?"

"She did."

"I wonder if you'd mind writing her and asking what she seasoned them with."

"I'd be happy to."

They couldn't have known how much their comments put him at ease, because they were said in an offhand way as they passed around roasted chicken, baked ham, mashed potatoes, fresh baked bread, and more vegetables than he'd seen in a month. He was convinced their comments were sincere when the bowls with his mother's vegetables reached him. They were close to empty. He took a small spoonful and passed them on. He had more put up in his pantry, but she would be tickled when he wrote her about it.

The children returned to their play outside for another hour while the meal's cleanup took place. Though the women reigned in the kitchen, the men moved the benches that had been set up for the meal and spread them around the sitting area so that there would be more space for the gift-giving.

"We draw names at Thanksgiving, so each person has had a month to prepare their gift," Joshua explained.

"*Ya*, it was the same way in my family."

"I believe Abigail has something for your girl."

"That wasn't necessary. I explained to her we're visitors."

Joshua shook his head as they moved the last bench. "You don't know my wife very well yet. She keeps a box of small presents for situations like this. She'd never let a child go without a gift."

"Actually I haven't given her my gift. I brought one that I bought from the store, and then I'd planned to pick up the other from Miriam before we leave." Gabe pulled the red ribbon from the pocket of his pants. "I haven't had a chance to talk to her yet."

"She snuck away to take Pepper the ham bone. You'll find her in the barn."

Miriam knelt beside Pepper as he enjoyed his special dinner. "Merry Christmas," she whispered, rubbing him between the ears. He gnawed on the bone, pausing occasionally to glance up at her. She realized how foolish it would sound if anyone heard her whispering Christmas wishes to a dog, but fortunately she was alone for the moment.

"Do you always give your dog Christmas presents?"

Though her pulse jumped, she forced herself to remain still. "It's become something of a holiday tradition between us. What brings you out to the barn, Gabe?"

He pulled out the red ribbon. "I was hoping we could see if this would fit a certain gray kitten."

Miriam took the ribbon and fingered it. Did he have it lying around the house, or had he made a special trip to town to purchase it? "You've decided to let her have it?"

"*Ya.* Try looking into those brown eyes and denying her something. I do, mind you. I wouldn't want her spoiled completely rotten, but it's harder than you would think."

He sat down beside her and studied Pepper. "I could probably use a good dog around my place. Will he be fathering more litters?"

"Yes, in a few months. We receive half the pups. If you'd like, I could save you one."

"That would be *gut.* I'll pay you for it, of course."

"All right, if you insist."

The silence stretched between them, though it wasn't an uncomfortable one. She never felt awkward around him anymore, only that she needed to be careful. So many emotions fought inside herself, and she wasn't sure which were proper to show and which she should keep tamped down. Even as they sat there, watching Pepper, she found herself wondering how Gabe and Grace had spent Christmas morning. Had it been lonely?

"How was Grace's Christmas at home?"

"*Gut.* We had a nice quiet time together. Probably spent it much as you did." Gabe looked at her sideways without turning his head. "Except probably you didn't have to share a special Christmas blessing with a mouse in a box."

Miriam smiled broadly as some of the tension left her shoulders. "No. We did not have any mice around this morning."

"I suppose that wasn't what you were asking me, though." Gabe's voice turned serious, and he stretched his legs out in front of him, reached forward, and scratched Pepper between the ears. "It's hard to know how much Grace remembers about her *mamm* or if she misses her more on holidays. This morning she only said that heaven must have a real celebration on Christ's birth and then she asked if I thought they exchanged gifts after lunch as we do."

Miriam moistened her lips as she tried to think of what to say that might lessen the hurt she heard in his voice. She settled for reaching over and squeezing his hand.

"What did you tell her?"

"That I have no doubt the celebration there is grander and the gifts are even better."

Miriam nodded and then pulled her hand away when she saw that he was staring at her fingers.

"Your parents were almost ready to open gifts."

"Oh." Miriam hopped up and began dusting straw off her dress. "Let me get the kitten."

"Is he old enough?"

"Yes. He'll be fine. I even set aside a little crate for you to take him in." They walked into the stall where the kittens were. The mother was gone, but two kittens were left—Stormy and a calico. "David is taking the other one."

She picked up Stormy and held him while Gabe tried to tie the ribbon around his neck. The kitten yawned sleepily, not really bothering to wake.

Gabe's fingers hung up in the ribbon. He tried a second time with no better luck.

"Maybe we should switch," Miriam suggested. "You take Stormy and I'll take the ribbon."

They swapped with some tangling of the kitten, the ribbon, and their fingers. Miriam tried to ignore the heat that shot through her when Gabe's fingers brushed hers even as she tried to forget her embarrassment from a few minutes earlier.

She tied the ribbon quickly and then set Stormy into a small crate that held an old tattered blanket. "I've been putting him in here afternoons, when I'm home, so he'd be used to it. I don't think he'll cry at all."

Closing the lid, she picked it up and handed it to him.

"You're too kind to us," Gabe said quietly, his brown eyes so full of warmth and kindness that she wanted to reach up and run her fingers over his brow, wiping away some of his worry.

"Not at all." She took a step back. "Maybe you could leave him in the mudroom while we're inside."

"*Gut* idea."

They walked back to the house side by side, not touching, but close enough that they could have.

Miriam tried not to think what it would be like if they were a family, if she were going home with him after the gift-giving. She tried not to dwell on the fact that her life seemed empty with only teaching and her parents, with no real place of her own to belong, no husband or child to care for, no one's needs to tend. A small silent part of her wanted to throw herself in his arms and beg, "Take me with you. Take me back to your place, and we can restore it together. We can be a family—the three of us."

She wanted to tell him about the things she dreamed of before she fell into a fitful sleep each night.

But she didn't do any of those things.

Instead, she walked silently beside him, up the back porch steps and into the house—pausing only to leave the kitten and his crate in the mudroom.

Chapter 32

Though much in Wisconsin was different from what Gabe had grown up accustomed to in Indiana, the gift-giving was the same. He smiled as the women unwrapped quilting notions, new cooking gadgets, and a new set of sheets for Abigail—it seemed everyone had pitched in on that. The men oohed and aahed over farming tools and new suspenders, and one of Miriam's brothers received a new hat.

Grace was wearing her new gloves in the house, so apparently she liked them—that and the grin on her face was a sure giveaway.

"Do you like the psalm I stitched?" Grace asked.

"It's very *gut*." Gabe held up the embroidered cloth that had been fastened into a frame. "I didn't realize you knew how."

"The older girls have been teaching us, and the boys made the frames. I messed up a little on the S in Shepherd."

"It's beautiful, Grace." Gabe ran his fingers over the stitching. "Psalm 23 is *mammi* Sarah's favorite."

"I only had time to finish the first eight words—"

"That's all we need. They'll remind us of the rest."

"Nicely done, Grace." Abigail peered over their shoulder at the sampler. "'The Lord is my shepherd, I lack nothing.'"

"Abigail can read my stitching," Grace whispered.

"Did you pick that verse yourself?" Abigail asked.

"It was that or Genesis 1:1."

"I always was partial to the Psalms. It looks like you two are quite the artists. Gabe, I want to thank you for the walnut bowl. I don't know how you managed to work such a beautiful finish on it."

"It gives me something to do in the evening. I'm happy you like it."

"Grace, I have a gift for you."

Grace's eyes brightened as she accepted the package. Unwrapping it, a small squeal escaped as she saw first the black *kapp* and then the black apron over the green dress, and finally the black shoes like her own.

"I've been making Plain dolls for my *grandkinner* for years. I hope you—"

But Abigail had no chance to finish her explanation. She found herself wrapped in Grace's hug.

"I believe she likes it," Gabe said.

"They usually do." Abigail led Grace off to the kitchen, enlisting her help in serving cookies and dessert as the children began to scatter to play with various gifts.

He heard Miriam thanking her for the picture Grace had drawn and placed in the blanket chest after the school presentation. "A picture of Stanley. It's almost as though he's at the school with me."

Gabe was about to go and find a piece of dessert himself, even though he was sure he'd been stuffed full only an hour ago, when Noah moved beside him and nodded toward the men and women who were gathering in the sitting room.

"I believe you might want to join us to hear what David has to say."

"*Ya?*"

"It seems he heard more about Byron Drake, his tourist attraction, and the old hotel."

Gabe followed Noah into the sitting room, which was crowded now with Joshua and Abigail's family—all but the children, who were in the kitchen eating dessert.

"You're sure about this, David?" Joshua sat in the rocker near the stove, his voice calm and quiet.

"I heard about it on Friday and saw it for myself yesterday when I was in town picking up a few things at the grocer."

"Saw what?" Noah asked. "Tell it again, now that we're all here."

"A poster about the size of a calendar." David stretched his hands out the width of a wall calendar. "And twice as long. It showed the old hotel on front with Drake's name over the top. In big letters it said Renovation Project, and it gave the time for the information meeting that was to be held by the Cashton board of trustees."

"And the village president will be there?" Miriam worried the strings of her prayer *kapp*.

"Goodland? *Ya*. Sure, she will. All of them will. Next Wednesday at six p.m."

"In three days?" Noah's voice was a low growl.

"No. Most business in town grinds to a halt the week between Christmas and New Year's Day, especially municipal business. It's the next Wednesday—in ten days." David added as an afterthought, "I guess they don't expect that any of us will show up."

"Why would we?" Ida piped up. She was married to Noah, and with seven children to look after she was a bit more stern than her husband was, but not unpleasant. "When was the last time we involved ourselves in *Englisch* politics?"

"We haven't, and I don't know why we would start now." This from Simon.

Gabe caught Miriam watching Simon and his girl, Emma— watching them almost with a longing look in her eyes.

He missed something Joshua had said. "—the poster?"

"I stopped and read it word for word. It had Amish Abbey spread across it plain as day. You'd think a formally educated man like Drake would know that we don't have abbeys. I wonder if he even knows what an abbey is."

"I don't imagine such things matter much to him. The point is, it sounds slick and looks good when you put the A's together on a poster." Joshua caught a grandchild who came running into the room and launched himself into his lap.

"What concerns me is that he specifically mentioned the school and the students." Miriam glanced around at each of her family members, her gaze finally landing on Gabe. "It's as if he wants to put us on display. That can't be a *gut* thing."

Gabe squirmed uncomfortably, wanting to ease her worries but not knowing how. It wasn't his place to jump in the middle of this situation. He was new here. Best to sit back and let the others handle things.

"It's not our way to interfere in their matters, though." Noah ran his fingers through his beard. "Why would we make an exception this time?"

"Since I moved here, so many years ago with your *mamm*, we've been able to remain apart," Joshua said. "Wisconsin isn't like other areas—Pennsylvania or Indiana."

All eyes turned to Gabe and then back to Joshua. "Here there are fewer of us and we're more spread out. It hasn't been hard to remain apart, to not attract attention. And this is the way of doing things you all are accustomed to—what you all have known because you were raised here."

"I took a trip to Pennsylvania a few years ago." David rubbed at the upholstery on the arm of the couch. "Remember, *dat*? To go back and settle things to do with your *onkel*."

"*Ya*. I remember."

"It was different there. I could hardly believe the Amish there were really...Amish."

"I didn't raise you to judge, son."

"And I'm not judging. I'm only saying I wouldn't want to see our area go that way. Our district is more liberal than yours—it's true. Our cottage industries operate more directly with the *Englischers*. We have the Glick's woodworking shop, Barbara Hershberger's rug shop, and the cabins that Troyer runs down near the creek."

"All on the west side," Noah muttered.

"*Ya*. I'll admit it's different on the west side of Pebble Creek, even though it's only a few miles away." David's smile tugged at his beard. "We even have indoor bathrooms and such."

There was murmuring and a bit of teasing about David being

too good to use an outhouse. Gabe noticed he took the ribbing well. When the joking had died down, David's older brother picked up the discussion in a more serious tone.

"Those changes were decided by your church leadership." Noah turned a chair around and straddled it.

"Exactly. Those are changes made within our community, not imposed from without. I agree with Miriam. I worry that what Drake has in mind will affect the children, and that I'm against."

"It would be *gut* if we had someone's perspective who has been through something similar—an Amish perspective." Joshua began to rock in the chair as his grandson yawned and curled up in his lap.

"Gabe, you're from Indiana." Miriam's words were soft, but they carried across the room with the weight of his entire buggy. "Did your community deal with anything of this sort there?"

He thought of denying it. He thought of changing the subject or pretending it was time for him and Grace to leave, but he didn't. He knew if he was going to be a part of this community, if he was going to fully commit to it, then he needed to help the families gathered in this room in any way he could. And that included sharing with them all that he knew.

⌒ Chapter 33 ⌒

When Miriam thought about it later, she remembered that the night of the school play, Gabe had had a rather strong reaction to the initial news about Drake. At the time she'd been too caught up in all that was happening to pay much attention to that, but watching him now, watching him speak to her family, things began to make sense.

He'd been in their community for little more than a month, and he'd been careful to remain somewhat apart, somewhat separate at first. Until the night Grace was lost—then he'd come out of his shell a little. Now he was taking another step forward, and it seemed to her, observing him sit up straighter and begin to talk, that it was more than a distance of a few inches—it was a distance of miles in regards to the heart. It was as if he were walking into the stream of the community around him.

"*Ya*," he admitted. "We dealt with something very similar."

"How so?" Noah asked.

"The town I was from—it was near Nappanee. Have you heard of it?"

A few murmured that they had.

"Nappanee was quite the tourist spot for *Englischers*, but our little town wasn't, and we had no desire to be." He cleared his throat and began again. "There were many within our district who were adamantly opposed to any changes and what the *Englisch* developers first had planned. We did not think it was respectful of our faith or our history."

"So you talked to them?" Now Ida was sitting forward, listening closely.

"At first we did not. Like you, we had never interfered before. We thought things would work out one way or another."

Miriam noticed him glance out the window to where the *kinner* were playing once again in the snow. What was he remembering?

"There was some disagreement between those who wished to go to the *Englisch* council and those who insisted we stay apart."

"What made you finally decide to speak with them?"

Gabe ran his hand up and around the back of his neck. "Several things, I suppose. It seems it never is only one thing. The media descended on the town. It became difficult to do the simplest of things—such as go to town to do the weekend shopping. They took many photos, especially of the young ones, though we would try to shield them."

He glanced up and met the eyes locked on him. "We finally took to leaving them at home when possible, but that didn't seem fair either. You should be able to take your *dochder* into town for an ice-cream cone or your boy in to help you pick up feed."

"It sounds terrible," Emma murmured.

"I don't mean to make the *Englischers* sound all bad. Often when we would ask them to take no pictures they would put the cameras away, but you probably don't understand how much an area can change when something like this happens. Automobiles lined up along the road next to my *onkel*'s place, snapping pictures while he plowed his fields."

"But it's private property," David said.

"The land, yes, but not the roads." Gabe placed his hands on his knees and pushed on with his story. "I think because we waited, it was harder to present our concerns. We went to the town manager and council when things became even more difficult, but they said contracts had already been signed and there was nothing they could do."

"So talking about the matter did no good?" Joshua motioned to Abigail to come and sit beside him as she entered the room.

"I'm doing a bad job of telling how things happened." Gabe looked directly at Miriam and smiled slightly, and her heart flipped like the pancakes on the griddle her mom often used for making breakfast. "If it had not been for the strong leadership within our church, things would have been much worse. The roads were becoming dangerous due to traffic, the *kinner* didn't feel comfortable in town, and then came word that another large corporation planned on purchasing land in town to build something similar to what Drake is planning...at least, to me it sounds similar."

"Was it as bad as an Amish Abbey?" Abigail asked.

"Oh, *ya*, I believe it was." Gabe's smile was genuine now. "These people had no interest in educating about our faith or accurately sharing about the history in the area—Amish or *Englisch*. They merely wanted to create an amusement park of sorts and put an Amish label on it."

"So what did you do?"

"We joined with leaders from other faiths—Mennonite, Episcopal, Methodist, Baptist, and Catholic. We all came together and petitioned the town's leaders to reconsider the business plan in light of our desire for religious clarity."

"And they agreed?" Noah shook his head. "I have a hard time believing that. In my experience, the dollar usually rules such decisions."

"Perhaps someone in the group was owed a favor, or perhaps someone on the council had a real desire to do the right thing—the godly thing. I can't say. I only know that without the interference from the leaders within our community, matters would have turned out badly. Not only would we have been sorely misrepresented, but our town would have been a difficult area to live in—and a much more expensive one, as the land prices were rising because of the corporation's interest."

The group digested what Gabe had related in silence. Finally David asked, "What happened with the new building?"

"They created something like what they have in Shipshewana—the Menno-Hof. It is a museum of sorts, but it was built like a traditional barn raising with the help of the local community. It teaches about the Hutterites, Mennonites, and Amish. It's very nice. And the tourists are happy to go there rather than photograph my *onkel's* farm. It's better for the tourists, better for my *onkel*, and better for the cattle. And, at the museum, they have hands-on exhibits where the children can help feed the animals and such."

"That sounds like a *gut* compromise," Abigail said.

"Most everyone thought so, though some would have preferred that things never change at all."

"That is an option we're not offered." Joshua stood slowly, careful not to disturb the child now asleep in his arms. "Gabe, would you be willing to repeat what you've just said to our church leadership?"

Miriam didn't wait to hear his answer. She knew he'd say yes, so she moved out of the sitting room as the family meeting broke up. It was time to check on Stormy and make sure he was ready for his trip to his new home.

She couldn't help noticing the way Emma smiled at her as she hurried out of the room, though.

Had Emma guessed at her feelings for Gabe? Had she stared at him overly long? Had she blushed when he glanced her way?

When had this happened? When had she fallen *in lieb* with Gabe Miller? And most importantly, what was she going to do about it?

Chapter 34

The week between Christmas and New Year's was usually one of Miriam's favorite times at school. The students were calmer because the excitement of Christmas was past. The stress of planning for the holiday presentation was over. She was also done working nonstop each evening on Christmas gifts, though it had been worth it—her mother had loved the shawl, and her brother's wife, Ida, thought the crocheted scarf, hat, and gloves were perfect.

Now, in the evenings, she could work on whatever project struck her fancy, or maybe none at all. Tuesday evening she sat staring at an unopened book.

"You look terrible," Esther said, bringing her a cup of hot tea.

"Really? Because I feel worse." The words sounded right when she formed them in her mind, but they came out resembling, "Ree? Be-oz I fee hearse."

"Still stuffed up, huh? Why don't we try steaming it out of you? I'll put some water on the stove—"

Miriam shook her head as she sipped the tea, but the first swallow went down the wrong way and she began coughing, and then she couldn't stop.

"Say, you sound worse than you did yesterday." Esther moved next to her on the couch. "Worse than you did in class today, even."

222

"I'm fine." Miriam blew her nose and then said, "Honest. I swallowed wrong, is all."

Putting the cup down, she pulled the layer of quilts up to her chin, and clenched her teeth together. Esther was doing the best she could, but their apartment was freezing! How cold was it outside?

"Miriam? Have you taken your temperature tonight?" Esther's cool hand on her forehead startled her out of the dream she'd been slipping into. "Your temperature, honey. Did you take it?"

"No."

"Let's do that. What about Tylenol? Have you taken any?"

Miriam tried to shake her head, but the pounding was too intense. "This morning," she murmured.

"All right. Sit up a little."

Next thing she knew, Esther had popped the thermometer they kept in the medicine cabinet in her mouth and was bustling into the kitchen, pouring juice into her mug. "Take two of these with the juice. It will go down better."

Removing the thermometer she held it up to the light and squinted at the numbers. "Oh, my! You won't be teaching tomorrow. I guess we'll be having Eli notify the substitutes for the morning. Maybe you'll feel better by afternoon."

Miriam wasn't better by afternoon, but she did wake up warmly ensconced on her mother's couch, covered in quilts.

"It was *gut* of Eli to bring you home," Abigail said. "We wouldn't want you around the students, spreading germs. Did you not realize how sick you were?"

"No, *mamm*." Miriam snuggled into the couch and stared out the window.

"Perhaps you did and you were being stubborn. We both know how you can be when it comes to missing a day of school."

Miriam closed her eyes. Better to pretend she was asleep than argue with her mother. The shivering was the worst part. If she held herself very tight, then she could force her body still, but then she'd relax, and the spasms would start again.

"It's only the fever, dear." Abigail laid a cool washcloth on her forehead. "Stop fighting it. Give it forty-eight hours and you'll feel much better."

She tried to remember when she'd first begun to feel badly, but it all fell away from her, like when she was a girl and tumbled into the waters of Pebble Creek. The water and summer and sounds in the kitchen merged until the back door slammed, pulling her from her sleep.

"Seems there's a lump on my couch. Where's a man supposed to sit?" Joshua bent and kissed her on the forehead. "She's soaking wet, Abigail."

"*Ya?* That's *gut.* Probably her fever has broken. And can you tell me why you let that dog into my house?"

Miriam stirred when Pepper pressed his nose between the quilt and pillow, seeking her face. "Hey, boy." Her voice croaked worse than one of the frogs Luke was prone to sneak in the classroom.

"See there? She'll speak to the dog, where she won't even open her eyes for me." Joshua settled in the chair across from her.

"Hi, *dat.*" Miriam smiled at him as she ran her fingers over Pepper's silky ears.

"How's my girl?"

"Better."

"You sound terrible. Can't say as you smell too great, either." Joshua winked and reached for the *Budget.*

"I guess I'm going to live."

"Glad to hear it." Joshua lowered the paper, all the teasing now gone from his eyes. "Next time you ring the school bell right away instead of waiting until the next morning when something's wrong. I don't like the idea of you girls being there alone with one of you sick."

Instead of answering Miriam nodded, staring down at Pepper as tears clouded her eyes. Had she been that sick? Had her fever been that high? Surely it hadn't or they would have called Doc Hanson.

Then she saw the prescription bottle on the table in front of her. Doc Hanson had been here? And she didn't even remember?

She struggled to sit up as Abigail walked into the room.

"When was Doc here?"

"Yesterday."

"But..." Miriam ran her fingers through her hair. "But I was at school yesterday."

Abigail set a tray of food down on the stool in front of her. "Honey, today is Thursday. You haven't been at school since Tuesday, and Esther sent you upstairs for most of the day then. Let me take that washcloth and fetch a fresh one. It looks as if your fever finally broke."

"Thank *Gotte* it did," Joshua said, once again behind his paper.

"Doc Hanson was here? I don't even remember that."

Abigail returned with a fresh washcloth and tried to place it on her forehead, but Miriam pulled it away from her hands and began running it over her face and down her neck. The cloth felt wonderfully cool and clean. "So he left medicine for my fever?"

"*Ya*, and the influenza. You had a nasty case of it. Looks like the medicine worked though." Joshua peeked over the top of the paper at her.

"Maybe it was his medicine that worked." Abigail sat in her chair and picked up her knitting. "Or it could be time, my chicken soup, and the herbs I've been using worked. Who knows?"

"Is that what I smell?" Miriam asked.

"Proof that you're feeling better when you can complain." Abigail stared out over her reading glasses. When had she started wearing them to knit? It occurred to Miriam that her parents were aging, and the thought made her start to cough.

"I have some licorice root mixed up. It will sooth your throat. Let me fetch you a cup of tea with it—"

"*Mamm*, I don't need the licorice root. Where did you even find it this time of year?"

"She dries her medicinal herbs now," Joshua said. "You should listen to your *mamm*. Even Doc Hanson admits to their effectiveness."

"Have you been pouring it down my throat as I sleep?" Miriam's hand went around her neck as if she could protect herself. "I have the most awful taste in my mouth."

"Probably because you haven't brushed your teeth since Monday."

"I'll take care of that now." She threw back the covers, causing Pepper to whimper.

"Joshua, I'll thank you to take that dog outside while I make Miriam's tea. Then I believe dinner will be ready."

"Yes, dear." Joshua stood, called the dog to him, and walked back out of the house, pulling on his coat as he did.

"Miriam, there's a chamber pot set up for you in the mudroom."

"I don't need a chamber pot!" Heat flooded her cheeks as she shook the blankets away and reached for her robe.

"I hope you're not thinking of going outside." Abigail shook her head. "Walking in the cold air is the worst thing you can do. You need to be careful, or you'll miss another week of school."

"*Mamm*, cold air doesn't make you sick. It's viruses that do that." Coughing, she reached for the back of the couch.

"If you know better than I do, all right, then. But if you change your mind, the chamber pot is in the mudroom on your way out. I know the students miss you and will be happy to have you back, but you do what you think is best."

Miriam hobbled to the back door, intent on ignoring her mother's words. Most of the time Abigail could be so reasonable, but in other ways—such as with the herbs and the idea that cold air would make you sick—there was no use arguing with her. Moving slowly through the mudroom, Miriam snagged her scarf from the peg by the door and then stepped out into the January afternoon.

Her dad and Pepper were already on their way toward the barn door, Pepper jumping and barking at a bird, her dad pausing to watch a deer lope across the southern pasture.

The first breath of fresh air was joy—the second a little less so.

She didn't remember the outhouse being quite so far from the house before. Shuffling through the last remnants of Christmas snow, she took care of her business and then hurried back inside.

By the time she was once again settled on the couch, she gladly accepted the licorice tea—not because of its healing powers but because it was warm.

She never did learn what they were to have for dinner. She heard Joshua in the mudroom, hanging up his coat and talking to her mother, but her eyes were too heavy to keep open. Curling back down into the bed her mother had made for her, Miriam slipped back into a deep, restful sleep.

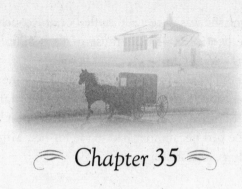

⌒ Chapter 35 ⌒

It had been the longest week of the school year for Grace, longer even than the week before Christmas.

She was worried about Miriam. Esther told her not to worry. Eli, Sadie's dad, told her not to worry.

Even her dad told her not to worry. He told her to pray for Miriam every night, and she did, but she still had a rock in her stomach. She couldn't stop thinking something terrible might be wrong, like when her *mamm* had been sick. She didn't say that out loud to anyone, but she thought about it almost all the time.

She thought about it when she did her lessons, and when she did her chores, and even when she played with Stormy. It seemed as though she couldn't stop thinking about it.

One night she thought about it so hard she started crying, like a baby. She tried to be quiet and cover her head with a pillow, but her dad must have heard. He was old, but he was still able to hear well.

"What's wrong in here?" he asked, sitting down on the edge of her bed.

"Miriam still wasn't at school today." She rubbed at her cheeks and tried to make the tears go away, but they kept running out of her eyes.

"Eli said she's better."

Grace nodded. He'd told her that too, but she wasn't sure she could believe him. Maybe he was just saying that, the same way everyone had told her things would be okay with her mother—only they weren't okay.

"Still worried?"

"*Ya.*" It came out all shaky and wobbly, like "yaahah," as she rubbed the back of her hand across her nose.

"Can I show you something?" Her dad had brought a lantern into her room, and now he stood up and turned the light up brighter. When she nodded, he walked to her dresser and picked up her Bible.

He sat down on her bed again and started fumbling through it. First he went forward, and then he went back, and then forward again. "Sometimes I have trouble finding a place," he admitted, smiling at her.

Finally he stopped in the book of Matthew and found chapter 10. Running his finger down the page, he came to the twenty-ninth verse. Grace sat up straighter, so she could follow along as he read aloud. The words were a little blurry because she was still crying some, but she rubbed her eyes again and tried to focus on the print.

"Are not two sparrows sold for a penny?"

She loved listening to her dad's voice—it was deep and rumbly and warm.

"Yet not one of them will fall to the ground outside your Father's care. And even the very hairs of your head," he paused, patted the top of her head with his hand. "And even the very hairs of your head are all numbered. So don't be afraid; you are worth more than many sparrows."

"Are we the sparrows?"

"I suppose so. In this case, yes."

Grace wanted to ask about her mother. Had she fallen to the ground? Had *Gotte* cared? But instead of asking, she put her hand in her dad's. She liked how it felt there. She liked how big and strong his hand felt around hers.

"I know you're worried about Miriam, Grace." He pulled in a

deep breath. "Maybe you're also thinking about your *mamm*. How she was sick and how she didn't get better. I wish I could explain that to you, but I can't. What I can tell you, what I can promise you, is that this isn't like that. Miriam only has the flu, and she already is better. In fact, we're going to see her tomorrow and—"

Before he could finish, Grace had climbed into his lap and thrown her arms around his neck.

She couldn't figure out how he'd known what she was afraid about, how he'd known she was thinking about her mother. After he hugged her back and then settled her down again under her warm quilt, she fell asleep wondering if her dad was the smartest man in the world.

As she sat in class the next day, watching the morning substitute, she still couldn't puzzle it out. Dads were funny that way. Sometimes you were sure they had no idea at all what was going on, like when you simply could not eat oatmeal one more time. Then other times they seemed a step ahead of you, like last night.

And the Bible verse he'd read, well, she'd written down that verse on a slip of paper as soon as she'd popped out of bed this morning. She'd carried it around in her pocket and sneaked a peek at it whenever she could, and now she had it memorized. It eased her worries when they tried to creep back inside.

Finally, Esther rang the bell that said they could put their things up for lunch.

Luke's mother, who had been substituting for Miriam all morning, gave Luke and Adam a severe look and they sulked off to the outhouse.

"They certainly act different when their *mamm* is here," Sadie said.

"*Ya*. They haven't thrown a wad of paper all morning. Could be they have the flu too."

"Or could be they're afraid of being punished." Sadie followed her outside. "How many different teachers does that make?"

"With your *dat* this afternoon, Grace, that will be eight." Hannah lined them up in the cold wind to use the outhouse.

"Your *dat*'s coming?" Sadie turned to smile at her friend.

"*Ya*. Bet the boys won't be throwing paper wads this afternoon, either."

They didn't, but they weren't quite as serious as they had been all morning. It had been a hard week with Miriam gone. Esther had done a good job, but Grace figured minding thirty-eight children couldn't be easy. Two had gone home sick, but that still left thirty-six.

The substitute teachers each looked fine when they walked in, and a bit overwhelmed when they left—usually in something of a hurry. Miriam and Esther always made it appear easy, but perhaps there was more to teaching than Grace had figured. So far they'd had two other dads who each substituted for one afternoon. The other mornings and afternoons had been filled in by three moms, including Luke's, and two grandmothers. The grandmothers seemed to fare best.

She'd figured out the tally of teachers with Sadie and Lily while they ate their lunches. What a crazy week!

As she watched her dad walk in and take a seat at the front of the room, she did her best not to giggle, but it was hard. He looked too large for the chair, and the book he picked up to read to them seemed small in his hands.

"Esther tells me you have story time after lunch, so I'm supposed to read where you left off here." Grace had seen him reading the book the night before, so he must have been studying. That idea made her smile. He pulled the marker from the book, but dropped it on the floor. When he bent to pick it up, he nearly toppled out of the chair. The entire class burst into laughter, including Gabe.

"It's hard to believe I was once very coordinated, even somewhat talented on a baseball field, isn't it? As you grow older, the chairs grow smaller." The laughter died down, and he studied the front of the book. "*Little House on the Praire* by Laura Ingalls Wilder. I'm sure you all know that Mrs. Wilder was born not too far from here, and maybe a few of you have been to Kansas, where this story takes place, or some of your family have."

One of the older boys in the back raised his hand.

Everyone, Grace included, turned to look at the boy and then back at Gabe. "I'd be interested to speak with you about that, maybe at our break this afternoon. I've been there myself, though I only passed through the area and wasn't able to stop. It looks different now than how it's described in these pages, but I can imagine what Laura, Pa, Ma, and Mary saw."

"And baby Carrie," Sadie said.

"Yes, and baby Carrie." Gabe smiled at her before glancing down at the book in his hands. "It seems you've read the part where they moved into the Indian Territory near Independence."

"Pa traded the horses for mustangs," Adam said. "I've never seen a mustang."

Gabe glanced over at Esther. "Maybe we could find a picture of one."

"*Gut* idea," she said.

"What was the name of those horses?" He searched through the pages the way he'd done with the Bible the night before.

"Pet and Patty," several of the younger students called out.

"Now I remember." Her dad smiled at them and then leaned back in the chair, his legs stretched out in front of him. "We're at the part where Mr. Edwards is helping Pa to build their house..."

The reading time passed so quickly that there were groans when Esther rang her bell, indicating it was time for afternoon lessons. Gabe did almost as well with the lessons as he did with the reading and only needed help with the geography once, but the health lessons had everyone laughing again. As he was correcting Lily's history worksheet by looking at the teacher's book, he'd thrown up his hands and admitted, "I've completely forgotten these things, and I bet you thought I was so old I lived during this time!"

When it came time to put up their books and clean the schoolroom, he actually looked relieved. Grace heard him confess to the older boys, "Cleaning I know how to do."

She loved school, and most Fridays she was sorry to see the week end, but when they walked out the schoolhouse door and headed to Miriam's buggy, Grace almost shouted with glee.

"*Gut* thing Eli gave me a ride in at lunch, or you would have had to drive Miriam's buggy, *ya?*"

"*Dat.* I'm too little to drive a buggy."

"You are?"

"I could drive a cart, though, if we had one."

"You could?" Gabe rubbed his chin as if he'd never thought of buying a cart or of teaching Grace to drive.

"*Dat.* You said maybe this year."

"I did?" He helped her up into the buggy.

"*Ya.* You did."

"I guess we'll see, then."

Grace glanced around at the buggy, surprised to find it looked just like theirs. She'd ridden in it before, on the Friday before Christmas, but she'd been so worried about the speech lesson she hadn't dared to look around.

Why had she thought it would be different? Did she think it would have the word "teacher" stamped inside it? Or maybe there would be a special shelf of books in the backseat? Glancing over into the back, she saw there was nothing different at all.

"Lose something?"

"No." Grace turned around and plopped down on the seat, happy to be riding home, happy to be going to see her teacher—finally, after a week of worrying and praying. "*Dat*, how are we going to get home from Miriam's?"

"I left our buggy there at lunch, and Eli gave me a ride in as he came back toward town in his buggy. Miriam was too sick to drive it herself when Eli took her home Wednesday morning." Gabe glanced at her. "You didn't think I was going to make you walk, did you?"

"Maybe."

"Well, it just so happens Abigail invited us to dinner, so it would be dark. I can't have you walking a mile in the dark."

A visit with her teacher and dinner with Abigail. Fridays didn't get any better.

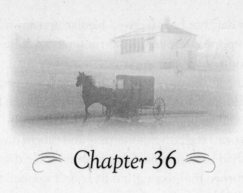

~ *Chapter 36* ~

It had been one thing for Gabe to read the Scripture from the Gospel of Matthew to Grace. It had been another thing entirely for him to stop the worries robbing his own sleep.

When he'd first heard from Eli how sick Miriam was, he'd wanted to run over the check on her. He'd resisted all of Tuesday when Eli had first told him Miriam was too ill to teach, and he'd even stayed away Wednesday morning when Eli had rushed her home to her parents—but only by tackling twice the normal amount of work he would hve attempted behind the old barn. Then Eli had driven up early Wednesday afternoon, pulled him aside, and told him that Miriam's fever was worse.

He had only waited until Eli's buggy had pulled away. Now, riding beside Grace in the afternoon sunlight, he ran his hand over his face, amused by the memory. Certainly he had looked foolish showing up on the Kings' doorstep. He hadn't even thought to have an excuse for coming. He'd simply ridden up and banged on the door, demanding to know if she was okay, if they had called the doctor, if she should be in the hospital.

Joshua had walked him to the barn and calmed him down. Actually, Joshua was the one who had reminded him of the Scripture from Matthew, the very words he'd read to Grace. He hadn't seen

Miriam that day, but he'd received regular updates from Eli, and Joshua had stopped by yesterday afternoon to ask if he could bring her buggy home.

Something in the man's eyes told him it was a ruse, but Gabe hadn't called him on it. Truth was, he wanted to see her for himself, so he'd said yes and thanked Joshua for coming by. When he'd dropped his own buggy off this morning and caught the ride in with Eli, Miriam had been standing at the window. She'd waved at him, and he'd returned the greeting, but he hadn't stopped to talk.

What would he say to her?

Their relationship was complicated.

He'd decided almost two weeks ago that he wouldn't pursue his feelings for her. He didn't even understand those feelings, but one thing he did know. She would be better off with Aden Schmucker. This week's illness only confirmed that in his mind. If she were living in a more liberal district, she wouldn't be walking outside to use the outhouse and as subject to the elements. Life was simply easier there, and she deserved a chance to live that way.

He hoped she'd had time to come to the same conclusion.

What was he thinking? She'd never said she had feelings for him.

His emotions and thoughts were jumping all over the place. He was worse than a boy on his *rumspringa*. Grace bounced on the seat next to him, pulling him out of his reverie.

"Maybe Abigail will let me help cook dinner."

"I let you help cook dinner." He tried to sound offended as they pulled into the Kings' lane.

"*Ya.*" Her voice croaked a little. That still happened once in a while. She cleared it and continued. "But mainly we heat up salted meat and warm the canned vegetables *mammi* Sarah and *mammi* Erma sent."

"Huh. You mean there's another kind of cooking?" He directed the horse to the barn, where Joshua was waiting for them.

Grace was immediately distracted by Pepper, which lasted about three minutes until she remembered she was there to see Miriam.

"She's resting in the living room, Grace." Joshua winked at Gabe and waited until Grace had skipped toward the house before he added, "For a minute there, she looked as worried as you did."

Gabe reddened but didn't rise to the bait. "I'll help you with the horse."

"*Danki.*"

They found another hour's worth of work to do—hoping to give the women enough time to finish their talking and also attempting to stay out of their way. Gabe was anxious to see Miriam for himself, but he figured he'd raised enough eyebrows storming his way up the porch on Wednesday. Obviously she was fine, because Esther said she would be back in the classroom on Monday.

Joshua had just opened the door to the mudroom when Grace's piercing scream split the afternoon's quietness, followed by a loud cry. Joshua sprinted into the kitchen before Gabe could stop him, before Gabe could push in front of him.

The cry ended abruptly, followed by an unnatural silence. The silence sent a shiver through Gabe's heart. It reminded him so much of that other time, the time he hadn't responded to her cries quickly enough, the time that had sent Hope's father into such a rage.

He hurried across the mudroom to gauge Joshua's reaction, but the man had stopped near the table, halfway through the kitchen. Gabe was right behind him. He barreled into the room and nearly ran into Joshua's back.

Grace was standing on a stool positioned beside the stove. She'd been stirring a pot. The spoon she'd been using lay on the floor. Dumplings trailed across the top of the stove and down on to the floor, and the smell of burned dough and chicken broth filled the air.

Abigail was next to Grace, trying to see her finger.

Miriam stood near, wrapped in two sweaters, her gaze worried and moving constantly from Grace to Joshua to Gabe.

But it was the expression on Grace's face which tore at Gabe's heart. He knew immediately, knew even before he'd crossed the kitchen in four long strides, what had happened and why there was a look of terror on his daughter's face. She cradled her finger, the one with a blister rising on it, in her other hand.

But her hands, both of her hands, were clasped over her mouth, as if they could hold her mouth shut and keep any more screams from escaping. As if her hands could silence her voice.

Her eyes were wide with fright as she stared at Miriam's father.

Gabe didn't say a word. He merely went to her and placed both of his hands gently on her shoulders. He'd seen her this way before. Mostly after Hope had died, while they were still staying with Erma and Micah. Once or twice even after they had moved to Cashton, when she'd wakened from a nightmare.

But Grace didn't seem to see him, or even Abigail, who was murmuring softly and trying to pry the blistered finger away. Grace's eyes were focused on Joshua, and the fear—the terror on her face—tore at Gabe's heart.

"Did you burn your finger, Gracie?" Joshua's voice was soft, low, and kind.

Grace nodded slightly, still not daring to move her hands away from her mouth.

Joshua moved forward slowly until he stopped just in front of her, and then he bent down so they were eye to eye.

"I bet that hurt."

Again the nod.

"I burned my finger last summer when I was clearing the fields by burning brush. It hurt so much I let out a holler that made birds take flight."

Grace's eyes widened even more in disbelief.

"I believe it helped some to holler that way. It let out some of the pain." He held out his right index finger to her. "I still have a small scar, but mostly it's healed."

Grace lowered her hands to touch the scar on his finger, which was large, old, and calloused. When she began to speak, the words and the tears came tumbling out at once. "I dropped...dropped the spoon and tried to pick...pick it up. When...when I did the stove was hot, like Ab-Abi-Abigail warned me."

She hiccuped as the tears tracked down her cheeks.

"Aloe vera is just the thing for that. Joshua, could you—"

"I know which plant it is. I'll go and fetch a leaf for you." He winked as he stood up and moved toward the windows on the kitchen's south side. Gabe hadn't noticed when he was there for Christmas, but the window ledges were filled with plants.

Before he could ask, Miriam said, "*Mamm* is something of an herbalist."

"Common sense, is all. Grace, come sit at the table and I'll show you how to do this, and then I'll send a cutting from the plant home with you. It would be *gut* to start your own plant in case your *dat* is as clumsy as Joshua. You'll need to learn how to care for him, and aloe vera has many uses."

As she proceeded to slice the leaf from the plant open and apply the gel to Grace's finger, Joshua and Gabe finished with the dinner preparations. Miriam tried to help, but they shooed her away.

"I'm practically well, you know."

"*Wunderbaar.* We like the practically well people to wait in the other room until we call them." Joshua handed Gabe the cornbread pan as he dished up the chicken and dumplings into bowls.

By the time they had placed everything on the table, Grace's finger was bandaged, and she was completely distracted by Abigail's knowledge of herbs.

Gabe was relieved the situation had calmed so quickly. He was relieved Grace's burn was minor. And he was especially relieved to see that Miriam was indeed on the mend.

However, he knew he had some explaining to do, and he knew he wouldn't leave the King house without doing it. Miriam sent him the occasional worried glance, punctuated by more than one long stare. Yes, he would be explaining to Grace's teacher what had happened earlier. Correction—he would be explaining to his *freind* what happened. He owed her that much.

The question was when.

And the answer came when Joshua took Grace to the barn to feed scraps to Pepper. Abigail insisted on taking care of the dishes alone. Gabe and Miriam were in the sitting room, playing a game of checkers next to the iron stove.

Miriam had taken two of his pieces. What he had left was cornered on his end of the board.

"Give it up," she said. "You can't win."

"What a terrible thing to tell your houseguest."

"I'm being honest with you."

"Ya, but I could—"

"No, that won't work. You tried it the last game."

"How about—"

"Uh-uh."

"Oh. Ya, you're right." Gabe tapped the table, hoping another idea would come to him.

"Stop staring at the board and explain to me what happened with Grace earlier."

He would rather endure losing another game of checkers again, but she wasn't going to be satisfied letting him suffer silently in defeat—so he pushed back from the board, looked across the table, and tried to think of how to begin.

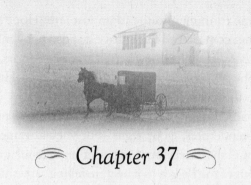

～ Chapter 37 ～

Miriam wanted to shake him.

He'd already wasted twenty minutes playing checkers and making small talk. He wasn't good at either. Soon Grace would be back and they wouldn't be able to speak openly.

"Gabe, she was terrified. Why?"

Scrubbing a hand over his face, he stared out at the inky night, as if he could find something there that would make the telling easier. Finally he turned and met her gaze.

"Her *mamm* died at her parents' home, and we were there—Grace and I." The memories came slowly, softly, but with a wealth of what he was feeling packed inside each word. "My *fraa* had been sick for many months. The night she passed, Grace woke from a dream, crying for her *mamm*. I had been by Hope's bed for two days. I..."

He looked again into the darkness and then down at the checker board. "I didn't want to be away at the end. Maybe it was my fault. Maybe I should have spent more time with our *dochder*. She was such a little thing, and she didn't understand..."

His words drifted off, but his eyes locked onto hers, sending a tremor through her heart.

"What happened, Gabe?"

"She came running into the room just after Hope passed. I...I didn't see her come in or I might have stopped her. I might have at least tried to explain. She threw herself at the bed and tried to crawl up on it. She was crying and screaming, and then Hope's father walked into the room. It was the dead of night."

There had been so much emotion in his voice as he described that night—tenderness, agony, regret—but when he came to this part of the story, Gabe's voice went flat, as if he were relating an event he'd read out of the *Budget*, as if he were telling something that had happened to someone else.

"I've replayed that moment in my mind many times. Though Micah was harsh, I believe he did only what was natural to him. He's a hard man, and he'd just lost his *dochder*. No doubt he was hurting, but he was merely—merely keeping it inside." The last four words were a whisper.

"He shouted at Grace to be silent. He told Erma to take her from the room. He said that he *would not have such a display in his home*." Gabe shook himself free of the memory and smiled weakly. "He was like the wrath of *Gotte* come down on that room."

Miriam pulled in a deep breath. "So that's why Grace was afraid tonight?"

"I suppose."

"She was afraid my *dat* would...shout at her for crying?"

"It was *gut* for her to see that not all *grossdaddis* respond so harshly to tears."

Miriam swallowed past the lump in her throat as she saw Grace and her *dat* walking from the barn to the house, holding the lantern between them. She knew the answer to her next question, but she had to ask it nonetheless.

"Gabe, is that why Grace didn't speak when she first came here?"

"*Ya*. Micah told her to be silent, so she was. She was silent for more than three years."

They went home soon after that. They were there long enough to share dessert and for Grace to play one game of checkers with Joshua. Gabe and Miriam's *mamm* talked about the meeting that was to take place after church on Sunday. There was to be discussion over whether to elect four from among them to go and speak to the *Englischers*.

If a group was elected, they wouldn't attempt to stop the building of Amish Abbey, but they would present their concerns about the project.

Gabe and the Kings were in agreement. All hoped the vote would be in favor of speaking with the *Englisch*, but Joshua wasn't optimistic. Word was that Bishop Beiler and Clemens Schmucker were against it—two of the strongest voices among their group.

Gabe and Grace both asked about Miriam's health again before they left, and she assured them she was fine. Actually, she had felt restless all day. She'd stayed home when Abigail had pointed out it would be difficult to teach with her frequent trips to the outhouse.

She didn't remind her mother that the outhouse issue was due to the herbal remedies. They had helped with her congestion, but there were...side effects.

"Will you be back to school on Monday?" Gabe asked.

"Definitely. If I stay here, I'll float away in *mamm*'s tea." She said it after her mom had hurried back inside to fetch the leftovers she was sending home with Gabe.

"I'm glad you're doing so much better. Grace was worried." He reached out and touched her arm. "We both were."

"*Danki.*" She felt warmth rise in her cheeks and knew it wasn't from the fever. She was grateful they were standing in the darkness of the front porch.

As she said good night and watched Chance trot off down the lane, pulling the Miller buggy into the darkness, she tried to straighten out the feelings tumbling around inside.

She'd accepted in the last few days that she cared for Gabe and for Grace. His story tonight of what had happened with Hope's dad had only strengthened those emotions.

Why did Gabe Miller confuse her so? She turned to head back into the house and nearly collided with her mother.

"Help me with the dishes?"

"Sure." Miriam was a little surprised, because she'd heard nothing from her mother since coming home except "Rest," "Stay in bed," and "Don't you have something to read?"

Standing at the sink and rinsing the dessert dishes, she was surprised to find that the warm water actually calmed the thoughts whirling around in her head.

"It was nice having Gabe and Grace over tonight."

"Yes, it was." Miriam's instincts went on instant alert. Abigail wasn't one for idle conversation.

"He's such a nice young man."

Uh-oh. They'd had this chat before, every time an unmarried man came within a field's length of their home.

"He is a nice man, but we're not going to have *that* conversation again, especially not *this* late in the evening. Are we?"

"What conversation do you mean, dear?"

"The one where you remind me I'll soon have gray hairs peeking out from under my prayer *kapp*?" Miriam smiled as she accepted a *kaffi* mug from her and placed it in the rinse water.

"I thought it might help you to talk about Gabe. You seemed... worried after your time alone with him in the sitting room."

Miriam wondered if what Gabe had told her was spoken in confidence but decided he wouldn't mind her parents knowing. It would probably help if it were to happen again when Grace was over, and as they were the Millers' closest neighbors, Grace would undoubtedly visit often. So she told the story of Hope's death, Grace's reaction, and how Micah had frightened the child into silence.

Abigail handed her the last dessert plate, released the plug on the water, dried her hands, and sat at the kitchen table, pulling her needlework toward her. "That certainly explains what happened tonight."

"And why she didn't speak when she came to school. Why she

didn't speak for *three* years. What a horrible thing for her own *gross-daddi* to do to her."

Abigail didn't answer. Instead, she peered at Miriam over her reading glasses and waited.

"The look? That's it? You're giving me the look?"

"Don't be quick to judge, Miriam. You're older and more mature than that."

"Abigail, is there any pie left?" Joshua called from the sitting room.

"I've already put it all up for the night." She wagged her sewing needle at Miriam. "Your *dat* doesn't need that pie. Have you noticed he's beginning to gain weight?"

"I heard that!"

"Hears well, but still—I believe he is gaining weight. I meant to have Doc Hanson check that."

"Or we could weigh me on the scale I keep in the barn."

"Back to Gabe and Grace," Miriam said, ignoring her father. "Surely you agree it was a terrible thing for her *grossdaddi* to do."

Abigail selected a different color thread and took her time fitting it through her needle. "We weren't there when it happened."

"But—"

"And we can't really know what occurred or how it occurred. Gabe was deep in his grief, no doubt."

"Still—"

"How many times have you corrected a child in the schoolroom, only to be told later that you hollered at them?"

"I hardly think this is the same thing."

Abigail stitched a row on the baby quilt she was piecing together—Miriam could see now that's what it was. Small ducks and rabbits took turns peeking out of the squares. She suddenly wished she had something for her hands to do, something rather than pick at loose threads on her sweater.

"You're probably right," Abigail admitted. "This is not the same. We don't know this man, Micah, so we shouldn't be judging him. That's my point."

After sewing for another moment, Abigail lowered her voice and continued. "Many Amish men suffer from depression. This is something we don't speak of, Miriam. Our life is hard, and we won't be complaining about that, but this Micah...what do we know of his life? What has he been through? After much suffering, perhaps, in the middle of the night his *dochder* dies and his *grossdochder* is screaming and he breaks. He snaps. He yells for her to stop. In his grief, he made a mistake—perhaps. It is not for us to judge."

Miriam nodded, slowly, as she continued to pull on the thread she'd succeeded in unraveling from her sweater. "Gabe said something similar. He said maybe Micah was hurting, but keeping it inside."

"Gabe seems mature."

Miriam stared down at her hands. "I thought *that* was what you wanted to talk to me about—Gabe."

"Is there anything to discuss?"

"I don't know. Maybe. Maybe not." Miriam stood and began moving things about the already clean kitchen.

"Maybe you want there to be?"

"It seems one moment we are growing closer and the next..." She picked up a dish towel and wiped off the clean counter.

"Yes?"

"The next moment he's talking about Aden Schmucker. Why?" She smacked the counter with the towel. "Can you tell me why he's so intent on pointing out what a respectable, successful person Aden is?"

Abigail smiled as she clipped her thread. "I might have noticed that he mentioned Aden a time or two."

"'Aden has a *gut* job in a buggy shop.'"

Abigail nodded.

"'Aden has purchased a nice small farm.'"

Abigail's eyebrows went up when Miriam dropped into the chair across from her.

"'Aden comes home to Cashton at least once a month to check on his parents—what a respectful thing to do.'"

Abigail actually laughed. It might have only been a chuckle, but it counted.

"Why? Can you explain Gabe Miller to me?"

"I can't. No more than I can explain your *dat*."

"I heard that too, and I'd still like another piece of pie."

Miriam put her head in her arms and began to consider sleeping there at the table. She heard Abigail stand, put up her sewing, and turn out the light.

When she felt her mother's hands on her shoulders, kneading her sore muscles, Miriam almost groaned with relief.

"Perhaps Gabe merely wants what is best for you."

"And that is Aden?" Miriam looked up at her *mamm*, feeling suddenly small and unsure of herself.

"I don't know." Abigail patted her arms as she smiled. "But it does sound as if he's trying to convince himself that Aden might be best."

Miriam kissed her hand.

"I like Gabe—a lot."

"I know you do."

"What if he's best?"

"Then we'll have to pray he figures that out." As she was leaving the kitchen, she added, "Be sure and mend that sweater where you dug a hole in it."

⌒ *Chapter 38* ⌒

New Year's Day. Grace had been on such an emotional seesaw that she'd forgotten all about New Year's Day! First there'd been the sheer joy of receiving her kitten, Stormy, on Christmas morning. After that she'd plunged into despair worrying over Miriam, worrying she might stay sick or even grow worse. When they'd had dinner on Friday evening, Grace had been happier than she'd been in ages—happier even than when her *dat* had handed her Stormy with the ribbon around his neck. Up and down her emotions had gone over the last week, exactly like the seesaw behind the schoolhouse.

All of which explained why she'd forgotten about the letter. Or maybe she'd just pushed it to the back of her mind, the way she sometimes pushed thoughts of her *grossdaddi* Micah. She remembered him in her prayers at night, and she wasn't mad at him. Her father had explained to her that her mother's father loved them all in his own way, but her memories of the man were bad, and she didn't want them in her mind.

The letter was a good thing, but it made her heart hurt a little, so maybe she had forgotten about it on purpose.

When she came to breakfast with her Sunday clothes on and her Bible in her hand, her *dat* was already sitting at the table.

"New month, Gracie. Time to turn the calendar page."

She'd skipped across the kitchen. She loved turning the calendar page. To her way of thinking, it was like opening up her sketchbook to a clean white piece of paper. A new month was filled with new days to spend with Sadie, new weekends at home with Stormy, and there was no telling what new things might happen around their farm, which seemed to be adding new members each week.

Only this morning there wasn't a new page to turn. Instead there was a new calendar on the kitchen counter, and she was supposed to place it on the hook on the wall. The calendar was filled with pictures of puppies and kittens. Her *dat* must have bought it at the store in Cashton while he was Christmas shopping.

She picked it up and slipped the hole at the top of the calendar over the hook on the wall.

January 1.

Letter day.

Her heart tripped a beat, and she almost dropped her Bible.

When she turned back to the table, she expected to see her mother sitting there, right beside her *dat*.

Of course she wasn't.

Her *dat* was alone, as always—his old mug clutched in one hand and the breakfast rolls Abigail had sent over on the table, warmed up already.

Sitting between them, though, was the letter.

She slid into the seat beside him, bowed her head, and they each silently prayed—or they were supposed to pray.

Not a single word came to mind.

Grace's mind was blank. She didn't know what to say to *Gotte*. What could she possibly hope was in that letter? She kept last year's in the little box where she put all of her special things. She read it, but not too often. She was afraid if she read it too often the words might lose some of their specialness.

"Want to eat first?"

Grace shook her head. She knew she wouldn't be able to swallow a single bite.

"Grace, do you remember why your *mamm* wrote you these letters?" Her *dat's* voice was low and gentle.

"*Ya.*"

When he didn't say anything else, she closed her eyes and swallowed. "*Mamm* wanted me to be able to hear her voice and her words. She wanted to leave me notes."

"That's right. And she wanted you to start each year—"

"With my heart full of her love." Grace wasn't sure if it was love she was feeling right at that moment. It sort of felt as though something else was twisting inside of her.

Gabe reached for the letter. His fingers traced the handwriting on the front of the envelope, and then he handed it to her. "Your *mamm* didn't realize how sick she was, or maybe we didn't want to admit it. She thought she had more time. This is the last letter."

He cleared his throat, but Grace didn't look up. She didn't want to know if he had tears in his eyes, because then she'd be crying and they would both be a puddling mess. "Do you want to be alone while you read it?"

"No, *dat.*" Grace scooted her chair closer. "She loved both of us. I'm sure she wanted us to read it together."

She carefully tore the seal on the envelope and pulled out the single sheet. Did she smell her mother when she opened the letter? Certainly she recognized the handwriting, even though she had to keep blinking back tears. She would recognize her *mamm*'s handwriting if she lived to be one hundred.

Dearest Gracie,

Another new year and you are eight years old now.

What a lovely girl you must be. It's

not possible for me to put on this single sheet of paper how proud I am of you.

You are the best thing Gotte has ever given to me.

I pray for you always, my dearest Grace.

Never doubt my love for you—it is strong like your dat's love for you, like Gotte's love for us.

Laughter, love, mercy, and grace—these are all gut things He has given us, Grace. I pray this year and all your years are filled with them.

With many hugs and kisses,
your mamm

Grace folded the sheet of paper, placed it carefully back into the envelope, and then she crawled into her *dat's* lap.

≈ Chapter 39 ≈

Gabe was more surprised than anyone when his name was mentioned in the vote on Sunday. He'd been well schooled in *gelassenheit*, so he didn't ask for it to be removed. To do so would have drawn attention to himself.

As he drove toward the meeting on Wednesday evening, it occurred to him that possibly Joshua or one of Miriam's brothers had mentioned that he had experience with situations similar to Amish Abbey while living in Indiana.

He was uncomfortable in a leadership role. He had been in his old life and would be here. That wasn't the point, though, as his parents had often reminded him. When he was baptized thirteen years ago, he'd promised to serve as a leader if ever elected to do so. At the time he'd envisioned that being as a bishop, minister, or deacon, and he hoped it would never happen. He truly didn't believe it would happen. He had enough trouble stumbling his way through each day, and God was his witness to that.

His father was fond of saying that many a man with the very same thought had been called to serve.

Gabe had only shaken his head and said, "*Ya, dat*. Let's agree *Gotte* knows what He's doing and leave it at that." The drawing of lots had happened twice in his old district, twice since he'd been baptized and married. The first time he was only twenty and his name wasn't mentioned. The second time he was in the midst of Hope's illness. Though his name had been whispered to the bishop by two members, he'd counted it a blessing that three votes were required to be included in the lot.

Pulling up in front of Bishop Beiler's home, he was grateful that this time he was only serving on a committee and not for life. The responsibility was still great but not overbearing. Maybe his dad had been right. Maybe God knew what was best.

Eli pulled up in his buggy as Gabe was securing his horse.

"*Gut* to see you, Gabe."

"*Ya*, it's been a long time."

"At least two hours." The older man slapped him on the back as they walked toward the bishop's front door.

Gabe hadn't been to Beiler's house yet, but he was impressed by it. Unlike Schmucker's, it was modest. Unlike his, it wasn't falling to pieces. Instead, it was well kept but unassuming, with acreage bordering on two sides. Woods shouldered up to the back of his property, but he could tell by the power lines that an *Englischer* was his neighbor in that direction.

"Beiler doesn't have much land?"

"No. He had to sell it off to pay taxes. He's doing better since he opened the buggy shop attached to the west side. He taught young Aden the trade. Now Beiler's sons tend to the fields, and he tends to the buggy work."

Gabe processed that as they climbed the two steps of the modest house.

"Where's Grace?" Eli asked.

"I took her to Abigail's. I believe she's learning to make apple pie tonight."

"Sounds like you're going to win out there."

"*Ya*. I think so too. I don't know what I'd do without Abigail and Joshua." The words were barely out of his mouth when they again heard the sounds of a horse and buggy. Miriam pulled up in front of the house, followed by Samuel Gingerich, one of the school board members.

Gabe hadn't had a lot of interaction with Samuel. He'd spoken with him a few times at church meetings—never at length. The man seemed to be sour, and his sentences tended to be short and declarative or long and heavy on Scripture. Gabe could read Scripture as well as the next person, so he didn't feel the need to have it recited to him. The short and declarative statements always left him feeling restless and that he should go and chop some wood.

Still, Samuel was one of the four elected, probably because he'd been on the school board so long. Miriam was also there to represent the school. Eli was there to stand for the community as a whole, and Gabe was there—well, he supposed he was there because he could offer an outside view.

Jacob Beiler opened the door and invited them all in, though there was no smile on his face. At least he didn't treat one man, or woman, different than another. He simply took life very seriously. It hadn't occurred to Gabe until he'd walked into the house that perhaps he had cause to do so. There was nothing there to indicate a woman's touch.

No shawl hung by the door. No sewing basket in the corner. No smell of fresh baked bread.

Was their bishop a widower like himself? Searching his memory, Gabe tried to remember if he'd met Beiler's wife. There were many woman and children at church meetings, and Gabe still hadn't sorted out who everyone was.

Why hadn't he thought to ask?

"*Danki* for coming," Beiler said. "I know you all are tired after a hard day's work, so we'll keep this brief."

No refreshments were offered, but at least he suggested they sit down at the table. For a moment Gabe had the idea they would be forced to speak standing near the front door.

"I asked you here because you will be representing our district to the *Englisch* in the matter of the hotel renovation. I spoke with the bishop of the western Pebble Creek district. For now they prefer to allow you four to represent both districts. I don't need to tell you it is not our policy to interfere, and we will not interfere in this matter. It is one thing to state our concerns. That is enough. That is more than enough."

Having expressed his opinion, he sat back and waited. Because Gabe had no idea what he was waiting for, he glanced across the table at Miriam, who looked to Eli, who scratched his beard and stared at the ceiling.

Samuel broke the silence. "I will speak plainly, Jacob. Myself, I would not have voted to form a group or to meet with the village board."

"But he's going to use the school. We'll become a stop on their tourist—"

"I heard your arguments on Sunday, Miriam." Samuel hushed her with a glare. "I was saying I would not have voted to form this group, but since we did..." He paused to study each person at the table. "Since we are going to meet with the village board, I consider it my responsibility to be sure we do *not* intervene. To be sure that *we do not conform to the pattern of this world, but be transformed by the renewing of our minds. Then we will be able to test and approve what God's will is—His good, pleasing, and perfect will.*"

Samuel's voice rose as he quoted the passage from Romans.

Gabe stared down at his hands, sure that if he glanced at Miriam he'd find her eyes laughing.

Jacob finally cleared his throat. "*Danki*, Samuel, for focusing us on the Scripture. I was going to suggest that someone make a short list."

"I would be happy to do that," Eli said. There was a small notepad and pen in the middle of the table, and Eli pulled them toward him.

"*Gut.* As Miriam pointed out, our members' main concern is the children. Although we will not be rude to visitors, we'd rather the school not be a regular stop on any guided tours. Their education is important, and it's best if that is not interrupted."

Samuel grunted as Eli made notes.

When he'd finished writing, Eli turned the pad where Miriam could read it. "Are you satisfied with the way that's worded, Miriam?"

"Ya. The children are my main concern."

"It will help to have you there," Jacob said. "In addition, I believe that because the village president is a woman, perhaps she will respond more favorably to you."

Gabe noticed Miriam didn't react to this, but she did meet his gaze, a smile tugging at her lips.

"The second concern among our members is about the name." Gabe noticed that Beiler, who had rarely shown any emotion, actually had a tic above his left eye. "If there is a way you can gently point out we have no affiliation to the Catholic church, that would be *gut*."

"Okay. No school tours, and we don't meet in an abbey for church." Eli was the only one having any fun at this meeting, but then Gabe had never known the man when he didn't see the humor in a situation.

Beiler's left eye twitched again. "The rest of the concerns expressed on Sunday can be summed up into one other category, I think."

He pulled out the sheet of paper which David, Miriam's brother, had given to Joshua—and Joshua had given to the bishop. The paper bore the marks of having been folded again and again. More than that, it had been passed from hand to hand until in places the letters were worn nearly off the sheet.

Gabe didn't doubt for a second that every person attending church three days ago had seen the marketing poster for the new facility, the one Jacob stared at now. The words "Amish Abbey" were typed in large letters across the top, and in the bottom right-hand corner was the contact information—funded by the CEO of Chester Entertainment, Mr. Byron Drake.

"This is no concern of ours," Jacob said slowly. "What the *Englischers* choose to do within their own business, inside their own building, is not our..."

Beiler's mistake was in searching for a word to express the degree to which they needed to remain separate from Chester Entertainment's doings.

While he ran his finger over the spot above his left eye, attempting to locate the phrase that would convince them of the gravity of this point, Eli doodled on his pad, Gabe and Miriam once again exchanged pointed glances, and Samuel saw his chance to jump in.

"It is not our place to be *yoked together with unbelievers. For what do righteousness and wickedness have in common? Or what fellowship can light have with darkness?*"

Gabe had to cover his mouth to keep from chuckling. No doubt Samuel meant well, but he sounded like a cantankerous old bull. Who was he to remind Jacob Beiler of the Scripture? No doubt the bishop quoted that very verse to the congregation several times each year. And how did such a grumpy old guy father the sweet little girl he saw playing with Grace and Sadie each Sunday?

Gabe decided to stare at Eli's writing, which was when he saw that he'd drawn lightning bolts in the margin of his notes.

Fortunately, Miriam started coughing, and that seemed to bring them all to their senses. "Excuse me. I believe I need a glass of water."

She stood and helped herself in the kitchen.

"Well," Jacob said. "My point was that some of these suggestions, as they relate to us, may be in poor taste." He pushed the paper to the middle of the table.

"Amish Acoustics, Amish Afghans," Gabe said, running his finger down the poster.

"What do you suppose an afghan is?" Miriam asked from the kitchen.

"I believe it's a blanket, like what you knit or crochet." Eli turned his page over to a fresh sheet.

"Then why not call it an Amish blanket?" Gabe asked.

"Apparently Mr. Drake is fond of alliteration." Miriam returned to the table with her glass of water.

When they all stared at her, she cocked her head to the side in disapproval. "Apparently English wasn't your favorite subject. Alliteration, as in—"

"Soon the sun's warmth makes them shed crystal shells, shattering and avalanching on the snow crust." Jacob's expression hadn't changed at all, but his eyes had softened, and Gabe saw him for a moment as he must have been.

Before what? Before life had rubbed off the soft edges. Before he'd learned to keep himself apart emotionally.

"Yes." Miriam actually clapped her hands. "That's right, and those are beautiful lines from Robert Frost's poem 'Birches.' He uses the S sound to give us the delightful sense of the snow melting and falling away. I'm afraid Mr. Drake hasn't been quite as successful with his A's."

"What is an Arcade?" Eli asked.

Surprisingly it was Samuel who answered, and not with Scripture this time. "I saw one at the bus stop in Madison. It's a room crammed full of game machines. There was lots of noise and shooting."

"Pretend shooting? The children were doing this?" Miriam took another drink from her glass.

"Ya. Even the little ones. Parents too. Booster seats for the youngest ones so they could see the screens. Terrible things."

Eli shook his head and dropped the pen on the table. "When they say Amish Arcade, you don't suppose Mr. Drake means to develop games with Amish people inside of them, do you?"

"We can't know." Jacob pressed his hands flat against the table. "You four will go to the meeting, listen, and present them with our first two points. The third point—Eli, you may write this down—can simply be that we are concerned about the presentation of our Amish lifestyle within his business."

Eli began to write, but stopped when Miriam stayed his hand.

"That's it?" she asked Jacob.

"Ya, and I doubt that will do any gut. He's there to make money, and he won't be caring if it hurts our feelings or not."

Gabe cleared his voice. He'd been silent for most of the meeting, but he sensed it was nearing the end and they were about to be dismissed. While he didn't relish stirring up a storm, he also felt the responsibility of having been chosen by the people of his church—the parents of Grace's friends.

That was what he'd thought on the most as he'd driven from home. His daughter would be growing up in this community. His neighbors and their children would be living in the midst of whatever was built. They had chosen him to *do* something, not to simply go with defeat as a foregone conclusion.

It was time for him to step forward and say something, even if it meant the disapproval of Samuel and Jacob. Gabe didn't do so lightly. Though Samuel was cantankerous, he was on the board where Grace attended school. He was influential in the community.

And Jacob was his spiritual leader for as long as he lived here in the Cashton district.

Gabe didn't see himself moving and uprooting Grace again.

So when he made his mind up to speak, it was no light decision. There was an important lesson he had learned from his daughter, though, and it was worth remembering.

He had learned that staying silent came with a price.

⌒ Chapter 40 ⌒

Miriam knew Gabe well enough to understand when he was struggling. No doubt he'd been trying to keep quiet, to let remain unspoken those things Samuel and Jacob would be reluctant to hear.

When he began to speak, she realized he was once again taking a step forward—as he did on Christmas afternoon before her family. The step forward this time appeared to be just as difficult. She now realized that the first day he walked into her classroom, holding on to Grace's hand, he must have been determined to remain apart.

So what had happened over the last two months?

He'd learned to tolerate the help of others—yes, but what else was at work here? Was he finally a part of their community? Was he committed to staying? What had changed his mind?

Miriam wanted that. She had even prayed for that. The thought that he might pack it all up and move back to Indiana had become one of her deepest fears.

When he first began to speak, it was as if he was finally letting his true feelings through. Instead of listening, she found herself watching the three other men at the table and their reaction to Gabe. Samuel continued to stare down at his hands, Eli leaned back and studied him, and Jacob leaned forward in interest.

"The businesses in Indiana—"

"We're in Wisconsin," Samuel pointed out.

Gabe glanced around the table and started again. "The businesses in Indiana found that it was beneficial if they worked with the Amish community rather than against it."

"We have no desire to yoke ourselves with the *Englischers*," Jacob reminded him.

"Yet as I've learned even in two short months, many of our families depend on side work to supplement their farming income. The *Englisch* tourism—especially one such as Mr. Drake's, could bring additional customers to our cottage businesses."

"How is that possible?" Jacob asked. "They won't be needing a barn built or wanting someone to shoe their horse."

Miriam knew Gabe had to move carefully now, because it seemed that their bishop was finally listening. And it wasn't only that she wanted him to win this argument—it wasn't their argument to win. It was that she truly did want what was best for their community.

"You're right there. *Ya*, they might not need a barn built, but they might need carpentry work done on a summer place. And though most don't own horses, they are interested in them. Many would like to take a ride in a buggy."

"This is ridiculous. So now we're supposed to use our farm animals to ferry around *Englischers*?" Samuel nearly spat out the words.

Gabe stared down at the table for a moment before responding. When he answered, his voice was calm and quiet, but sure. "If you fight this man, and if you turn the village board against you, then you're more likely to find yourself diapering your horses every time you're on a public road. Do you realize the cost of that?"

"*Gotte* will provide—"

"I know *Gotte* will provide, Samuel. He also gave us common sense and called us to be *gut* neighbors."

"Maybe it would help if you explained what happened in Indiana." Eli stood and stretched. "I think that's one of the reasons you were voted onto the board. The community wanted someone who had experience with the *Englischers*."

Miriam was curious too. Though she had never been farther than fifty miles from Cashton, she had heard that Indiana was quite different from Wisconsin.

"Much of Indiana is practically overrun with tourism, and a lot of that tourism has recently been focused on the Amish communities."

"Why do you think that is?" Jacob asked.

"Some say it's nostalgia. Others that it's disbelief...their world is now so different from ours. Many can't believe we're able to survive without technology."

"They could too if they ever had the need," Samuel said, staring down at his calloused hands again.

"And perhaps those are the questions they come seeking answers for. Questions about their own abilities. Whatever the reason, they come in droves."

"To stare? To mock us?" Jacob's frown deepened.

"Some of our community thought so at first. When it became clear that we could not win against the builders and developers, when our land prices started going so high that we could no longer buy any additional acreage for our sons..." Gabe shook his head. "We sent a group to several neighboring districts to speak with their leaders."

"What did they learn?"

"That many of the *Englischers* who come are *gut*, *Gotte*-fearing people looking for a place of respite, and they seek it among our community."

The room became quiet as they considered Gabe's words.

Miriam was the first to speak. "We have the occasional visitor, even now, in the schoolhouse. They are usually older, and they tell me how much our ways bring back memories of when they were a child, of how the schoolhouse reminds them of simpler times."

She cleared her throat, shaking her head and causing the strings on her prayer *kapp* to brush forward. "It's not that we mind visitors. Perhaps *Gotte* brings them into our life for a reason. It's only that we aren't sure we could handle so many."

Eli returned to his chair at the table. "So we have our list." He tapped it with his finger. "Are you suggesting anything in addition to this?"

Gabe sat back, crossed his arms, and rubbed his chin. "You're right. This isn't Indiana. You know the people of our district far better than I do. I'm only suggesting that perhaps we could point out to Mr. Drake how we could work together in a beneficial way, rather than him coming up with ideas like..."

He spun the paper around so he could read from it again. "Amish Astronomy or Amish Angels."

Frowning, Jacob rubbed his forehead. "You're not saying we offer to work in his hotel, his shops?"

"Nooo..." Gabe drew the word out. "Unless some of our young men and women on their *rumspringa* choose to. That's something that would have to be discussed with you, Bishop."

Miriam thought it was interesting that Gabe addressed Jacob by his title at that point. Jacob didn't seem to notice, but it was a nice show of respect. She adjusted her position in her chair and watched the others as if she were watching one of the *Englisch* theater presentations. It wasn't that they were acting, but Gabe knew how to read people better than she realized.

Did he also know how to read her? The idea caused her cheeks to warm.

Catching her staring at him, he winked.

"A matter for another time," Jacob decided.

"What else did you do in your old district?" Samuel asked.

"In Indiana, which *ya*, is decidedly more liberal, we started out by offering some of our goods that we made at home in the *Englisch* stores. At least then people had a chance to see honest Amish craftsmanship versus something made overseas that has been labeled Amish but has never seen the inside of a Plain workshop."

"Several of our young men could certainly use the income with their furniture and woodwork. David, Miriam's *bruder*, has even started making toys in the winters. Because his acreage is so small, there's not as much work." Eli folded his hands as if he were praying. "The women too. They make quilts and rugs, even knitted items, and you've allowed them to set out signs by the roads, Jacob. But not many people see them and stop, especially during the winter months when they could use the income most."

"It could be a *gut* compromise," Jacob admitted. "The buggy rides I will have to think on, but selling the goods in the store...this might make sense."

"We'd have to pay Drake a percentage," Gabe reminded him.

"*Ya*, but it would be worth it if we sold more." Eli stared down at the list, which still didn't have a number three. He tapped the sheet. "Could we offer to work with him to better portray Amish lifestyles and craftsmanship in his stores?"

"Possibly including offering some of our goods there," Miriam added.

Eli wrote quickly to add the words to the sheet, and then he glanced around the small group to be sure everyone was in agreement. When they all nodded—even Samuel—he tore the list from the pad and put it in his pocket.

It seemed to Miriam that Gabe hesitated, but then he pushed on with sharing what was on his mind. "Many *Englischers* have a genuine interest in the old ways. I read an article in the *Budget* my *mamm* sent me. Often they pay to bring schoolchildren on tours, or retired people. Some like to come out and see how the buggies are made. It could be *gut* for your work too, Jacob."

Standing and adjusting his suspenders, Jacob nodded. "You've set out your reasons well, Gabriel. What your bishop told me about you is true."

They had all stood and Samuel was already walking toward the door. Miriam noticed Gabe's head jerk up and around. Eli didn't. He was busy pushing in the chairs and making sure Jacob's dining room was back to the spotless condition it had been in when they arrived.

"And what was that, Jacob?"

"Don't be offended."

Now Samuel had turned back and was listening.

"It's my responsibility when a member of my district is as new as you are and they have been chosen to lead. I take that responsibility seriously. If one day you are chosen for the position of minister or deacon, then you will know what a weighty thing it is."

When Gabe nodded, he continued. "I considered this a matter worthy of a phone call to your old bishop. Ezekiel spoke highly of you. He also said that you put the needs of the community first. I'll count on you to continue to do so."

"*Ya*, of course I will."

"Very *gut*. Eli, be sure that you have the list with you when you attend the informational meeting with the village president and board of trustees in two weeks. I would ask you all to make this a matter of priority during your prayers. Samuel and Miriam, *danki* for coming."

Everyone murmured their goodbyes as they stepped out into the cold evening air.

Miriam wanted to ask Gabe what he was doing for Old Christmas. The January sixth celebration of Epiphany would include a large family feast and no school. She was about to speak to him about his plans, but then she heard him ask Eli what they could bring for the meal. Her heart sank, but she forced a smile when he turned toward her.

"I hope you have a *gut* Old Christmas, Miriam."

"You too, Gabe."

"Perhaps Aden will be home to see his *dat* again, *ya?*" he said as he helped her into her buggy. She thought about running over his foot with the buggy wheel. He was so determined to bring up Aden's name every time they were together. Maybe she could train him otherwise, the way her dad had trained Pepper not to chase on a hunt until he gave him leave to do so.

"You're smiling now, and you were frowning a second ago." Gabe stepped back so she could lower the flap and shut out the cold.

Instead of answering him, she changed the subject. "You know, Gabe, sometimes I don't understand men at all."

"Is that so?" He pulled at his beard as if he should give that some thought. "I suspect you're not the only one."

"But when I don't understand something, it makes me want to puzzle it out all the more."

Now he was the one frowning, and that did lighten her mood. "I'm headed back to the school now. Tell my *mamm* hello for me when you pick up Grace, would you?"

"*Ya*, of course I—"

But instead of waiting for his response, she dropped the flap, enclosing the buggy in darkness and a little warmth. Then she murmured to Belle, who trotted off at a pretty clip.

She didn't know what was going on with Gabe Miller or why he insisted on pushing her toward Aden Schmucker. She had decided one thing while watching him tonight, though. She was going to find out his reasons. And when Miriam set her mind to something, sooner or later it was done.

⤳ Chapter 41 ⤳

Grace didn't remember auctions from their old home, but she was sure they had them. Her dad described them to her as they drove toward Hannah's home. But it was as though he was describing something from one of her dreams. Some of it sounded familiar—or maybe she was confusing his memories with hers. Maybe she only remembered him talking about them.

None of that mattered.

Grace couldn't imagine a better weekend. The weather was cold but sunny, which was just what she'd prayed for. There was still a little snow on the ground, but not enough to mess things up.

"Remember not to stay outside. You'll have your nose frostbit."

"I won't."

"All the items will be in the barns or the house."

"*Ya*, you told me."

"Hannah's *dat* said there will be places to play in the barns as well—so there's no need to wander around outside."

She turned to stare at him. There was no threat of a blizzard. Was he worried she'd walk off and become lost in a crowd of people?

He shrugged and she went back to watching out the front of the buggy. There had been a forecast for rain earlier in the week, but it had changed two days ago. Her dad had said God had taken care of it, and she supposed he was right.

Yesterday they had spent Old Christmas at Eli's house. She'd had hours and hours to play with Sadie. Had there really been a time when she hadn't known her? As she sat forward in the buggy, peering out over the front of Chance's rump and looking for her best friend, it was hard to remember. Now she saw Sadie almost every day, and when she didn't she wrote her a note or drew her a picture.

"Lots of buggies," Gabe said.

"*Ya*, and cars too."

"Stay close to me so you won't get lost."

"*Dat*, I'm not a baby." Grace turned to give him the look and saw something painful pass over her dad's face. Maybe he had gas again. She scooted to the far side of the buggy.

"What, do I smell?"

"You got that look, like you might be about to do something."

"Oh, I did, did I?"

His hand crawled across the seat, and Grace let out a squeal as she tried to move farther away. He hadn't tried to tickle her in ages. Why was he acting so strange all of a sudden?

As he pulled Chance to a stop, she glanced back out over the crowd and saw Sadie's dad standing beside his buggy. "They're here. They're here."

"*Ya*. I told you they would be."

"There are so many people. Even more than when we have church."

"That's *gut*. More people means we'll raise more money for Laura Kiems. If you see her, you remember to tell her that we're praying for her and that you made a cherry pie to be auctioned. Abigail said you did a fine job on it."

Grace nodded as she hopped out of the buggy. She hoped the auction raised a lot of money to help Preacher Kiems' mother. She had something called heart disease. Miriam had explained to the class last week what that was—how your heart could get tired and not work so well.

Grace waited for her dad to hand her the cherry pie from the box in the back of the buggy. She'd asked him if his heart was old, if he'd need a benefit auction. He'd promised her it wasn't and that he still had a lot of years left. But she still put her head to his chest to listen to his heart beat whenever he hugged her good night. There was nothing wrong with checking.

She'd told that to Hannah, and Hannah said some things you have to trust to God. That was a little hard to do, especially given their past.

Grace still didn't understand what had happened to her mom or why God had let that happen. But then, on the other hand, she could have died in the snow cave, and she didn't. God was hard to figure out, let alone trust, but she was trying.

Sadie met her halfway between their buggies. "I made cookies. What did you make?"

Sadie had worn her dark blue dress and black apron, of course. Grace could just make it out underneath her coat. They always wore their black aprons. They giggled about being older and wearing a white one, but Grace wasn't in any hurry to be older. Grace looked down at her clothes, identical to Sadie's, and smiled. She liked it when they dressed the same.

"I made cherry pie. It's the first time I didn't burn the crust."

"Let's take them to the tables together."

"Do you girls want me to go with you?" Her dad had caught up with them.

They turned around and stared at him, and then they both shook their heads. Gabe had that look on his face again. Grace was just sure he had a stomachache. Maybe his breakfast had been bad. He tried to smile, though. "All right. Be careful, and I'll see you at lunch."

"That was weird," Grace said.

"My *dat* did the same thing."

"Honest?"

"*Ya.* He even offered to carry the cookies for me."

That started them giggling, and they had to walk closer together through the cold sunshine so they wouldn't drop their auction items.

Once they had dropped off their baked goods in the kitchen, they headed out to the livestock barn to look at the animals that were being auctioned. As they were headed out of the house and toward the pens, they passed the preacher's mom.

"Uh-oh," Sadie whispered. "We could skirt around."

"Can't. *Dat* told me I had to stop and talk to her. And she's seen us."

"Come here, you two, and let me have a look at you." Laura Kiems reached out a bony hand, and Grace almost stepped back, but she didn't because she saw the lonely look on the old woman's face. So instead she allowed herself to be pulled closer. "Now, Sadie, it seems you grow more every time I see you."

"My *mamm* says the same thing."

"And Grace. You look just like my *dochder* described you. She told me all about your going up front in the church service with your *dat.* I wasn't there to see it on account of..." she pulled in a deep breath and rested a second. "On account of my heart."

"We brought baked goods," Grace said.

"That's *gut. Danki.*" Laura patted Grace with one hand and reached for Sadie with her other.

Though her fingers were awfully thin, they didn't feel as scary as Grace thought they might. They actually felt soft, like Stanley. She imagined you had to be real careful with someone as old as the preacher's mom so she wouldn't break. Looking down at Laura's hands, she saw they were thin and bony, and she could even see the veins, same as she could with her mouse. Which is why she would never let Stanley out around Stormy. That kitten just played too rough.

"One day, before you know it, you will be wanting to catch a boy's heart. I don't mean the one that beats inside. I mean the one that flutters when you see someone special." Laura pulled in another shaky breath. "Baking helps in the area with boys and men."

Grace glanced at Sadie, and they both began to giggle.

"Go on now. I saw that you were headed toward the auction animals. Go and see how they look."

They started to skip away, but then Grace remembered the lonely look.

"Wait for me," she whispered to Sadie. Running back to the preacher's mom, she hugged her gently, as softly as she would hug Stanley if he were big enough to get her arms around. "We'll be praying for you every night."

Without waiting for an answer, she was gone.

They went over to the barn and watched the animals for a while. There were two bulls, several cows, and even a couple of horses. Someone had donated some pigs, and a donkey stood in a stall at the very end of the barn. He came to the door that was half open, and the girls found a crate to stand on so they could bend over and touch his nose.

"I'd love to have a donkey," Grace admitted.

"Ask your *dat*."

"I don't think we could afford it. Not right now, anyway."

After they had looked at the animals, they decided to go and check out the other auction items. The second barn wasn't as big as the first, but it smelled better. Long tables were set up in it, like the ones they used for dinner at church meetings. On the first row of tables were baskets of every size and shape. They had sheets of paper beside them where people wrote down the price they were willing to pay. Every hour someone picked up the sheet and called out who the winner was.

The same was true for the hand-stitched pot holders and table runners. Once the persons picked up the items they had bid on, new items were put out and it started all over again.

The most amazing thing in the second barn was the clothesline strung down one aisle. When they came to it, Grace stepped closer to Sadie and linked her fingers with her. "I've never seen so many quilts on a line before."

"*Ya*. I heard my *mamm* say they are the reason the *Englischers* are here. They could bring in more money than the animals."

"These are amazing. Can we walk through them?"

"Sure. We just have to be careful not to touch. We wouldn't want to dirty them."

Grace counted a dozen in all. Each had a number clipped next to it, but no sheet of paper.

"They will be auctioned before the noon meal," Hannah explained as she walked up behind them.

The girls turned around and each gave her a giant hug.

"I remember *mammi* Sarah quilting like this," Grace said. "*Mammi* Erma did too, but I don't think I could ever do it."

"Of course you can, Grace. It's just a matter of practice." Hannah walked the girls to one of the quilts at the end of the line and showed them a mistake in the stitching on the border.

"How did you find that?" Sadie asked. "I would never have seen it."

"My *mamm* and I made this one. Those were my stitches when we began. I wanted to pull them out, but she wouldn't let me. She said imperfections are important too, and that I'd be able to see how much I'd improved if I left them."

Grace heard Hannah's words. She even understood what she'd said, though she'd have to talk to her *dat* about the imperfection thing. There was one thing she knew for certain. She was going to have to ask Abigail about giving her quilting lessons.

Cooking was great and all, but you did the work and then someone ate it. What did you have to show for the hours in the kitchen?

Quilting, now there was something that would last.

"I'd best go help with the baskets. You girls have fun."

Sadie and Grace watched her leave and then turned round in a circle.

"I guess we've seen it all," Sadie said. "What do you want to do now?"

"Where are the boys?" Grace asked. "I haven't seen any of them from school, but I've seen most of the girls."

"They're in the old barn playing ball."

"Hannah has three barns?"

"*Ya*, but the old one, it has a hole in the roof. Wanna go watch the ball game?"

"Okay. But I'd like to be back in time to see who gets the donkey." Still holding hands, they swung their arms as they hurried out of the barn with crafts and across a small pasture to a crumbling structure. It reminded Grace of their barn before the men had come and helped her dad fix it up and make it better. It reminded Grace of some of the pictures she'd drawn when they had first come to Wisconsin, pictures she'd labeled *Sad Barn* and *Droopy House*—only the barn didn't look sad anymore, and the house now felt like home.

"We'll be able to hear the auctioneers. Don't worry. They talk fast and very loud. They use some kind of microphone-thing that makes me want to cover my ears."

"Who's the auctioneer?"

"There are several, but my *dat* is one." Sadie started laughing again, and then Grace started laughing. They were both laughing as they walked around the corner of the old barn, which is probably why they didn't hear the hollering at first.

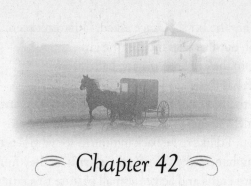

~ Chapter 42 ~

Miriam tried to control her temper as she stared at Aden Schmucker.

His face had turned as red as honey crisp apples in the fall, so there was no doubt she'd heard him correctly.

"Why would your father be discussing me?"

"I'm sure he—"

"Tell me why your *dat* would be discussing my personal life!"

"I wasn't there, Miriam."

"You weren't there. Yet you're certain I was the subject of conversation. That my personal life was the subject of conversation not once, but twice!"

"If you look at it that way, I suppose—yes, you're correct."

Miriam wanted to scream. She wanted to pick up something, anything, and chuck it at him. Unfortunately, at that very moment she saw the edge of two black *kapps* peek around the corner of the barn and then draw back.

Stepping closer to Aden, she whispered fiercely, "Don't move."

Then she stormed around the corner of the barn. Sadie and Grace were standing with their backs against the old barn wall, their eyes as wide as half dollars.

"Girls."

They both nodded in greeting but didn't say a word.

"Awfully cold morning."

"*Ya*," Grace said.

"It is," Sadie offered.

They stared at her as if she were wearing three *kapps* instead of one. It wasn't as though they had never heard her raise her voice before. She'd shouted only a few days ago when she'd opened the janitor's closet and a family—an entire family—of mice had run out toward her.

"Why don't you both go on inside the barn? I expect you're looking for the other *kinner*."

"*Ya*, we were." Sadie scooted past her, holding fast to Grace's hand.

Grace looked back once and then disappeared into the barn.

Miriam pulled in a deep breath, resolved to count to ten and made it to three, and she then turned back around and stormed toward Aden.

"All right. I asked you about this because Gabe has been acting a bit strange around me. If I had the time, and if I didn't have a pounding headache at this moment—"

Aden stepped toward her, but she held up her hand and stopped any forward progress. "I would go and find him and perhaps your *dat* also and we could straighten this out. But because I'm scheduled to help with the luncheon, there's no time for that."

"I can see you're upset, Miriam, but *dat* meant no harm by it." Aden stepped back when she didn't speak. He was a clean shaven, nice-looking young man, but she was having trouble letting go of her anger in this situation. "When I came home yesterday, he said that perhaps I should ask again if you'd like to go to the singing with me next week. That I should catch a ride home again if you would."

"And you said—"

"That you'd turned me down before, and I didn't expect a different answer."

Miriam felt a small twinge of sympathy, but she squashed it. "And he said—"

"That this time might be different, seeing as he'd had a talk with Gabriel."

Miriam paced back and forth in front of the barn. Her toes were nearly numb and she could see that Aden was miserable. Usually confident, he was out of his element with this conversation, but that was too bad.

How dare they talk about her this way! And to think Clemens Schmucker had told Gabe—

"You're *sure* your *dat* told him I wouldn't consider courting a relative of a student?"

Aden took off his hat and rubbed at the back of his head.

"Say it, Aden. We're going to freeze out here and there's nowhere else for privacy."

"It's only that it's not just my *dat* who has heard you say such things. You *have* said such things, Miriam. You've said it to several men in the district. It's common knowledge."

She glared at him a moment and then turned to stare out over the fallow fields. "I may have, but a woman has the right to change her mind, especially when..."

"When you've had a change of heart? Is that what you were about to say?" Aden's voice was low and solemn.

She knew he deserved an answer, but she didn't turn back to him. She didn't need to because she could tell he'd walked up behind her. Instead of answering, she asked another question of her own. "Tell me the truth, Aden. Did you move away so I would consider courting you?"

"Partially, yes. But there was more. My *dat* has a heavy hand in his dealings. I never had a *rumspringa*, and I've had no urge to try *Englisch* things, but there is a different Amish way, Miriam. Life does not have to be as hard as it is here. Just a few miles to the north and east, where I'm working, is a district that is more liberal."

"And is liberal always better?" She turned now and looked him full in the face.

"Is it always worse?"

"I don't know."

It seemed they had nothing else to say, but as they began to walk back toward the house where she would help prepare the luncheon, she reached out and touched his arm.

"I apologize if I've hurt your feelings in any way, Aden."

He smiled then, and she saw the boy she had played baseball with behind the very schoolhouse where she now taught. "I bounce back easily."

"I would appreciate it if conversations *about* me *included* me."

"*Ya,* that seems fair."

Gabe had been trying to have a private word with Miriam all day. It was almost as if she was avoiding him, which was ridiculous. There was no reason for her to do so.

The benefit for Laura Kiems seemed to have gone very well. Her medical expenses for the heart surgery would be high, but Gabe had heard Eli say they had raised more than half of what she would be required to have not just for the surgery, but also for the medicines and recovery. The other half had already been set back, so her immediate needs were taken care of.

The same had been true when Hope was sick. It had been a huge burden off his shoulders, not to worry about the financial end of things. It did his heart good to see this community pull together in the same way. Many things were different between Indiana Amish and Wisconsin Amish, but much was the same.

Grace was nearly out of breath as she ran up to his side, conspicuously alone. No Sadie? They had been together every time he'd seen his daughter since they had arrived.

"Miriam and some man were having a fight earlier," Grace whispered as they made their way toward the animal barn.

"What's that?" Gabe forced his voice to remain neutral.

"A fight. She was hollering at him."

"Grace, were you listening in on someone else's conversation?"

"Nope. We didn't hear nothing."

"Anything."

"Huh?"

"You didn't hear anything."

"We didn't. How did you know that?"

Gabe sighed. "Why are you telling me this, sweetie?"

"Because I thought she looked sad or maybe mad. I'm worried about her."

"Your teacher's a big girl. I think she'll be all right." Gabe wanted to ask whom Miriam was fighting with, but he didn't know how to ask without sending Grace the wrong message.

"That was him. That man there."

At least she didn't point at Aden Schmucker as he walked ahead of them into the barn. Tugging on Gabe's hand, she instantly changed the subject. "All of the animals are gone, *dat*. All except one. Sadie saved a place for me up front. They are about to auction the donkey."

"Let's go watch, then," he said, following her inside. "Should be fun."

"Can we bid? Please?"

"The last thing we need is a donkey."

"He's so soft and sweet."

"Do you remember your *grossdaddi*'s donkey? That animal was nothing but trouble."

"And his name is Gus."

"I'm not doing it, Grace Ann. We can't afford another animal, and I probably wouldn't buy it if we could."

"But *dat—*"

As they approached the auction area, Gabe saw several things at once. Joshua King was standing behind the auctioneer stand. Miriam and Esther were standing to the right of the stand. The donkey was to the left, and holding the lead rope was young John Stutzman. Still in eighth grade, the boy was all arms and legs.

What caught his attention, though, other than Miriam, were the ten stacks of wood spaced out and set in front of the auctioneer's podium. Next to each block of wood was an ax.

"I'd take care of Gus," Grace added. "I would see to his feeding."

Gabe pushed through the crowd until he stood beside Eli, who turned and grinned at him.

"The entry fee is twenty dollars, folks," Joshua called from the auctioneer's stand. "This is the last event of the day. The last chance to contribute to the benefit and work off some of the desserts you ate."

Good-natured laughter mixed with the chatter.

Eli opened his wallet, pulled out a twenty, walked forward, and dropped it in a black hat that had been turned over for receiving entry fees. Then he walked to a block of wood and picked up the ax.

"We have our first competitor. Are you young men going to let Eli have it?"

Again laughter.

"I'd even clean out his stall," Grace said, tugging on his arm.

"Remember, not only will the winner take home this lovely donkey donated by Clemens Schmucker—"

"I promise." Grace moved in front of him and put her hands on his suspenders.

"You'll also win dinner at the schoolhouse, cooked by my *dochder*, Miriam, and Esther Schrocks."

"Please..."

Aden stepped forward and dropped money in the hat, and then he picked the spot next to Eli.

"What's wrong, Grace?" Sadie asked.

"I want that donkey, and my *dat* won't even look at him."

Four other men stepped forward, followed by two gentlemen Eli's age. Now there were two spots left.

"Not to mention, you'll be providing the schoolhouse with enough chopped wood to see the children through the winter." Again, laughter rippled through the crowd.

"Why did your *dat* say you can't have the donkey?" Sadie asked.

"He hates them."

"Oh."

Gabe heard Grace and Sadie discuss the donkey. He heard Joshua explain the competition. Neither affected him much.

Then Miriam turned and glanced at him. She had been speaking to Esther, but when she turned, found him in the crowd, and smiled, Gabe groaned. He was sunk. Those gray eyes could ask him to plant a field of roses instead of hay, and he would do it.

"So he doesn't like donkeys. I don't like vegetables much, but I eat them," Grace said.

"*Ya*, and I don't like baths in winter, either. I wonder if donkeys need baths." Sadie hopped so she could get a better look of what was happening up front.

Gabe only had eyes for Miriam.

Another contestant walked to the front, or rather was pushed there by his family.

Gabe reached for his wallet, pulled out a twenty, and put it in Grace's hand. "Go place that in the hat for me."

Kissing her on top of the head, he reached the last open spot, the spot next to Aden Schmucker, as Joshua turned back toward the microphone. "Looks like we're ready to begin, folks. Ten fine men and two hundred dollars for Laura Kiem's medical fund. Feel free to add some to the hat if you haven't contributed today because you're about to see some wonderful entertainment."

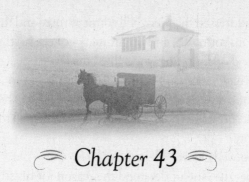

≈ Chapter 43 ≈

M iriam watched Gabe walk to the front of the room and pick up the ax.

What had just happened?

She'd been talking to Esther, and when she'd turned back toward the people in the barn, he'd been staring at her. And not just at her, but into her. The look he'd given her had nearly pulled the breath out of her chest.

Then he'd handed Grace his entry money and walked up to the last open spot.

"Whom should we root for?" Esther teased.

"Hush."

"I'm just saying that if you have a favorite, I could whisper a quick prayer."

Miriam gave her assistant teacher the most withering scowl she had, but Esther only smiled and nodded back toward the men.

"Bishop Beiler," Joshua said, "you helped me count the wood in each stack. Is that correct?"

"*Ya.* Correct." Beiler didn't seem completely at ease with the competition they were having. Miriam supposed he was allowing it because it was for a good cause. Surely there was no harm in splitting wood. It wasn't as if the winner would receive a ribbon.

Joshua addressed the men. "I'll count to three and then you may begin. Pick up your axes, and on my mark—one, two, three!"

The sound of chopping wood filled the air.

Miriam had watched her father and her brothers chop wood hundreds of times. Never before had it caused her heart to race. Never had it caused her palms to sweat so that she had to wipe them on her apron.

Esther moved closer, "He's ahead by two."

Was it because she understood the reason for his strange behavior now? And did that change anything between them?

"Aden's catching up."

"I can see, Esther."

Esther was clutching her arm, and Miriam suspected she'd find bruise marks there in the morning. Somehow she didn't mind. It helped to have her friend so close.

The men were all breathing heavily now and wood chips were flying. They were down to their last few logs. Aden reached for his next to the last piece, dropped it, and had to bend for it again.

Gabe glanced at Aden once, realizing now that the two of them were ahead. He grabbed his last piece of wood, set it on the block, and put the ax through it in one smooth stroke.

Applause and laughter filled the room.

Gabe turned, but instead of looking to Joshua, he again found Miriam. This time his gaze left her confused. Before she could think what he meant by it, he'd turned back to Aden, who was congratulating him on giving him a solid run for the prize.

And what was the prize? Had Gabe entered because of the donkey?

Gabe stepped closer and said something to Aden that no one else could hear. Aden glanced toward the back door and nodded once.

Suddenly, Grace ran into the picture. She greeted her dad, jumping up and down, and she hugged Sadie, whom she'd brought with her. Miriam had last seen the girls before lunch when they had interrupted her conversation with Aden outside the barn.

Her conversation with Aden—

Gabe glanced at her once more. It seemed his eyes lingered on hers, sending a trail of goose bumps down her arms. Then he reached down for Grace's hand, and together they went to collect their winnings.

Had Grace told Gabe what she'd heard? What had she heard?

Miriam thought to go and ask Gabe. It certainly was past time to straighten this out while they had the chance, but then the crowd came between them. Esther and Joshua began talking at once. When she looked for them again, Gabe and Grace were gone.

Gabe walked up to the schoolhouse on Thursday evening more than a little self-conscious in his Sunday clothes. What do you wear when both teachers are cooking you dinner?

He'd received a note in Grace's lunch box. Yes, he checked it every night now. The note asked him if Thursday would be agreeable to collect on his prize for winning the woodchopping contest and suggested he take Grace to stay with Abigail.

Interesting. Adults only?

Because he'd already picked up the donkey he'd won, he figured he might as well get this over with. No doubt it would be awkward for all of them, but he couldn't think of any way out of it.

What had he been thinking?

He hadn't been. He'd seen Aden walk up to the block, he'd remembered Grace say that Miriam and Aden had been fighting, and he'd simply reacted. That was usually not a good thing where he was concerned.

And, yes, he'd spoken with Aden afterward, but only for a moment. Aden had been in a hurry to catch his ride back to his district. The conversation had cleared up one thing and muddied another.

"Gabe, perfect timing." Esther opened the door of the schoolhouse for him.

He stepped inside and was surprised to see they had moved things around some. Several of the desks were pushed out of the way and Miriam's desk was covered with a dining cloth. It had also been pulled closer to the stove near the front of the room. Two chairs were positioned on opposite sides. Only two?

"*Danki* for having me."

"You won fair and square. We were happy to do our part to help in the benefit." Esther's eyes practically danced as she motioned him to the front of the room. "Miriam has been cooking since the *kinner* left. I'll go and see if there's anything I can do to help."

She vanished up the stairs before Gabe could ask any questions.

He stood by the chair but didn't sit. Glancing around the room, he noticed the students' drawings fastened to some string that bordered one wall. It was easy enough to pick out Grace's. The children's abilities varied from a crude drawing, as he would do, to the most detailed and sophisticated—his daughter's.

Had her drawing grown out of her time of silence? Or was it a gift from God?

"Grace is a talented artist," Miriam said, walking up behind him.

"I didn't hear you come downstairs." He turned, not realizing how close she was, and found himself inches from those beautiful eyes. Something inside of him twisted, and he admitted to himself, maybe for the first time, that he might be ready to move on with his life.

Would Hope want him to do that?

They had talked of it, at the end, but they hadn't talked of when. They hadn't talked of how.

A fist closed around his throat. He shook his head and turned back to the drawing.

"She is," Miriam insisted, misunderstanding his reaction. "I've seen many students come through this room with many different talents. Grace's gift is in the way she sees things and then her ability to translate that to pencil on paper."

"*Danki.*"

"It wasn't a compliment, Gabe. It was my opinion." She had put a hand on his arm while she was talking, but now she pulled it back and motioned toward the desk. "Shall we sit?"

"*Ya*. I'm starving."

Her laugh surprised him. He put a hand to his hair to check that it wasn't sticking up from where his hat had been. It certainly wouldn't be the first time his appearance had made someone laugh.

"I'm not laughing at you," Miriam assured him. "It was something else—"

"Go on." He pulled out her chair for her before walking around the desk and sitting down.

"When you said you were starving, it reminded me of something my *mamm* is fond of saying." She blushed but continued. "'No woman can be happy with less than seven to cook for.'"

"I've heard that one too."

"I suspect your Hope enjoyed cooking for you. It seems you always have a healthy appetite."

Gabe took a long drink from his glass of water, allowing himself time to think how best to answer. "*Ya*. She used to say we'd have to watch my waistline, that by the time I became a *grossdaddi* I would be needing sturdy suspenders."

Miriam fiddled with her silverware, her eyes everywhere but on him.

"I think maybe Hope was like Abigail," Gabe added. "Like your *mamm*, she wanted her dinner table to be full. She wanted a big family with lots of sons."

"Is that what you wanted?" Now she was looking directly at him.

"*Ya*, I suppose so. But boys or girls made no difference to me." He shifted in the chair. "Now, after Grace, I think anything will be easy, though I've heard twins are hard."

Miriam's eyebrows shot up. She started to speak, but then she stopped herself, so Gabe helped her.

"I'm not that old, Miriam. I do still think about having other children. It's what Hope would have wanted. And she would want Grace to have a *mamm*."

At that interesting moment Esther brought them dinner and then excused herself, claiming she'd already eaten. They bowed their heads for a moment of silent prayer and then started in on the meal of chicken casserole, salad, and fresh bread.

Gabe thought about ignoring the look on Miriam's face, but then he decided it was best to put their concerns on the table. "You look worried over there."

She set her fork down. "So you have considered marrying again?"

When he didn't answer right away, she continued. "I don't mean to be bold..."

"It's all right, Miriam. We're *freinden*."

She had been staring out the window but glanced at him sharply at the word *freinden*. "It's only that you've told me three years have passed since Hope's death."

"*Ya.*"

"Most men would have already remarried."

"Perhaps."

"And some men don't remarry at all—like Bishop Beiler."

Gabe nodded as he finished the casserole and reached for another piece of bread. It had occurred to him that he didn't wish to arrive at old age alone and stern as it seemed Jacob Beiler was. He wanted a woman in his life. He wanted the love and the laughter a wife brought. And he wanted more children.

"Perhaps it took me longer to feel that Grace and I were ready to move on, or perhaps..." he set his empty plate aside and folded his arms on the desk, leaning forward a bit so he could study her eyes, her expression...everything about her. "Perhaps I was waiting to meet the right person."

The color came into her cheeks slowly and her eyes widened, but she never took her gaze from his.

"And now you have?"

"Possibly."

Esther interrupted them with dessert—shoofly pie.

"My favorite. Are you sure you won't join us?" Gabe asked as he accepted the coffee she also offered.

"Oh, no. *Danki*, but I had some earlier. I couldn't resist. Right now I'm grading papers. I can't believe there are so many of them."

"It seems wrong to let you wait on us."

"No. That's my part of the prize." She smiled at Miriam. "I didn't do any of the cooking."

"You cooked all of this, Miriam?"

Miriam nodded and pushed her fork through her pie.

"It's excellent."

He thought he saw Esther wink at Miriam as she scooted away. Could be this was a setup, but he wasn't sure. There was one thing he was sure about, one thing he needed to make clear, and it had been weighing on his heart since his talk with Aden.

"Miriam, I spoke to Aden."

Her fork clattered onto her plate. "About?"

"It wasn't about you. He wouldn't say a word about you, not that I didn't try." Why a smile spread over her face, he wasn't sure. "The man clammed up like he had the toothache. But he did talk to me about the Amish community he works in, and I have to say—it sounds closer to the type of community we had in Indiana."

"Are you thinking of moving?"

"Me? No. I don't want to uproot Grace again."

"Then why—"

"Miriam, before you make any decisions about..." Gabe reached across the desk and claimed one of her hands as she began to fidget. "About how you think you want to spend the rest of your life, you owe it to yourself to at least consider the alternative."

"With Aden Schmucker?" She flung the words at him.

"I don't know." Gabe pulled in a deep breath and then said the words that had been weighing on him since the auction, perhaps much longer than that. "I do know that before I ask someone to be my *fraa*, I want her to be very sure she has considered all of her options. I want her to be sure she knows her heart. I want there to be no place left for doubt."

⁓ Chapter 44 ⁓

Miriam didn't speak directly to Gabe as they waited to enter the public meeting in downtown Cashton.

She'd mulled his words over and over in her mind for the last six days. At first they had made her angry. She was so tired of people trying to tell her what was best for her future. Then she'd remember the tender look in his eyes and the way he'd leaned forward in earnest. She'd thought about the soft touch of his hand as he'd stood, thanked her for the dinner, and walked out into the cold evening.

Eventually her anger had melted away, leaving only confusion.

The weather hadn't helped. It had done nothing but snow since their dinner.

Cold, gray January days. Perhaps they were to blame for her mood.

Or perhaps she knew, deep in her heart, that he might have had a valid point, that she should at least consider both sides before making her decision.

"Big crowd," Eli muttered.

"More than I expected." Miriam smiled an apology as she bumped up against Gabe.

He caught her arm to keep her from slipping on the icy pavement.

"Samuel's standing at the back. It looks as though he saved some seats."

Indeed, he was easy to spot with his Amish hat standing out amid the baseball caps and his customary scowl plastered on his face.

"Been here for an hour. *Gut* thing I came early. Never seen so many people interested in a new hotel."

"Technically it won't be a hotel any longer when—"

Samuel waved off Eli's comments. "The village president woman is about to begin."

Gabe took the first seat, next to Samuel. Miriam sat next to Gabe, and Eli took the last seat.

She tried to focus on the people at the front of the room and not on how close she was seated beside Gabe. He brushed his hand against her as he removed his coat.

"Sorry," he murmured.

"No problem."

His eyes met hers, and she had the craziest notion that he was going to reach up and straighten her *kapp*, push her hair back into place, or touch her face. Her heart beat faster, and she moistened her lips.

"I want to thank you all for coming. My name is Janice Goodland, and as most of you know, I'm the village president. I'd like to introduce the board to you, in case we have any newcomers."

Miriam pulled her eyes away from Gabe and toward the speaker.

The woman stood on a stage that was elevated about a foot above the rest of the room. Several others were on the stage with her, but it was plain she was in charge. In her forties and thin, with short black hair, she looked to be very serious about the meeting. Miriam had been so busy studying Mrs. Goodland that she'd missed most of what the president had said.

Sitting up straighter, she inwardly vowed to concentrate.

"We're here tonight to provide information about the renovation of the old hotel in the downtown area."

"Don't need information," an old man from the back hollered. "Need a job."

Several folks murmured in agreement.

"We will have a handout regarding possible employment, but first let's watch the presentation Mr. Drake has sent."

What followed was a short video highlighting other projects Chester Entertainment had completed in the last ten years. Miriam noted that none of them involved Amish communities.

Before the lights had even come back on, a woman seated two rows in front of them stood up. "I'm a single mom, and I have a job, but that old hotel is a danger. I can't be watching my boys all the time, and twice last year they got to playing around that building. One of my sons hurt himself on broken glass. If you ask me, one less deserted building is a good thing for Cashton."

Again there were murmurs of agreement.

"I vote we tell Mr. Drake to get started. What's he waiting for?" This was from a middle-aged man in a white dress shirt and charcoal-colored slacks. He looked vaguely familiar to Miriam. "The sooner the hotel opens, the more people I'll have frequenting my bank."

That would be why she knew him. As a girl, she'd accompanied her father a few times to the bank when he had business to take care of.

"We want to move in an expeditious but reasonable manner for all village business. Now, if there are any questions you would like answered at this time, Mr. Drake has sent two of his assistants here tonight."

A young man and young woman, dressed in nearly identical black suits, waited near the right of the podium.

Samuel was the first from their group to stand. When Mrs. Goodland called on him, he spoke up loud and clear. Miriam found herself praying he wasn't going to quote Scripture. Somehow she didn't think it would further their cause here.

"We'd like to know where Mr. Drake came up with the name for his new facility."

Mr. Drake's two appointees eyed each other. Then the man, a redhead with a small goatee, stepped forward to answer Samuel.

"That is an excellent question. We had a marketing team come up with a name that would catch the attention of—"

"What I mean is that Amish folk..." Samuel glanced to the right at the three of them, the only other Plain people in the room. "Amish people don't meet in an abbey. So the name seems more than a little inappropriate to us."

There was some rumbling around them, and the man at the front turned to the young woman. Together they began consulting their notes, and then she pulled out her phone and pushed some buttons.

"Perhaps we could move on to the next question," Mrs. Goodland said.

"But they haven't answered the first one," Samuel protested.

"I understand, Mr.—"

"Gingerich. Samuel Gingerich, and I tell you *the love of money is a root of all kinds of evil. Some people, eager for money, have wandered from the faith*—"

He was quoting Scripture from First Timothy to the village board in a public meeting? Miriam wanted to put her head in her hands.

Gabe sat quietly to her left, though his fingers had begun to tap out a nervous rhythm on his leg. When she glanced at Eli, there was no doubt about it. A smile tugged at the corners of his mouth.

"Quiet." Mrs. Goodland tapped her gavel against the podium as everyone began talking at once. "Quiet, please."

Instead of hushing, the crowd only grew noisier. No one seemed to be listening to her, so she turned and spoke to one of the persons behind her. That person stood and hurried off the stage.

Gabe wasn't surprised when one of the board members walked up to their group. Mrs. Goodland had ended the meeting somewhat abruptly with "More information will follow in the paper."

As far as Gabe knew, they didn't have a local paper, so perhaps she meant the *Lacrosse Tribune*, which sometimes covered events in the smaller local towns and villages. Other than that, if you wanted to know something, you asked a neighbor, listened to the radio, or had *kaffi* at the diner, where the old folks met.

How did he know these things after living in the Cashton area such a short time? Because some things were the same no matter where you lived. And because he listened more than he talked, especially when he went into town for supplies.

A young Hispanic woman approached them before they could make their way out of the building. "Mrs. Goodland would like to have a word with you in the boardroom, if you have a moment."

"Do you work for the village president?" Eli asked.

"I'm the clerk. Technically, I work for the citizens of Cashton."

"I suppose that means you work for us," Gabe said with a smile. "Lead the way."

They walked into the boardroom in the same order they had sat in the row—Samuel, Gabe, Miriam, and then Eli.

Janice Goodland greeted them cordially, everyone introduced themselves, and then she offered them all seats—which they refused. She didn't bother with small talk.

"Obviously, you have some concerns about the project."

"*Ya*. We have a list." Eli pulled the small sheet of notepad paper from his pocket. When he noticed the expression on her face, he added, "It's a short list. Only three items."

After Eli had gone over their three points, Mrs. Goodland turned to the other members of her board. A tall, wiry man named Jim—Gabe thought he'd been introduced as the tax assessor—only shrugged.

He did remember that the shorter and rounder one handled money. That man shook his head adamantly and rubbed the bridge of his nose. He didn't offer an explanation, but the frown and gestures were enough. Gabe was sure he was saving his comments for a private conversation with the other board members.

Miriam cleared her throat. "Surely you can understand my

concerns as a schoolteacher. It's my job to teach and, to some degree, protect the children under my care."

"Yes." Mrs. Goodland fiddled with the cap on a bottle of water. "I wouldn't want one of our schools to be a stop on anyone's tour, but I'm not sure that's what Drake was intending."

"Perhaps if we could speak with him," Gabe suggested.

"I was thinking the same thing." Mrs. Goodland walked over to a calendar laid open on a desk.

"We are not here to interfere in *Englisch* ways," Samuel pointed out.

Mrs. Goodland had been running her finger down the calendar. At Samuel's words, she paused and studied him a moment. "I'm sure you're not. I've been president here for twelve years, Mr. Gingerich. In all that time, I've never had a group of Amish persons attend a public meeting. You strike me as quiet, private, law-abiding citizens."

She circled a date in the book and closed it.

"You've also never failed to pay your taxes." She looked at the tax assessor when she said this. "Wisconsin now has the fourth highest Amish population of any state, as you probably know." She tapped a finger against her lips. "Actually, I wouldn't mind having more Amish in Cashton. And while not everyone in that room tonight would agree with me, that's all right. I don't mind a little dissension. They would point out that there's the occasional young Amish person on their..."

"*Rumspringa*," Eli offered.

"Yes. And there are the horse droppings, the buggies that slow down traffic, and now and then conflict with the FDA over raw milk."

"Natural milk," Gabe corrected her.

"Call it what you like. My point is that I'll put my crime rates beside a non-Amish community any day. Plain people make good neighbors, and I represent you as much as I represent everyone else who gathered here tonight."

Gabe stared at her in surprise.

No one moved. He could tell the others in his group were as astonished as he was. Could they actually have found an advocate in the village president?

Mrs. Goodland reached for her bottle of water and began fiddling with the cap again. "But I do represent everyone else in that room as well, and they need jobs. Whether you like it or not, Amish communities increase tourism."

Miriam shook her head, Eli stuck his hands in his pockets, and Samuel looked as if he were trying to decide which Scripture to spout next.

Gabe jumped in before the tone of the meeting could deteriorate. "We're not here to stand in the way of anyone's job, Mrs. Goodland, but these three things Eli mentioned...surely there is a way to present them to Mr. Drake. Surely there is a way to have both the jobs which people need and still maintain respect for our way of life."

"A compromise?" she asked.

The room was quiet, but it was obvious everyone was in agreement.

"Okay. Two weeks from Friday," she said. "I'll set it up with Drake. We'll meet here."

⁓ Chapter 45 ⁓

The driver Miriam's father hired arrived early Friday morning. "I'm glad you're going with me," she confessed as they walked toward the car.

"This is an important decision in your life. Besides, your old *dat* could use a day off the farm." He tugged on his beard as he opened the car door for her.

Her parents had been incredibly supportive when she'd explained her predicament. Although she couldn't believe there would be anything that would appeal to her in the New Order district where Aden was living, it seemed best to go and see. Abigail offered no words of wisdom, no proverb, as she checked that they had their overnight bags.

"Are you sure you won't go with us?" Miriam asked.

"No. Your *bruders* are coming with the *grandkinner*. I promised we would make popcorn." She paused to kiss the top of her daughter's head, which spoke enough to the seriousness of the occasion—Abigail King was not one to demonstrate affection, especially in front of *Englischers*.

Jocelyn, their driver, waited until everyone had buckled up before starting the shiny blue automobile and driving down the lane. Miriam had ridden in cars before, but not often and she didn't relish a drive that would last nearly two hours. She missed her mare already. Immediately Jocelyn had Joshua talking about the weather and if the snowfall they'd had meant good planting in the spring.

Miriam stared out the window, watching the fields, hills, and creek she'd grown up around sail past her like leaves caught in a wind. How would it feel to leave all she'd ever known behind her? How would it feel to move away from this, returning only for the occasional holiday?

The road unwound like a skein of her mother's yarn as they drove north and then east through a few towns, then more country-side, and finally to the community where Aden had settled.

"My sister lives north of here," Jocelyn said. "It worked out well for me to drive you because I've been wanting to come up and see her. Are you sure you want me to drop you off here at the mercantile? I would be happy to take you to the home you're visiting."

"*Nein.* Aden said he would pick us up at noon." Joshua helped Miriam out of the car and then claimed their overnight bags from the backseat.

"I'll meet you back here tomorrow at six."

"*Gut. Danki*, Jocelyn. We appreciate it."

Miriam remembered to add her thanks at the last moment. She was busy staring at the store in front of her, where Amish families were walking in and out.

"It looks no different than our store," she whispered.

"Perhaps a little bigger." Joshua said. "Plain is Plain, Miriam. Don't expect to see much that is different here."

But there were differences. Joshua soon had his head stuck in the hardware section, asking the salesperson to explain how the gas stove worked and walking around the refrigerator, shaking his head.

When Aden found her, Miriam was staring at an *Englisch* coffeepot.

"This is for Amish use?" she asked.

"*Ya.* There's no electrical cord. You set it on the gas-powered stove."

Miriam shook her head, but she could feel a slow smile working its way across her features. "You New Order Amish are like children with your play toys. My *dat* is fascinated with the refrigerators."

"Can you blame him? No more cutting blocks of ice from the lakes. A man could get behind that." Aden waved a hand to Joshua and then walked her toward the coffee shop in the corner of the store. "Have you eaten?"

"*Nein.* We were waiting on you."

Aden's answer was a smile that pricked at her heart. Had it been fair to agree to come and visit him? Could she return his feelings?

Joshua bounded up like a pup let in from the outside. "Aden, have you seen these contraptions they are selling to put your food inside?"

"I have. All the families here have them."

"And your bishop allows it?"

"*Ya.* No electricity needed."

They ordered sandwiches and soup. While they waited, they discussed everything from the condition of the roads to happenings in Pebble Creek. What they didn't talk about was the real reason for their visit. It sat on the table between them, like a giant Thanksgiving turkey no one had the courage to carve. Finally, Joshua sat back after accepting a refill of coffee from the waitress. He cleared his voice and gave both Miriam and Aden his serious, fatherly look. "My *dat* often said to me that if you want good advice, consult an old man."

Aden smiled uncomfortably, and Miriam stared down into her tea and then back at her father.

"I don't consider myself old. I also don't know enough about your feelings for each other or enough about this community to offer either of you advice."

Miriam glanced at Aden. This time she didn't look away. She had a sudden urge to reach across the table and push the dark-blond hair back and away from his blue eyes.

Instead they both waited for her father to continue.

"I can't say the gadgets here don't interest me, but marriage is about more than what is convenient and what doodads a community allows. Aden, I assume you moved here for a reason, and I'm sure those reasons were *gut*. It speaks well to your hard work that you've been able to purchase your own place already—"

"It's small," Aden said.

"Many of us started on a small place. No need to apologize for that. We came to visit today because none of my *kinner* have moved more than a buggy ride away. Before I give my blessing for such a thing, I wanted to meet some of the families from your district, and Miriam—"

He waited, but she didn't offer any explanation.

"Miriam is still searching her heart."

Aden lowered his gaze to the table. When he looked up again, the boyish smile was back. "I think I understand."

"*Gut!*" Joshua set enough money on the table to pay for their meal. "First, I'd like to see this buggy shop where you work. Our bishop wants me to bring back a report about where his young apprentice is employed."

Miriam was happy to be in a buggy again. Jocelyn seemed to be a *gut* driver, but the ride in the *Englisch* car had made her a little *naerfich*. Buggies were more natural, in her opinion, and Aden's gelding was a real beauty. His buggy, though—it was like the coffeepot in the general store. It was different. There was a gas heater inside that ran on a small propane cylinder. Though he still kept lap blankets stored on the backseat, it was definitely warmer than her old buggy back home.

She thought it was the fanciest buggy she'd ever seen, and Miriam began to wonder if Aden had forgotten his vows of humility. But then they arrived at the shop, and she soon saw that the buggy he was driving was the cheapest model sold there. There were buggies with leather seats and buggies with dual heaters. All of the buggies were the same color on the outside, so that when passing on the road no family would seem more prosperous than any other, but she couldn't help thinking of her buggy waiting for her back in Pebble Creek.

Aden had worked extra hours all week so that he could have the afternoon off. He took them to his farm next, which was indeed small. "I have the option of buying additional acreage as long as I do so within five years."

"From an *Englischer*?" Joshua asked.

"*Ya*. He is retired and can use the money, but he's not in a big hurry for it."

The home he was staying in was an old hunter's cabin. There was no electricity, but he did have small gas appliances—heater, stove, and mini refrigerator. He also had running water and a small corner bathroom.

"It looks like your *bruder*'s home, Miriam."

"You mean the bathroom? *Ya*. David would be comfortable here."

The laughter helped to ease the tension as she stood in the middle of Aden's one-room cabin. Aden waited until Joshua walked outside onto the porch, and then he stepped closer.

"I would never ask you to live in this cabin. You know that, right?"

"Aden, I'm not ready to talk about—"

"*Ya*, I know. But it's just that when I look at this one room through a woman's eyes, well it doesn't look so *gut*. I wish you could see what I see." He turned from her and walked to the window, frustration tightening his shoulders.

"And what do you see, Aden?"

He glanced back to decide if she was mocking him. Satisfied that she wasn't, he pointed out across the fields. "There, tucked in the shade of that grove of trees—a home. Not large at first, but well constructed. A barn to the west of that, and animal pens, of course."

"You're happy here. Aren't you?"

"Yes. Except—"

Miriam waited, dreading but knowing there was no way to stop him.

"Except that it's lonely." He turned now and walked across the room until only a few inches remained between them.

"Aden, I know there are women here, *gut* Amish women."

"*Ya*."

"Except?" She echoed the word back to him.

Now the boyish grin returned. "They are not you, Miriam King."

"You sound like a student with a childhood crush."

"But I'm not a student, and it's not a crush." He cupped her elbow in his hand and walked her out onto the porch. The sun was shining down on his fields and she could picture it, could imagine what he had described. She could even envision the way Grace would draw it, and that thought made her smile. The question was—could she see herself in that picture?

The rest of the evening and the next day passed quickly. The home she and her father stayed in was warm and inviting. The women were kind and didn't ask too many questions. They did let slip that several of the young ladies in the community had expressed an interest in Aden Schmucker. For some reason it eased the worry in her heart. Should her answer be no, she didn't think Aden would be living on his small farm alone for very long.

She didn't speak of her decision on the drive home, while the road unwound beneath the tires of the *Englisch* car.

Neither did she talk about her feelings as she and her father laughed about the percolating coffeepot with her mother, or told of how the gas heat left the downstairs rooms warm but felt rather dry on their skin.

Miriam stayed at the kitchen table on Saturday night, long after her parents went to bed. She opened her Bible, searched her heart, and prayed that her decision wasn't a selfish one. Then she wrote a letter to Aden.

The next morning she woke feeling ten pounds lighter.

There was no church that day, so they would do only the chores that had to be done, followed by breakfast and Bible study in the sitting room.

It was during lunch, when her parents noticed her humming, that they finally asked.

Miriam selected a cold slice of ham and another piece of bread, one baked yesterday in her mother's wood-burning oven. "I'd like my children to have a creek wandering through their childhood."

"*Ya.* That's important," Abigail agreed. "I always loved that proverb."

"I suppose I'd trade a feed bag of modern conveniences for one *gut* creek," Joshua said, reaching for the butter a second too late.

Abigail moved it away from his grasp and shook her head.

They didn't ask Miriam about her feelings, but she loved her parents all the more for that. And she positively wanted to laugh when her mother said, "Did I mention that Gabe and Grace are coming for dinner tonight? I promised to give her another quilting lesson."

Could it be that her mother was matchmaking?

If so, she'd have to thank her for it. But first she needed to clean up these dishes and make sure the checkerboard was out and ready for their guests. She was ready for a rematch with one Gabriel Miller.

≈ Chapter 46 ≈

Grace didn't understand adults. She didn't understand donkeys, either, but at least they made more sense than adults.

"Watch your stitches, Grace. I believe they are getting bigger there." Abigail's voice was kind as she pointed to the border of the lap quilt Grace was piecing together.

They had been having lessons since the auction. Grace thought she was getting better, but she was still glad they had started with something very small. She had a small lap, so it was a small quilt. Abigail said it would be just right.

"My stitches grow worse when my mind wanders."

"Where was your mind wandering just then?"

"Two different places. Toward grown-ups and donkeys."

Abigail chuckled and reached to put another piece of wood in the iron stove. It was comfy where they were sewing in the sitting room. Grace loved Sunday afternoons spent with Abigail and Joshua. Being home was good too, and Sundays when church meetings were fun, but Sundays when they visited? Those were her favorite.

"Want to talk about the donkey first?"

Grace leaned forward so that she could peek at her dad and Miriam sitting at the table in the kitchen. They were supposed to be playing checkers, but far as she could tell no one ever moved a piece on the board. That made no sense at all. Didn't they want to win?

"*Ya.* Donkeys might be easier."

"How is Gus?"

"He's *gut.* He likes being with the horses, but if you ever leave him alone..." Grace shook her head as she sewed three stitches that ended the row. Turning the quilt, she glanced up at Abigail. "He can find a lot of trouble for such a small animal."

"Donkeys are herd animals. They tend to find trouble when left alone."

"That's what my *dat* said. When we tried to pull him out of the old chicken coop—I don't know how he even got in there—well, we couldn't do it. My *dat* pulled and pulled, and he's real strong. Gus wouldn't come. He sat down and brayed and wouldn't come. *Dat* was mad and stomping around in the cold."

Abigail nodded as she reached into her sewing box for her scissors. "Is he still there?"

"No!" Grace started giggling as she bent back over her quilt. "We finally went and got Chance. Gus just loves that buggy horse. He'd stay with him all day long if he could. When he saw Chance, he came right out of the chicken coop, dragging old boards and rotten hay behind him."

"Donkeys can be trouble."

"That's what my *dat* said. He didn't want Gus to begin with. I still don't understand why he entered that woodsplitting competition."

They both stopped sewing and peered into the kitchen.

"Adults make less sense than donkeys," Grace whispered.

"Sometimes it seems that way," Abigail admitted.

Grace sewed the entire length of her quilt before she asked the question that had been bothering her. "Is Miriam going to move? I know she went with her *dat* to visit some other people out of town. We had the twins' *grossmammi* for a substitute, and she smells kind of funny."

"I hope you didn't tell her that."

"*Nein.*"

The sound of the crackling fire filled the silence between them.

"Did you ask Miriam if she plans to move?"

"*Nein.* I didn't want to be nosy."

"But you're still worried."

"*Ya.* Some."

"Well, I wouldn't worry about Miriam. She told me she plans on living in Cashton and raising her children here."

"Children? But she's not married."

"Maybe she will be one day. *Gotte* has a plan for her life, and I suspect it includes a family of her own.

Grace felt a heavy weight lift off her chest and float to the ceiling. She put her sewing down and walked over to Abigail's chair. When Miriam's mom looked up, Grace slipped her arms around her neck.

"I love you," she whispered.

"I love you too, Grace Ann."

There was still the problem of Gus behaving himself, and she still didn't understand adults, but at least there wouldn't be any more change—not for a while. That was all she needed to know to make this Sunday absolutely perfect.

⌾ Chapter 47 ⌾

Gabe pulled his buggy up in front of the Cashton Village Community Center, Miriam sitting at his side. He'd picked her up from the schoolhouse, glad to have the time together in the buggy alone. They hadn't spoken of anything important, but sometimes those moments were significant in a relationship.

Did they have a relationship?

Before he could answer the question, even to himself, Samuel arrived in his buggy.

"Samuel," Gabe nodded to the older man as they both secured their horses to the hitching posts that had been provided for local Amish.

Samuel frowned and pulled at his beard. "I saw Eli on my way in. His buggy threw a wheel and he'll be late."

"Should we go back to help him?"

"No. He had help. Said he'd be here as soon as he could." Samuel scowled at the building. "I'm still not sure we should be here, but let's have this over with."

Miriam stepped closer to Gabe, as if she were lending her support, as if she understood they needed to stand together. "The meeting doesn't start for another five minutes," she said.

"Better early than late." Samuel shook his head. "Being our

schoolteacher, I thought you would be instructing the younger ones in such things."

He entered the building without them. The man had been chosen to serve, and he would fulfill his duty. However, there was no doubt in Gabe's mind that his heart wasn't in it.

Gabe and Miriam waited by the buggies, watching down the street for Eli, the afternoon wind pulling at their clothes. It was cold but not unpleasant. Gabe had always preferred the outdoors to inside, especially when inside included a meeting of any sort. This meeting was bound to be confrontational. The thought made a muscle in his jaw twitch.

"It could be worse," she murmured. "It could be Clemens Schmucker in there with us."

The name Schmucker brought a dozen questions to Gabe's mind. He knew Miriam had been to see Aden with her father. What had she thought of that community? Had she fully weighed the differences in what her life would be like there, with him, versus here with Gabe?

Would staying be a decision she would regret?

He glanced her way and saw the smile playing at the corners of her mouth. It was an expression that succeeded in pushing his questions back where they belonged, back into the corners of his mind.

"*Ya.* Clemens could have been elected."

"It would be the shortest meeting the *Englischers* ever had, because Clemens' declarations are fairly short and his listening skills don't exist."

"Miriam King. That's a little judgmental of you." Some of the tension melted from Gabe's shoulders as he put his hand on her elbow to guide her along the sidewalk, which still had a bit of ice on it from the recent snow and cold nights.

"Not judging, Gabe. Only observing. It's one of the things I try to instruct the children in." Now her grin widened as he opened the door for her.

As he smiled back, Gabe thought about how their district was

comprised of an odd group of personalities. But what group wasn't—
Englisch or Amish? And perhaps there was hope in that. Perhaps all
of the *Englisch* were not as excited about this building plan as Byron
Drake.

The village president walked up to them as they came in the door.
Gabe still wasn't accustomed to seeing such short hair on a woman,
but there was no mistaking the friendliness in her welcome.

"Miriam, correct?" She shook both of their hands. "And Gabe.
I'm so glad you both could come again today. I was just saying to Samuel that I believe our board of trustees can only make an informed
decision if both parties are represented."

"We are happy to represent our district as well as the other Amish
district in the Cashton area," Miriam said. "We believe the development Mr. Drake is proposing will affect us all."

"And we definitely want to hear your concerns. If you would like
coffee or a cold drink, there are some beverages at the back of the
room. We'll be starting in a few minutes." Mrs. Goodland excused
herself to go and greet others who were finding their places around
the table.

Several nodded in greeting, though they didn't walk over and
attempt any conversation.

"I believe they think we bite," Gabe muttered.

"Perhaps we should make the first effort."

"*Ya.* Maybe so."

At that moment Byron Drake pushed through the front doors—
"pushed" was the only word for it. Both doors opened at once, and
the man came through with a burst of February afternoon wind.
He was followed by three other men, all in black suits and red ties.

Drake also wore a red tie, but he sported a gray suit made of some
sort of silvery material. Gabe didn't usually notice what other men
wore, but these four looked as if they were dressed for a parade. He
had never met Drake personally, but there was no mistaking who he
was or that he was the leader. There was no doubt they were a team,
same as Gabe's workhorses. He yoked them up to plow a field, and

they pulled together with one mind, one goal before them. These four appeared ready to attack the assembled group with their folders and briefcases.

Drake's head was as bald and shiny as it had appeared in the *Englisch* newspaper, but he was younger than Gabe had expected. How did a man his age lose all his hair? He was also fit, which was somewhat unusual in *Englischers*—at least, that had been true in Gabe's experience.

The three behind him looked pastier, as if they didn't see the sun much. And while Drake worked the room, shaking each person's hand—even shaking Samuel's hand—the three behind him stood back, as if waiting to see what their leader might need.

Miriam watched with amusement as Byron Drake made his way around the room and then toward her and Gabe. She wasn't sure this man was evil, but she was convinced that what he was planning to do would ultimately harm her students.

That brought out her urge to protect.

She had to plaster on a smile as he came forward.

"And you must be the schoolmarm."

"Teacher. Miriam King."

"Pleased to meet you. I've wanted to tell you how impressed I was with your Christmas program. It's part of what convinced me to choose Cashton for our development."

Miriam snapped her mouth shut over the retort that came to mind. Both of her parents had warned her against saying anything she, or the community, might regret.

"And you are?"

"Gabriel Miller."

"Ah. I'd be most interested in having your photo on the front of our brochures. You're a fine—" Miriam had no doubt he was about to say "specimen"—"example of Amish life and how healthy it is. Exactly what people will be coming to see."

"I'm not interested." Gabe dropped his hand. Miriam noticed the muscle in his cheek tick again as it had out on the street. Was he that worried about the damage this development might do to their community? Somehow the realization endeared him to her even more, which she hadn't thought possible.

"Perhaps you don't understand how much we would be willing to compensate you. Or maybe you think modeling is only women's work. It isn't. I myself have—"

"I'm not interested." Gabe's voice didn't change in tone or volume, but there was no mistaking the resolve in his words.

"Oh." Drake was apparently not used to being denied. He took a step back and then glanced toward a minion, who scuttled forward. "Tell Goodland we're ready to begin. I have a schedule to maintain."

Without another word, he pivoted away from them and walked across the room.

"Well, that was a *gut* first impression." Miriam picked up a bottle of water from the refreshment table.

"From both perspectives, no doubt."

"*Ya.* He was very taken with you."

"He probably wanted my workhorse in front of his cameras too."

Janice Goodland walked to the middle of the room. "If you all would take your seats, we'll start this meeting. It appears everyone is here who is going to make it. We understand Mr. Stutzman had some transportation problems and will join us if possible."

Someone muttered, "Get an automobile, buddy."

Mrs. Goodland ignored the comment, if she heard it, and put on her reading glasses. Miriam thought she was a beautiful woman with a pleasant personality, even though she was very different from the Amish women she knew. It seemed odd that she'd grown up in the Cashton area but had never had cause to meet Mrs. Goodland before.

Other than herself, there were only two other women in the room, which had become rather crowded while they were speaking

with Drake. There was the woman who worked for the village president, the one who had spoken with them during the last meeting.
Miriam recognized her. There was also another woman standing
near the back of the room, and Miriam was sure she'd never seen
her before.

Missing was Drake's female associate from the last meeting. Had
she been reassigned to another project? The redheaded man was not
present either. Perhaps the two were back in the tall office buildings
of Mr. Drake, working on his renovation plans.

"I'd like to begin with everyone making brief introductions."

There was Drake and his three merry men. Miriam barely caught
their names, as Drake introduced and dismissed them with a casual
wave of his hand.

The board of trustees consisted of President Goodland, the clerk,
the treasurer, and the tax assessor. Though Miriam had met them
previously, she still had trouble putting the correct name with the
correct face. As soon as her attention moved from one to the next,
the previous person's name slipped through her mind like sand
through an hourglass.

However, the name of the woman at the back of the room she
wouldn't forget, because her name sounded like words in a poem—
Rae Caperton. With shoulder-length hair and a dark tan, she looked
about Miriam's age. She was now sitting at a smaller table, and she
was typing on a laptop as they introduced themselves. She had taken
Drake's picture with Janice Goodland when the man first walked
in. When she introduced herself, she said she was a reporter with
the *Lacrosse Tribune*.

"Another person to request your photo," Miriam teased Gabe in
a whisper.

"Did you notice she put her camera away, though? She didn't
even attempt to take our pictures." Gabe regarded the reporter
thoughtfully as Samuel introduced their group.

"Excellent. That's everyone, I believe."

The words were barely out of Mrs. Goodland's mouth when Eli

came through the door. His clothes were a bit disheveled, and he seemed somewhat out of breath from hurrying, but he'd made it.

"Mr. Stutzman?"

"Yes."

"We heard you had buggy problems."

"*Ya*, I did. A wheel broke, but an *Englischer* stopped and gave me a hand with it." He took the seat Miriam had saved for him. "I'm sorry if I held you up."

"Not at all." Mrs. Goodland looked down at her notes again and then addressed everyone in the room. "I'd like to thank you all for coming. We have busy work schedules, and I don't abide useless meetings. What Mr. Drake is proposing will significantly affect all of the residents of Cashton, but perhaps none more than those assembled here. In light of that, we're holding this meeting to allow him to present his plans and then to listen to concerns from representatives of the Amish community."

She paused and removed her glasses. "I want to go on the record as saying that nothing said in this room today is binding. There will be no decisions made at this meeting. It is an exchange of information only. Am I clear?"

All present nodded, though Miriam noticed that Drake was examining his fingernails as he did so. She wondered if he had a splinter or hangnail, or perhaps he was bored.

"Excellent. Mr. Drake, I'd like to begin with you, and I ask that you keep your presentation to two minutes."

Drake stood and straightened his jacket. "It will be difficult to present the scope of the marvelous plans we have for Cashton within two minutes."

"I'm sure you'll find a way. Pretend you've paid for a commercial spot."

Drake tried to pierce Mrs. Goodland with a stare, but she'd sat and was fumbling in her purse to turn off her cell phone. Miriam's opinion of the village president rose the more she was around her. It was apparent she wasn't swayed by expensive suits or wealthy men.

"Very well. My corporation plans to refurbish the abandoned hotel downtown. We've contacted the owners and made a very attractive bid, which only a fool would turn down."

Running his hand down the length of his tie, he continued. Miriam couldn't help but notice that he wore a gold ring with a diamond embedded in it on his right hand—not a wedding ring, so what was it? "Our business proposal includes a marketing plan that highlights the local Amish community."

He nodded toward one of his people, who popped up and began distributing glossy folders. On the front was a picture of the old hotel. Across the top, in large words, was printed Amish Abbey and below that Cashton, Wisconsin. The front of the building had been redone though to look like a Catholic church—St. Mary's up near Norwalk. Miriam was afraid to touch her folder, afraid to even open it. Her anger was building, struggling against feelings of hopelessness. When the *Englisch* made their minds up to do something, they were like big bulldozers on the freeways. Stopping them seemed nearly impossible.

"If you'll open your folder, you will see that we envision quite a few businesses, including Amish Accents for home furnishings, Amish Accessories for women's needs, Amish Acoustics to highlight—"

"We're not Catholic."

"Excuse me." Drake peered at Gabe as if he were a lesser mortal, as if he were in fact something stuck on the bottom of his shoe that he needed one of his minions to scrape off.

"I said we're not Catholic." Gabe held up the folder. "You've redone the hotel to resemble a Catholic church and printed the words 'Amish Abbey' across the top."

"Your point?"

"We're not Catholic. We're Amish."

Drake smiled—tightly, in an unfriendly way.

Miriam noticed that Samuel had also not touched or opened his folder.

Eli, on the other hand, had not only opened his, but had the sheets inside spread out on the table in front of him.

"What difference does it make?"

"It makes a big difference to us. Amish Abbey is like saying Catholic Temple, but Catholics don't worship in a temple, and we don't worship in an abbey."

Drake's face turned pink, and he again stroked his tie. Miriam glanced down and saw that Gabe's hand had tightened around the pen he was holding. The two looked as if they might begin shouting at any moment.

Should she say something? Should they even have attended the meeting?

When it seemed the tension could grow no worse, Mrs. Goodland rose from her seat.

~ Chapter 48 ~

Gabe tried to force his hand to relax, but the picture on the front of Drake's folder had nearly sent him over the edge. Amish Abbey!

The man was worse than arrogant. He was also ignorant. And though his associates must have told him about the previous meeting, it seemed that he had no intention of changing any of his plans.

Mrs. Goodland glanced from Gabe to Drake. "Perhaps we could note Mr. Miller's concern about the name of the project and revisit that particular issue in a moment."

The members of the board focused first on Mrs. Goodland, then on Drake, and then they stared again at Gabe—as if he were the odd man out. It was as if they were watching a volleyball match, only this wasn't a game.

Cashton was where Gabe's daughter lived, where his friends lived, and he didn't appreciate this strange man coming in and changing the entire makeup of the village in order to earn a dollar.

"I think you're overreacting, Mr. Miller." Drake drew his shoulders back and raised his chin higher. "Amish Abbey is merely the facility's name. Perhaps you should leave the advertising aspects to us. Now, if I may continue—"

"I have a question." Eli raised his hand, reminding Gabe of one of the schoolchildren in Miriam's classroom.

Mrs. Goodland sat down with a sigh, and Drake directed his plastic smile to Eli.

"It appears you took these pictures of Amish children during our school play. I can't imagine how. I was there, and I don't remember seeing anyone with a camera."

Gabe watched Drake closely. He didn't admit or deny taking the photos at the Pebble Creek school. He only waited for Eli to continue.

"Are you aware that we do not allow photography of our people?"

"Oh my heavens." Now Drake stared at the ceiling as if he might find help from that direction. "Of course we will seek a release, and if necessary provide compensation—"

"Exodus twenty, verse four." Samuel spoke for the first time, his voice echoing through the room with authority. "*You shall not make for yourself an image—*"

"What is he saying?" Drake turned to one of his employees. "Why is he speaking to me that way? Does he need a bottle of water? Is that why his voice is gravelly? Find out what he's saying to me. He sounds like one of those televangelists. You know I can't abide being preached at."

Samuel wasn't deterred by anything Drake said. In his short time in Wisconsin, Gabe had learned Samuel wasn't one to stop in the midst of quoting the Bible. "*...or on the earth beneath or in the waters below.*"

"President Goodland, I would think you could conduct your village business in a more seemly matter." Drake walked back to his table and began collecting his things.

"Does this mean you've finished with your presentation?" she asked.

"I'm finished here."

His three merry men fell in line behind him as he turned toward the outside door.

"I don't need your approval to purchase a building," he reminded her.

"You do need our approval for building permits."

Drake stopped and turned on her, reminding Gabe of a spring storm reversing course. "I would not suggest that you stand in my way—you and your small-minded group of people. I have lawyers who could bankrupt this village with legal filings, and in the meantime I will still build my abbey. I will build it—" he glared at Gabe and then took in Samuel, who now looked as if he had bowed his head in prayer. "I will build it, and I'll call it *whatever* I please."

Stepping closer to Mrs. Goodland, he lowered his voice enough to sound menacing but not enough to conceal his words. "Maybe you didn't have your people google me quite enough. For all I know, you don't even have people to do your meeting prep work for you."

The thought seemed to disturb him, but he pushed on. "Whatever the reason, it's apparent you don't know whom you're talking to. I didn't have to stop by this little hovel of a town. You're barely on the Wisconsin map, but you will be after I'm done with you, and one day you'll thank me."

He pressed his tie down again, and Gabe saw his diamond ring sparkle in what was left of the afternoon sun. "I'll be back. I want the papers to have a picture of me on the steps of the despicable little hotel as it is now—all crumbly and rat infested. Then they will see what a difference I can make in three months when the shops are ready to open. Watch for the press announcement as soon as the papers are signed and the money transferred—within the week. I suggest your little Amish group forget about any idea of trying to stop me."

The door rattled as his group exited the room.

For a moment there was silence, and then everyone began talking at once.

Mrs. Goodland was surrounded by her board, who were throwing around words such as "revenue," "litigation," and "property rights." Gabe had no idea what it all meant, and he didn't really care.

He pushed his folder away and stood up from the table. They hadn't accomplished much, but at least he'd be able to pick Grace up from Abigail's earlier than he'd planned.

Miriam put her hand on his arm. "We're not leaving yet, are we?"

"*Ya.* It looks like the meeting is over."

Her lovely face was all scrunched up in her worried look. Funny how he'd come to recognize that. He'd learned a whole lot about her in the near three months he'd known her. Some days he feared the next thing he'd be learning was that she was moving, marrying Aden, and starting a family in the other district. Well, wasn't that what he'd told her to consider? Didn't he want what was best for her? Was that best?

He pushed the questions away.

"But, Gabe. We need to come up with a way to stop them."

"It was foolish even to come here." Samuel placed his hat on his head firmly. "Didn't I tell you that from the beginning? But I was elected to join you, so I did. Now that you see it was a futile thing to do, we can go back to our people where we belong."

"I don't like the looks of this," Eli muttered. "It's as bad as we feared, and he shouldn't have photographed our children. That was wrong."

Miriam moved behind him and stared down at the pictures, photos of her students. "What can we do about this? As he said to Mrs. Goodland, he'll take them to court, and we're not going to fight this in the *Englisch* legal system."

"Maybe you won't have to." They all turned as the reporter walked up and joined their group. "Maybe there's another way you can bring Drake around to your point of view."

When they all simply stared at her, she held out her hand and introduced herself again. "Rae Caperton, *Lacrosse Tribune*."

Gabe had seen the paper once or twice but never read it. Like most Amish, he read only the *Budget*.

Glancing at their little group, Gabe understood their suspicion of the newspaperwoman and her intentions. No doubt she was a nice enough lady—but she was *Englisch*, and she worked for the press. Both were things that as a group they preferred to avoid. "I'm not sure what you had in mind, Miss Caperton, but I doubt it's something we'd entertain. As a rule, Amish folk—"

"Avoid intervening in *Englisch* affairs. Yes, I know, which is why I was surprised to see you here."

Samuel jingled the change in his pocket. "If you understand it was a stretch for us to be here, then you probably also know we don't often speak to news reporters."

"I understand that, Mr. Gingerich, and I think I even appreciate why. It's not often that the Amish community is represented fairly in the media."

Gabe knew when someone was pulling on his suspenders, but Rae Caperton appeared genuine and concerned. He could see from the way Miriam stepped forward that she was interested in hearing the woman out, but he was surprised when Eli spoke up.

"If you have a solution to this chicken fight, I'd be willing to listen, but perhaps this isn't the best place." Eli glanced pointedly over toward Mrs. Goodland and her trustees, which was when the shouting started.

Chapter 49

Miriam wanted to wade into the middle of the argument, pull the offending parties apart, and send them to the chalkboard to write sentences correcting their behavior. She didn't, but the urge was strong.

"In case you haven't noticed, the village's monetary chest isn't overflowing." The treasurer was a short, round man with longish hair who pounded the table as he spoke. "We need his money, and we need his jobs."

"We still haven't collected on the back taxes the previous owner of the hotel owes," the assessor admitted. Tall and wiry, he worried his glasses as he spoke. "My sources say we'll receive all of that and more with this new development project. It's not a deal we can turn our backs on, Janice. Not if we want our jobs next year. I have children in college still. Do you think that tuition will pay itself?"

Mrs. Goodland hadn't exactly lost her composure, but her face was flushed. "You're not offering any solutions, Jim. I know we need the taxes paid."

"And the jobs. We need those jobs here. Folks need work—"

"I have it," she barked. "I've studied the unemployment figures same as you. There is no need to remind me about them. I'm not senile."

"Don't jump down my throat." The tax assessor slumped into his chair. "Amish Abbey could be the biggest thing Cashton has seen in decades. And Carter's right about the village treasury. It's not overflowing by any means."

"We manage to balance our budget," Mrs. Goodland said.

Carter cleared his throat and nodded toward their audience.

"Perhaps we should be going," Miriam murmured as Mrs. Goodland stood up and made her way toward them.

"I'm sorry that didn't go well. I had no idea Drake had such a temper. I'd read he was flamboyant and I knew he was rich, but I never thought he'd go off like that—" Her hands came out in front of her, waving away the situation. Miriam almost had pity on her, but not quite. She was the one person who had the ability to make this situation go away.

"You're going to allow him to build this place?" Samuel asked.

"I'm not sure we can stop him. We could slow him down perhaps, but legally I don't know that he's breaking any laws. He has a right to do what he will with the land he buys, once he buys it." She glanced back at her treasurer, assessor, and the clerk—Miriam had forgotten her name.

Elia, that was it. She was a young Hispanic woman, with beautiful dark hair pulled back by a hair clip. She was currently stacking all the papers together and straightening the room.

"So you won't do anything to stop him?" Gabe asked.

Mrs. Goodland pinched the bridge of her nose. "I sympathize with your position, Gabe. I do, but I'm not sure I *should* try to stop him."

"And can he move as quickly as he said? He'll begin by next week?"

"I suspect he was ready to close on the deal before he even came here. He probably never meant to negotiate with us at all. This was merely a public relations stunt only marginally important to him."

"Did you look at the rest of this brochure?" Eli asked. "Amish Afghans—the Amish don't make afghans, Mrs. Goodland. Phase two is worse. He's putting in an Amish Astronomy. What do you suppose that will be? And Amish Aerials? What's an aerial?"

She held up her hand to stop him, but Eli was on a roll. "Amish Alley is going to include a bar."

"As long as he meets the ordinance requirements, alcohol sales are permissible."

"It's not the alcohol sale we object to," Miriam explained. "It's our name paired beside it. Imagine how you would feel if—"

"I don't need to imagine. I told you. I understand—"

"Do you?" Gabe asked. "Take this one, for example. Amish Angels. I expect Mr. Drake will make little dolls with Plain clothes, wings, and beautiful ceramic faces, never stopping to learn that we don't put faces on Amish dolls. It goes back to the Scripture Samuel quoted earlier."

Samuel perked up, suddenly interested in the conversation again. "Exodus twenty, verse four. *You shall not make for yourself an image*—"

"I remember, Mr. Gingerich. My father once made me memorize that very verse. I know it well, but I can't impose the Bible on a business deal."

"And possibly worst of all," Gabe continued, "is this one—Amish Arcades. How did you describe this one, Samuel?"

"Games. Video games that children play. Surely you've seen them when you've been in town. They kill things."

"Kill things," Eli echoed.

"No. Not really. It's only pretend, on a screen." Mrs. Goodland's voice had lost all conviction.

"Do you see? This shouldn't be done with our name attached. There has to be a way to convince him that it's wrong." Gabe glanced at Rae Caperton, but the newswoman shook her head slightly, as if to say "Not here."

"I'll think on it," Mrs. Goodland said. "I don't want to raise any false hopes, though. While I don't like his plans the way they stand, he doesn't seem to be a man who changes his mind often. I wish I could be more helpful."

She turned and walked back toward her group, and Miriam understood that they had been dismissed.

"I have an idea," Rae said. She glanced back over at the board. "Let's go across the street. The cafe's still open, and they have pretty good coffee."

Miriam figured they didn't have anything to lose. Gabe shrugged.

Eli said, "Sure. They have *gut* pie too."

Samuel blustered. "We have wasted enough time today. I suppose I'll be heading home."

"We need you on this, Samuel. We're a group—the four of us." Miriam reached forward and placed her hand on his arm. "We were all elected to represent the district. If we go back now, we go back with nothing."

"Which is what I told you would happen before we came."

"If we listen to Miss Caperton, there's at least a chance she will have an idea," Gabe reasoned. "What will it cost but another twenty minutes?"

Samuel shrugged, nodded, and followed them out of the building, but Miriam heard him mutter, "*Kaffi* ain't free in that café, you know."

A few minutes later they were sitting around a table at the café across the street. Miriam had been there maybe a dozen times, but she could tell it was Gabe's first visit. He took in the checkered tablecloths, red country curtains, and grandmotherly waitresses—and then he glanced across at her and smiled. Her heart nearly tripped a beat.

He was amused with the decor, not with her.

Possibly. Or was he?

She still had not figured out Gabe Miller. From the night he'd had dinner at the schoolhouse, the night he'd leaned forward, took her hand, and told her he planned to marry again, she'd allowed herself to hope. She'd even gone to Aden's community and spent the weekend there with her dad. She'd gone to see their lifestyle firsthand so she could tell Gabe that she'd considered it.

She just hadn't found the courage yet to bring up that conversation with him. What would she tell him?

Yes, they had bathrooms in the house. Yes, they had gas stoves and refrigerators. Yes, her life would be marginally easier. But why would any of that matter without him? Without Grace?

Her pulse beat faster whenever he looked her way, and no matter how she tried to slow down the dreams of her heart, his was the last face she envisioned when she went to sleep at night.

But he hadn't brought up the subject of marriage again. He visited her parents' home often enough. They sat and talked, even took walks together, but the topic of their relationship—it hadn't been broached.

Perhaps he was regretting that he'd ever mentioned it.

The waitress brought everyone a cup of *kaffi*, and all but Rae ordered pie. Samuel nearly smiled when he bit into his Dutch apple. Miriam hoped Rae spoke quickly. The sugar was the only thing keeping the old codger there.

"What's your idea, Rae?" Miriam took a small bite of her chocolate pie and studied the newspaperwoman.

"I believe Mrs. Goodland is right. She probably can't stop Drake. People like him aren't afraid of litigation. It almost seems to me that they thrive in courtrooms, same as bees flourish in the heat of summer." She shook her head, her dark hair falling forward over her shoulders. "Maybe it's the drama. Maybe it's the winning at any cost. Personally, I think it would be foolish to fight him on those grounds."

"Do you know Byron Drake?" Eli asked, looking up from his cherry cobbler with interest.

"I did some research before my editor sent me here to cover this story. This isn't the first time he's swooped in and made a big controversial splash in a small town."

"Huh." Samuel swirled his fork through the ice cream that had begun to melt over his pie. "Can't say as I'm surprised. He seems like the type who would go around from one place to another causing trouble merely because he can."

"I suspect partly it's about the money, and partly it's about the power. Whatever his reasons, if you want to win you need to attack on a different front."

"We don't attack," Gabe said quietly. "We're Amish."

"Yeah. I understand that part, but what if there was another way? What if there was a quieter, gentler way to win? Wouldn't it be worth it for you to try?"

Her question hung in the air over their table. Miriam knew how she would answer, because her first concern was the children, but she also understood that their principles ran deep. As they went from chair to chair, answering what they thought the rest of their district would agree with, the ball of tension inside of Miriam began to loosen. It had been there since the night of the students' presentation, growing and tightening.

She began to hope that the problem might have a resolution, and with that hope it almost seemed as if the first warmth of spring filled the little cafe.

"It would be worth it," Gabe said. "In my opinion."

"Suppose so," Eli agreed.

"Maybe." Samuel sat back, pushing away his empty plate.

"What do you have in mind?" Miriam asked.

"Use the media against him. You probably don't realize how much the general population sympathizes with your culture."

"We already told you." This time Samuel picked up his fork and waved it at her. "We don't abide being photographed."

"I understand that, and Drake's blatant disregard for your religious customs will be a point in our favor." She pulled the folder from her shoulder bag. "From the cover to the last page, this entire plan neglects to consider a single aspect of your beliefs."

"Ya. That's what we were trying to say." Gabe accepted more *kaffi* from the waitress.

"He never planned to listen to you, but he *will* listen to bad press. No one can afford that, in spite of what Donald Trump says."

Miriam had popped a forkful of chocolate pie into her mouth. "Who?" came out sounding like an owl, which started Gabe laughing.

"You don't know who Donald Trump is?"

"No," Eli said. "Should we?"

"Not necessarily, but that's what I mean. You and Drake operate in different worlds. He's invading yours, and the way to win is with my newspaper."

"Not to be rude, Miss Caperton, but why are you willing to help us?"

"It's a good question." She picked up her napkin and began to fold it. When she did speak, she looked up, first at Miriam and then at the men. "The easy answer is that I'll get several good stories out of it, and that will make my boss happy."

"Without pictures?" Samuel asked.

"Without identifying pictures of any Amish person."

"She does know our ways," Eli muttered.

"There's another answer?" Miriam asked.

"Yes." Rae sipped her cold *kaffi*, choosing her words carefully. "I was raised on a farm east of Wilton. When I was twelve an Amish family purchased the property bordering ours. They had a young girl my age, and we became close *freinden*."

The word slipped off her lips as a smile tinged with sadness caused her lips to turn up slightly.

"What happened?" Miriam asked. One part of her didn't want to know, but she could sense that Rae needed to tell. It seemed they were bound together now, the five of them. Sitting in the café on the first Friday in February, all of them pulling together—yoked together—against Drake and his massive business machine.

Rae's voice calmed her nerves and reminded her of the essence of all they fought for, even as the woman's heartache bled through her words.

"Katie was driving her buggy on one of the side roads in the early hours of an October morning when an *Englischer* hit her. He'd been up all night drinking, and he came speeding over the top of the hill. He said he never even saw her."

"Oh, I remember that, honey." Their waitress had stopped to pick up their empty plates. "It was about six years ago. The fool's attorney claimed he wasn't at fault because there were no buggy signs."

"Right. He was still convicted of vehicular homicide, but they pled it down. Instead of ten years in prison, he received one." Rae had been staring out the window, but now she gazed at each of them and finally at Drake's brochure. "One year for killing a nineteen-year-old girl. All because there were no buggy signs, even though his blood alcohol level was twice the legal limit. The media ran stories, which seemed to me to go along with his point of view, discussing how dangerous it was to have horses and buggies on the roads, etc."

She sipped her *kaffi* and then glanced briefly around the café. "They never interviewed a single Amish person for any of the stories. That was when I decided I wanted to be a reporter and an advocate for Plain folk whenever possible."

All were quiet as they processed her story and the tragedy of her friend. Miriam knew, though, that although Rae had a sincere desire to help them, she didn't completely understand the Amish way. Katie's family would have been counseled that it was *Gotte's wille* for her to perish that October day, just as Gabe had been told it was the destined time for his wife to die.

She glanced up, met his stare, and wondered if he was thinking the same thing she had been. Their eyes locked, and it seemed that a heart full of emotions passed between them. She tried to remember the reasons he'd suggested, reasons she should consider Aden, that she'd be happier living somewhere else, that he was not the person God intended for her—but she couldn't recall a single word or hint from that conversation.

"So now you know. You know why I try to catch these assignments. I do what I can to be an educator regarding the Amish community. It's my way of being loyal to Katie's memory."

Their waitress had moved on to help an elderly couple who had walked through the front door.

Eli cleared his throat. "It's a *gut* thing you are attempting to do, for sure. But what exactly do you have in mind? How do you think we can succeed in using your paper to change Drake's plans?"

This time Rae's smile was bright and confident. She pulled out a pad of paper with notes she'd written. "I was hoping you'd ask."

It only took fifteen minutes to outline what she wanted to do. By the time she was finished, even Samuel was leaning forward and listening intently.

Her ideas were bold, but they might work if the group could convince the other members in their district and if they could time everything right.

And if it was *Gotte's wille.*

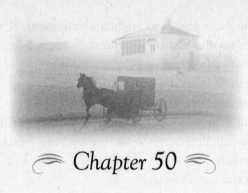

~ Chapter 50 ~

Grace could hardly sit still as she rode in Eli's buggy. Sadie sat on her right side, next to the window. Hannah sat beside Lily on the seat in front of them. Even though Hannah was older, and Grace had never seen Hannah nervous about anything, her cheeks were red and she kept glancing out the window as if she expected to see an *Englisch* car pull up beside them and snap their pictures.

Adam and Luke were in the seat behind her, and she didn't even mind. The bishop was right—miracles did still happen!

This might be the most exciting day Grace could remember.

It was more exciting than when they exchanged presents on Christmas, though she loved Stormy more than *mammi* Sarah's shoofly pie. Still and all, a school outing was the very best. And one to town? There wasn't a single student who could ever remember such a thing.

"Will there be a lot of people, Hannah?" Grace leaned forward so Hannah could hear her over the buggy full of students and the clip-clop of the horses.

"Don't know, Grace. Maybe."

"What about cameras? Miriam said there might be cameras." Sadie practically bounced on her seat.

"Don't you worry about that. Remember when Rae came and talked to the class?" Hannah leaned over to pick up the song sheet Lily had dropped.

Grace and Sadie sat back and whispered, comparing what they remembered about the newspaperwoman, Rae.

"Hannah, what if the other newspaper people don't listen to Rae?" Grace smiled when Sadie reached over and laced fingers with her. They were best friends, and they were going to stand beside each other when the time came for songs. Lily would be next to them.

"Our parents trust Rae, and they think this is best."

Grace turned around and tried to see out the back of the buggy. She moved to the right and the left, because mostly she could only see boys' Sunday hats, but finally she was able to make out Chance. Behind their buggy horse would be her dad and Miriam.

Sometimes when she was going to sleep, she would dream about her *dat* and her teacher marrying. She knew that was only a dream that she wanted to come true. She was older now, nearly nine, and she knew the difference between pretending and what was real.

When folks were planning on marrying for real, they went riding in buggies alone and stayed for dinner. There were signs. Her dad and Miriam didn't have the right signs. Miriam hadn't been over for dinner once, and they never went for buggy rides alone. Grace had even offered to stay home by herself. She'd told her dad that she was old enough if he wanted to go out driving, but he only laughed and told her he was fine sitting and reading the *Budget* again.

Sometimes she did catch them looking at each other funny, and then she'd think maybe...but so far, nothing.

She'd talked to God about this...but again, nothing.

Abigail, Miriam's mom, said praying could take a while. She said sometimes it took years.

Grace turned around in her seat and smoothed out her dress. For her dad's sake, she hoped this prayer worked a little faster. He might not have years if he was looking to marrying. She'd noticed a little gray in his beard one morning this week. When she'd mentioned it, he'd laughed and laughed, which made no sense to her at all.

She was about to turn to Sadie and ask her if her dad ever laughed about things that weren't one bit funny, when the buggy began to slow as they entered town. The streets were lined with lots of people—Amish and *Englisch*, and there were cars everywhere.

"Say, look at that truck," Adam whispered to Luke.

"Never seen one with lights on top like that."

"It's for spotlighting deer," John said.

He was sitting behind the two boys. Though he could have driven a buggy if he'd wanted to, he'd chosen to ride along with them. Grace wondered if it was because he liked to be with Hannah, but then he didn't sit with Hannah. The boy-girl thing was all very confusing to her.

"What's that mean, spotlighting?" Luke asked.

"You shine a light in their eyes so they don't move, and then you shoot them." John sat back without another word to let the boys decide for themselves if the truck was still something they liked or not.

Grace didn't care about the *Englisch* cars, but she'd certainly never seen so many of them—not even when they had ridden on the bus from Indiana. Of course, she'd slept much of that trip, which was last November. Thinking about it, that seemed to have happened years and years ago. It seemed as though it were someone else who had stepped onto that bus holding her dad's hand.

"I see her!" Sadie said. "I see Rae."

As soon as she pointed, Grace saw her too, standing back near the hitching posts and handing out sheets of paper.

What was on those sheets of paper?

"We're here, *kinner*." Eli murmured to the horses, pulled them to a stop, and then turned around to face everyone in the buggy. "Out slow and careful to keep your clothes clean. I tried to park away from the mud, but that wasn't so easy to do with all of the traffic."

Esther's buggy had parked to the left of theirs, and her *dat* and Miriam were on the right. Hannah walked out of the buggy first and John stepped out last. By the time Grace and Sadie hopped out, fingers still laced together, she felt as though she were in the middle of a church service.

There were so many Amish around her that she couldn't see anything but trousers and long dresses.

When would she grow taller? At least she could hear well enough.

As the adults were guiding the children to the steps in front of the building, a man stepped up and started speaking into something that made his voice loud. Grace thought it only made him sound noisy. In fact, he reminded her of the bull in the pasture when he was in one of his moods. He could stomp and snort and make the craziest sounds. That was what this man sounded like.

Was he why they were here? Miriam said they were here to sing their songs and show people what it really meant to be Plain.

Grace watched her teacher and Esther as they arranged everyone on the steps, tallest in back and shortest in front. She tried not to listen to the man speaking, but some of his words leaked into her head.

"Proud to announce a new business venture..."

"Venture" was a word she didn't know yet. She'd have to look it up in the big dictionary at school.

"Joining hands with the people of Cashton..."

She had never met this man, she was sure of it. She had met some *Englischers*, like Doc Hanson. Was he in the crowd? Yes! He was standing by the newspaper people with their cameras.

Oh. The cameras. Goose bumps popped up on her arms, but then she noticed that the cameras were only around their necks. They weren't looking through them. Maybe Rae had put something on her sheet of paper. Maybe Rae had explained what it meant to be Plain.

Now the man wasn't talking anymore. Instead a woman was. Her voice was better.

"Before Mr. Drake reveals more about the renovation of the hotel, we thought it would be nice for the press to hear a presentation from our local Amish schoolchildren. As you know, this is a rare treat, and I personally want to thank the schoolteachers—Miriam King and

Esther Schrocks—as well as the school board of the Plain School on Pebble Creek for bringing the children into town today."

There was a smattering of applause. The woman waited for the crowd to quiet, and then she continued talking. "We consider the Amish citizens of Cashton and the surrounding area to be a vital part of our community. As such, we always want to respect their unique lifestyle, their beliefs, and their history."

Grace couldn't see her, but she could hear the smile in her words. "A member of our local media has given you a handout that highlights basic facts about the Amish in general and the Cashton Amish in particular—facts anyone can easily verify if they are so inclined. And now I hope you enjoy the songs of the schoolchildren."

Suddenly Grace didn't mind that she was still short, because she could see Miriam, and she could see her dad standing behind her with the rest of the church members. When Miriam held up her hands to signal for them to start, the voice that came out of Grace's mouth was stronger than ever before. And that was a miracle.

Singing out loud was so much better than singing in her head.

All of the songs were her favorites—one was in German and two in *Englisch*. She didn't have to worry about forgetting the words because they were ones they sang in school and church every week.

When they were finished, everyone in the crowd clapped. This time they clapped louder and longer than they had for the woman who spoke. Then Miriam motioned for them to sit down on the steps.

The man with the angry voice started speaking again, and he didn't sound any happier. If anything, he sounded as if he wanted to be somewhere else. Grace knew what that sounded like because for a long time she didn't want to be here—but now...well, now here was home.

≈ Chapter 51 ≈

Miriam couldn't help laughing at the pile of lunches on the front table. Each year she tried to think of something different to do for Valentine's Day, but this year her heart wasn't in it—no pun intended.

Probably because her own love life had come up against a quarry wall. Not that she had anyone to blame but herself.

Aden had come home again over the weekend. He'd received her letter, and they had talked about it. She reminded him that she still counted him as an important *freind*. He'd taken it well, ducked his head, and smiled. She'd seen the hurt beneath, but knew it was best to be honest with him rather than to pretend to care for him in a way that she didn't. As her *mamm* was fond of saying, "You can't make cider without apples." Perhaps that particular proverb didn't specifically refer to love and marriage, but to Miriam's way of thinking, it fit perfectly.

So Valentine's Day had crept closer, and she'd had no inspiration. Esther had gone through her folder of ideas and chosen the lunch swap activity she'd used years before.

"I think they must have enjoyed preparing for the day from the looks of things." Esther pulled a chair up beside her. "Everyone is washing up."

"*Gut.* I wasn't sure we'd ever settle the twins down after recess."

"*Ya.* They have a lot of energy." Esther glanced back over the room. "Did I tell you that Joseph heard Mr. Drake is completely changing the renovation concept?"

"Rae stopped by our house on Sunday and said the same thing. The new name for the business is Amish Anthem."

Esther beamed at her. "I love it! I wasn't sure what he was going to do after the speech he made last week. Honestly, those statistics he quoted made no sense in my opinion. All that talk of expenditures and job projections. Sounded *narrisch* to me."

"Apparently, Drake goes a little crazy when he's made to look the fool in front of the press, but there was nothing he could do about it. The children singing was the final bit of push the media needed to win the town over—"

"That and Rae's Amish information sheet."

Miriam nodded. They had won the battle with Drake. He'd even agreed to a much scaled-back retail model that was without arcades, astronomy, and acoustics.

So why didn't today feel like a victory?

Hannah and two of the older girls let loose a harmony of giggles from the middle row.

Esther shook her head, as if that hadn't been her a few short years ago. "Did you notice the lunch John made? I'm sure he's hoping Hannah will choose it. He set it way at the back so the younger students wouldn't see it."

"That, and there's an *H* on the heart he glued on the outside." Miriam sent her a sideways glance. Young love could be so poignant. Most years she would laugh at such things. Today it made her want to climb the steps to her room, crawl into bed, and pull her oldest, most favorite quilt up over her head.

"The cookies and punch are set out at the back for afternoon games," Esther said. "I'll start everyone on the lunch exchange."

Moving to the front of the room, she began pulling names from the Valentine box. As she pulled each name, the student would come forward and select a lunch from the table. Everyone laughed when Luke chose the pail with pictures of mice all over it. There was no doubt Grace had decorated it and that it was meant for Sadie, but the girls were good sports about it.

Sadie leaned over to Grace and said, "I still have your valentine card," while Luke pretended to be confused about the entire thing.

"What? I like mice. They're interesting creatures."

He wasn't fooling anyone. He'd taken to sitting with Grace during recess every morning, though he still hung around the boys at lunch.

When there were only two lunches remaining, Miriam stood to select hers, but Esther moved forward. "I'll go next."

There were quite a few giggles as she chose the nicer of the two boxed lunches that were left—one that Miriam had seen Eli give to his middle child to bring into the room that morning.

A solitary lunch box remained on the table. It was simple and undecorated on the outside, though it had paper handles glued to it in the shape of hearts.

"This is going to be a hard choice," Miriam murmured.

Now the girls were all whispering to one another, while the boys were watching her intently.

Had she missed something? Surely they had not placed a rubber snake into her box.

Suddenly her memory slipped back to the year she had first used the lunch swap for Valentine's Day. Daniel Lapp had been in her class then. He'd thought it clever to fashion a false bottom into a lunch box. When the young lady had picked it up, the bottom had fallen out. Her entire lunch had fallen out on the floor, to the delight of the class.

She lifted the lunch carefully, one hand holding on to the paper heart handles and one hand supporting it from underneath. Nothing popped out of the top. Nothing fell out of the bottom.

"Aren't you going to look inside?" Esther asked.

Miriam noticed that all eyes were riveted on her.

"Of course. Yes. I'll look inside right now." She set the box back on the table and opened it slowly, leaning back slightly as she did. When nothing sprang out, she stepped closer to gaze inside.

There appeared to be dozens of hearts cut from paper that had been colored red, purple, and blue. They were all different sizes, but none larger than the palm of her hand. And they were all blank. Who had taken the time to cut out so many?

The laughing in the classroom increased as she continued pulling them out and setting them on the table. She could feel something solid underneath, so surely there was food down below, but there was something else on top of it—a larger sheet of paper.

By now the girls were giggling so hard they were bending over. Miriam couldn't help but join them. "Seems a real Cupid made my lunch."

She pulled out the final sheet of paper. It was a large heart cut from red paper.

This sheet was not blank.

When she opened it up and read the words written there, tears began to sting her eyes.

Blinking rapidly, she folded the heart and placed it in her pocket. "Time to eat," she declared and then she turned so she was facing away from the class.

Esther stepped in front of her.

"Are you okay? I thought it was a *gut* thing..."

Miriam closed her eyes and forced herself to gain control over her emotions. "Can you watch the children?"

"Of course."

She didn't bother to carry the lunch box, but the note—that she took with her.

Gabe was working in the barn when he saw the buggy coming down his lane. At first he thought something might be wrong, but then he realized it was because of the note. Of course it was the note. Had he really expected her to wait until after school was out?

He'd be lucky if she didn't box his ears.

Walking out into the afternoon sunshine, he met her before she'd made it to the pasture fence.

"Miriam."

"Gabe."

As he helped her from the buggy, he noticed she was clutching the red heart in her hand. She glanced at him once and then walked over to the workbench he'd pulled into the doorway of the barn.

She ran her hand along the stall door he was sanding. "Almost finished with the barn renovations?"

"Almost." He waited, but she didn't pick up the conversation. She only stared out over his pasture. "I suspect that isn't what you came to talk to me about."

"*Nein*. It isn't." Opening the valentine, she ran her palm down the crease in the sheet of paper. "I wasn't expecting this."

"Really? You can honestly say you didn't know how I feel about you?"

When she finally looked at him, the tears in her eyes drew him closer, until there was only the old sawhorse between them. "But you told me to consider an alternative."

"Did you?

"*Ya*."

"And?"

She shook her head no.

Instead, she asked what had been wounding her heart for weeks. "Why? Why did you ask me to go to him? To see his district? My feelings have been obvious for a long time—"

"Look around you, Miriam. This place...it still needs so much work. I was hesitant to ask you to commit yourself to such a life of labor."

"Why?" Her hand came down and whacked the red heart. "That's my decision to make. You can't decide that for me."

A single tear escaped and traveled down her cheek. Picking up the sander he'd been using, she carefully set it on top of the heart. He made his way around the sawhorse, but she held a hand up, stopping his progress.

"It's for me to choose, Gabe."

"I know that. I know it now." He cleared his throat and pushed on with what needed saying, with what wouldn't fit on the heart. "I knew it when I heard you went to see Aden but still came back to Cashton. I waited, and you didn't leave again, and I hoped that meant—"

"Aden is a *gut freind*, but that is all. I don't choose him. I choose you."

Now happiness struggled against his fear. "Are you sure, Miriam? I'm a little like this old farm—falling apart in places, showing promise in others. I'll take a fair amount of work. Are you positive?"

For her answer she flew into his arms, and he wondered why he'd ever doubted her.

She was a strong woman, Miriam King. Strong enough to teach at the Plain School at Pebble Creek all those years. Strong enough to bring along the farm beside Pebble Creek. Strong enough to care for both him and Grace.

He ran his thumb across her lips, along her cheek, and down her neck—and then he did what he'd wanted to do since the first day he'd stepped into the schoolroom. He kissed her.

When they finally pulled apart, her stomach gurgled.

"Didn't you eat the lunch I sent?"

"No." She laughed and laced her fingers with his. "I didn't even see what you sent. I read your note and then drove out here."

"I suppose we should go and fetch it." Gabe walked her to her buggy.

"Can you leave your work?"

"*Ya.* I'm my own boss here. A few hours off in the middle of the day is okay. It only means I have to make it up later this afternoon." He winked before reaching out to help her in the buggy.

"Oh, the heart—" She hurried back to the barn door and pulled the piece of paper out from under the sander. "I wouldn't want this to blow away while we're gone."

"No. That would be terrible."

"I'm going to show this to our *grandkinner*, Gabe. So they'll know what a *wunderbaar* writer their *grossdaddi* is."

"Indeed." They climbed up and settled close to each other, and then he called out to Belle. He turned the buggy around, completely content with Miriam tucked in beside him as they headed back toward the school their *kinner* and *grandkinner* would attend, the school Grace was waiting at this very minute.

As they made their way down the lane, Miriam read aloud the words he'd labored over the night before. They wouldn't win any awards—Amish or *Englisch*—but they had expressed what was in his heart. That she was sitting beside him was proof of that, and he'd be on his knees thanking the Lord tonight it was so.

I'm not a poet, Miriam.
But if I were, I'd write on a red heart
Words to describe my love for you.
You are the reason *Gotte* brought us to live
Here among these rich valleys and hills.
Will you share our life?
Will you be my bride?
I can offer you days filled with Grace
And nights of love and peace.
If you share my love,
Marry me and share our
humble home,
Along the banks of
Pebble Creek.

~ Discussion Questions ~

1. Have you ever been slow to learn something about someone? Did you feel somehow betrayed? Sometimes there are good reasons as to why people keep their history, even their wounds, private. Yet it does help us to know how to help and how to pray if we're aware of those things. Is Gabe justified in waiting to tell Miriam about Grace's issues?

2. In chapter 18, Esther starts the day with the children reading Psalm 125:2. We learn this is one of Miriam's favorite verses. She thinks that it is "Simple enough for the younger ones to understand, and yet with enough wisdom for the older students." Do you agree with this sentiment? Are the Psalms, or Scripture in general, simple enough for young children to understand, yet provide wisdom for our teens?

3. Miriam is confused at the disparity in how much the Scmuckers have versus how little Gabe has. It is sometimes hard to see this economic difference in our communities. What is your reaction to this in your town? What do you think God would have us do?

4. In chapter 25, Grace gets into a small pushing match with two boys. One of the older boys, John, reminds her of the words in Romans 12:18-19. This is a tenet of the Amish lifestyle that many of us have trouble with. Do you agree or disagree with the way John explains it to the girls? How would this change our lives if more situations were handled in light of these verses?

5. In chapter 26, Gabe faces his real fear, that perhaps a whole home wasn't "God's plan for him. Perhaps he was to learn to be satisfied with the piece of happiness he had." Has there ever been a time in your life when you thought God wanted you to be happy with less?

6. Gabe comforts Grace when she's worried about Miriam. He reads her a verse from Matthew. "Are not two sparrows sold for a penny? Yet not one of them will fall to the ground outside your Father's care. And even the very hairs of your head are all numbered. So don't be afraid; you are worth more than many sparrows." In this scene we see again that Gabe isn't a perfect father and doesn't claim to have all the answers, but he is trying to raise his daughter lovingly and with a strong faith. How do you think he's doing? What makes a good parent?

7. In chapter 39, we get a peek into the bishop of Pebble Creek, an austere man who doesn't show much emotion. Later, in the meeting with Gabe, Samuel, Eli, and Miriam, his stern mask slips and he quotes Robert Frost. What does this indicate about Jacob Beiler?

8. At the benefit auction for Laura Kiems, the little girls are looking at the quilts, and Hannah shows them one she has done. She shows them a mistake she made in the quilt and explains, "My *mamm* and I made this one. Those were my stitches when we began. I wanted to pull them out, but she wouldn't let me. She said imperfections are important too, and that I'd be able to see how much I'd improved if I left them." What do you do imperfectly?

9. When Drake is unmoved by Eli's or Gabe's concerns, Samuel once again begins quoting Scripture. Samuel is an interesting character. When I first started writing him, I'll admit I didn't much care for him, but he grew on me. Yes, he's grumpy, but what's unique about him is that he relates to other people

through God's Word. It literally is the lens through which he sees the world, and sometimes people don't know how to respond to him and his pronouncements. Do you know anyone like this? And if you do, what is your response to them?

10. The story ends with Gabe putting a note in Miriam's lunch. Is this at all realistic? Why wouldn't he just show up at the schoolhouse and speak to her, face-to-face? Do you know of any men or women who are more comfortable expressing their feelings on paper? And how does this relate to God's ultimate "love letter" to us?

Glossary

Ausbund	a collection of hymns
boppli	baby
bopplin	babies
bruder	brother
danki	thank you
dat	father
dochder/dochdern	daughter/daughters
Englisch	something in the non-Amish world
Englischers	non-Amish people
fraa	wife
freinden	friends
gelassenheit	humility
gem gschehne	you're welcome
Gotte's wille	God's will
grandkinner	grandchildren
grossdochdern	granddaughter
grossdaddi	grandfather
grossdawdi	grandparents
grossmammi	grandmother
gudemariye	good morning
gut	good
in lieb	in love
kaffi	coffee
kapp	head covering
kind	child

kinner . . . . children

Loblied. . . . . the second hymn of praise

mamm. . . . . mother

naerfich. . . . . nervous

narrisch . . . . crazy

nein. . . . . no

onkel . . . . uncle

Ordnung . . . . Amish oral tradition and rules of life

pappi . . . . grandfather

rumspringa. . . . . running-around years

schweschder . . . . sister

wunderbaar . . . . wonderful

ya. . . . . yes

If you loved A *Promise for Miriam,* you won't want to miss
Book 2 of the Pebble Creek Amish Series

A HOME FOR LYDIA

Prologue

Wisconsin
April

Lydia Fisher pulled her sweater around her shoulders and sank on to the steps of the last cabin as the sun set along Pebble Creek. The waters had begun to recede from last week's rains, but the creek still pushed at its banks—running swiftly past the Plain Cabins, not pausing to consider her worries.

Debris from the flooding reached to the bottom step of cabin number twelve. She could have reached out and nudged it with the toe of her shoe. Fortunately, the water hadn't made it into the small cottages.

Almost, though.

Only two days ago she'd stood at the office window and watched as the waters had crept closer to the picturesque buildings nestled along the creek—watched and prayed.

Now the last of the day's light was nearly spent. She should harness Tin Star to the buggy and head home. Her mother would be putting dinner on the table. Her brothers and sisters would be needing help with schoolwork. Her father would be waiting.

Standing up with a weariness that was unnatural for her twenty-two years, Lydia trudged back toward the front of the property, checking each cabin as she went.

All twelve were locked and secure.

All twelve were vacant.

Perhaps this weekend *Englisch* tourists would return and provide some income for the owner, Elizabeth Troyer. Guests would also ensure that Lydia kept her job. If the cabins were to close, if she were to lose her employment, she wouldn't be able to convince her oldest brother to stay in school. Their last conversation on the matter had turned into an argument—one she'd nearly lost.

Pulling their old black gelding from the barn, she tied Tin Star's lead rope to the hitching post, and then she began to work the collar up and over his ears.

"You're a *gut* boy. Are you ready to go home? Ready for some oats? I imagine you are."

He'd been their buggy horse since she was a child, and Lydia knew his days were numbered. What would her family do when he gave out on them? As she straightened his mane and made sure the collar pad protected his shoulders and neck, she paused to rest her cheek against his side. The horse's sure steady breathing brought her a measure of comfort.

Reaching into the pocket of her jacket, she brought out a handful of raisins. Tin Star's lips on her hand were soft and wet. Lydia rubbed his neck, glanced back once more at the cluster of small buildings which had become like a small community to her—a community she was responsible for maintaining.

Squaring her shoulders, she climbed into the buggy and turned toward home.

Chapter 1

Aaron Troyer stepped off the bus, careful to avoid a large puddle of rainwater. Because no one else was exiting at Cashton, he didn't have to wait long for the driver to remove his single bag from the storage compartment. He'd thanked the man and shouldered the duffel when a buggy coming in the opposite direction hit an even bigger puddle, soaking him and his bag.

The driver had managed to jump out of the way at the last second. "Good luck to you, son."

With a nod the man was back on the bus, heading farther west. A part of Aaron wished he was riding with him. Another part longed to take the next bus back east, back where he'd come from, back to Indiana.

Neither was going to happen, so he repositioned the wet duffel bag and surveyed his surroundings.

Not much to Cashton.

According to his uncle and his dad, the town was about the same size as Monroe, but Aaron couldn't tell it. He supposed new places never did measure up to expectations, especially when a fellow would rather not be there.

The ride had been interesting enough. They had crossed the northern part of Indiana, skirted the southern tip of Lake Michigan, traveled through Chicago and Rockford, and finally entered Wisconsin in the south central portion of the state. Aaron had seen more cities in the last twenty-four hours than he'd visited in his entire life, but those had been oddities to him. Something he would tell his family about once he was home, but nothing he would ever care to see again. But passing through the Hidden Valley region of southwestern Wisconsin—now that had caused him to sit up straighter and gaze out of the bus's window.

There had been an older *Englisch* couple sitting behind him. They'd had tourist brochures which they'd read aloud to each other. He'd caught the highlights as he'd tried to sleep.

He heard them use the word "driftless." The term apparently indicated a lack of glacial drift. His *dat* would laugh at that one. Not that he discounted all aspects of science, but he had his doubts regarding what was and wasn't proven as far as the Ice Age.

According to the couple's brochure, Wildcat Mountain to the east of Cashton was teaming with wildlife and good hiking. Any other time he might be interested in that piece of information, but he wasn't staying so it didn't matter much to him.

He also learned small towns in the Driftless Area were at risk of major flooding every fifty to one hundred years.

Staring down at his damp pants, he wondered how much rain they'd had. How much rain were they expecting? He hoped he wouldn't be around long enough to find out.

Aaron glanced up and down the street. He saw a town hall, a tavern, a café, a general store, and a feed store. A larger building, probably three stories high, rose in the distance, but he had no desire to walk that far because it could be in the wrong direction. Already the sun was heading west, and he wanted to be at the cabins before dark.

There were several streets branching off the main one, but they didn't look any more promising. Pushing his hat down more firmly on his head, he cinched up the duffel bag and walked resolutely toward the feed store.

Instead of heading toward the front door, he moved down the side of the building to the loading docks, where two pickup trucks and a buggy were parked.

Fortunately, it wasn't the buggy that had sprayed him with rainwater and mud. He would rather not ask information of that person, though in all likelihood the driver had no idea what he'd done. Folks seldom slowed down enough to look outside their own buggy window—even Amish folk. It appeared some things were the same whether you were in Wisconsin or Indiana.

He approached the loading docks, intending to find the owner of the parked buggy.

"That duffel looks heavy...and wet."

Turning in surprise, he saw an Amish man leaning against the driver's side of the buggy. Somber brown eyes studied Aaron, and a full dark beard indicated the man was married. Which was no surprise, because a basket with a baby sat on the buggy's floor. The baby couldn't have been more than a few months old, based on the size of the basket. He couldn't see much except for a blanket and two small fists waving in the air.

"The duffel wouldn't be wet if someone hadn't been determined to break the speed limit with a sorrel mare."

The man smiled, reached down, and slipped a pacifier into the baby's mouth.

"That would probably have been one of the Bontreger boys. I'm sure he meant no harm, but both of them tend to drive on the far side of fast."

He placed the walnut bowl he'd been sanding with a piece of fine wool on the seat, dusted his hands on his trousers, and then stepped forward.

"Name's Gabe Miller."

"Aaron Troyer."

"Guess you're new in town."

"Ya. Just off the bus."

"Explains the duffel."

Aaron glanced again at the sun, still slipping west. Why did it seem to speed up once it was setting?

"I was looking for the Plain Cabins on Pebble Creek. Have you heard of them?"

"If you're needing a room for the night, we can either find you a place or take you to our bishop. No need for you to rent a cabin."

Easing the duffel off his shoulder and on to the ground, Aaron rested his hands on top of it. "Actually, I need to go to the cabins for personal reasons. Could you tell me where they are?"

"*Ya.* I'd be happy to give you directions, but it's a fair piece from here if you're planning on walking."

Aaron pulled off his hat and ran his hand over his hair. He replaced it slowly as he considered his options. He'd boarded the bus ten hours earlier. He was used to long days and hard work. Though he was only twenty-three, he'd been working in the fields for nine years—ever since he'd left the schoolhouse after eighth grade. It was work he enjoyed. What he didn't like was ten hours on a bus, moving farther away from his home, on a trip that seemed to him like a fool's mission.

"Sooner I start, sooner I'll arrive."

"The Plain Cabins are on what we call the west side of Pebble Creek."

"You mean the west side of Cashton?"

"Well, Cashton is the name of the town, but Plain folks mostly refer to the area as Pebble Creek, after the river."

"The same river going through town?"

"Yes. There are two Plain communities here—one where the river runs to the east side of town, and one where the river runs to the west. I live on the east side. The cabins you're looking for are on the west. The town is sort of in the middle. You can walk to them from here, but as I said, it's a good ways. Maybe five miles, and there are quite a few hills in between, not to mention that bag you're carrying..."

Instead of answering, Aaron hoisted the duffel to his shoulder.

Throughout their entire conversation, Gabe's expression had been pleasant but serious. At the sound of voices, he glanced up and across the street, toward the general store. When he did, Aaron noticed a subtle change in the man, like light shifting across a room. Some of the seriousness left his eyes and contentment spread across his face.

Following his gaze, Aaron saw the reason why—a beautiful woman. She had the darkest hair he'd ever seen on an Amish person.

A small amount peeked out from the edges of her prayer *kapp*. She was holding the hand of a young girl, who was the spitting image of the man before him. Both the woman and the child were carrying shopping bags.

"I was waiting on my family. Looks like they're done. We'd be happy to take you by the cabins."

"I don't want to be a bother."

Gabe smiled, and now the seriousness was completely gone, as if having his family draw close had vanquished it. As if having his family in sight had eased all of the places in his heart.

Aaron wondered what that felt like. He wanted to be back with his own parents and brothers and sisters in Indiana, but even there he felt an itching, a restlessness no amount of work could satisfy.

From what he'd seen of Wisconsin so far, he could tell he wasn't going to be any happier here. He'd arrived less than thirty minutes ago, and he couldn't wait to get back home.

Gabe was already moving toward his wife, waving away his protest.

"If it were a bother, I wouldn't have offered."

To learn more about Harvest House books and
to read sample chapters, log on to our website:

www.harvesthousepublishers.com

HARVEST HOUSE PUBLISHERS
EUGENE, OREGON